D1521350

To Jen
my best friend

...and to Tony
the best friend
I got to marry

THE WAY WE MET

Friday, September 1, 2000

Gage

I found her in the bushes.

Or, not exactly in the bushes, but the in-between space, wedged in the small opening between what Layla, the girl I slept with more than once last spring, called a lilac bush. They were her favorite flowers, Layla whined once, and it wouldn't hurt me to pick her one sometime. She thought we were dating, I thought we were screwing, and that miscommunication led to a lot of weirdness between us. She was wrong, by the way. I did try to pick her one and the damn things were a lot more tree-like than flower-like, which meant I could not "pick" one so much as hack away at one. I found these rusty shears in the basement of Delta Beta – and believe me, that basement should have been condemned a long time ago – and then I tripped on what seemed like a five-hundred gallon vat of bleach, leading to a huge chemical burn, a broken thumb, a tetanus shot, and forty stitches where the shears bit into my thigh like deranged possum. *You look like some kind of X-Files lizard-monsterman,* Ace had told me on the way to the hospital, because, you know, the bleach had won the fight with my skin, and I basically looked like some kind of X-files lizard-monsterman. *Fuck you* seemed the appropriate response. Layla and I were pretty much done after that, and I say "pretty much" because there was no denying Layla was the crazy kind of hot and the hot kind of crazy that drew me in like an addict. And also when you shear your leg apart for some chick, she owes you at least one last sympathy screw.

Anyway. *This* chick was behind what used to be lilac bushes. Like me and Layla, they eventually withered and died, and exactly like me and Lay, nobody really cared or did anything about the withering or the dying. And why would we? We were a bunch of drunk guys sharing the same house. When did we ever think about lilacs and bushes? Since Layla was gone, never, that was when. Or, almost never. Because of now. Because I was staring at a girl back there.

Beer cans and a spillover of people from a party grown too large littered the rest of the yard, but here in the bushes the air was as still and quiet as that girl. I don't know how she got there, and I was drunk enough to forget how I got there. But there we both were.

"Are you dead?" I questioned her body in a voice way too loud, as if yelling to a dead body would somehow rouse it. I was surprised at my lack of concern as to whether or not she was actually dead, but, hey, what could you do? I stuck out one sneakered foot and watched – totally impressed with my balance and coordination - as the toe of my checkered Vans sank into her tee-shirt, into the soft skin of her shoulder.

She looked bad. Nobody wore sweatpants to a frat party. Okay, correction: No underclassmen wore sweatpants to a party. Some of the senior girls did, but they wore those yoga kind of sweats, the kind with *Juicy* and *Secret* scrawled across their asses. And those yoga girls were mostly the girlfriends of brothers. This chick and her sweatpants, though. Yikes. It looked like maybe she painted her Grandma's basement in them. Or found them at a crime scene.

The toe of my Van sunk deeper into her. She moaned.

I sighed, which sounded both drunk and relieved. Not dead. We would not have to report some chick's death to Delta Beta. We would not have to go through interviews and be sanctioned and fined and suspended and all that tedious shit.

With a groan, Chick rolled over. Her body swam before my bloodshot eyes. Chick was not dead, but she was definitely drunk. Maybe as drunk as me. Maybe drunker. Or maybe not quite as. It is kind of hard to judge things after hammering down your eighth Jager Bomb.

Her eyes popped open, and I'm not ashamed to admit it freaked me out enough for me to move one halting step back. She stared at me and I stared right back at her, the beer forgotten in my hand.

"My dad's dead," she said finally, slurring a little over the words. "Don't ask me about it." She started muttering then. Whispering like some creepy ghost from those Japanese horror films Ace's girlfriend was forever making us watch. The kind of horror films that made me piss my shorts - just a little – not that I would ever tell anyone about that.

And that ends the freak show portion of the evening, I thought as I put myself into reverse and backed away pretty quickly

I didn't belong here. And even more, she didn't belong here. Not in the bushes. Not at the party. Because now that I saw her face clearly, a memory surfaced. I had seen her earlier in the house. Actually, I saw her at a lot of our parties. With Roxie. Roxie, her friend, her gorgeous friend, always by her side. *What a butterface*, Ace had said. About her. The chick. Not Roxie. *What a butterface.* *More like butter...everything*, I replied with a grimace. It was all we had to say about her before discussing Roxie, a much more interesting topic.

"Fare-thee-well," she called out now to my retreating form, and I stopped. It was that stupid *Fare-thee-well*. Seriously, what kind of person *fare-thee-wells* strangers? Probably the same kind who can't even take care of herself and ends up in the bushes speaking in tongues about dead fathers. Despite myself – and probably because I was shitfaced - I felt a wave of sympathy wash over my mostly dead heart. Who knew a fare-thee-well could stir such emotions from a mostly dead-inside frat brother?

"Can you feel guilt when you're drunk? Can you feel anything at all?" She asked.

Oh, God, she was one of *those* drunks. The existential, crying kind. Chick was the drunken philosopher. I cringed.

She started crying then, and of course I felt bad. I felt bad because her dad was dead, and also because she looked...wow. Bad. Should I feel guilty because I felt worse that she looked so awful?

Yeah, I decided. You probably should feel guilty, you heartless, drunk monster. Her dad is obviously dead. When did you become some caricature of frat life?

Yep. You can feel things while drunk. Lots of things. Guilt definitely being one of them. Because my family was at home. All of them. Mom, Dad, Kristen. Our dog Toby. Not that I should feel guilt. The girl's dad was dead, sure, but my own family had been barely functioning since I was in middle school. I tried to rub the guilt from my mind by wondering who Mom was having an affair with this year.

I scarcely thought of the family. Rarely called. It's not like they expected a call. This was college. This was what I was supposed to be doing. They got summers and Christmas. College got the rest of my time. Kristen, though. She was probably alone right now. Playing her piano. Journaling? Whatever else she did alone there in her room. I should talk to her more. Annoyance seeped through the edges of guilt. At this chick. This waste-of-my-time chick in the bushes.

Yeah. You can feel a lot of things when you're drunk; you can feel damn near everything. It's not like I was never drunk before. But this was most definitely the first time I felt everything when I was drunk. It was suffocating. I felt my body sag, sway. I had not thought this hard while drunk in a long time. Hell, I had not thought this hard while sober in a long time. Then I got pissed. At her, for being here. At myself, for finding her. Even at Kristen, for being alone at home.

Screw this.

"Uh, I have to…uh." I kind of thumbed the space behind my shoulder as I made my escape yet again.

The porch door banged in the distance. Laughter. The motion detector did its job. Light flooded the backyard, crept into the bushes. I could see her face clearly now. Eye glazed. Was it the drunk or tears? Her jaw worked back and forth. "Don't ask me about it." The words whispered out of her in a way that made her sound hollow.

You're the one who brought it up, I yelled to myself as I fought with the guilt that washed over me yet again. She was the one who told me not once, but twice, not to ask her about it. Didn't psych 101 tell me something about this? I should ask. She probably wanted me to ask. It was now my duty to ask. I clamped my mouth shut tight.

You could at least sit next to her. For a minute. I checked my watch. Ten minutes tops. Enough time to make sure she doesn't kill herself or something. I sat down next to her. The ground was soft and damp. I could feel it soaking through the pockets of my jeans. But, I decided as I swore under my breath, I wasn't going to ask, which meant we sat in silence for a good long while.

She sat up with an unsteadiness that had me reaching out to her before I froze, changed my mind, and tucked my hands into the pocket of my hoodie. She surprised me then, when she fell against me, her weight sagging unevenly into my chest. My body had become used to this movement from girls. My head automatically tilted to the sky so that she could move closer, and, without thinking, I pulled one hand from my pocket to wrap over her shoulder. Like every other girl, her head fit right under my chin. Her hair was softer than I predicted, and I was definitely predicting a rat's nest, maybe, I don't know, rolled around in a dumpster; she looked that bad. It smelled good too, like mint and maybe flowers or something, and there was lots of it. The smell alone had me folding my fingers into her arms, pulling her tighter to me. She was tiny, her bones like a bird or something, a fact her baggy tee-shirt covered up.

What the hell are you doing, Gage? Let this chick go.

"You want to sleep together?"

My body tightened. My head snapped up. "What?"

"Let's take a nap." She slurred. "Right here."

"Oh." Relief filled me so swiftly, I almost laughed out loud. "We can't sleep here. Your friend is probably looking for you."

"Roxie?"

"Yeah."

"Where's Roxie?"

Envy tugged at my gut again. God, I wanted Roxie. She was so happy and funny and ready for anything. And she was gone while I was stuck here playing white knight to this girl's drunkenness. And just as quickly I felt shame. For wanting to leave. But, God, did I want to leave.

"I don't know where she is," I replied. "Should we look for her?" Yes, say yes, and it will be over. I glanced at my watch. Ten minutes was up three minutes ago.

"Are you drunk?" The girl whispered, and I could feel the vibration of her voice in my chest.

"I'm definitely drunk." I swallowed over the lump in my throat. I wouldn't be feeling all this ridiculous pity for her if I were not drunk. I would have left long ago. She never would have known I was even there.

"I think about my dad when I'm drunk."

I couldn't think of an answer. So we sat there, this girl tangled up in me, her hair smelling like mint and flowers. She sighed a lot as the minutes ticked, like maybe I was supposed to ask her things or talk to her. There was nothing I wanted to know.

"Are you cold?" She finally asked.

"No." Why would I be cold? It was barely autumn and I was wearing hoodie. The alcohol was burning through my blood, too, flushing my skin.

We sat in silence some more.

"I'm kind of cold," she said.

"Yeah?" I asked absently and stared into the distance before realizing, finally, through my haze, what she meant. "Oh!" I started tugging off my hoodie. It pulled the back of my tee-shirt up a little when I pulled it over my head, exposing a strip of skin to the night air. It was colder than I thought. "Here." I shove it roughly into her hands. "Wear it. I don't care."

She kind of smiled, and then reached out to touch my hair. "It's messy." She ran her fingers through it. "Your hood. It messed it up."

My eyes closed at her touch. You're drunk, Gage. You are way too drunk.

"What happened to your arm?" My eyes snapped open at her question and I took in the scars the bleach had left.

"Oh." I shrugged at her question. "Nothing."

"That means something."

I shrugged again, even though I knew she was waiting for a different answer. With other girls – like both Jessica B. and Jessica S. this past summer - I would say "picking flowers" and it produced a lot of confusion, but also a lot of sympathy. With this chick, I produced no other answer, and she sighed deeply. "What do you do?" she asked, and I felt like we were on a terrible blind date.

"What do you mean?"

"Here. At school. What do you do?"

"Oh." That was an odd way to phrase the question. Usually people asked your major, not what you did. I closed my eyes again. "I change my major a lot."

"What was it?"

"Earth science. Education. Psychology."

"Well rounded."

"Yeah. I guess."

She waited a beat, probably for me to say more. I ran my tongue over my teeth and stared at the dead bushes around us.

"You know what they say about psychology," she finally said.

"No. I don't know what they say."

"The only people who go into psychology are the ones who want to fix themselves."

I rubbed my forehead. This had to be the worst night of my life, and that included telling Kristen about Mom's first affair. "Nobody says that."

She shrugged, picking at the grass. "What is it now?"

"What is what now?"

"Your major."

"Finance," I said. "And accounting. Business management minor."

"That's a lot."

"I want to make a lot of money."

"That makes sense," she agreed in a voice that drifted and flowed and smelled like wine coolers.

I ran my tongue over my teeth. Was she my responsibility now? Was I supposed to carry her home? The automatic light near the porch abruptly flicked off, leaving us in darkness.

"Literature. With a focus in composition. I want to make a lot of words," she answered the question I was supposed to ask, but never did.

God, I was such an asshole. I couldn't even force a conversation. But I didn't even want to be here. So, really, should it matter if I talked to her? How much do you owe someone you connect with only because of crippling alcohol-induced guilt?

"My dad's dead."

"So you said," I answered irritably. Then I felt bad for getting pissed off at her, because, really, Gage, her dad is dead, can you not, like, spare her some compassion? My arms tightened around her, and I wasn't quite sure it was the crushing guilt or a great need for her to shut up that made me do it. Her hair still smelled good.

"So are you smart? With all the majors?"

She was drunk. That's why we were switching around all the topics. Nothing really made sense.

"Uh. I guess so." When I wanted to be. *Apply yourself, Elliot. Apply yourself. Don't be so stupid.* Mom's words rung though my head until they hurt like the hangover I was sure to experience tomorrow. *It would be precisely like you to let a good opportunity go.*

"What else do you do here?"

Nothing. "This." Meaning the parties, not comforting drunk girls in the bushes.

"That's sad. That's a sad life."

Really? I squinted into the distance, into the crowd of people crushed in our lawn. They looked happy. And not long ago I was one of them. Sad? It didn't seem that sad. Would you know your life is sad when it's the only life you've known?

Oh, God, the girl was an evil witch. Now she was turning me into one of *those* drunks.

"He died with my dog. I was ten."

God, her dog died too? *With her dad?* Jesus. How? Nope. No, Gage. Don't even ask. I didn't want to know. *That's* a sad life. I didn't say it out loud; it seemed as if she already knew that fact.

"I didn't die though," she said, as if she were convincing herself. "That's what they told me."

That was the punch to the gut. I squeezed her tighter to my chest. Tighter. Until it felt like we both might burst. "I know." Even though I didn't know anything. People had to remind her she wasn't dead? Good Lord.

I thought of Kristen back home. She practiced the piano six hours a day, every day. She went to Grace Prep Day School for the Gifted and Talented, a school with a long name that meant everything to her. Kristen cried the night I told her about Mom having an affair. The first one. The one I found out about. I shouldn't have told her, but who else was there to tell? Not Dad. Never Dad. And the secret had been killing me; it was tearing me apart. Kristen cried. Kristen was Dad's favorite. He never said it, but he didn't need to. She cried so hard it shook me.

Aw, hell. "What's your name?" I asked.

"Jendy," I heard her mumble into my shirt.

"Maybe you should go home." Nice, Gage. Nice. How compassionate. "I mean, maybe I should get you home. You need, like, sleep or something, Jendy."

"No--" she started to argue.

"Come on. Let's go." I shifted, intending to help her to her feet. "You'll feel better tomorrow."

"No, no. Not that. Jen*na*. *Na*," she corrected. "My name is Jen*na* Gressa."

"Hmm. I like Jendy better." I nudged her, trying to lighten the mood. How long do people feel grief? I was a psychology major for two semesters. What did they say about grief? It comes and goes? You move through it or something like that. Yeah, maybe I needed more than twelve credits before I started psychoanalyzing. Maybe I needed to be sober as well.

Jendy shrugged. "I'm too drunk to care what you call me."

I laughed.

She wasn't Roxie, but she wasn't awful. Maybe Ace and I had been hasty in our initial assessment of her. She didn't look so bad in my hoodie. Her hair. It would probably look halfway decent out of that ponytail. Plus, she was drunk, and like she said, she thought about her dead dad when she was drunk. How could anyone be expected to be attractive when they were a depressing, existential drunk?

"Don't make me go home," Jenna said in a voice that bordered on pleading. "Not now. Not tonight."

An uncomfortable silence engulfed us.

"Okay." I filled in the unnerving silence.

"Thanks," she said with gratitude that was definitely disproportionate for the favor of allowing someone to sleep in the dead bushes in your backyard. She's just drunk, I told myself. Heightened emotions. Girls get strange when they are drunk. Any nice gesture is equivalent to lying on a live grenade.

"Really. Thank you." Her eyes met mine and they were deep and brown and shined with the power of probably six or seven wine coolers. She touched my chest then, leaned into me, her hair, her scrubby ponytail brushing my face, the scent of it filling my whole body.

Good God, she's beautiful, I thought for the first time about any girl. Then the words *what are you thinking* filled my whole body. I stared at her hand. Her fingers moved, splayed across my shirt. Then she gripped it, hard, wrinkling the front of my shirt into a tight fist. I touched her, lightly, my fingertips grazing her shoulders.

"Roxie is a really good friend," she said with the kind of sincerity that comes only with drunkenness.

"Everyone likes her," I agreed, though my interest in Roxie had been more than platonic.

My hands moved down her shoulders, over her arms. She watched my hands, her stare focused, intent. Then she looked back at me, surprise swimming in her eyes. "What do you think is happening?" She whispered.

"I don't know." I answered, with complete honesty that comes only with drunkenness.

"How did we get here?"

"I don't know," I said again, looking at the bushes surrounding us. "But it smells terrible," I added, and it made her laugh.

She had a good laugh. She wasn't that bad. Was she?

I was holding her hands now, a whisper of fingers not quite locked together.

"Are you still drunk?"

Very. "Eh." I rubbed her fingertips, her thumbs, in mine. "Not really," I lied. "Are you?"

What are you thinking, I asked myself again, a question that, in my drunkenness, I could not answer. So she did. She pulled her hands away, and I stared at my now empty hands. They looked different, and I was not sure why.

"Yes," she answered. She looked at me with a half-smile then pushed on her lips with one finger. "I'm very drunk. I think my mouth is going numb." She smacked her lips together.

I laughed and shifted into a lying position, my arm still around the girl in my sweatshirt, and she tumbled with me. I couldn't help it. And there she was. I saw her. I thought about Toby again and how Dad bought him for me, a present for my eighth birthday. A boy needs a dog. Dad fiercely believed stereotypical sentiments like this. He was the only one surprised when Toby took to Kristen immediately and rarely left her side.

Jenna smiled at me.

My body felt sticky hot, and I was drunker than ever.

She smacked her lips together again. "Yep. Totally numb."

I propped myself up on one elbow, and stared down at her.

"Numb? You're numb, Jendy?" I reached a thumb out and rubbed it across her lower lip. "You feel that?"

She shivered, her eyes on mine.

Our faces were close now, my mouth nearly on hers.

"What are you doing?" she asked.

My hand stopped on her stomach right under the hem of the hoodie. "What are *you* doing?" I asked, hoping she couldn't see me shivering like her.

Her eyes cleared, as if she finally realized she too was touching me, pulling at my tee-shirt, pulling me close to her. Her eyes met mine. They held and then they swallowed me whole. If I believed in souls at all, I'd guess mine just met its mate.

"Did you feel that?" Jendy asked, and she sounded breathless. She touched my face. Her hand ran over my cheek, gripped the back of my neck.

I did.

Yeah I felt it. Yeah. I felt the crippling fear ripping through me.

Jesus.

Reality slammed into me. I imagined bringing this girl to parties. This girl in sweatpants and rumpled hair and no make-up. Jesus. Even her hands were dirty from sitting back here, and she probably got the dirt all over me, all through my hair and on my face and down my neck.

I blinked.

So this is how it would go.

I shifted. Off of her. Away from her. Even though what could have passed for a soul inside me protested. I sat up. "This needs to be done," I said. "You need to go home." I always knew I was kind of an asshole when I needed to be, but this time, the pain of the realization was so real, a hot, searing bullet to the gut, that I squeezed my eyes shut. It was a decision I could never take back. I opened my eyes, and she was still there. She definitely had not anticipating my abrupt rejection. Confusion settled into her features. She sat up quickly. "What?"

"I don't know, Jendy. What the hell is with all of this?" I gestured to her body. My insides were ripping apart.

"What do you mean?" Her confusion was quickly melting into anger.

"Who the--" I stopped. Did I really want to do this? "Who the hell wears sweatpants to a party? You got dirt," I scrubbed my hands through my hair, "all over me. This is really weird."

Her eyes widened, her lips parted in shock. Then she bristled. "You're an asshole," she said, less accusatory and more like a sad revelation.

I saw the tears burn in her eyes. Three minutes and she would be gone. You can make it through three minutes.

"I'm just being honest," I said.

"What is wrong with you?" She pushed me away, exactly where I wanted to be.

"I don't know." I must have looked as strange as I felt because she hesitated for one second.

"Screw you." The curse ripped out of her, and she hurled a red cup that seemingly materialized from nowhere at me, emptying the contents all over my shirt. Wine cooler. I was right. She pushed off the ground and immediately fell right back down onto me.

"No!" Jendy screeched when I moved quickly to help her to her feet.

"Let me walk you home," I offered. I did not want to walk her home.

"Are you kidding me? No. No," she said more forcefully, pushing at me. "I'll get home on my own. That's right. I'll do it myself. Gage. *Gage*. Yeah, I know your name. I know *you*, Gage. How 'bout that?" She was rambling, and she must have known it because her face flamed scarlet. "Stop laughing at me."

"I'm not laughing at you," I said. "Just…just…wait. Jendy--"

"Don't call me that," she screeched, and pushed at me. "Don't *ever* talk to me again. You're an asshole." She said it again with the same astonishment.

"What did you expect?" I asked because though I had been called an asshole many, *many* time before, this was the first time it had been said out of disbelief, as I were capable of being anything else.

"Gage," she said. "You are an asshole." I hated hearing her say my name. She knew me. She knew me as soon as she saw me.

"No, no. I'm sorry. I'm sorry." I struggled with her even as she pushed me away. "I'm sorry. Come on. I'm sorry. Let me take you home."

"Leave me alone."

"I'm not leaving you alone."

"How chivalrous of you. How lovely and kind of you."

I winced. She pressed her hands to her forehead, ran them over her face, red and raw. "Then go. Go find Roxie. I want to go home." She sat down in the grass again.

I hesitated. The irony of it all.

She looked up at me. "Go! Go find her!"

And she didn't cry over her dead dog. And she didn't cry over her dead dad. But she cried now. My head pounding, I looked to the house, then back to her. She curled in a ball, pulled the hood of my favorite sweatshirt over and around her face. My heart pounding, I lay down next to her. Not far from us, people laughed. Somebody howled. A group of girls shrieked and screamed in reply.

"I hate you," Jenna said.

And I didn't say anything. I rolled to my back. The humid night, the damp ground, soaked through my tee-shirt. And we fell asleep like that. There in the bushes.

Jenna

Jenna woke up with a start. She woke up like this sometimes. Fast and alert and in panic mode, a paralyzed feeling running deep through her. When she was younger, they thought it was some sleep stage disorder. She was getting caught in one stage and couldn't move to the next. At her first foster home, she'd scream and scream, sleeping and waking in this state until someone got fed up and wasted a co-pay on the sleep study. Which found nothing. It was her brain that failed her, they said, sending her into dizzying panic at night. Meds were prescribed. Meds for her brain and her sleeping problems. The meds that made her feel better until they didn't. The meds that Jenna took until she didn't. Then she'd start the cycle all over again. She was in a "no meds" cycle right now. One of those cycles where she thought she was better than her own brain, better than the meds. She was wrong. Jenna was always wrong.

Deep breath. Deep breath. You're okay. You're not dead. You're alive. You're here. She learned that in therapy. The second foster family took her to that psychiatrist. They were the woo-woo family. The ones that ate organic and burned sage in the mornings. The doctor would click sticks around Jenna's head and tap her body on random spots and send her home with spiritual meditation music and a prescription for diazepam and the latest SSRI re-uptake inhibitor.

Jenna didn't have to start every day like this, convincing herself she was alive. But she did have to start some days like this.

This day was one of them.

Jenna finished her deep breathing and, with a groan, she dropped her aching head into her hands. Time to start my medicine again, she thought. She thought this every time she spiraled on down. So, she would start again. That morning. Her doctor could never convince her to take the meds regularly. Whatever. Right now all she could think about was her hangover.

Her brain was on fire and her eyes itched in places eyes should not itch and her finger swelled over the cross ring her dad gave her for her First Holy Communion. It barely fit her pinky normally. But now it felt like she would need it surgically removed.

A hangover. Jenna didn't drink often, but when she did, it was always to the point of hangover. She groped around her and realized she was outside. Outside? She scrunched her face in confusion as the ground beneath her buried itself into her fingernails. What was she doing outside?

She looked down at her shirt. A hoodie. Delicately, Jenna pulled the fleece material away from her chest with a forefinger and thumb. Not her hoodie. She stared at the sweatshirt a full ten seconds before she remembered. Her eyes widened in horror, and her gaze flew to the ground next to her.

He wasn't there. She was alone.

Thank God.

Jenna looked up. It was dawn, and it was beautiful, and it was, she looked at her watch, the day after her dad died.

She made it.

She sighed with relief.

It wasn't exactly the day after her dad died. It was ten years later, the day after her dad died.

But that didn't matter. Time never felt linear when it came to death. Jenna was never one hour or five months or ten years away from her father's death. When it was there, it was there. Right there. It was the day, the hour, the exact minute.

And she spent the day, ten years later, getting drunk then sleeping in the bushes with Gage. Jenna had seen him before that night. Roxie had dragged her to the parties. *Let's do something fun tonight.* He was there, always there. Typical frat boy, one might have assumed. But Jenna saw something in those parties. Yeah, he was picking up girls. But she also saw him pick up a girl. Literally. From the floor. She had fallen. She was very drunk. Everyone ignored her.

Actually walked around her. Jenna was sober then. And she had seen. She was pushing through the crowd to get to the girl. But he noticed first. And, easy as anything, Gage bent over and scooped her upright. Under her armpits. Nothing sexy about it. *You okay?* Jenna saw his mouth move. The girl giggled and nodded her head. It was a big nod, an over-exaggerated drunk and embarrassed nod. He patted it. Smiled. Then turned back to conversation with some guys.

Another party. Another girl. Struggling with a beer. He passed her. Stopped. *Need help?* He twisted the top off with a smile. Handed it back. *Thank you.* She looked eternally grateful. Of course she did. Gage was beautiful in a way no man should be beautiful, and it seemed like he barely cared to acknowledge it. *No problem.* He brushed off the gratitude and kept moving.

"What is his name?" Jenna had asked Roxie.

"Who?" Roxie asked, and Jenna pointed. "Gage." Roxie answered. "I think."

He did nothing big. Nothing heroic or particularly honorable. Even after he pulled the girl up by the armpits, he let her go. She stood on her own, and it was not like he watched over her the rest of the night. Jenna knew because she watched him the rest of the night. He drank. He cheered on two girls as they kissed. He drank some more. He ran outside, jumped in the pool fully clothed, made out with two different girls in said pool who were not fully clothed. He drank even more. He was pretty much an animal.

But he had noticed that girl who fell. He had noticed Jenna. He noticed things nobody else did.

Jenna couldn't remember much of their conversation from the night before. He was studying a million things, and he wanted to make money. But he didn't do anything else. Right? She was fuzzy on the details.

She knew they almost kissed, and she knew he insulted her.

But she wasn't an idiot. She knew why he did it. She never thought of herself as particularly attractive, but she wasn't ugly either. Jenna was average and fine with it. She knew she could take off her glasses and straighten her hair and mascara her eyes and she was more than average. But Jenna really did not care what anyone thought of her clothes or her face or her hair or her anything. She had never really cared, because for her there was a lot more to care about. Some people cared about that kind of stuff - people like Gage - and while it always surprised her that there were people who cared so much, she understood.

What embarrassed Jenna the most about last night was how wrong she was about Gage. She had always prided herself on her gut instincts, that swift reaction she had to people and situations that was almost always right. *Almost* always. She was too drunk to be embarrassed then. Now, in the daylight, she was appalled at what she had divulged to a person she had judged so incorrectly. At *everything* she had divulged. She knew why he hurt her. She could even almost understand it. *Almost.* Still, she hated him. Or maybe she hated herself.

Whatever. If there was anything she learned from her first woo-woo foster family it was what's done is done and all that Buddhist stuff about not living in the past. Enough of sitting in the dirty, dead bushes. Jenna needed to get back to Roxie. Roxie was probably freaking out.

Jenna stood, her legs still a little wobbly. She stretched them and thought of her dad and her dog and Aspirin and scrambled eggs and Roxie and the guy who left her alone there in the bushes.

A pang of regret stabbed her.

She thought she knew him.

But he knew himself better.

And he was an asshole.

She felt the heat of embarrassment, of being so wrong, rise in her cheeks.

Coffee. She needed coffee with lots of cream and sugar.

Jenna wiped her face with the sleeve of the hoodie that still smelled like him and stepped into the expanding morning. She saw it immediately. There on the grass next to the pathetic looking lilac bush was a coffee, cooling in a paper cup, a note scrawled in black marker across the lid.

Curious, Jenna walked over to it. Bent down and studied it.

Gage. The barista had scribbled his name across the belly of the cup.

And on the lid, very different handwriting.

I didn't know what to do.

Anger flared through her. What a coward. Did he seriously think this would redeem him? Asshole. She nearly kicked the cup. She could already see the contents flying through the air. She felt the satisfaction spread through her. Like a fire. Which made her stop, foot still drawn back. Why? Why after she cried last night, after she told him she hated him, why had she let him stay?

She let him stay.

Leave the past in the past, she told herself. Easier said than done, she argued back. But she really needed some coffee. She felt her face burn. She could accept his stupid peace-offering cup of sludge coffee.

Still. She hated him.

Roxie was waiting for Jenna, pacing actually, when she got home. "Where were you? Are you okay?" Roxie rushed to Jenna and grabbed her hands. "You disappeared last night! I was getting ready to call the police."

"Aspirin." Jenna said. More like begged.

Roxie cringed. "That kind of night? God. I should have never let you out of my sight. You are not made for partying. What was I thinking?" She scurried around the loft, tripping over Terri, who was apparently asleep in a pile of laundry. "Sorry, Ter," Roxie apologized even as she flew through the air and landed with a thud. "Ouch." She massaged her hip with one hand. Terri grunted.

Jenna watched with an amused ghost of a smile. "Rox. It's okay. Really."

"You stopped for coffee?" Roxie pulled herself upright, still rubbing her hip, and nodded at Jenna's coffee. "It's so early."

Jenna had no desire to relay the story. "Hangover," she explained and took a sip of the already stone-cold coffee.

"Oh." Roxie found a plastic bottle and handed it to Jenna. "Water. You need water, not coffee."

Jenna accepted the offering happily and chugged.

"I can't believe you were drinking so much." Roxie shook her head and dug around in her purse. "Ah-ha!" She lifted her head in triumph, a bottle of pain-killers in her hand. "Here," she shook some into Jenna's cupped hand.

"It was last night."

"Huh?" Roxie's eyebrows drew together. "What was last night?" She looked at the calendar she insisted they all use, the squares penciled with appointments and highlighted. Then it registered. Jenna could see it in Roxie's eyes. Jenna was good at that. She was used to it, gauging reactions. She'd been doing it for so long, she hardly noticed when she did it anymore. "Oh, my God, *yesterday*? How could I forget? I am a horrible friend."

Jenna swallowed the pills, snapping her head back as she chugged the water. She winced. "God, I feel awful."

"I'm sorry. I'm so sorry."

Those words brought back a flicker of a memory. Gage. Did he apologize to her? Is that why she let him stay? Was that what this coffee was about? Jenna couldn't quite remember.

She shook her head, trying to wipe away the jumbled memory. No need to remember. "Roxie, I meant the hangover. Don't worry about it. I'm serious." And Jenna was serious. Death anniversaries weren't something you really remembered unless it was personal. It wasn't like Roxie should have scheduled it on the calendar. Jenna gulped the rest of the water. "I should have said something," She said, wiping her mouth.

"Yes. You should have." Roxie looked at Jenna. "I'm serious, too. You're not alone in this world, Jen. You think you are, but you're not. Okay?" Roxie always reverted to den mother, a fact Jenna pointed out during their freshman orientation after Roxie, then a sophomore and campus tour guide, led Jenna around with the precise navigation of a GPS, found her lunch, paid for it, and insisted she stay in her apartment after she learned of Jenna's situation (no parents, no money, etc,, etc.) Eldest of five, Roxie said simply as if that explained everything. And it did.

She put her hands on Jenna's shoulders, and Jenna tried to shake away more fuzzy details of last night. Shoulders. *Gage touched my shoulders. I think.* She looked at my hands. *My thumbs. That's where his hands ended up. Maybe?* She could almost feel them there right now, as if six hours hadn't passed. Jenna squeezed her eyes shut and tried to remember. Why that detail was important to recall, she didn't know, but, God, she wanted to remember.

"Hello? Okay?"

"Um…what? What's okay?"

Roxie gave Jenna a strange look. "You're not alone," Roxie said again, speaking as if Jenna were still drunk.

"Okay," Jenna conceded.

Roxie nodded, appeased for now. "It kills me to think you were alone last night. I could kick myself for that."

I wasn't alone.

The thought was so clear, the words so strong, Jenna thought she said it aloud. She blushed and turned away.

"Jen?" Roxie voice lifted curiously. "What was that?"

Jenna composed herself and turned around. "What?"

"That." She gestured to Jenna's face. "Are you blushing? You were alone last night, right?"

"It's the hangover. My limbic system is all out of whack." Jenna pressed a hand to her cheek and felt the fire of a deep blush. "That's the….that's the heating. And whatnot." *Heating? And whatnot?* Yikes.

"Ah, yes. The limbic system." Roxie did not look convinced. "It'll get you every time."

"I really…I really shouldn't drink," Jenna stuttered. She hated that she got all verbose when she was self-conscious. "My therapist says that drinking is--"

Terri moved on the floor, thankfully bringing Jenna's likely rambling to a halt. Her blonde head poked out from under a towel.

"Could you two, um, please shut up? It's," she looked at the clock, "six-thirty in the morning."

"It's actually quarter to eight," Roxie said, her voice low, so only Jenna could hear. Then louder, "Sure, Ter, we're leaving anyway. Eggs, Jen? Let's go get some omelets."

"Don't use my Fructis. It's expensive," Terri answered.

Jenna's face screwed up. "Your *what*?"

Roxie rolled her eyes. "Nobody is using your shampoo, Terri."

"Somebody is showering. I can hear it."

Roxie held up both hand. "Okay, Ter. Whatever you say." She turned to Jenna. "Omelets. Now."

"Eggs sound kind of horrific right now, but I could probably go for more coffee." Jenna said as she slipped one of the anti-depressants from her purse and shoved it in her mouth, hoping Roxie didn't catch her.

"And we can talk about your limbic system." Roxie pushed Jenna toward out door.

"Why is she sleeping in the laundry?" Jenna whispered right before the door shut.

Spring Semester

Sophomore Year

Tuesday, May 8, 2001

Jenna

She ran the coffee cart on the social floor of the university library. Which was a weird sentence unto itself. And also it was not completely accurate. Yes, there was a social floor of the university library, something Jenna's brain could not compute. And yes, there was a coffee cart on that floor. But Jenna didn't run that cart so much as manage it. She did not even manage it. She "night managed" it. Which meant that from four until ten p.m. – midnight during finals - five nights a week, Jenna was in charge of the coffee, some lackluster pastries probably salvaged from someone's carburetor, and one other co-worker.

Jenna hated the hours. She hated her co-worker, Ben, a third year theater student who drove a Lexus and consistently called in sick. And she really hated coffee. Okay. That was not entirely true either. She hated Charred coffee. And she did not like the name of the place either. How was the named Charred at all appealing to anyone? Who in their right mind would like charred coffee?

The coffee cart, however, was a huge success. Apparently Charred coffee appealed to everyone. Especially during the evening, when students were cramming both class notes and coffee into their sleep deprived bodies. And especially during finals week, which was this very week.

Ben called off. Of course he called off. He did that thing where he changed his voice, made it sound all croupy, which fooled Jenna several times back in the fall when he transferred to nights because nobody on the 7-3 shift could stand him. Which she guessed was a good thing considering his theater major. Ben probably could have fooled Jenna today, except that she had seen him at Taco Bell ordering three chalupas and a sixty-four ounce Baja Mountain Dew thirty minutes earlier.

"You have got to be kidding me," she said when he gave his excuse, which this time was walking pneumonia.

"It's true." Then he added. "I already called Pete. He said I can cover a shift tomorrow morning."

"Wow. Good to know walking pneumonia clears up so fast."

His reply was a grunt.

"You're an idiot," Jenna said, but only after she hung up the phone. *Fire him*, she jotted down next to his name on the schedule and hoped the general manager would actually fire him this time. Jenna considered her message then added three exclamation points. Satisfied, she nodded her head. Yeah, the exclamation points were definitely the apex of her argument. She should have gone into law.

"Hello? I don't know why you're back there pissing around, but you have a massive line." This special announcement came from an obviously irritated guy with green hair and lots of metal stuck through his ears and eyebrows. One girl, a typical looking college girl clad in flip flops and pajama pants, stood behind him reading from a notebook. Yeah. Massive line.

"Can I order?" He asked impatiently.

"Sure. Sorry about that," Jenna said brightly.

"Whatever." He rolled his eyes. "Get me a café latte, extra espresso. And if you could hurry up," he added, "that would be simply wonderful."

Simply wonderful, Jenna mocked in her head and imagined decaffing his drink. She smiled to herself. She was too nice to actually do it, but the act would be utterly satisfying.

"Jen! Jen!" Roxie skidded to a breathless halt at the counter.

"There's a line," Green Hair spat out at her.

She looked him up and down. "Relax, chief. I'm not here for coffee."

"What's up, Rox?" Jenna had gotten good at holding a conversation and waiting on customers. It only took two years and Roxie leaning against the counter nearly every night.

"There's a party tonight." Which in Roxie-speak meant *Let's go to a party*.

"It's a Tuesday, Rox."

"It's finals week, Jen," she countered, which to Roxie was a proper counter-argument.

Jenna handed the fully caffeinated latte to Green Hair. "Have an awesome day," she said with a smile. He dropped a penny in the tip jar and walked away.

Roxie made a face. "What a douche."

"I have a ton of studying to do." Jenna smiled at the next girl in line. "What can I get you?"

"Iced tea, please. Unsweetened. How are you doing today?" The girl was one of those overly-pleasant people pleaser types trying to make up for the last customer. Jenna loved those types. She punched her employee discount into the machine for the girl. She deserved some kind of reward to niceness. She probably got walked all over in everyday life.

"You have a 4.0." Roxie said. "You don't need to study."

"How do you think I got the 4.0?"

"Come on. One party." Roxie looked hopefully at Jenna. "You don't have a final until Friday. Let's live for Tuesday." Roxie declared the last part as if it were some motto of theirs Jenna was disavowing.

Jenna moved her shoulders, trying to stretch them out.

"And, may I add, I have a 4.0 as well," Roxie retorted. "Parties and all."

"Hey! I have a 4.0 too. I think I'm gonna do it." The girl waiting for her iced tea got caught up in Roxie's closing argument. "I'm going to go out tonight." She turned to Roxie. "Life is made for the living, right?"

"Good for you!" Roxie nodded her head approvingly at the girl and smiled sweetly at Jenna.

Jenna pushed the iced tea at the girl. "You have a good day."

"I will." The girl paid, gave Roxie a big smile, "I feel so good right now!" and practically skipped away.

Jenna turned to a nearly laughing Roxie, her expression flat. "You paid her to say that."

"I never thought of that. That is an excellent idea though." Roxie rubbed her chin thoughtfully.

"All right, all right," Jenna relented. "Fine. I'll go." Roxie squealed and jumped up and down clapping, making Jenna laugh and shake her head. "Where?"

"Delta Beta house," Roxie replied, and Jenna heard the sound of mentally screeching brakes.

"No. No. Absolutely not." Jenna had somehow miraculously managed to avoid Gage on their tiny campus for the past eight months. There was no way she was going to purposely set out to find him. She had also managed to take her meds every day for the past eight months. She had taken them for so long her brain was starting to do that thing again where it thought she probably didn't need them anymore. And Jenna did a miraculous thing. Instead of stopping, she kept taking them, which was a first. It probably had something to do with her embarrassing and weepy disclosure to Gage and her desperate need for that to never happen again. So, yeah, she should stay far away from him.

"No. Nope. That doesn't work. You already promised."

"I didn't promise anything."

"But why not? They throw the best parties."

"I'm tired of their parties," Jenna lied.

"Liar," Roxie correctly stated. "You can't be tired. You haven't been to one of their parties since September."

"Exactly."

Roxie's face screwed up in confusion. "What?"

"I'm not going. I really should study, anyway." Firm decision made, Jenna turned to a stack of boxes full of cappuccino mix.

"Jen?"

"Hmm?" Jenna was busy looking for her box cutter. That thing was always getting misplaced.

"Remember when I asked you back in September about that night? If you spent the night alone, I mean?"

Jenna stopped abruptly and shot upright. Thank God she wasn't facing Roxie. Jenna was never great at hiding that fact that she, too, was apparently a big, fat liar. "I *was* alone." Her voice didn't squeak at the end, did it? She bit her lip. She was already sweating. She should have remembered that Roxie didn't miss a thing. Roxie's mind was a steel trap, which was either the reason she decided on her criminology major or the very subject that encouraged the development of that kind of brain.

"You know you can tell me anything."

Jenna considered that. She knew she could tell Roxie anything. Roxie would always take Jenna's side. Roxie would sympathize and rant and rave and swear up and down they would never set foot in Delta Beta ever again. She'd curse the place and tell everyone they encountered what a bunch of scumbag trolls lived there. Picturing that pleasant scenario, Jenna smiled to herself, rubbed her sweaty palms against her apron, and took a deep breath to compose herself. Jenna could tell Roxie anything.

"Roxie?"

Roxie raised her eyebrows, expectantly.

"You want a coffee? On the house."

Roxie's mouth set in a straight line. She narrowed her eyes. "Sure," she said slowly.

Jenna smiled as she pulled the coffee. There was nothing more mortifying in Jenna's life than her night with Gage. She was so wrong about him. So incredibly, stupidly, disgustingly wrong. It was embarrassing how Jenna equated his good looks, his ropey muscular arms, his laid-back extraversion with being kind and insightful. She had only three credits of required freshman psychology, but she knew her brain had done something very wrong in judging him. What did they call that stupid thing your mush-pile of brain did when facing a hot guy? The Halo Effect? The Dumbass Effect?

Jenna could tell Roxie anything.

Except this.

"You know what? We should go to that party." Jenna leaned over the counter and handed Roxie her cup.

"Yeah." Roxie sipped her coffee. "Thanks for the coffee." She said, but really it sounded a lot like *I'll get to the bottom of this*.

Jenna ignored the tone and turned to the guy who wandered up to the cart. "How can I help you?"

It was late.

Much later than Jenna planned on staying.

She waved a hand in front of her face. No more blurry lines pulsating around it. She blinked twice, moved her hand again. Her hand. A clear and perfect hand. Which meant Jenna's vision was clearing. Phalanges. She wigged them. Yep. Perfect. There they were. All of her phalanges. The word didn't even make Jenna giggle. Which meant she wasn't even tipsy anymore. Which meant, yes, she really wanted to go home. She needed to find Roxie. She had ditched Roxie upon entering the house, mainly so Jenna could hide in the bathroom, drink alone like a weirdo, and hope to avoid Gage. And it had worked. She hadn't seen Gage all night.

Now Jenna had come full circle to sober and felt no need to push her luck in avoiding every single person there. And maybe one person in particular.

"Roxie? Have you seen Roxie?" She asked this question to groups of people. Everyone knew Roxie. Everyone knew Jenna as Sweatpants, Roxie's roommate, even though she had taken to wearing yoga pants lately. Jenna shrugged at the thought. Lemmings, all of them.

A group of girls nodded upstairs, and Jenna moved to the top floor.

"Roxie?" She called out. Hopefully Roxie wasn't sick in a bathroom. Jenna never should have ditched her. Wasn't Roxie's mother always telling them to stick together? That sounded like good advice. They should really consider following it sometime. Jenna pushed at a door.

The room was not quite dark; dim light radiated from a corner of the room. It also smelled kind of like feet and sweat and some sort of room deodorizer, the cheap fruity kind that reminded Jenna of a gas station bathroom. But this was not a bathroom; it was a bedroom. Oh, well. Jenna poked her head in anyway and called out to the void. "Roxie?"

It was then she saw the bed and the two forms on it tangled in each other.

One form was definitely Roxie. She saw the creamy skin of her back. The long cascade of deep brown curls Jenna had watcher her straighten the re-curl into a waterfall of perfection hours earlier.

"Oh! God! I'm sorry, I'm sorry." Jenna backed quickly from the room. "Rox! I'm sorry. I'm sorry." She pulled the door shut tight and leaned against it. Face heating, Jenna covered her mouth squeezed her eyes shut.

"Jen?" Roxie's voice cut through the thin panel of wood between them.

"No, no, no. It's cool. It's cool." Jenna heard the muffled reply of the guy with whom Roxie shared the room. Jenna squeaked with mortification. "She's gone, babe."

"That's Jen. I think that's Jen."

"It's fine. Hey. Hey. It's fine."

There muffled voices argued some more as Jenna cringed. I should go. "I'm gonna go!" Jenna called out a little too cheerfully. She heard some clattering, some bumping, fumbling, one loud thud followed by a groan. That was definitely Roxie, who for all her beauty, was an enormous klutz. Then louder, "Jen, wait up. Jen!"

Jenna's eyes flew open. Roxie must have thought Jenna had run away. She backed away from the door as Roxie flew through it, plowing directly into Jenna. "Oh! Jen. I thought you were--"

"I'm here!" Jenna answered brightly. Too brightly.

"I'm drunk," Roxie proclaimed. "We should go. You shouldn't walk home alone. Right? Right. I'm right, right?"

Slowly, Jenna nodded her head. "Right."

"I'll walk you home!" Roxie teetered then fell then burst into wild laughter.

"Right. Okay. You walk me home." Jenna looked at Roxie and helped her to her feet. She glanced back to the door. It was open again, and a figure emerged, dark against the light spilling out of the doorway.

"Bye, Roxie," he said, a flat monotone that matched his expression. He was smashed. Completely. Eyes red and bloodshot. Stumbling a bit, fumbling a bit.

"Oh. Oh, yeah." Roxie teetered on her heels and smiled back at him. "I'm drunk," she said with the wide-eyed seriousness only a completely plastered person could muster.

He tucked his tongue in his cheek. "We are." He said with a drunk, wavering smile.

"You want to walk us home? Me and Jen?"

"Yeah!" He exclaimed companionably. "Yeah! I can walk you home. You and Jen."

"No," Jenna said quickly. "No. We're fine."

"Oh, no." Undaunted, he waved one hand dismissively. "I would love…*love* to walk you home." Drunkenly, he sagged against the door.

"Nope." Jenna gathered as much cheer as she could and said through her grinding teeth, "We are perfectly capable." As if to punctuate the sentence, Roxie fell to the floor again. Jenna sighed the frustrated cry of a person rapidly losing patience. She pulled Roxie to her feet again. "Say bye, Roxie."

"Wait!" Roxie dug around in her purse, pulled out a fat, purple sharpie, and scribbled something into his palm. "Find me."

He stared at his cupped palm. "Will do."

He wouldn't. There was no way he'd come looking for Roxie after tonight. Jenna was absolutely sure of that. Especially not after seeing her. "Come on, Rox. I'll get us home," Jenna said in what could be mistaken for an important tone, as if she were responsible for far more than the five minute walk. She wasn't feeling important though. Jenna was feeling hurried. Hurried and embarrassed and, truthfully, a little queasy.

Roxie smiled, proudly, and made her way back to Jenna. "We live together." Roxie excitedly gestured back and forth between Jenna and herself. "You could visit us!"

"Yeah. I could," The guy said, his eyes burning into Jenna's, the ghost of a smile on his face. Jenna's mouth dropped open. He wasn't embarrassed? He wasn't ashamed? He should be. He was the one who ruined everything. And now, with Roxie? *Roxie*? Jenna's heart clenched.

"Stop it." Jenna's voice came out taut as an over-tuned guitar.

"Jendy." He regarded her through his watery eyes.

"You're disgusting," She hissed.

He smiled. "Fare-thee-well, ladies!"

Jenna felt the fire of anger burn through her body and reach her eyes. She pushed him. "Grow up, Gage." Jenna whirled indignantly, and Roxie, still leaning heavily on her, let out a squeal of delight at the spin they performed.

"You should go into pairs dancing," he said. No, he slurred.

Roxie laughed, delighted at the suggestion.

"Shut up." Jenna shot a harsh look over her shoulder. If the words were bullets, he'd be dead.

"Oh, be careful there, babe. If looks could kill."

"Or maim." Jenna glared at his crotch for one second then met his eyes.

The laugh he let out was wild and drunk and high.

Roxie squealed with laughter then tripped, pulling Jenna to the floor with her.

"You need help?" Gage asked amiably.

Jenna glanced back at him as she struggled to upright Roxie. He hiccupped twice then sagged into the doorframe. "Don't touch us," Jenna huffed as she pulled Roxie along, even though he wasn't trying to touch them. Her leg burned with pain, a pain that would never go away, and she really wanted the help he offered.

"Why are you pissed? I'm a good guy," he argued.

Jenna kept walking, dragging Roxie and her pained leg behind her. Roxie sang something under her breath.

"I'm tired," he announced to no one.

"Shut. Up." Jenna yelled.

"Maybe you're pissed about something else."

Jenna heard him fall to the floor after that declaration. He probably passed out there, alone and helpless. Good.

She never looked back.

It was eight months later, even though, to Jenna, in that moment, it could have very well been that same night.

Gage

Mom and I were in the middle of a nuclear meltdown.

It started the weekend I went home, but in retrospect, should not have started at all.

Dad. It was Dad. Kristen was always worried about Dad, who grew gradually stranger and more withdrawn as the years passed. She called in, not really a panic, but sort of a tizzy.

So I went home only because of Kris and Kris was all giddy to see me, probably because she was the only one left to bear the increasing bitterness between Mom and Dad. Kristen could also barely stand Mom and preferred to spend most of her time either with Dad in the backyard building things, or if he wasn't around, alone in the piano foyer (yes, Mom actually had a foyer solely for the piano) consumed in her music. People called Kristen a prodigy. I wasn't so sure. Not that she wasn't talented, but prodigy? I don't know. I did not know much about prodigies, but I wondered if they hated their lives too, and if you hate your life while at the same time have an insane mother who "encourages" you to practice until your fingers pretty much bleed, *and then* end up being unearthly great at something, are you a prodigy or just a person with a lot of escape time and an insane mother?

So I was home - on Cinco de Mayo of all days - when I could have been celebrating with the guys.

"Mom's cheating on Dad again," Kristen said to me as I ate breakfast alone Sunday morning. Mom was working her typical eighteen-hour day. Dad had taken to making these little wooden birds and selling them on the Internet when he wasn't at work. Today he was at work. Still, the table was littered with little wooden birds that Kristen painted gold or blue or purple during her free time. She was currently painting one gold. They were good, like really good. Was Dad a prodigy or happen to have a lot of time and an insane…wife?

"Did you tell Dad?"

"Of course not." Kristen pursed her lips then lowered her voice. "To be honest, I don't think he'd care if I did, Elli." Kristen was the only one who could get away with Elli.

"So…he knows?"

"How could he not?" She gestured to all the birds, as if to say *look at all these fucking birds.*

"And he doesn't care?" I asked, picking up a bird poised for flight, but cemented into place with wood glue.

"Things are *very* different around here, Elli. Like, you don't even know how different."

"What is going on?"

"Nothing terrible," she replied. "Just, like, if two ghosts got married..." Her brush poised over the wing of a bird while she thought. "I'm terrible at analogies," she said finally. "What do old people say? Ships passing in the night? I don't think they have talked since Christmas."

"Jesus."

"I don't even know if I should--" Kristen hesitated.

"Say something?" I finished. "To Mom?"

"I mean, does anyone even care?"

"I don't really want to say anything." I said, confirming that, nope, I did not care anymore. I was tapping out.

Kristen looked sullen. "I hate living here."

It struck me then. This conversation. With my teenage sister. How completely absurd. Kristen abruptly stood, and looked around as if unsure of herself. "Um, I think I'll go practice."

"Kris," I called, stopping her.

I absolutely did not want to say something to my parents. Not to either one of them.

Kristen turned. Looked. Her face was small and round. Pale. Like porcelain. I recalled vividly when she was a baby and would hold onto me, wrapping her tiny fingers around mine tightly. I hated that I remembered that. I cursed then, low and slow under my breath. I was going to say something.

"I'll say something." And felt the weight of the words crush my chest.

That night I found Mom in the kitchen. Dad and Kristen were down in the basement painting birds.

I had no idea how to say it, so in true Gage fashion, I blurted it out. "You're having an affair."

I don't know what I was expecting. Mom wasn't inclined toward histrionics. But, I don't know, maybe I expected at least a shocked jaw drop? A denial? Anything?

Instead, she swiveled on one heel and gave me a measured stare. Then she turned back to the cupboard. She reached for the cereal, some bran kind high in fiber. She poured a bowl that was as measured as the stare she gave me. She took a bite, chewed. Then finally, "And how, Elliot, does my business pertain to you?"

So I was the one with the reaction. How ironic. It took a full three seconds to pick my jaw up off the floor. "It's our family," I whispered incredulously.

She laughed, an indulged one an adult gives a toddler. "Oh, Elliot. Your father ruined our family long ago."

"No, he didn't!"

"You mean to persuade me that his behavior is normal?"

"And yours is?" I countered.

"My behavior is purely reactionary."

Her replies were so robotic, I wondered if she already had the defense of their imminent divorce ready in her head.

"What about Kristen?" I asked.

"What of her?" Mom took another bite of cereal. "Kristen is fully capable of taking care of herself."

"Kristen is fifteen!"

Mom fussily brushed hair from her eyes. "And?"

"She's a child!"

"Elliot. Don't be silly. She is already teaching piano lessons to kindergarteners. *Those* are children." She put her empty bowl into the dishwasher, fastidiously wiped the spotless counter, and checked her watch. "Now can we wrap this up? I have an appointment with my personal trainer."

"Sure you do," I replied, full of acid.

"Elliot, I'm really trying to understand your position, but, you are making no logical sense, dear." She rolled her eyes impatiently, as she pulled a gym bag out from under the kitchen table.

"Are you kidding me?" I seethed.

"Your behavior is inappropriate."

"*My* behavior? That's hilarious," I said without laughing.

"Elliot, please try to remember. This is my life. Not your life. You are quite welcome to take care of your own affairs. *I* would never think to intrude into your decisions."

My head exploded. It had to have, because I had no control over anything that came out of me. "You," I said, voice shaking, "are a horrible bitch. No wonder Dad is losing it."

Mom turned then, and I saw the first stoke of emotion in her eyes. She walked to me. Slowly, her mouth set in a grim line. She stared at me. I stared back, challenging her.

The *crack* of her hand against my face stung, but it didn't hurt. The slap was more weird that anything. I was twenty-years-old, and she was still slapping me?

I nodded. "I see," I said, working my jaw.

"You are not welcome here," she said and pointed to Kristen's bedroom door. "Say your goodbyes."

"My goodbyes?"

"You're lucky you are even getting that."

Incredulous, I could only stare.

"You, Elliot, owe me an apology." She picked up her gym bag. "Call me when you grow up." Mom's new sneakers squeaked against the wooden floorboards all the way to the door.

I picked up a bird and hurled it at the window. I missed. It bounced off the wall and fell to the floor, stuck within the confines of this house.

So there was Roxie, three days, six shots, and half a bottle of vodka later.

"You look sad, chief," She had said.

Three days after the Mom nuclear meltdown.

I needed to forget, and Roxie was the kind of girl who could make you forget anything. Beautiful Roxie, with her lightning fast grin. Beautiful Roxie plying me with gin.

Anything to forget my mother.

"This tastes like dead bodies," I had proclaimed after the first shot.

"I'm afraid to ask how you know what a dead body tastes like," she answered wryly, and we both laughed. I caught her eye, and she grinned that way that girls grin when they know they are being cute. "Anyway, I think it tastes like Christmas. And I *love* Christmas."

"To Christmas," I toasted, one hand on my shot, one on her knee.

"And dead bodies!" She added as we smashed our plastic shot cups together. Two more shots down the hatch.

"Look at these cups! These widdle, widdle cups," Roxie said in a baby voice. "They're so cuuuute."

"Ace bought these cups from a guy he met at Pretzel Twist in the mall. They threw in a five pound bottle of caramel topping."

"What did you do with the caramel?"

"It's in my room." I said and took another shot. "In my closet."

"I think I could figure out something to do with it." A sly grin bloomed on her face.

I grinned and fell into her, running my hand through her hair. She had left it curly that night. "You're a pretty, pretty girl, Rox."

"And you're a pretty, pretty guy, Gage." She ran a hand down my back.

And then it was shots and shots and shots later.

And then we were laughing, hands locked as the room spun around us. She was pulling me up the stairs, her jeans tight across her legs, straining against her ass with each step. *Show me your room,* she said. *Don't forget the vodka,* she said.

She had on one of those little tank tops, the ones for which every guy survives the winter just to catch a glimpse of in May. She was on my lap. She was leaning over me. Grinning. Laughing. Both of us dizzy with gin and vodka.

When our lips met, everything I was trying to forget slammed into me. Mom. Kristen. Dad and how pathetic it seemed that he painted birds in the basement on his days off. How nobody really gave a shit anymore about anything. Then all I could think of was Jenna. I should not have been thinking about Jenna. But I had been. So, in summation, eight months ago I was with Jenna and thinking about Roxie. And now, Roxie, thinking about Jenna.

So I kissed Roxie harder.

And Jenna, who I didn't even know was at the party, came barging in the room like a fucking queen at her coronation. *For God's sake*. And *what the hell*. And all those other phrases that run through a stunned and drunk guy's shocked mind. In my utterly wasted state, I convinced myself that my guilt had conjured up Jenna's presence right out of thin air.

Jenna said some stuff. Some mean and angry stuff. She was right. What a lousy asshole I turned out to be. So basically everyone on this goddamn planet hated me. Including Jenna, who in eight months never once noticed me as I passed her near daily in the campus commons on our way to classes.

I noticed her though. I noticed her then, and I noticed her now as she swung into and back out of my life like a raging hurricane.

I'll make it up to her, I thought.

I'll make it up to you, Jendy. I'll make it right. I thought I said it; I was sure I yelled it across the ever increasing expanse between us. But when I woke up the next morning, in the hall and still in the same clothes, I realized I had never yelled anything. Instead, I had passed out right in my doorway.

Wednesday, May 9, 2001

Jenna

Ben called off that morning at Charred.

Pete, the day-manager, called Jenna to cover. She covered. She always covered. They could count on her for anything. You'll have to open alone, he told her. Early mornings in the library are slower than evenings.

For once, Jenna was happy about Ben and his unlimited sick days. She needed to avoid Roxie, avoid the questions Jenna desperately wanted to ask about Gage and Roxie and what exactly happened between the two. Jenna needed to avoid Roxie, at least until she had a few hours to process everything. Because Jenna could never ask. Roxie would never forgive herself for hooking up with Gage if she knew what happened between Jenna and Gage eight months prior. Not that it was Roxie's fault. Even if Roxie had suspicions about Jenna's night eight months ago, she never could have guessed who. Jenna needed to know what happened. But Jenna would never know.

So she would have to walk alone, think to herself, talk to herself, sort the problem out. Maybe therapy did work after all. Maybe she shouldn't have stalked out of Dr. Trager's office three years ago after deciding that he would not be able to find his way out of a car if someone opened the front door. Which reminded her. Jenna checked her backpack. She'd have to take her meds as soon as she got to work.

The quiet of the Wednesday morning was nice. Jenna rarely worked mornings. Few students occupied the social floor at quarter 'til eight. They were all asleep or getting ready for class. Or not feeling very social. Some kid photocopied a book in the corner of the room. Another girl slept on a worn brown chair, her feet propped up on a bookcase across from her.

Jenna opened the till and settled into the monotony of morning routine. The silence and routine of opening for the day lulled her. She knelt by a box, ready to emptied it of its contents. She debated with herself on whether to tell Roxie. No. She could never. But shouldn't Roxie know? Especially with the way Roxie was going on and on about Gage on their walk home last night. Hot, Jenna. I mean incredible. And funny. And you should feel his abs and wouldn't it be awesome if he came over and hung out and would Jenna mind so much if…Jenna stopped listening after that, because she was ninety percent trying to basically do the walking for both of them, seven percent dreading a future filled with Gage and Roxie, and three percent wondering about Gage's abdominal muscles.

"I'll have a mocha." A voice pulled her from the depth of her thoughts, and she jumped.

"Sure! Give me one sec--" The smile faded from her face as she turned around.

Gage.

Because, yeah, sure, why wouldn't it be Gage at the very moment she was thinking about his midsection?

"Sorry. Didn't mean to startle--" His face lit up like they were old friends. "Jendy!"

Panicked, she spun away again. *Why? Why are you here?* She wanted to scream. To shake him. She dug through her backpack and grabbed a Xanax from a pack she marked Emergency! She clung to the bottle. *Save me, save me, save me*, she begged it as she chased the pill with a chug of water. Fists clenched at her sides, Jenna faced him. She set her face hard, her lips tightened against her teeth. "A mocha what?"

He raised his eyebrows. "Coffee? I assume you've heard of them."

Jenna tugged a cup from the stack. "Of course I've heard of them," she muttered to herself. "There's a lot of mocha things you could order."

"What was that?" Gage leaned over the counter with a smile.

"Nothing," Jenna answered, voice full of false brightness. She gave him a tight grin.

"You looked nice last night. Graduated to yoga pants I see." He practically sang the words.

The Xanax was not working. Jenna held her breath and counted to five, a trick Dr. Trager taught her. A trick that worked as well right now as a fan in a desert. She was right all along. Dr. Trager was incompetent. She spun on her heel, cup in hand. "Are you serious right now? Are you actually serious?" She would have added a hard curse if she wasn't at work.

"What? I can't compliment you?"

"No. No, you can't." She blinked once, the tight smile still plastered to her face.

"You look weird," he said slowly, a strange expression on his face. "Like a...robot."

"Ah, there he is! He's back!" Jenna slammed the cup. "Mocha whatnow?"

"Uh...mocha. Plain, normal mocha." He dipped his head close to hers. "Are you okay? Are they holding you against your will? Blink twice if they are."

Jenna looked up, eyes wide.

His eyes narrowed at her, he tilted his head. "I'm waiting."

"It takes a couple minutes to brew."

"No, for you to blink twice."

She dropped the false happiness that obviously was not working. "This?" She gestured back and forth between the two of them. "*This* is not happening."

"Aw, Jendy, everything is--"

"Don't call me that," Jenna interrupted.

He made a face like he was humoring her. "We can be friends. That was what, six months ago?"

It was last night. "Eight," Jenna answered sharply. "Eight months."

He was incredulously silent. Then his eyes widened. "You're counting." Then he grinned. "You're jealous?" Curiosity had creeped into his question.

Hide your emotions, Jenna. You can do it. Nope. Jenna snarled. "Jealous? About what?"

He didn't answer; he simply stared at her, amused and expectantly, so Jenna filled in the blank.

Roxie? He was right. It killed her, both the thought of Roxie and him together and the fact that he was right. Anger bubbled over. "I am absolutely not jealous. You--" she poked him in the chest, and regretted it. Immediately. She flashbacked. His chest pressing into hers eight months ago. Her face flamed red before she could control it. She steadied herself and tried again. "You are an imbecile."

"You didn't knock."

Confused, she stared at him.

"You didn't knock last night."

The humiliation would not quit. He did not know when to quit. What was wrong with him?

"You're jealous," he egged.

She dumped the coffee in the cup. Mocha. Whipped it. All that barista stuff. "Do you want sprinkles?" She practically spat the question at him. It was probably the best cup of coffee she ever made. And she was selling it to this asshole. What a waste.

He shrugged good-naturedly. "I like sprinkles."

God, she hated him. "Chocolate or rainbow?" Her eyes, dead, stared into his. They were glittering. Charmed. Slapping him. Yes. Slapping him would be amazing. Quite possibly the best experience of her life.

"Rainbows are nice. They're really nice over in Ireland. I saw one once on this hike. Wicklow National Park, I think it was."

Go screw yourself. She lightly dusted sprinkles over the whipped cream.

"So how have you been, Jendy?" He leaned over the counter and watched her, then pointed to the cup between them. "You're good at that."

"I didn't know it was happening," she said, her voice low.

"Didn't know what was happening?"

"The…you know." Jenna lowered her voice. "With Roxie."

He smiled and slowly pushed himself upright. "You can't even say it."

She started to push a domed lid onto the mocha.

"Oh. No, no." Gage's hand stopped her. "That's a work of art. Wouldn't want to ruin your creation."

She rolled her eyes and murmured something low and inaudible.

"What was that, Jendy?"

"My boss would rather me not repeat it."

He grinned. "Oh, Jendy. That cup of coffee is museum quality art. We need to call a curator."

She stared at him silently.

He stared at her.

A challenge.

Which she lost. "I didn't know."

"Didn't know what?"

"I didn't knock because I didn't know," she bit out.

He laughed. At her. He was laughing at her.

"There was a light were on." She blushed, recalling the scene. "In the corner."

"*A light was on*? God, are you kidding me?" He laughed. "You're a child."

Jenna ignored the insult. "Your room stinks, by the way."

"Ouch." He didn't look that upset about it.

Jenna couldn't take it anymore. She had been holding the question inside for so long, she might explode.

"Were you with her?" Her heart twisted. Did she really want to know? Yeah. She did. It shouldn't matter anyway. She spent approximately six hours with the guy eight months ago. And it ended so horribly, the answer should not matter. "Were you with her," Jenna repeated, "or was it was like…the before stuff?"

"The *before* stuff? Are you serious? Who has romanced you?"

Jenna punched some numbers into the till. She up-charged him for everything. It wasn't bad. She was supposed charge for extras. It was just that she normally didn't do it. She considered herself the Robin Hood of caffeine; it seemed almost sadistic to charge a college student for sprinkles. Now, she pressed the buttons with near glee. Extra mocha, whipped cream, sprinkles, the works. Bing. Bing. Bing. Bing! "Seven dollars."

"Seven dollars? For a medium coffee? I don't know about that." He dug around in his wallet. "Pete usually charges me four."

She shrugged. "Seven dollars."

"You are such a child. You cannot be twenty years old."

"I hate you," She said, proving his point. She didn't care.

"The lights were on." He couldn't stop snickering over that.

"Leave me alone."

"I was scared of you that night. I was actually intimidated by you." He said it like he couldn't believe it.

That made Jenna pause. He was intimidated by her? Was one of the chunks she forgot? He had to be kidding. She tilted her head and studied him. "You're mocking me."

"Yes. I'm mocking you."

"You are such an asshole."

"Oh, honey. You wound me."

"I am not a honey."

"And I'm not an asshole."

"You don't even know me."

"And you know me?"

"Yes. I know your type."

"Yeah. Right."

"I read."

"Let me guess, second year psych major. Knows it all. What do you read, psychological profiling? Serial murderer memoirs?"

Jenna worked her jaw and averted her eyes. "No." She read romance novels. Victorian era romance novels. And dirty middle-English poetry. And that poetry was *dirty*.

"Ah." His grin was back. The same one that made her melt into him eight months ago. The same one that probably made Roxie melt last night. "What do you read? I'm intrigued."

Jenna stared at him now. So full of himself she could just puke. Just puke everywhere.

"You know what? Nobody likes you," she said matter-of-factly, "unless they're drunk. How 'bout that?" She punctuated her declaration by slamming his coffee down. They both watched it spill all over the counter.

"I see." He grinned. Jenna fumed. "You're only making more work for yourself." He glanced at the puddle of mocha spilling all over the glass countertop.

That was it. Jenna wasn't sure why that was it. But that was it. Her breaking point. The anger that coursed through her was suddenly gone. It dissipated as quickly as it had gathered, a ripping tornado gone before it even started. And underneath all that anger was grief. Deep and strong. Grief. It was as basic as that. Jenna was utterly full of grief. Grief was a roiling unhappiness that Jenna hid well, hid easily after all these years. But this guy. He could find it. He could twist it. And worst of all, he didn't even know it. She broke.

"You apologized to me." Jenna whispered furiously, her voice cracking as she reached for the rag under the counter. "You apologized to me. I remember that."

His demeanor changed like lightning. The smile that filled his face dropped. His eyes, they changed, somehow, someway Jenna could not describe. But they were different. He was different. Gage fell quiet. Jenna knew quiet. She sat through a lot of quiet. She immediately understood this quiet. And it scared her. It was an honest quiet. Bad things happened at the end of an honest quiet. Her dad died at the end of that kind of quiet. He took the dog with him. And her home. Jenna lost everything at the end of an honest quiet, so she did what she had to do to make it stop.

She talked over it. "None of this even matters. You know?" She shrugged casually, wiping the rag over and over the spill, never stopping even after it was gone. "This doesn't even matter." Jenna looked up at him, her eyes hovering somewhere below his face because she did not want to read what was in his eyes.

He swallowed. Jenna watched the lump move up and down in his throat. His hands gripped the edge of the glass counter. Hard. Jenna could see the way his knuckles changed from pink to white.

"Maybe we should stay away from each other." Gage picked up his cup and what was left of his mocha.

Jenna finally looked at him. "Yep."

Jenna remembered jumping out the window when she was ten years old. She remembered hitting the picket fence, the ground, rolling over the paved sidewalk. She remembered the blood. She didn't even feel it. Not until hours later. Hours later, she felt it all.

"Nothing happened, Jenna," he said. "Nothing happened with Roxie."

Jenna swallowed hard. "You need to leave," she said abruptly. "I have customers."

Gage nodded. He dropped bills on the counter. Ten one dollar bills. "Keep the change," he said, his voice softer than it needed to be.

Fall Semester

Junior Year

Tuesday, September 11, 2001

Gage

Cody was new to the house. A sophomore, he had moved in under dubious circumstance. He was on some sort of academic probation, having what he called "debatable" drinking charges pressed against him – nobody was quite sure if it was a DUI or an underage drinking or public drunkenness. His father's lawyers were working on it, he said. Public drunkenness was nothing. The president of Delta Beta had three public drunkenness charges that he was currently expunging from his record. Underage charges we could deal with. Academic probation we could skirt around. DUI? Eh, that was pushing it. But nobody really knew for sure what charges Cody was hiding, and since everything against him was up in the air, and he was a senator's son, and he was pretty much was an all-around cool, laid-back guy, we gave him a pass. The kid knew how to talk his way into or out of anything.

Cody and I were the only ones awake at nine that morning. Me because I had a paper due at noon. Him because he hadn't gone to bed yet. He was drinking some kind of concoction he blended in a Nutri-Bullet that he bought from a guy selling pot and kitchen appliances from the back of a pick-up truck. It's a great deal, he convinced me, after he made me pull over to buy both the bag of pot and the Nutri-Bullet. I'll get him to throw in a Toastmaster. He did. The Toastmaster caught on fire two slices of bread later and was now somewhere under a pile of clothes and next to a vat of very, very old caramel in my closet.

Cody took anyone's presence as an invitation to talk, so as soon as he spotted me hunched over my laptop, he switched on the television and started in on his insomnia, which by now I presumed was not so much insomnia as it was a drinking problem. The kid drank like a monster and never wanted to stop. Currently, Cody was mixing all sorts of fruits and vegetables in the NutriBullet. I watched him dump half a beer in it, felt my face contort in incredulous disgust, and turned back to my paper.

"Shit, man. That building blew up."

"Huh?" I glanced up to a burning building on television. "What happened?"

Cody stared at the television as he dumped the rest of his coffee into his putrid green brew, making it a mud brown sludge. I didn't gag until I actually watched him slug it down. "A bomb?" He wiped his mouth with a tee-shirt he found on the table. "I don't know, man. It just happened."

"Okay," I replied, because I wasn't sure what else to say, and I had a paper to finish. I looked back down to my laptop.

The shock of the burning building was enough to keep him quiet for five minutes. Until information started pouring in.

"Commuter plane, they're saying. Hit the building. That's wild, man. Could you imagine?" I heard the hiss and pop of the beer can he opened.

Cody ran open-commentary like that, giving me the play-by-play in-between alternating gulps of beer and green-brown sludge.

I was barely listening to Cody. Once in a while, I would glance up or mutter in agreement to a statement I didn't even hear, but mostly I wanted to tell him to shut up so I could concentrate. I hunched my shoulders and hunkered down at my computer. Twenty page paper. Due in three hours. If I typed fifty words per minute and never stopped...hmm. I could change the font. Fourteen point. Courier New. Yeah, that might work. Chart, I thought. Add a chart. That'll take up, like, what, half a page? Where were my headphones? Maybe some music would drown out Cody's voice.

"Whoa!" Cody's yelp startled me. "Did you *see* that?"

"Dude, can you give me, like, one minute? I have to get this done." Irritated, I looked up. "Wait." I squinted at the picture in front of us. The other building was on fire. "What is—that's not really—what?"

"The other one. They hit the other one."

"Who hit the other building?" I asked. "A bomb?"

"No, man. How are you not watching this?" He leaned forward, beer forgotten in his hand. "A plane. A plane hit the building. Both of 'em."

"Where?"

"New York, dude. New York City. The world is burning down, dude."

Cody was drunk 24/7. So he was probably wrong. Nevertheless, my fingers stilled on the laptop. "What the hell are you talking about?"

"Look at the television, Gage. Shit. It's terrorists," he said, eyes glued to the television.

"I thought you said it was a…some commuter plane. An accident."

"Well," Cody gestured to the television, "it's obviously not."

"Two other planes are missing."

"What?"

"True story."

"Where?"

"They're missing," Cody said slowly.

"In the sky?"

"Yes. In the sky." He was still addressing me as if I were a dumbass. Then he changed his mind. "Well, I don't know. They could have crashed already." Cody made an explosion sound and moved his hands. "Gone."

I looked at my laptop. I looked back at the television. Back to my laptop. I had eleven pages done. Was it wrong for me to ask the question? It was probably wrong and also stupid and selfish to wonder if we had class anymore now that two buildings were burning. But

Cody wouldn't care. He was probably still drunk. "Do you think I need to finish this paper? Do we have class today?"

"Why wouldn't we?"

"We're under attack."

"No. That doesn't happen here." His voice was skeptical with a hint of are-you-kidding-me. "It can't get worse than this."

Famous last words and all that cliché garbage.

Jenna

Somebody hit the World Trade Center.

The words ripped Jenna out of a deep sleep.

"Wha--" She heard Roxie's mumble drift up from her bed across the room.

Jenna stumbled to the edge of the loft and glanced over the railing to see Terri, stunned, sitting in front of the communal television, her feet propped up on the coffee table next to her forgotten bowl of Frosted Flakes.

"What's going on?" Roxie's voice, still gravelly from sleep, made Jenna jump.

"I don't know. I think she's watching something on television."

Confused, Roxie looked to the television, and then back at Jenna. Jenna shrugged. "It's just a television show," Jenna whispered. "She's really into it. You know how she gets."

Roxie suppressed giggle. "What movie are you watching, Ter?"

"Not a movie. See?" Terri pointed at the burning skeleton of a building. "It's the news."

By then, Jenna and Roxie had dragged themselves down to the makeshift living room of the suite. Boxes littered the living room. Stacks of newspapers and empty cosmetic containers and bottles of lotion covered nearly every surface. Terri was a hoarder, her closet an explosion of clothes and scarves, and sometimes she stole Jenna's medication. Jenna knew this because she counted them after she caught Terri reading the bottle once. Jenna never said anything because she secretly hoped they would work and Terri would be able to clean out the loft without hysterically crying every single time. Living in excess was a strange experience for Jenna, who after the age of ten, possessed only three rolling suitcases of items.

"This is for real?" Roxie asked.

Terri nodded her confirmation.

Jenna squinted through her glasses and pushed them closer to her eyes, as if they were not on straight, and she was not seeing things correctly.

"Oh, my--" Roxie was wide awake now.

"God." Jenna finished for her.

They watched in silence for a little bit, trying to piece together slivers of news and speculation.

"When did this--" Jenna started to ask.

Then chaos broke out as a plane smashed into the other building.

All three girls jumped.

Roxie screamed.

Jenna's hands flew to her mouth, cupping it in shock. "Was that…was that a…" She could not finish her question.

"Yes." Roxie answered.

Terri gawked at the television.

Fire and smoke, thick and choking, poured from the gaping hole left in the buildings.

A stunned silence engulfed everyone. And then they were all talking at once.

"Did you see that?"

"That didn't…did that just…what happened?"

"Was that a…that wasn't a…plane?"

"That was not a plane. No. No way, Rox."

"There's no way that was a bomb," Terri touched her newspapers, her lotions.

Jenna eyed her Xanax on the counter. Should she offer Terri one? Terri probably already took one.

Roxie interrupted Jenna's thoughts. "It wasn't bomb then? The first one? It was a plane too?"

"What is going on?"

"No way. This is not..."

Jenna noticed something very strange, very curious. She leaned closer to the pictures streaming across the television. "What is that? What is falling out of the building? Paper?" Was it office paper? No. Whatever was dropping was falling way too fast to be paper.

"I think it's...I think it's...people," Terri finished and started crying. She hugged a newspaper to her chest.

"No. No-no-no-no-no."

Roxie turned slowly to Jenna, concern filling her eyes. She said nothing, but she reached for her hand and gripped it tight. "You're still here," she whispered.

But they're not. Jenna swallowed the scream that wanted to peal from her raw throat. Eyes washed with tears, she nodded.

Then Terri was running for the phone. "I need to call my mom."

"Let me use that next, Ter," Roxie called out. "I should too."

Jenna's stare, her morbid fascination, glued her to the television. She found herself unable to pull away from the carnage of fiery buildings. So far from where she sat. Yet somehow so close.

There was no one for Jenna to call.

Eventually Jenna heard Terri call out, "The lines must be jammed. I can't even get a dial tone."

Roxie acknowledged Terri with an absent nod as she moved next to her, watching buildings burn. Together, they watched the first building fall, collapsing in on itself.

Jenna cried.

Roxie grabbed her hand, linking them together.

Television news anchors anxiously updated and speculated. Terrorists. Other planes. Washington D.C. Planes crashing into the Pentagon.

"The Pentagon was hit," Terri said mechanically, as if Roxie and Jenna had not heard. The pentagon was less than an hour away.

"Are we going to die?" Terri asked.

Nobody answered.

"Oh, my God."

"This can't be happening."

"We're still here," Jenna reminded everyone. "We're still here."

"Classes are canceled,' Roxie looked up from an email on her laptop.

"I need to call my mom. She's probably freaking out," Roxie said. Jenna looked at her. She knew immediately. "She'll be worried about you, too, Jen. We need to let her know we are okay."

"The lines are down," Terri reminded her.

"What about cell phones? Are they different?"

"Maybe. I don't know."

Jenna watched as Roxie chewed on her cheeks. Roxie always did that when she was nervous. She didn't know anyone noticed.

"Who has a cell phone?"

None of them. Only a handful of students on campus had cell phones.

"Gage has one," Roxie finally said. "I saw him on it at a party last week."

Gage had a phone. Roxie needed to call her mom. Jenna wanted to make that happen; she needed to make that happen.

Jenna would have to find him. She would have to run. She could already feel it. Her legs would scream from the sprint across campus to frat row, to Delta Beta, the last house on the street. Her lungs would ache. The run would hurt.

Jenna was supposed to hate Gage.

But today felt like the wrong day for hate.

"Let's find Gage," Jenna, still pajama-clad, opened the door, and fled the room, without waiting to see if anyone followed her.

Gage

Dad was, for lack of a better word, an interesting man. Grew up on a farm. Served in the army. Fifteen years. Then he walked away. Mom complained he could have done more. Could have gone the distance. Made it far up in the ranks. But he was done. They asked him back a few times after he left, Mom told us; they told him he was the best. Kristen would always cry after Mom told the story. Mom would tell her to pull it together, that some people weren't made to go the distance. And that's everything Dad was to Mom.

To me, Dad was mysterious, and as distant as he was brave. Everything he did for us and with us was done from a distance. I played soccer in kindergarten, and he sat in the car watching from the parking lot. I hit my first homerun in fifth grade and there he was, standing alone on the other side of the park, hands in pocket. When I scored my thousandth point in the varsity basketball state playoffs, there he was…listening on the radio at home.

Kristen had it a little better than me. For her, Dad at least sat in the audience fully and obviously uncomfortable.

He never regaled the tales of his army days to Kristen and me. He was a sniper, was all he said, before we really understood what sniper meant. When we were old enough to understand what sniper meant, we were too afraid to ask.

When I was a teenager, he and I sat next to each other at Kristen's piano recital. The room was dark, and Kristen had chosen a Rachmaninoff Prelude. Neither Dad nor I knew anything about pianos or Rachmaninoff, except for the small excerpt printed in tight script under the name Kristen Rebecca Gageby in the program. By the end of her piece, Dad was crying. And not little sniffles of pride either. His huge, gulping, wracking sobs mortified me as I noticed people two rows ahead of us turning to stare. As distant as my father had always been, he had chosen the perfect moment to be very present. We sat there, almost painfully sat there, as the last notes dissipated, me trying to figure out who took over the hard, stoic body of my father, my father trying to contain himself in that same body.

Kristen stood, bowed, gave a small smile and played with the ends of her hair as she awkwardly accepted the audiences' praise. All three of us there in the same room, uneasy in our bodies in our own ways.

"Elliot." Dad turned to me. I was well into high school by then, and only my family called me Elliot anymore. "I wasn't really made for it."

I stared at him. Really looked at him. His face looked older, and it kind of scared me the way the tears ran like rivers down the jagged scar crossing his cheek. I could have said something, could had said anything. I could have asked a question, a question as simple as, "What Dad? What weren't you made for?" I swallowed - the audience was now clapping for the next pianist – then got up, clambered over some irritated people and jetted out to the parking lot, where I gulped huge mouthfuls of air then shared a cigarette with a bored-looking girl in a black dress.

Dad never brought it up again, and there was no way in hell I was ever going to bring it up again either.

Dad got really into running after that. Running and cigarettes. Because, apparently, people are complex and confusing beings, full of inconsistencies and ironies. When he was done running five miles, he would smoke a cigarette. When he was done running ten miles, he smoked two. After he ran the marathon, he ate a greasy double cheeseburger, chain smoked in the car, got out, stretched, threw his lighter in the trash, and did not touch a cigarette for five years.

Then he began a vegetarian.

Kristen and I were confused. We stopped talking about Dad; we stopped trying to figure him out. Dad, all we could agree on, was a man with one scar on his face and a whole lot of other scars inside.

When he took the job at the Pentagon, when he told us over dinner that we were moving to Washington D.C., we all accepted it with the ease of people used to living with impulsive. Well Kristen and I accepted it. Mom laid into him. *Stupid. Selfish. And what am I supposed to do? Simply quit the practice? You'd just love that, wouldn't you?* Mom had finally made partner at Shields and Rafferty. You knew I was doing this, he countered. We did know. The process was unending and discussed over numerous dinners. I did not think you would actually accept, Mom argued, and I had to admit that for once in my life I had agreed with her. Mom rattled on. We all had lives, things we cannot drop so easily for his whims, surely he knew that? And this vegetarian stuff, she added. We're supposed to bend our eating to you? She threw her fork down with a clatter. She paced. Got up. Looked through the phone, checking the caller identification, before pulling the phone into her room and making a quick call. She left then, excusing herself to get a burger at some fancy bistro down the street. I was not sure why, but I knew deep in my gut that she was having an affair.

Dad ate his broccoli rabe in silence.

Stupid, I thought. Selfish. But I did not know exactly who I thought was stupid or selfish in this situation.

Kristen and I side-eyed each other over our dinner plates, but we accepted it. We eventually accepted all of it. The Pentagon. The affair. It was how our family worked. Our family was made of pent up rage boiling under a thin skin of passive-aggressive acceptance.

Now, I was sitting in the grass, thinking about Dad and staring at my cell phone. A Nokia I bought over the summer. It was expensive. The cell phone guy talked it up. Equipped with an FM radio, he told me. Stores sixty-four megabytes of music. Much to my dismay, I bought it. I was weak and easily persuaded, so unlike my father. Frivolous, Mom called it. Spoiled. What kind of person needs to store music on a telephone?

The selfish kind, I thought but did not say. And you raised him.

The phone didn't seem so frivolous now as I stared at it.

If only it would ring.

A figure neared me, breathless. I could hear the panting, see the shadow cast out from the burning late-morning sun. It was nice out. What a beautiful fucking day.

I squinted, shaded my eyes. "Jenna." I was surprised the way I said it so easily, as if I was expecting her, though it had been four months since we last spoke.

I had seen her on campus a lot. She hadn't seen me. Or she had done as good a job as hiding it as I had.

"Gage." She looked frantic. Or in pain. Maybe both at once. I was having trouble reading her, probably because I didn't know her. She was virtually a stranger, and I didn't know what to say.

"How was your summer?" The question shot out of me like a reflex, some pre-programmed politeness I did not recognize. I don't know. Sometimes you say weird things when you're in a panic and don't want anyone to know.

"Uh--" she stammered. Jenna's face slid from confusion to deeper confusion. "Terrible," she replied in a tone that said her answer should have been obvious to me. "They're always terrible."

"Hmm," I said then ran out of things to say to her.

Jenna eyed me warily. "Did you see the news?" She rubbed at her leg.

"Yes." I nodded at her. "What's wrong with your leg?"

She ignored the question. "I don't want to fight."

"We are not going to fight," I answered dully. Tired. I was so tired of this.

Jenna nodded slowly. "Can I use your cell phone? Roxie needs it."

"Can you use it later? I'm waiting on something."

"On what?" Jenna's temper exploded out of nowhere, catching me off guard. "And what could *you* be waiting on? Pizza delivery?" Her voice sparked with anger. "Roxie needs to call her family. They're probably freaking out. We live right near D.C." Jenna reminded me. As if I needed reminding.

"I know." My voice cracked.

"Please, Gage. Give it to me. We need it."

I stared stonily at the phone. "We're not fighting, remember?"

"Why are you such a jerk?"

"My dad." I said, my own anger rising. "He works at the Pentagon."

"Oh." But it came out more like an *Ugh*, a shot to the gut. "Gage."

"No, Jenna," I said sharply. She pissed me off. With her stupid shot about me ordering pizza. As if I wasn't a part of this day, a part of this huge disaster. As if I had no family to call. As if I was spawned from an *X-files* lizard monsterman. If there were ever a time I wished the ground could open up and swallow a person whole, the day had come. "Don't *Gage* me. I don't want your pity. I don't want to talk. I want to sit and wait, and I absolutely do not want to talk."

"Yeah. Of course," She tried to hide the pity in her voice, but I could hear it.

I didn't want to fight, but I also didn't want her here. "Can you leave? Not to be...blunt or anything," I added.

Jenna looked torn. "You don't want to be alone. Trust me."

It wasn't the first time I had considered the possibility that my father was dead, but it was the first time someone else confirmed my fear. I relented, and nodded to the space on the grass next to me. "Don't be nice to me though."

"I would never," She answered in mock seriousness as she dropped to the grass beside me.

If someone took a picture of us and looked back on it ten years later, we would look like a couple of college kids sitting in the grass. In front of a sprawling white framed house. A house with a porch and a wide lawn and a maple tree shifting leisurely from green to red. They wouldn't see the mad desperation filling our eyes as we stared at the cell phone between us, willing it to ring. They wouldn't see the grip of fear holding us still, strangling our voices. They wouldn't feel the agonizing pain of the wait to hear if someone was dead. They wouldn't know that we were together, but completely alone.

We sat and sat. I don't know how long. Ten minutes? An hour? Time blended into one long abyss. Jenna was nice, nicer than she had to be. She told me some story about her roommate Terri and how sometimes she stole Jenna's Xanax and slept in the laundry for days because "it was warm and smelled nice."

It should have surprised me that Jenna took Xanax, but it didn't. Not because she was crazy or anything, but just because, I don't know, it didn't. I didn't tell her this, and I probably never would, because it was way too creepy Freudian for me to admit, but Jenna reminded me way too much of my dad.

I offered to get her food. Pizza? I suggested. There was some leftover and cold in the fridge. She declined, blushing, though I had no clue why. She offered to get a radio. To listen to the news. I declined. I don't want to know, I said. I don't blame you, she answered. Then we fell into a comfortable silence.

"Where's your posse?" I eventually asked. "Terri and the crew." I meant Roxie, Jenna knew I meant Roxie, but I could not bring myself to say Roxie's name in front of her, and that was a feeling I was not used to.

"I thought they were following me. They didn't. Terri thinks we are going to die." She picked at some grass. "I think they were afraid to leave the room."

I looked up at her. "Jenna wasn't afraid."

"Oh, Jenna was. Jenna ran so fast she nearly shit herself."

Shocked, I let out a laugh again. The girl surprised me sometimes.

"It hurt, running here."

"That's good."

She laughed and punched me. "I guess I deserved that. Can I blame the panic on my lack of manners?"

"You can blame whatever you want. Today, and today only, I'll accept any excuse." It was my peace offering.

She looked down and smiled to herself. She had shredded at least a handful of grass.

"You know about regrets?" I asked.

She didn't look up like I expected. She raised her eyebrows at the pile of grass and blew out a breath. "Yeah. I know a little bit about regrets."

"I shouldn't have said those things to you," I blurted out.

"You gave me coffee." She shrugged it off. "The past is the past."

"Jen." She looked at me kind of shocked. "It was shitty of me."

"Okay," she said quietly.

I didn't want the moment to get uncomfortable, but it did. Very uncomfortable. It was almost as bad as my dad at the piano recital. Jenna hugged her knees to her chest, sending a shower of grass to the ground. I willed up the courage to ask what I needed to know. "Jendy?"

"Hmm?"

"Your dad died?"

She looked me dead in the eye. "It was awful."

"That's what I thought." I stared into the distance.

She could have lied. I guess I was grateful she did not.

"It's...today. This. I'm..." I trailed off. I ran my tongue over my teeth, then swallowed the lump forming in the back of my throat. I realized then if I finished the sentence I'd probably start crying, and there was no way that was happening.

"I'll be here," she said. It wasn't some bullshit she was saying either. She was merely saying it, a statement that she would be here. It was as simple as that. Our knees were touching now. Her eyes, pained but steady, gazed into mine. She was reading my future, and she didn't like it.

Inwardly, I cringed.

The shrill ring of the phone had us jumping away from each other, scrambling to our feet. Jenna brushed at her shirt, her sweatpants, sending more shredded grass flying as I fumbled for my cell. I looked down at the phone in my hand. Back to Jendy. I saw her throat convulse, and it made me want to hold her tight.

I looked back at the phone. The phone with the FM radio and sixty-four megabytes of music storage. My frivolous phone.

That phone was going to tell me everything.

Jenna

Don't answer it, Jenna almost screamed when saw his finger hover over the green button. This was the moment, a moment she knew well. The moment when one reality hovered over another one. It was the moment she decided to jump out the window. The moment before she hit the ground. The moment where she floated between two terrors, and nothing seemed real. Jenna had been safe. Until she wasn't.

She didn't want Gage's worst nightmare realized. She could tell he felt the same. He let it ring three times.

"Hello?" His voice shook, and he coughed to cover it up. Jenna looked away, because she was feeling pity for him and she knew he did not want pity. "Kristen, hey. How's....We're all fine....Yeah, I'm with someone. I'm here with, uh, my, um, friend....Yeah, I know. It took forever....The lines are messed up or something...Did you hear from....Oh...Oh, God...I can't believe --...Ok, ok....No, I'll be ok. Don't worry about me..."

He talked some more. A lot. Asking this Kristen girl about his mother. Asking about his dad again. Asking this Kristen if she was okay. Jenna watched his face carefully for any changes, but she didn't know he was raised by a sniper.

He hung up, and then looked at Jenna.

Jenna's legs cramped and she realized she hadn't moved since he answered the phone. She wet her lips and waited.

He said nothing, simply stared at her.

Finally, Jenna asked. "So. Um…"

"His part of the building was hit."

Jenna clamped a hand over her mouth, felt the tears welling.

"But he wasn't there. He wasn't there, Jendy." Gage's voice sounded very far away. "He was taking my sister to school. High school. First day of senior year. She had a flat. She needed a ride. Then he got stuck in traffic. He wasn't there, Jendy." He looked like he could hardly believe the story he was retelling.

Jenna imagined him telling it over and over again. He probably would tell it over and over. At class. At the bar. Years from now, at some fancy job. It was the miraculous kind of story you told over and over again. It was not the kind you kept inside, locked away forever.

"He wasn't there." Jenna shook her head in disbelief.

"He wasn't there." Gage caught Jenna's eyes and he shrugged.

Jenna imagined they could have kept repeating those same three words back and forth to each other for the rest of eternity if it wasn't for the laugh that broke out of her. His shrug. It was so out of place.

He answered her with his own laugh.

Then they were both smiling, relief quickly flooding out the despair that had glued itself around them.

And then he was tackling her, hugging Jenna, and she was hugging him, and they fell backwards to the grass, laughing. His father was alive. A little part of Jenna, one that was so tiny she had never noticed it until that minute, opened. And, in that moment, Jenna did not need anything else.

Except maybe to borrow his cell phone.

Part Two
The Way We Were

Senior Year

Fall Semester
Friday, November 1, 2002

Gage

Head pounding, I scanned the room, attempting to process my surroundings.

Morning. It had to be morning, because the light was scorching the retinas out of my eyes. My brain creaked and groaned as I scrubbed a hand over my face, shielding my face from the blinding sun.

When did we land on the surface of the sun?

Day of the Dead. Day of the Dead. Day of the Dead. That chant along with some pounding bar music earwormed through my brain. I groaned, pressing the heels of my hands to my temples, and squeezed my eyes shut tight.

Day of the Dead. Day of the Dead.

Stop, I silently command the chanting in my brain. *Stop.*

Naturally, it did not stop.

I opened my eyes. Slowly. Took in my surroundings. Splashes of pink. One hand dropped to the bed. Sheets. Some kind of blanket. I looked at the comforter. Soft, probably filled with feathers, and lots of ruffley things on it. I think Jendy had one of these that she bought before summer break. She dragged me to Target and spent way too long agonizing over the decision between blue one that liked and a fugly brown one that was on clearance. For God's sake, buy the blue one, I said and threw an extra twenty at her. Then she got pissed at my "cavalier attitude" and how she would not accept my charity even if she were dying in a gutter and all she had left to her name was that fugly brown comforter – she said it exactly like that - and some lady in the aisle near us chuckled and commented to the dude with her about how it was probably our first fight or whatever. I rolled my eyes and stalked out of the store, waiting in my car until Jenna came walking out with the fugly brown one tucked under her arm. I left for break like that. She threw the twenty at me. You're being ridiculous, I said, and stuffed the twenty into the ashtray of my car. I left for summer break like that, both of us pissed at each other, the twenty untouched. It was not until the month after I went home, though, I realized I had exactly nobody to talk to, as Kristen Kristen had won some kind of musical scholarship to some piano thing out in California and jetted as far away from the sucking void that was our home.

I had found myself alone with Mom, who even though we were talking again, worked seventy hour weeks, and Dad, who had taken an early retirement and spent every waking hour in the backyard, mostly staring into the distance or mowing the lawn or building a shed that I hoped was to store his birds which had overtaken the basement and Kristen's bedroom. The house was unnervingly quiet, and by mid-May I couldn't wait to get back to school. Kristen was not exactly right when she told me Mom and Dad had quit talking, because I remembered a tepid exchange between them about Italian leather around Memorial Day. Mom wanting it, and Dad, in an obvious progression, had become a vegan.

In June, I spent most of my days sleeping and most of my nights at the bar, either ending up at random girls' places or checking us both into a hotel downtown because there was no way I was bringing them back them back to the house that hell built.

By July, Mom received the credit card bills revealing my weakness for sleeping in seven-hundred-dollar-a-night hotels in downtown D.C., and that was pretty much the end of that. Credit card gone. Part time job at Radio Shack found. I then spent most of my days in Radio Shack texting Cody or Ace and half-heartedly convincing (mostly women) to buy absurdly priced cell phone plans. I spent my nights helping Dad with the shed and then drinking all of Mom's vodka and replacing it with water. Dad rarely spoke unless he was talking about the shed; he was fixated on measurements and lumber. I checked his locked medicine cabinet – last year I had found where he hid the key – and saw he was on two new medications. I spent an entire week Googling the side effects of drugs I could barely spell or pronounce.

In August, with nearly zero income and no more credit card, I went grocery shopping with Mom. Some upscale place called Fare Trade Market Dining Bistro or whatever that sold mozzarella marinated in olive oil and six different kinds of crab salad. Jendy, who lived on a diet of mainly Ramen and Gatorade and fought me bitterly over what was now known as the Fugly Brown Incident, would have been horrified.

Your father only looks out for one person Mom had said bitterly as she filled a plastic container with green olives from the longest olive bar on earth. And we all know who that is. She plucked an olive and popped it into her mouth with a shrug. They won't miss it. She pulled out her phone to text. I glance over her shoulder and saw a man's name and immediately assumed it was an affair and not a client. I might have been wrong but I didn't care. We moved on to the cheeses.

I wanted to text Jendy pictures of the mile long gourmet cheese bar, but she could not yet afford a phone. It was then, thirty days before the start of our senior year that I realized fully what a complete dick of a friend I was to Jendy. There at Fare Trade Market Dining Bistro Club for the Rich and Important, I thought about how she couldn't afford a phone. I had known for a long time she couldn't afford a phone, so why then of all times it struck me as depressing, I am not sure. I felt an impatient urge to know everything about her. I wondered what she did for summer break. Did she live at school? Work in the summer? Who paid her bills? She couldn't seriously be paying her own tuition, could she? Was her life as quiet and miserable as mine was right now? How had I never thought to ask her these things?

At the beginning of the semester, the vodka went down even smoother than the year before, mostly because I was so grateful to no longer be at home. Parties felt like an oasis after a long, dry, lonely desert walk. Jendy had almost seemed uncomfortable when I hugged her at one of them. Because of lingering ill will from the Fugly Brown Incident we weren't buddy-buddy or anything at that point, but it was a surprising relief to see her meandering around Delta house like a lost hitchhiker, I didn't even try to stop myself from reeling her in. She babbled, obviously overwhelmed, when I asked her all the questions I had thought about over the past month. The more she babbled, the more I realized what a dark and deep place she lived in most of her life, and I felt like a dumbass about throwing twenty dollars at her in Target. She was riddled with anxiety, frequently took herself off medications – an idea that seemed about as smart as Cody's Chextini creation, a concoction of Chex Mix, vodka and don't even ask me what else. Jenna also lived paycheck to paycheck, was racking up lots of debt from student loans, and spent most of her summer reading obscure novels that bored me into a cocoon of sleep and writing morose stories that freaked me out enough to make me count her pills when she wasn't looking.

My roiling stomach pulled me back to the present. To the bed. The ruffled bed. Day of the Dead. All that garbage that filled both my head and her room.

My head pounded with no regard to the fact that I had to sneak out of this place quickly. And quietly. I shook it. That was a huge mistake. My skull definitely cracked open. My brain spilled all over the bed. I felt bad for whoever was lying next to me; she'd have to sleep in the brains. And speaking of whomever was lying next to me…maybe I should figure that out.

I squinted, trying to take in the rest of the room through bloodshot eyes. They settled on the ungodly amount of pictures plastered on the wall in front of me. The face I saw the most began to look familiar.

That's where the earworm had started. With that girl. She had been chanting "Day of the Dead" all night long at Grady's to the beat of whatever song was playing. It was annoying, but she was beautiful and dressed up like something weird. A slice of cake? Pie? Maybe a taco? Eat me, she kept saying. Eat me. She somehow made that bizarre costume really hot. At least, I think. I couldn't quite remember.

I looked over my shoulder. The girl. Her hair, long and brown and everywhere, spilling over her back, curling down to her waist.

What was her name again?

Gage, you're losing it.

My stomach lurched and rolled. It prepared to drain is contents all over what's-her-face's apartment floor. I sat up fast.

I needed to get to the bathroom. Quick.

My eyes darted, searching for the bathroom. Only one door. Only one room.

A dorm. I was in a dorm.

Ugh. I would have to use the communal bathroom. And it was probably the girls' bathroom at that. I stumbled out of bed and fell to the floor with a loud thud. Immediately, my head shot up to the bed. Surely she would wake up and see me naked and tangled in that stupid, ruffled bedspread.

Nothing. Not a groan, not a wince, not one movement.

Jeez, was she even alive? I stared at her carefully, checking for breath, sighing with relief when I saw her back rise and fall.

Whew. Now to get the hell out of here.

What was her name? I wracked my brain as I searched the floor for my pants. I'd remember it. Eventually. I needed to make my escape before whoever she was woke up.

And coffee. I needed some coffee.

Jendy. Jendy would go to breakfast with me. That was one of the great things about girls. They were always willing to get breakfast with you. And speaking of, I had to get out of here before this one wanted breakfast with me.

I hastily pulled pants over my legs, crashing into things as quietly as possible, discovering too late that the pants I tried to squeeze into were her jeans. The alarm clock screamed, and I made a stumbling dive for it before smashing into a stack of books. I looked at it as I set it upright. 6:15 a.m. An absurd hour. I hit the snooze. I had five minutes to get out.

Jendy, I thought, as I searched for my jeans. Jendy would be awake. She had an 8 a.m class; she was the only senior I knew who took an 8 a.m. class. I could talk her out of it. Maybe. Probably not. But I could talk her into breakfast. Coffee. At least coffee.

I jumped into my jeans.

I stopped to look at the girl, certain her name would come to me if I concentrated hard enough. Enough guilt filled me at the fact that I couldn't remember it that I contemplated leaving a note - a quick note couldn't hurt. I ran my hands over her desk, searching for a pen, a Post-It. Anything.

My stomach turned ominously, a warning that the puking was imminent.

Forget it, I thought and ran out the door. The two girls talking over the sink barely acknowledged me as I dashed into the bathroom.

Sheena. That was her name. I sighed with relief then mercilessly heaved the contents of my stomach – and maybe even part of my stomach – into the toilet.

The girls outside the stall did not even break conversation.

"You look terrible." Jenna's voice croaked at me, like this insult was the first thing out of her mouth that morning.

"I could say the same to you, beautiful." I leaned against the door casually. I knew getting Jenna to skip class for breakfast would take effort. I figured that should be a piece of cake what with a splitting headache and all.

She rolled her eyes and padded back into the room, which meant I could follow. "I guess that means you had fun?"

"I don't remember. So yeah, that means I had fun."

"Good. I'm glad," she said, but she sounded like she didn't really care.

"Did you have fun?"

"I went to the Lit party, so yes," she replied.

"What does that even mean?"

"The Literature Club Halloween party."

"My God. You are worse off on a normal day than I am right now."

"Ha-ha," She said without humor. "It was fun," She insisted.

"Good," I said, not really caring to argue about whether a literature club's Halloween party was fun or the most pathetic thing a human could possible conceive, and walked in to her bathroom. "You have Tylenol?"

"Yeah. Top shelf. You shouldn't take it though. It's hard on your liver," she lectured. "I dressed up like Hyper-Chicken."

"That rooster on Bugs Bunny?" I searched her cabinet.

"The chicken lawyer on Futurama."

"You dressed up like an old chicken?"

"I had a lot of time this summer to watch television."

"You, Jendy, never cease to amaze me." I said flatly, no trace of amusement at all. Even with my back turned, I could see her eyes roll all the way back into her head.

"Extra strength? Forget what I said. You're a goddess." I walked out chewing four.

"Dear God, that's awful. How do you do that?" Jenna winced.

I saw a bowl of already poured Cap'n Crunch waiting for her near the sink.

"Years of hangover practice," I said.

"Want some?" Jenna nodded to the bowl and started to dig into her cereal.

"No," I grabbed the spoon from her hand.

"What the--" She reached for the spoon, but I held it out of her reach. "Gage," she griped impatiently.

"Have breakfast with me."

"I have class."

"I know you have class, baby." I wiggled my eyebrows at her. She gave me a look. Okay, so I couldn't be on my best game after the second worst hangover of my life. I dropped the charade. "Skip."

"I'm not skipping class."

"Come on, Jendy. Just this once. It's your senior year."

"How does that matter?"

"You never skip."

"That's a lie," she pointed at me. "You got me to skip on my birthday last year."

"One time. *One* time."

"I've skipped more than that."

"Not this year."

"It's only November first."

"Which means you should have skipped at least three classes by now."

Wide eyed, Jenna looked at me. "I have no idea how you are graduating."

"Jendy, everyone skips. It's not like you're not going to graduate."

"Don't you have class?"

"I never have class."

"Well, that's true."

"That's the spirit," I said and wrapped an arm around her shoulder. "You can go in that." She was wearing red sweatpants, a stretched out tee-shirt and tube socks with slip on sandals. "You look great."

"You're an idiot."

"Well," I said with a pause, "You look normal."

"I hate you," she deadpanned.

"You love me," I said, bumping her shoulder. "Come on. One "

She rolled her eyes.

"Hey. I drink tea with you. On a purple comforter. A purple comforter, Jendy." I raised my eyebrows at her. "Purple. With ruffles."

She looked quite nearly defeated.

"Wakey wakey eggs and bakey?" I took her hands in mine and shook them a little trying to make her dance with me.

"I *could* use a good cup of coffee. Roxie bought this stuff from the clearance section." She sniffed. "I'm telling you, I think it's *supposed* to be coffee, but I don't know, Gage. I just don't know."

"And one more thing," I requested. "A non-sequitur, if you will allow."

"Proceed," Jenna said with the generosity only seen in popes and kindly queens.

"Can I puke in your toilet?"

"Oh, my God. Get away from me." She pushed me to the bathroom. "Go. You are the foulest person on the planet."

There was a pause as I rummaged through her cabinet.

"I'll go to breakfast," she yelled through the door. "Only because of my unending well of benevolence."

I grinned, picking up the Pepto and guzzling it straight from the bottle. "I'll never forget it Jendy-girl."

"But you have to pay."

"All right."

"And you have to listen to a fifteen minute lecture about the dangers of alcohol poisoning."

"Five minutes."

"Ten."

"Deal."

"Perfect." Then I heard the grin in her voice. "I only have enough material for ten anyway."

I pushed out of the bathroom. "Let's go," I grabbed a random coat and started wrapping her in it before she could change her mind.

"You weren't even sick," she said accusingly, then looked at the coat. "This is Terri's."

"I was. Very sick." I zippered her into the coat. "Why are you two still rooming with Terri?"

"Entertainment value? Is that mean?"

"That's very mean, Jenda. You are a bad person."

She narrowed her eyes at me. "You weren't sick in there," she said, nodding to the bathroom.

I shrugged innocently. "Let's go. I'll tell you all about the slice of cake I slept with," I said as we walked down the hall.

"No." Jenna stopped dead. "Do not tell me you ended up with her."

"How do you know Cake? Sheena," I corrected.

"I was there with you for the first hour, or do you forget?"

I had forgotten. "I didn't forget."

"I know all about Cake."

"What's wrong with Cake?"

"Typical. Oh, how typical." She spun around, a sly smile on her face. "Gage."

"What?" I followed the laughter that trailed her down the hall. "What?"

She laughed again, throwing her head back, reached her hands into the air like she was grabbing the world, spun in a circle. She ran her hands threw her hair, still smiling, obviously amused at herself, and pulled her hair into that stupid, ugly ponytail.

Monday, December 9, 2002

Jenna

"So what are you two?" Roxie asked Jenna as they dashed across campus to Magee. Jenna had a final in three minutes. She was thinking about theories and methods of literary analysis and all the stuff she crammed into her head about Marxist theory and feminism and some kind of major political interpretive approach to literary analysis - in other words, all the stuff she missed in class taught on the day Gage conned her into breakfast. Instead of political analysis, Jenna was subjected to Gage's two hour discourse about the Cake girl.

"What are who two?" Jenna asked, distracted. So, wait, who were the Western authors influences by Marx again? Jenna ran through the list in her head as she spared Roxie a glace.

Roxie stared at her pointedly.

Jenna mind screeched to a halt. Gage. Gage? Roxie seriously wanted to ask about Gage right now?

"Roxie," Irritated, Jenna bit out her name, "if you knew the crap-ton of theories I'm trying to keep straight in my head right now, you would not be asking me this."

Jenna was sick of the question. Sick of girls at Grady's asking. Sick of girls at frat parties asking. *So, um…what are you two?* They'd giggle and scrunch up their noses and waggle their pointer finger back at forth between us. *Friends. Just friends*, Gage would say sometimes. Other times, *Nothing. We aren't anything, honey.* He'd shoot Jenna some stupid chummy grin and she'd grin back and fight the urge to slug him.

One morning last week when Gage was making pancakes and Jenna sat studying in the living room, Cody walked into the kitchen. "What's she doing here?" It was asked in a whisper Jenna wasn't supposed to hear.

Gage shrugged. Jenna had spent the night. She fell asleep next to Gage. They had been talking. Jenna studying, Gage drinking a double mocha, and planning a powerhour, as he called it, of typing his term paper. It was the first time that had happened. The sleeping together, not the powerhour. Jenna didn't count the first time in the bushes, because they both were drunk and really she had no idea if Gage actually stayed the entire night, being that she was alone the next morning. It was weird when they woke up, Jenna and Gage in the bed together, fully clothed, she underneath a blanket, he on top. She wondered how she had gotten there, under the sheets, and flushed at the thought of Gage covering her up. Jenna was sure he had felt as awkward – he had woken up as she tried to sneak out, but instead kind of tripped over him and fell from the bed to the floor - but they acted like everything was normal until, eventually, it did seem normal.

"What is she, man? Like, your girlfriend?" Cody asked, and Jenna's head snapped up from her book. It wasn't the first time it was asked, but it was the first time the question had been asked by one of Gage's friends in her presence. Jenna, trying to act nonchalant, reached for her coffee and peeked at them from the corner of her eye.

"Nothing," Gage had answered.

Jenna's hand stilled, the mug inches away from her waiting lips, the book forgotten on her lap.

"What number is she?"

Gage looked pained. Or pissed. Or maybe not. The flash was so fast Jenna barely had time to catch it, let alone decipher it. And she was supposed to be busy reading anyway. "She's not a number."

"Well, bitch is weird anyway."

"She's not a bitch, dude." Jenna watched Gage wrestle with barely contained anger. His grip around the pancake turner tightened. By the time Cody turned around, beer in hand, Gage was Gage again. But Jenna wasn't Jenna anymore. Her eyes were saucers. She had never heard Gage take that kind of tone, never seen him that angry.

"Don't say that again." He said it lightly, but Jenna had seen his face. There was nothing light about it. "We're friends. You can't say that shit."

"Oh." A genuine look of surprised flashed on Cory's face. "Dude. Sorry. Okay? I thought you said she was nothing."

Jenna, both a friend and nothing to Gage, slipped quietly, book in hand, out the back door, while Cody and Gage made pancakes because she was confused as to whether or not she should be hurt.

And now, right now, on the way to class, on the way to a final, Roxie started asking. It was inevitable, the question, and Jenna was sure Roxie had held out for far longer than she had been wondering. In the three minutes before a looming test, that fact didn't matter to Jenna. Also, it was cold and windy, and Jenna hated the cold. It was snowing too, and not the pretty kind. The slushy, dirty kind that stuck to the bottom of Jenna's pants and dripped off under her seat in class. Jenna hated walking in the icy snow, especially when she slept in and had now two minutes to make it to class. She could blame all of that for her cranky mood, right? The cold. The finals. The question she was sick of hearing.

"You…slept there last week," Roxie pressed.

"So what? You and I live together. *Muy scandaloso!*" Jenna exclaimed her best Telenova impersonation.

"That's different. We share chromosomes."

"You could say the same about me and Gage." Jenna upped her pace to a jog. "The X's." She didn't want to be reminded of last week because all she could think about was Gage and Cody's conversation and how she still wasn't sure if she should be upset. Especially because of the secret Jenna was keeping. The secret Jenna had been keeping since late summer. The secret she kept so well even ever-suspicious Roxie had not caught on. There was so much swirling around in Jenna's mind right now about Gage and her secret, she wasn't sure what to do or how to feel. You know who would know? Roxie would know. But Jenna wouldn't ask Roxie, because then Jenna might be admitting to something Jenna had no intention of admitting to, even though she wasn't sure what she'd be admitting to. Something shameful. It had to be shameful if you didn't even know what the problem was. Roxie would know what Jenna was admitting to, and Roxie would be happy to inform Jenna.

"You're not dating," Roxie said it like she could trick Jenna into admitting, *No, Roxie, we are dati*ng.

"Nope," Jenna answered matter-of-factly.

But if there was one thing Roxie could *not* do it was drop the subject.

"Are you sure?"

"Jeez, Rox. You're not a detective yet, you know?"

"What do you think he thinks?" Roxie asked, brushing aside Jenna's statement.

"I don't know what he thinks…care what he thinks," Jenna corrected, but Roxie was quick to pick up that morsel and chew it relentlessly. Her eyes lit up. "I think you should date him," she said in a tone so casual Jenna knew she had to be walking into a trap.

"Oh, my God. I am not asking him anything. That would be humiliating," Jenna said and noticed the intrigued look that crossed Roxie's face. "*And* I don't even care…to know." She added quickly.

"What if he wants to date you?" She proposed.

"He would tell me."

Roxie rolled her eyes. "As if."

"Does he look like he wants to date anyone? He was with some girl last night."

"How do you know?"

"Because he took me to breakfast this morning."

"Oh." Roxie made a face. "That's weird."

Yes. Yes it is.

"Does he tell you that stuff?" Roxie lowered her voice. "About the girls?" She added in case Jenna didn't get her drift.

"Sometimes."

"Did he tell you about me?" Roxie asked, her eyes wide.

"No." Jenna said, horrified at the thought. "God, no. I'd kill him. With my bare hands, and it'd feel really good."

"I'd support you in that."

"No jury of my peers would convict me."

"It's true."

Jenna's feet pounded through the snow-covered concrete stairs outside Magee. Nobody shoveled them yet. Nobody threw salt onto the ice underneath the inches of snow. She felt the freezing cold, wet clump of snow make friends with her ankles. Jenna grimaced and shook her leg, and the very action made her slip through the front door and fall to the floor.

"Still, you should date him," Roxie said as she fell on top of Jenna.

Jenna hated winter.

"What are you doing for Christmas?" Gage's voice cut through the bite of the wind as they hurried into Golden Wok. "And more importantly, what are you getting me for my birthday?"

Jenna ducked under Gage's arm as he pulled the door open and rushed through the entrance. "Nothing, Gage. The answer is the same for both questions." She shook the snow from her hair. She normally stayed with Roxie's family for Christmas. But this year Roxie's family planned a two-week ski trip and, to Jenna, nothing sounded worse than a two-week ski trip over Christmas.

Gage grabbed two paper menus and handed one over to Jenna as he looked for an open table. "Thanks." Jenna scratched her cheek as he steered her to an open booth, his hand on the small of her back, a gesture he did so frequently it barely registered with either of them anymore. "I think I'm gonna get a number three. And two number sixes. Yep. Two number sixes," She confirmed to herself as they slid into their seats.

"What? Are you serious?"

"I have PMS, okay? Get over it."

"I mean the present." He reached through the space between them to punch her shoulder.

"Ow! I'm not one of your frat buddies. You need to give me twenty percent strength, not fifty." Jenna rubbed her shoulder, muttering. "I think I might have flunked a test too."

"You did not flunk a test." He punched her again.

"Gage! That was forty percent." Jenna shrugged him away. "You're hurting me."

"Oh, I am not," he answered companionably. "But really? You have no defense for not even planning to acknowledge my birthday?"

"I didn't say that. In fact, I can buy you an egg roll right now," Jenna suggested as unwound the scarf wrapped around her neck. "That's it though. Money's a little tight right now." Something had happened with her student loan and processing and blah blah blah. Jenna also lost about five hours a week at Charred this past semester because she had thought it was a great idea to take eighteen credits and promptly found out she was not, in fact, superwoman despite taking the Zoloft that gave her the false confidence that she was, and then she had to drop some work hours in favor of studying and not, you know, flunking out of college. And speaking of Charred, she had a shift starting in an hour.

"Stop checking your watch." Gage pouted. "You make me feel unimportant."

"You're such a narcissist."

"Maybe you could recommend a good medication for that." They had reached a place in their friendship that Gage felt okay enough around her to rag on her need of medication, and Jenna felt okay enough around him to know he was rarely serious.

"Shut up, aaaand," Jenna drew out while checking her watch again, "you're dumb." She was terrible at come-backs and would never admit the hours she spent scouring the internet forums for good comebacks. Because to Jenna, everything was an academic pursuit she could eventually figure out with the right theorems and/or published studies.

"Seriously. Stop checking your watch."

"Stop making me late for things, and I'll stop checking my watch."

"Twenty-two, Jendy."

"You're ordering a twenty-two? Good God, Gage. That's, like, a family meal." Her eyes scanned the menu. "For seven. Do *you* have PMS?"

Clearly not impressed by her joke, he sighed. "No, Jendy. *I'll* be twenty-two."

"So that means your birthday doesn't matter anymore. This is the exact year your birthday stops mattering."

"Cold, Jendy. So, so cold." He turned to the waitress who had appeared in front of them. "And how are you doing today? Number 8, if you could be so kind. Pepsi. And she probably wants tea." He nodded at Jenna and added a wink for the waitress.

She did want tea. But it was an extravagance she couldn't afford right now.

"I'll buy." Gage said, reading her thoughts.

Jenna hesitated.

"Jesus, Jen, aren't we past this yet? Do not make this the Fugly Brown Incident all-over again. I respect you as an independent human woman in this world," he said quite robotically.

The waitress watched them carefully, eyes volleying between them, pen poised over her pad. And Jenna dropped it, because she did know him well enough now to know that he only called her "Jen" when he was serious, when he actually was telling her that he respected her. Also, they were in a Chinese restaurant, and the waitress was watching them carefully and smiling a little bit.

"I'll have the tea," Jenna said.

The waitress grinned now, a full-on megawatt smile that nearly blinded Jenna. "Good. Good choice. Good boy. You have good boy here. Very good boy."

After the waitress left, Gage turned to Jenna, eyebrows raised, tongue in cheek, and grinning like he won the Oscar for Best and Kindest and Most Generous Person in the Restaurant Category.

"Narcissist," Jenna muttered.

"Medication?"

"No. Years of therapy. Years and years and years of therapy."

"I've got the time."

Jenna tucked her tongue in cheek. "Am I supposed to think I am beholden to you now? Because you bought me a two-dollar hot tea?"

He thought for a minute. "Yes. Absolutely."

"I don't."

He laughed. "You're really not getting me anything?"

Jenna realized he was serious. "I'm not even going to see you, Gage. We'll be on break." Was she supposed to feel bad? They hung out sporadically. Once or twice a week. Picked up breakfast on Sundays.

"Well, that's a fine friend." He sulked.

Nothing. She's nothing. The words echoed through her head. She did this sometimes, this confusing job of trying to sort out Gage and what they were and who she was to him and what they meant to each other. Because to Jenna, everything was an academic pursuit. Jenna focused on her hands which were rolling a bottle of soy sauce. "Well, now you're really laying it on thick. Trying to weasel guilt and presents out of me."

"I'm not going home for Christmas this year."

Startled, Jenna looked up from her hands. "Why not?"

Gage shrugged and took the soy sauce bottle from her. He looked at it for a few seconds then mimicked her earlier movement, rolling the bottle over and over.

"But what about seeing your Dad?" Jenna thought of a time a little over a year ago, when Gage had asked what it was like to lose a father.

"Dad and I. We…we're having some trouble." Gage wouldn't meet her eyes. "He hasn't really--he's not the same." He set the bottle down with finality. "And you know about my mom."

The divorce happened. Remarried to a guy who had full custody of a little boy. The topper being that Gage's mother was pregnant. All in fifteen months. Gage didn't like to talk about it. Roxie said it was the strangest tale she ever heard, and being a criminology major, she heard and read about a lot of strange tales.

"Everything is so effed up." Gage looked up. "Is that normal?"

Jenna watched Gage unwrap his chopsticks then play them like drums on the table, on the napkin holder, finishing with a flourish on Jenna's arm.

He smiled.

It didn't reach his eyes.

"I'll stay with you." Jenna blurted out. "I'm always here anyway." Jenna had originally had other plans, secret plans. But this was the crux of the problem. Gage. And her secret. She wasn't sure what to do.

He nodded, and Jenna knew by now that a nod meant thank you.

Then he stared at her carefully.

Jenna touched her hair self-consciously. "What?"

"You look," he pursed his lips, "different. Just right now. Exactly right now, you look different. What are you thinking?"

"Nothing!" she said a little too defensively.

"You have a secret?"

Jenna's eyes grew wide. "No! Well, I mean, you know, everyone has secrets. You have secrets too, Gage."

"Hmmm." He didn't look convinced.

The waitress thankfully interrupted his interrogations by setting five or six plates on the table. "So much food for two. And such a skinny, little thing. You'll break in the wind." She pinched Jenna's arm. "You take good care of her," the waitress said to Gage.

"Always."

She's nothing. Jenna remembered the words again. Everything was always so confusing when it came to Gage.

They looked at the food before them. It *was* a lot of food.

"You left last week." Gage said. He had a piece of sushi between his chopsticks. "You left when I was making you pancakes."

Jenna worked her thumbnails against each other. "I know."

Jenna and Gage stared at each other, sharing a look Jenna didn't want to decode. Because of the secret.

"Jendy. You're a great friend."

"Shut up." She laughed a little too loudly, trying to cover up her discomfort.

"Really."

"Ah…ok. And you're a…great friend…too, Gage."

"Good. Glad we cleared that up."

"What do we…do…now?"

"We hug it out. And never speak of it again."

Jenna pursed her lips in contemplation. "Well. Sure. That seems healthy."

"It's not twenty-two, Jendy. It's twenty-six," he said after the hug.

"What are you talking about?"

"The birthday that stops mattering. It's twenty-six. Because we can't rent a car and run away together until I'm twenty-five."

Jenna laughed, but she felt an odd quivering in her belly at the thought of running away with Gage. Everything. Every single thing was so confusing about Gage.

Gage

"She's in love with me."

Cody and I were drunker than his norm of "very fucking drunk." I liked Cody. Over the years, he had somehow grown on me. Probably because he was the only one who instinctively knew what I was talking about without any context whatsoever.

He burped. "She said that? Jenna. That chick said that?"

"She didn't say it. But, you know," I waved the air around us; "she said it."

"But she didn't *say it* say it? She wasn't like," Cody made his voice go all high and quivery, "'Gage, I love you. Marry me and make weird babies with me!'" His voice fell back to normal. "She wasn't like that?"

"No." I downed a shot of something honey-brown and vile tasting. Maybe I was wrong.

"She's not in love with you," Cody said with a grimace and a definitive shake of his head.

"No?"

"No."

We sat in silence then, getting a little bit drunker. Minutes and shots ticked away. "She could be, bro," Cody said out of nowhere. "She could be in love with you," Cody completely reversed his position within the span of a minute.

"You think?" I asked, ready to agree.

"'Cause, you know, she's in love with you."

"What?"

"Man, I'm very drunk." He blew out a breath. "She's in love with you."

"I don't know. I think so." I shook my head. My confidence in my earlier statement waned. "I don't know if she's in love. She was saying stuff. About having a secret and...stuff."

"She said that? She said she had a secret?" Cody burped again.

"No, bro. No, she didn't say that."

Cody squinted at me. His mouth was half open, like a caveman learning to breathe. He shook his head a little bit. "What?" He finally said.

"She didn't *say* it," I waved the air around me. Everything was getting fuzzy. "But she said it. Virtually said the words."

"Oh." Cody drew out the word. "What you say then?"

"What was I supposed to say? Declare my love? Climb her trellis?" I shrugged it off, and flapped my hand dismissively.

"Climb her trellis. Dude." Cody said. "Climb her fucking trellis. Dude."

"Oh, dude, yeah." I turned to him.

We nodded quite seriously at each other.

"And you're in love," he said plainly, gesturing with his beer. "With her."

"No." I paused. "No."

"But you're, like, you know. I mean, come on." He switched on the television and surfed the stations.

Maybe Cody could instinctively make sense out of garbled sentences, but I couldn't. "I have no idea what you're saying."

"Guys and girls can't be friends. Like, you're not friends with her." He stopped on MTV. A rerun of *The Real World* was on and everyone was fighting.

"No. No, I am. I'm friends with her."

"Nah, bro. Nah. You were never friends with her." He turned his attention back to the show. "That chick is hot," he said, no longer talking about Jenna, but about some girl who pitilessly threw an entire pitcher of margaritas onto her roommate.

"I like her," I conceded.

"Yeah, she's hot," Cody agreed, staring at the blonde now tearing at the hair of her roommate.

"Nah, bro. I mean Jenna."

"Yeah," he agreed as if this was obviously. "So you want to date her."

I chugged my beer. "She has this...Code, she has this messed up existence. Like...like, I don't even know if I know the half of it."

"She sounds like..." Cody stared into his empty beer can as if he was choosing the words straight from the vessel, "like a real piece of work. She's a bad decision. One, big wreck of a decision."

"Yeah, she is."

"So, yeah." He shrugged and popped open another can. "You should date her."

"No way, man." I took another swig. "No...I don't think— you think?"

"Yeah, dude, do it."

"No. I shouldn't."

"Then...you know." He stopped the channel surfing, settling on a Japanese game show.

"What?"

"Maybe you two could screw. Like, she probably wants to...too."

That. Yeah. That sounded like a good idea.

"I mean, yeah," I agreed. "I think everyone would like that."

"Yeah, dude. *Everybody* likes that."

"We could still be friends. Me and Jenna. We could still be friends." With no attached responsibility to her other than friendship.

He shrugged. "Yeah. Heck yeah. Friends."

I nodded my head and leaned back, on the verge of falling asleep.

"Well, dude, you need to think of a plan."

"What kind of a plan?"

"A plan to sleep with her. I don't know, like, be nice to her and shit." He waved his hand. "Girls love that stuff."

"Yeah. Yeah. That sounds good."

"Cheers to Jenna, dude." He held out his can and I slammed my bottle against it.

"Cheers."

I thought about that. The plan to sleep with her.

Then I passed out.

Tuesday, December 31, 2002

Gage

"I'm blotto."

"Jendy, nobody uses those words anymore." I lifted her bodily from the floor where she had tripped over her own feet and fallen into a heap of giggles, threw her over my shoulder, and carried her up the stairs. It had been a long time since Jenna had been drunk, but tonight was apparently the night making up for the dry spell.

"You could put me down. My feet work." She grabbed a shot glass full of vodka from the table we passed.

"I don't think they do. You remember how you got on the floor?"

"I 'member everything." She tapped her head with the glass. "Steel trap."

"More like rusty trap." I set her on my bed. "Maybe you should slow down there, buddy." I snatched the shot glass from her hand and downed it before she could react.

She watched in drunken stupefaction then pointed at me. "Hey." She drew the word out before collapsing onto my bed in a fit of giggles.

I awkwardly hovered over her.

"It's...very lonely here."

"I'm right here." Awkwardly hovering over you.

"In the bed," she said. "It's very lonely in the bed."

"You're drunk," I said.

"No. You're drunk." Jenna always sucked at come-backs. She was such a chick that way. And ever since I woke up from my drunken proclamation to sleep with her, I had been noticing more and more how much of a chick she was. Everything about her was so very female. She was soft everywhere and in a very good way. She met me after class one day, and she even smelled female. She looked exactly the same and smelled exactly the same as when I met her, but something about her was different. She was wrong though, too. I was not drunk. In a rare turn of events, Jenna was smashed, and I was completely sober. On New Year's Eve. Half an hour before my official birthday.

"It's lonely," she said again.

"I know. You already said that. I'm right here."

"I mean on campus," she whined. "Right now. It's lonely. Hollerdays."

"Holidays," I corrected.

She shrugged. "Potato. Pa-tah-to. Pa-shut-up." She laughed hysterically, and I remembered someone - some professor in some class - once saying how drunk people think they are hilarious while their sober counterparts find them annoying. Tedious, Jenna would say. But Jenna was right. Campus was a deserted wasteland of snow. Within one hour of completion finals two weeks ago, everybody had fled campus like it was the apocalypse. Jenna and I had been alone since then. Or nearly alone, since Cody, who forgot his entire families' Christmas presents, came back on Christmas Eve to pick them up. Then he needed to have a drink with us, which turned to complete shit-facedness, which led to me hiding his keys, which led to him waking in a hungover panic on Christmas morning, his mother screaming at him over his cell phone something about Mass and Grandma's brunch. The whole ordeal culminated in him proclaiming he'd never drink again, right before jumping into his car and screeching away.

"You could have gone with Roxie to Canada," I said. Or wherever the hell she and her family went skiing, which, to me, sounded like about the worst thing ever. What kind of person straps boards on their feet to discover and even colder, frozen tundra than the one they currently reside in? Especially when there are much warmer places to discover?

"You," Jenna pointed at my nose, "didn't get me anything for Christmas."

"What are you talking about? I'm giving you these excellent holiday memories you'll never forget."

"I'll never 'member them," she hiccupped.

"What about that steel trap of yours?" I argued

"What steel trap?" Jendy looked genuinely confused. I laughed.

"And these accommodations. I gave you these excellent accommodations."

"I hate hollerdays."

"Everybody hates holidays."

She gave me a pointed stare. "You know Roxie's family? They hug. Like...a lot. They hug like it's the eighties and they are in a family situation comedy."

"Okay. Not everybody."

"A situation comedy, Gage. Some families are a situation comedy."

Exhausted, I rubbed my eyes. Could she not just pass out already?

"They're skiing right now. *Shush, shush, shush.*" Jendy made skiing motions, which was a good effort considering her level of inebriation. And the fact that she was lying down.

"What do you want to do?"

"Act out a situation comedy for me!" She declared like a queen on a rampage.

"I'm not doing that."

"Come on. Be a sport," she slurred the *"S"* a little. "I loved Family Matters."

"I'm not doing that."

"*'Did I do that?'*" She laughed riotously and then snorted.

"Sleep," I suggested, feeling like I was in charge of a toddler right now. "How 'bout you go to sleep?"

"I'll miss the New Year," she said looking at the clock. 11:45 p.m. "I almost made it."

I thought about Ace and Cody and the others driving to Key West the day after Christmas. I thought about how they had asked me to come with them to the house they rented for the New Year. I could be in a bar somewhere in Key West right now. With a hot girl and a cold drink. Fifteen minutes before my birthday. I thought about how Jendy had told me she would stay with me. How birthdays really weren't supposed to count anymore. I sighed and reclined next to her.

"You want to sleep?" I suggested again. "We'll sleep." I closed my eyes.

"I'm too hot to sleep," she complained, and I lazily opened mine in time to watch her start to pull her shirt over her head.

"No." My eyes shot open as I sat up quickly. "No, no, no. Don't do that." I covered her hands with mine and shook my head at her. "Don't do that, Jendy."

"I'm hot, Gage," she pouted and fought with my hands.

"What's under your shirt?" A tank top. Girls wore that stuff under their shirts sometimes. Those silky kind. I didn't want to think about Jenna in some silky kind of tank top. But there was no way Jendy would lie naked with me on my bed on my birthday on New Year's Eve. There was no way she'd do that to me. Not when she was drunk and we were supposed to be friends. Yeah, I had that plan. But not when Jenna was drunk. No way when she was drunk and I was dead sober. "What's under there?" I asked again.

"My body."

I groaned inwardly.

"Can I at least wear your shorts?"

"Will you keep your shirt on?"

"Yes," she answered and held out her hand eagerly. "I'll keep her on."

I pulled a pair of shorts out of my drawer and threw them at her. "Change under the covers," I said with a self-consciousness I hadn't felt since high school. Since Gina Jilette, who invited me over to her house for Diet Coke and some other kinds of things girls like, maybe Milano cookies and these tiny little sandwiches? I was fifteen and Gina was seventeen and nothing was more intimidating. Gina wore those silky tank tops, I discovered that night.

"Wow. Gage is a prude." Jendy smiled wide as I turned my back on her. "Who wudda thought?" I listened to some rustling and tried not to imagine what was happening. "I'm ready."

I pulled back the covers. The shorts were hitched up, the hem running high on her thigh. I saw the scar quickly, easily. It would be hard to miss a scar like that anyway. Long and jagged, the line of skin knotted and tough like the bark of a tree, it ran from her knee, up her leg, and disappeared under the shorts. I swallowed roughly as I stared at it. Holy shit. That scar was scary real. Gina Jilette never had a scar like that. No girl I was ever with had anything like that. I looked up. Jenna, breath shallow, body still and tense, watched me warily. I flashed a quick smile and flicked off the lights, pretending I hadn't noticed anything and jumped into bed.

We sat there in silence, in the dark, staring at the ceiling, covers clutched up to our chests as if that would offer protection from something very real that had passed between us. We sat there for minutes, both knowing what the other had seen, but saying nothing, and the wait might as well have been years.

"You can ask," Jenna finally said. She sounded very coherent now, even though I knew she was nothing close to sober.

"What in God's name was that, Jendy?" I asked. Neither one of us could look at the other. Not that it would matter. The room was a black void.

"It's my scar."

"From what? Crashed your bike?" I said, knowing full well it wasn't from bike riding, but hoping, Jesus, praying, she'd say yes. Then I'd tell her about how I'd gotten a scar on my leg too - from roller skating - even though I told every other girl it was from skate boarding off a jump. And I'd tell her how I'd gotten the scars on my arms from tripping over bleach like an idiot and Jendy could know the truth and then we'd never talk about our scars again.

"It's where I was impaled."

"Jesus." Abruptly, I sat up. "Impaled?" Didn't that only happen in, like, the Dark Ages?

"A fence post."

"What?" I switched on the table lamp next to me and stared at her. Jenna appeared, covers still hitched up over her chest. "How in the holy hell does that happen?"

"All kinds of ways, I guess."

"Jenna." I waited until she looked at me. "How did that happen?"

"I had to jump out a window. I had to." She said like I was going to scold her. "It was either jump or die."

"Are you *kidding* me?" I asked, completely skeptical. Then realization dawned over me, immediately and clearly. "Your dad," I said. "That's how your dad died."

"Close enough. He died in the fire." She said, and my heart crushed when I saw the tears gather at the corners of her eyes. "He told me to jump. And I did."

"You were ten," I said, remembering her stilted drunken statements in the dark of the bushes that one September night from what now felt like a hundred years ago.

Jenna's voice was tiny, the voice of a child. "I looked for him Gage, I swear. I promise. I looked up. I waited. They said it was…it was…smoke inhalation. He died." Her face crumpled. "He told me to jump, so I did."

"You were ten," I said again.

"I didn't even know the fence was in my leg. I moved when I shouldn't have. That's why the scar's so long. I promise, Gage, I didn't know."

"Jenna," I said, and my voice sounded far away and nothing like myself. "Jenna. You don't have to promise me anything. You were ten." *Even if you were twenty; even if you were sixty.*

We stared at each other.

"What kind of fire, Jenna?"

"Gasoline. In the garage. I guess technically it was electrical to start. The socket was overloaded with plugs. But dad kept these pans of gasoline in the garage. Who keeps gas in pans? I don't know. When it hit the gas pans, it must have gone fast. Really fast. When it burns from the bottom and you're on the top, where do you go?"

I had no answer.

"There was no one after that. No one." She started crying abruptly, her face broken and contorted, and if I knew then that if I didn't hold her, I would never forgive myself. She cried, harder and harder until I thought we would both burst, and I said all the lame things people say when you're crying. *It's okay, Jenna. I'm here, Jenna. It's not your fault.* I said those things until I couldn't anymore. Because my chest physically hurt; it ached and burned and I realized it was not because I was talking so much, but because I was trying not to cry.

Then, as quickly as it started, it was over. She stopped crying. Her head fell to my chest, and she wiped her face against my shirt. The tears soaked through, leaving my skin cold and clammy. I ducked my head close to hers and looked in her eyes. "Jenna, where's your mom?"

"She was gone before that."

I swallowed. "Died?"

Jenna shook her head. "No. Worse."

"What's worse than death?"

Jenna turned abruptly from me and stared at the ceiling. "She left. She chose to leave."

"You never looked for her?"

"They tried. Social Services looked for her after the fire. Do you know how to look for a person who does not want to be found?"

"I have no clue."

"The world is a really big place when you are trying to find someone."

"But now, I mean. You ever try to find her?"

"No." A bitterness I never realized existed in Jenna escaped in that one, short answer. "The world is an even bigger place now."

"Never? You don't ever want to know?" Confused, I propped myself up on on elbow to lean over her. I watched her face. I searched her eyes. They were curiously blank, oddly calm. If she had answers to my questions, I could not see them.

She didn't answer me, and I kind of figured she wouldn't. At least not now. Sometime she would answer me. But not now. But I could not stop staring at her. Her face, her eyes, everything. Jenna looked so different now.

Jenna stared back with a look that dared me to defy her and finally said, "I'm not going to cry again, Gage. I swore I would never cry over her, and I'm not doing it. Not for you, not for anyone."

"Yeah. Okay," I agreed, and I hoped my voice did not sound as condescending as it did in my head. I turned away from her then, because I saw it. I saw the light go out in her eyes. I heard the way she choked on her last declaration. I turned away from her then, because I knew she was starting to cry, and my ignorance would mean more to her than my comfort.

I waited there in the silent space beside her and wondered how long you ignored someone's pain before it got weird.

I got my answer. Approximately five minutes.

I shifted uncomfortably. "Do you need medicine, Jenna? Do you need your medicine? I can get it for you."

"It doesn't work like that, Gage," she said, and she laughed, short and hollow. "My therapist. I thought he was an idiot. Maybe he's not. I don't know. He said loss is like an ocean. You're always in it. And grief is like the waves. High tide, low tide." I felt her wipe the tears from her face, but I still refused to look at her. "I cry at high tide. I think my life is over at high tide." She took a deep breath. "But you're here. You're here now. I think it's low tide."

I finally let myself steal a glance. I watched her tightly wrap her grief back up like a package. She moved through it then contained it. She looked at me then, and I felt like we would never look at each other the same way again.

"My leg is kind of messed up now. It's been messed up for a while."

"Yeah. It looks like it."

"On the inside, I mean. The nerves. The nerves in my leg got messed up when they tried to fix it. It hurts a lot. I shouldn't have moved. The fence impaled me, but when I moved it ripped through me. I didn't even feel it."

We were lying next to each other again, and my arm was still around her, my fingers brushing her neck. "Why don't I know any of this?"

"I don't like to tell people."

"I'm not *people*, Jenna."

"Okay," she said.

I wanted to kiss the top of her head. The compulsion was quick and swift and a kick to my gut. I turned my face away from hers.

"It hurts."

I jumped, moving quickly. "Am I hurting you?"

She smiled at me, almost like she was indulging a child. "No, I mean it hurts. In general. It always hurts."

"All the time?"

"It burns. When I walk. When I run. Especially when I run. I can't really run anymore."

"You can't run?" She ran to me September eleventh. All the way across campus.

"I mean, I can. I do when I have to. But it doesn't feel good."

What do you do when you want to pick someone up, carry them away from everything awful, but you can't, because everything awful is inside of them? My stomach clenched. She ran to me on September eleventh. And it hurt her.

"It hurts when certain things touch it. Jeans. They really hurt my leg. I don't know what it is. The material or something."

"Oh, God, Jendy. I'm sorry."

"It's been so long. I'm used to it. I can't really remember what it feels like not to hurt all the time."

"You know why I'm sorry," I said, and she sniffed and nodded silently.

"Gage?"

"Yeah?"

"Can I tell you something?"

"Sure."

"It's really stupid. You can't tell anyone."

"Okay."

"This scar is the toughest part of me. Sometimes when I was little, I used to imagine everything that hurt me got sucked up into the tough part. This scar, this was the mangled part, the part holding all the pain. Then the rest of me could be normal. Nobody would ever know."

"That's not stupid."

"Yeah. I guess. But is it stupid if I still do it?"

"No. No way." I pulled her close to my chest. Her hair smelled exactly the same as it did that morning. As it did two years ago. Mint and flowers.

"You're calling me Jenna a lot," she said and snuggled into me. We inched closer to each other. She was in my arms and she was real and here and I would be twenty-two in five minutes. Our noses touched. Her face nuzzled under my head, into my chin, and I felt her breath on my neck. I felt Jenna close her eyes, her eyelashes brushing my skin. I shifted to look at her face. She licked her parted lips. She opened her eyes slowly, looked up from her lashes. I felt my eyes close, one hand inch around her waist, and the other curl into her shoulders. Our bodies aligned, our hips touched. She was so soft. Our feet tangled together. My head dipped to hers.

"Is this a moment?" Jenna asked.

My eyes snapped open. Her voice was low and dreamy, but she might as well have screamed the question while throwing a bucket of ice water at me. "What?"

"Roxie says you can get moments back. It's cosmic or something. You think there's more than one moment?"

My senses flooded back to me. It hurt to swallow the lump in my throat. Jenna. Bogged with grief. I could see the tears still staining her cheeks. Jenna. Completely drunk. I couldn't hear the alcohol in her voice anymore, but I knew it was there. She was very drunk. So drunk she probably wouldn't remember much of this. And I was sober. Very, very sober. Roxie was right. In the span of time and two lives there was absolutely more than one moment. And Jenna was right. This was a moment. We had gotten it back.

Under the worst circumstances.

This moment, our new moment, was somehow even scarier than Gina Jilette. I was holding Jenna's heart, her entire soul, in my hands. And as much as I wanted Jenna, I still did not want that responsibility. I would be twenty-two in three minutes.

"Jenna...I don't know." My voice was cautious, controlled. "I don't think it would be...good. I don't know if there are," I swallowed hard, hoping it would hid my lie, "moments."

The mood shifted immediately.

"Yeah. I agree." Jenna did not sound certain at all, but she pulled herself out of my grasp and flipped on her back. "Roxie really doesn't know us. I don't even know about cosmic probabilities. I don't think that's even a thing."

"No. She makes up shit all the time." Grabbing the remote, I turned onto my back too. "You know Roxie," I said, and Jenna nodded in agreement. We did know Roxie. And Roxie had never made anything up in all the time I'd known her. She was, quite honestly, the most candid and outspoken person I had ever met.

Some New Year's Eve special blared from the television, the sound of a band blasted from the speakers.

"Let's watch this," Jendy said and propped herself up on an elbow to see over my body. We stared at the band, the picture, all static and fluttering in front of us. The antennae needed adjusted.

"I'm not fixing them," Jenna said as she flopped onto her back. "So this is what you do for the New Year."

I thought about Cody and Ace and the boys in Key West. Drinking. I thought about the girls they were meeting. The parties thumping around them. "This is what I do," I said.

"You're boring." Her voice was thick with sleep and alcohol.

"Only for you," I muttered and got up to move the antennae around, looking for the sweet spot.

The ball, slowly descending, came into focus.

"Jendy, it's happening," I said, turning to her.

"Hmm," she murmured, her eyes closed, one arm bent over her forehead.

I turned back and watched the last five seconds of the year slip away. Alone, in my shorts, in the glow of an eleven-year-old television.

People in party hats screamed the countdown.

"3..."

I thought of Jendy. When I first met her at the party. Sweatpants. Laughing. Falling asleep next to me. The way I hurt her.

"2..."

I dredged up that horrible day. September 11. When she could have hated me, should have hated me, for being such a dick to her, but instead she waited in the grass with me all afternoon. The astonishment I felt when I saw her look genuinely relieved that everything in my life would be okay after finally getting that call.

"1!"

And now, here we were. Jendy. Falling asleep in my bed. And I hurt her, when she had been nothing but kind, nothing but herself. She didn't show the hurt this time, but, God, did I hurt her.

"Happy New Year!" The drunken mass screamed on television, falling into each other. I wandered back to Jenna. She was asleep, I guessed, her hair all fanned out over the pillow, one leg under the covers, the other, the scarred one where all her tough stuff resided, flung out in the open. I took a pull from the bottle of beer that sat on my nightstand and stared at her.

"I'm sorry, Jendy," I whispered and hunkered down next to her. I would forever be apologizing to the girl.

Senior Year

Spring Semester

Thursday, February 13, 2003

Jenna

Jenna was keeping a secret, and Gage was painting her toenails. The two things were not related, but they were both happening at the same time. Jenna did not want to be keeping the secret. And she also did not want him to paint her toenails. Both the secret and the painting of toenails (especially by the likes of Gage) would lead to disaster. She gave him every reason she could think of to stop him. He was relentless.

Waste of time? *We're in college. All we have is time to waste.*

Toxins seeping through the polish and into her brain? *The science behind your theory is sketchy at best.*

You don't know anything about theories or science, Jenna had countered.

I know enough.

If Gage thought Jenna should have painted toenails, by God, he was going to give her painted toenails. Jenna laughed to herself. She couldn't fault him for being overly nice, even if it was out of character. He had been popping by doing strange things for her. Picking up lunch. Making her tea. Asking about her day. He was making up for something, and Jenna knew exactly what it was. She knew what he thought. That she didn't remember anything about New Year's Eve. He was wrong. She remember everything. It was like a weird, embarrassing miracle for which nobody prayed.

She knew all the stuff she said to him, she knew they almost kissed, she knew she asked if they were having a "moment", and worst of all, she basically begged him to sleep with her without saying a word. Jenna burned red thinking about it now. She should absolutely not have done that. Especially not with her secret. Thank God Gage was engrossed in his task. He had barely spared her a glance since starting.

She also knew that if he had agreed with her about *moments* and how maybe some people were lucky enough to get more than one, she would have kissed him. She would have slept with him. And felt incredibly guilty the next morning. Very guilty. Because of the secret.

The next morning, she thought about sneaking out, but they had been friends far too long for her to do that anymore. She also was smarter than that. She came up with a plan, and the plan was simple. Confirm his suspicions. Jenna remembered nothing. As far as Jenna was supposed to know, Gage somehow changed overnight, transforming from sometime-friend to new best friend.

He did remind her, one day as they walked to class together, that she told him about her scar and the fire. He brought it up awkwardly, a little hesitantly, and she smiled because she had never seen him so nervous. "Oh," was all she answered then she looked away, feigning uncomfortable shock, because she thought that's probably how she would answer if she had not remembered what she divulged. Jenna waited a beat, but he said nothing else, so she figured that was all he'd ever say about their night together.

And now he was here painting her toenails. And she was full of secrets.

Jenna didn't even like nail polish.

"You don't need to do this stuff for me because of my scar. You never did before."

"It's not because of the scar. Now shut up and let me work."

Jenna knew then that it was because of the kiss. Or almost-kiss. The guilt of it all. But one thing that bothered her is that she did not know if he felt guilty for almost kissing her or guilty for turning her down. Whatever it was, she had decided long ago to move on. It was best for both of them that she move on. Gage would understand. And that would be one less secret.

"I can't wait for spring break," Jenna said to Gage as she watched him. It was all she could do to not laugh at the ridiculous picture he made; a Frat-boy in a pink polo hunched over and staring intently at her toes.

"I don't know why. You refuse to go to booze cruising with me and the guys in Mexico. Building houses in Haiti," he scoffed. "For spring break. Who does that?"

"No need for flattery. I know you're impressed."

"I am. You're a better person than I. I keep thinking maybe it'll rub off on me."

"It won't," Jenna said grimly.

"So you are not as influential as I hoped. How very disappointing. Done," he said, pounding the nail polish bottle on the desk like a finished shot of vodka.

Jenna cocked her head to check out his work. "Wow, Gage. You can actually do it. I thought they'd be a hot mess."

Gage looked away, a ghost of a smile on his face.

"I'm impressed. How'd you learn this? Are you a secret toenail polisher? Do you pedicure yourself?" Jenna pulled at his shoes, trying to take them off. "Do you?"

"No," he laughed and grabbed her hands. "Jesus, Jendy. I had a girlfriend in high school. I did it for her."

That stopped her. "Aw. The Tin Man has a heart."

"She made me."

"No woman can make you do anything."

"What can I say? She had my heart in her hands." He held his cupped hands voice, "And she *crushed* it," he added, changing his voice, adding a thick Russian accent, smashing his palms together.

"Poor baby." Jenna poked out her lower lip.

"Your bogus sympathy is greatly appreciated."

Jenna shrugged. "I try."

Gage dusted off his hands. "I need to go shotgun some beers in a basement somewhere and feel like a man again."

"You offered," Jenna reminded him. "If you'll remember, I argued against this."

"I have no rebuttal." He stood to stretch then clapped his hands once. "Let's get drunk."

"Meh."

"Come on. It's the weekend."

"It's Thursday."

"Which is," he said, tugging at her wrist, "the first day of the weekend."

"I don't feel like it."

"We haven't been out since last semester."

"I've been to so many of your disgusting frat parties, I'm in need of a chemical shower."

"Out, Jendy. Out. Frat parties are inside."

"So is a bar, genius." She was getting better at her comebacks.

"We didn't go out for my birthday." They both were quiet, and Gage…blushed? Jenna squinted at him. Did Gage actually blush? He barreled on to cover up the silence. "And you refused to go out for your birthday."

Jenna, who didn't want to remember his birthday night either, also moved on. "That was nearly a year ago. You have issues."

"And you forced me into antiquing. The whole day." He shook his head. "No. You owe me."

"It wasn't antiquing. It was an indoor flea market. In April. Nearly an entire year ago."

"And you bought me all that used clothing. Used clothing, Jendy. I wore somebody's dead grandpa's shirts for you."

"Gage. It's time to let it go."

"It didn't smell good, Jendy. That shirt never was quite right."

"It was a nice shirt."

"And that lamp. My God, that lamp."

Jenna remembered the tacky lamp built of ceramic and stained glass Koi, the lightbulb held delicately in a fish's upturned mouth. "You should be thanking me for that experience. That lamp is a classic."

"A classic piece of garbage. You owe me for that *experience*."

"Cody loved that lamp," Jenna countered.

"He used it as a drinking vessel. He filled that trout's mouth with whiskey."

"See? It was perfect. I don't see why you're complaining."

"Come on. Let's go. Grady's." He pulled Jenna to her feet, then leaned over her desk. "Get your keys. Get your purse. Get all your girl stuff." He stuffed random things in her hands.

Jenna saw his hands hover over the papers she had hid under her purse. TERMS OF LEASE in huge block lettering across the top. "Wait. Gage."

Too late.

"Jendy, what's this?" Gage snatched the paperwork from Jenna's littered desk.

Jenna's secret.

"Nothing." Jenna dropped all the stuff she held and made a grab for it. "Nothing."

"Ooo!" He held the papers high above his head and well out of her reach. "That means it is interesting." He scanned the papers.

Jenna gritted her teeth, turned away to make her escape. She wanted to tell him; she needed to tell him. But that didn't mean she wanted to do it now.

"Whoa there." He grabbed her arm and pulled her back. She bumped solidly into his chest. "What is this? An apartment application? In Pittsburgh?"

"Yes."

"In Pittsburgh?" He repeated.

"Yes."

"You're moving to Pittsburgh."

"Yes."

"After we graduate?"

"Yes."

"Why does this feel like pulling teeth?"

"Why does this feel like an inquisition?"

"Why not New York? Isn't that where all the tortured writers go?"

"I don't need New York to torture me. This writer is tortured enough. Have you ever Googled the cost of living in New York City?"

"So you looked."

"Of course I looked. I'm a tortured writer."

"You could go to California. Be a famous screenwriter."

"Yeah. Ok." Jenna laughed. "Earthquakes."

"Snow. Ice. Tornados?" he countered.

"Pennsylvania doesn't have tornados." Jenna paused. "I think."

He stared at her. "Pittsburgh?"

"Pittsburgh," She stated with finality.

"But why?" He held up a finger, stopping her answer. "And *why* did you not tell me?" He said it with such gloom.

"Cheer up. It's not like I'm taking the summer off to walk through broken glass in Calcutta."

"You're not answering my question."

"I'm going to work there."

"Doing what?"

"Writing."

"I mean for money."

"Your confidence in me is overwhelming."

He cocked his head at her.

"Fine." Jenna sighed. "I'm going to work in a bagel and coffee shop."

"Jendy." His voice held an ocean of pity.

Jenna bristled. "I don't care, Gage. I'm happy. This is what I want."

"You're moving to Pittsburgh alone."

"I've always been alone."

He stared at Jenna. Jenna squirmed. "No. Nuh-uh. You're lying."

"I'm not lying!"

"Lying by omission?"

Jenna looked away.

"Ah-ha!" He pointed at her triumphantly.

"I know people there," she said elusively.

"You *know* people? Jenna Gressa knows people Pittsburgh."

"Don't be a dick," Jenna said.

"When did this happen?"

She stayed silent. Gage waited patiently, more patiently than she had ever given him credit for. He waited until she was uncomfortable, then he waited some more. She broke. "I met someone, Gage."

"You met someone? An agent? An agent for your writing? You don't have to move to where the agent lives, you do know this, right Jendy?" He laughed.

"No, Gage. I met someone. A guy. He's from Pittsburgh." Jenna shrugged through the shock quickly filling the space between them, trying to make the move seem less dramatic. Because it wasn't dramatic, she told herself. It was life. "He's a grad student in Pittsburgh. After graduation, I'm moving to be near him. I found a place to work until my writing takes off. A bagel shop in the South Side. It's really nice. I'm okay with that until my writing takes off." She realized she was blathering and abruptly stopped.

"You met a guy?" Was all Gage could ask.

Jenna pressed her lips together. The shock between them became electric, almost painful.

"Pittsburgh," he said, for the final time.

Jenna tried to smile, but felt it falter. "I'm moving to Pittsburgh to be with my boyfriend."

Tuesday, April 6, 2003

Jenna

She met him at Charred last July. He was lanky, pale skin stretching over his long limbs. He was pretty, too. Pretty in a way guys don't like to think they are, big eyes and lush lips, face perfectly symmetrical.

"Daniel Baxley," he said, reaching out to shake her hand. And she liked him because he introduced himself, something nobody had ever done to her before. "Do you sell food?" he asked.

"We have these little pie things," she said and gestured to the new display case of baked goods.

"Are they freshly baked?" He asked, contemplating them

"They came fresh from a freezer this morning," she admitted. She thought it would make him laugh, but it didn't. He did flash a smile though and he looked even prettier – which she had erroneously thought was not possible. He bought the pie and ate it with a fork and knife, cutting it up into equal and tiny parts. Jenna thought it was so adorably civilized and unlike most students who typically shoved the entire thing into their mouth. He ate there at the counter, which was perfect because she could ask him questions in-between waiting on other customers. He was studying astrophysics, chasing a master's degree in Pittsburgh, visiting Northern Virginia for use of their research lab.

He ordered a coffee after he finished his pie. Black. She liked that too. Simple.

He stayed for a month to work on research, leaving right before the fall semester begun. He liked to talk a lot and about anything. His research, his teaching assistant position, Pad Thai, the benefits of barefoot running, even one time about his leather jacket for half an hour. Jenna didn't care. She never cared when people didn't let her talk anyway. She never wanted to talk. He was so smart, and so much older. What could she possibly add to the conversation? The death of her mother? The death of her father? God, her life was shit compared to his and his barefoot running.

He started taking her to astronomy lectures on campus at night, which she would promptly sleep through, clapping appropriately at the end when she was startled awake. He never noticed, turning excitedly to chatter about whatever topic Jenna had slept through.

But Jenna liked him.

He'd introduced her around his cohort as Ms. Gressa, and he'd never comment on her yoga pants. In fact he seemed to really not care at all what Jenna wore or what she did or what she did or did not talk about. Which made Jenna happy. The day before he left, she asked him about moving to Pittsburgh after she graduated; he pursed his lips, looked into space for a little bit, and then said, "If you want to, I wouldn't mind." Then he went back to typing whatever he was typing. And talking some gibberish into a recorder, while she giddily searched for cheap lofts in downtown Pittsburgh.

Then he was gone and got really busy, teaching his classes again and grading papers, and they talked once a week for ten minutes. It's all I can spare, Jenna, he would say. She didn't care. She had to hide in the bathroom to take his calls and erase his number from the caller identification after they hung up.

Now, eight months later, Jenna excitedly dialed his number.

"Daniel," she said eagerly, barely noting his distracted grunt. "I got it. I got the apartment. It's tiny, but wow, it's so much cheaper than anything here, anyway, so I'm thinking it shouldn't be too bad to furnish it. It'll be sparse, but after I get a few paychecks--"

"Sounds good," He interrupted.

Jenna smiled. "So, I was thinking, I have the extra room in there, so if you ever need to spend nights, my place will be pretty close to--"

"Yeah, okay. Sounds good." Jenna heard the clack of keys as he typed. "I don't really have time for this. No offense, Jenna. I trust you to make the correct decision."

"Oh." She didn't really understand why she was disconcerted by his tone. He was speaking the same way he always did.

"All I'm saying, Jenna, is that if I need to spend the night, I will. It's completely logical. I'm not sure why we would have to discuss it."

"Right."

"And, obviously, if you need the funds for furniture, you can always borrow some money from me. There is no reason to worry."

"Oh, I could never take money from you."

"Borrow, Jenna, not take. You wouldn't need to worry. We could set up an agreement on paper. I don't even think we would have to add interest. I trust you to reimburse me."

"Um…yeah."

"It not like you would take my money and run. You have no family to run to. So, really, where would you go?"

Jenna swallowed the sick feeling threatening to bubble up. "Right."

"Now, I really need to get back to my dissertation."

"Yeah, I'm really busy, too," Jenna said looking to the pile of nachos she had been demolishing before she opened the email from her new landlord.

"Of course you would be. It's nearly finals."

"Will you be visiting?" Jenna asked tentatively.

"Would you like me to?"

"Um…would you like to visit?"

"Jenna. I don't really have time for this."

Jenna paced the room. Sometimes, she felt uneasy about their conversations. But, that was how he communicated. It was the way everyone should communicate, he had argued numerous times. Direct, Jenna, he told her. Everyone should be direct. Humans are too passive. And we have not yet evolved to mind reading. "I would like you to visit," she said finally. There was nothing wrong with being direct, she supposed.

"Then I will visit. And I'll be happy to visit."

Couldn't he have said that to begin with? But instead Jenna said, "Good. And maybe we could go out to dinner? You could meet Roxie. And Gage," she added hesitantly.

"If that is what you would like, I'll do it."

"I'd like to tell you something, Daniel."

"Go ahead. I have one minute."

"I love you," she said for the first time to a man. For the first time to any human being in more than ten years. The thrill of it washed over her. She was in love with Daniel Baxley. And, even if he wasn't sweet or grand gestures type of man, he was solid and he was there. And soon he would share a life with her. And furniture. With no interest added at all.

"Oh, Jenna," he replied. "I agree our experiences together have been very satisfying. Great."

The dead weight of his response landed with a thud in her gut. He isn't overly romantic, she reminded himself. Maybe not romantic at all. But he was honest. And direct. So if being with her was satisfying, no, very satisfying, that was something to celebrate. So she put a smile in her voice. "I'm glad to hear that."

And she was. Being satisfying was a step towards love, wasn't it?

"Jenna?"

"Hmm?"

"I really must go."

"Yes. Of course. Bye, Daniel. I can't wait--" And then she heard a dial tone. He had already disconnected.

Saturday, April 17, 2003

Gage

The calendar said spring, but it might have well have been winter. Sleet. Some kind of slushy snow-rain. Thirty-three degrees. Which was fitting, because surely I had died and gone to hell. Dante's hell. Ninth circle. You know, the one filled with ice and your best friend's tedious boyfriend and all that fantastic shit.vvThat could only explain why I was sitting across from Jenna and Dan Baxley at the most expensive restaurant in town. That, and it was Jenna's birthday.

At least Roxie had been invited too.

"What's he like?" I had asked earlier when Jenna was in the shower.

Roxie was sorting through graduate school catalogues. "I don't know. Weird?"

"Like Jenna weird or--"

"No. A whole different kind of weird." She flipped a brochure at me. "What are your thoughts about American University?"

"I never think about it." I flipped the brochure back at her. "What kind of weird?"

"I don't know how to describe it." She flicked through a different catalogue. "I've been in Virginia forever. Maybe I should move on. What are your thoughts on California?"

"Back up. How old is this guy?"

"I don't know, like, twenty-seven or something?"

"God, Rox," I spit out, hoping she did not detect the dismay I could feel, "you gotta come with me."

"No. I don't even want to meet this guy."

"So you told Jenna no when she asked you to come? Cold, Rox."

She brushed off my comment easily. "I told her I have a paper due and I really need to finish it. Told her I'd make it up to her. We already have something planned for tomorrow for her birthday. I'm making lentil soup. And vegan cake."

"Which sounds horrifying."

"Jenna loves vegan cake."

"I hate to break it to you, Rox."

"What?" Roxie stopped and looked up at me. "She doesn't like it?"

"She doesn't like it," I whispered.

"You're lying."

"I'm not lying." Maybe. I could have been. But maybe I wasn't. Truthfully, Jenna never talked about vegan cake. Or any kind of cake.

"Jenna doesn't like vegan cake?"

"Or lentil soup."

Roxie's mouth dropped open.

"Come on, Rox. You had to know. Nobody actually likes lentil soup."

"I've been gifting her lentil soup and vegan cake for years. This is bad. Why wouldn't she tell me?"

"Because she's too nice, Rox."

"She is way too nice. You know what he told her?"

"Who?"

"God, Gage, keep up. Daniel. Do you know what he told her?"

"What?"

"He told her he would loan her money. For furniture."

Because I was expecting so much more, like maybe *and then he forced her to shave her head and join a nunnery*, so when the story ended there, I must say, that was pretty much the most anti-climactic moment of my life. I raised my eyebrows at Rox. "So?"

"So?" Her voice squeaked. "*So?* So that crazy, that's what. He said he wouldn't even charge her interest on the loan, and that they could fill out papers. Like an application." Her voice dropped to a whisper. "And get them notarized. *Notarized.*"

Okay, that was a little more shocking. "He knows a notary?"

"That's not the point." Roxie flicked her wrist dismissively. "And then you know what? She told him that she loves him. Right after he said all that stuff about the notary."

"For saying the notary isn't the point, you really seem to be hung up on the notary."

"Oh, God. Keep up, Gage. She loves him. She *thinks* she loves him, Gage. She doesn't love him. She's just scared."

"Scared of what?"

"Being alone after we graduate."

"That's stupid though. She could live with me." I shrugged because this was a given. Jenna could follow me; she could live with me; whatever she wanted she could have with me. I didn't mind. "So why's she saying she loves this weirdo?"

"Because she doesn't even understand her own feeling about anything...or anyone." She looked pointedly at me.

I stared back. "What?"

Roxie lifted one eyebrow, which impressed me so much I tried to copy the look, but ended up wiggling both eyebrows.

She sighed and shook her head. "You two are ridiculous."

"What are you talking about?" I wiggled my eyebrows again, because I figured I if I put enough effort into this eyebrow move, it could improve conversations exponentially.

"Stop with the eyebrows, Gage! I'm serious." Roxie hit my shoulder, and I dropped the act. "I'm talking about Jenna loving Daniel. But not really loving Daniel."

"So what he say? About her declaration of love and whatever."

"He said, get this." She leaned in, and because it felt like something I should do to, I leaned in as well. "He said, 'You have been very satisfying.'"

The eyebrow move would be perfect for this. See? Improve conversations exponentially. But since I did not need one more hit from Roxie, I instead contorted my face with disgust. "Who *is* this guy?"

"She's like, convincing herself that she loves him, Gage. And that she's okay with his, pardon my French," Roxie waved her hand, "bullshit."

"How do I not know any of this?"

"Oh, she's not going to *tell* you, Gage."

"Why not?"

She spared me a glance long enough to let me know she pitied my cluelessness. "And here I am, feeding her lentil soup and vegan cake. Dating this asshole. She's miserable, Gage. And my lentil soup is a part of it."

Now I kind of felt bad about my vegan cake lies. But it gave me the leverage I needed. "Then you need to make it up to her," I said quickly, then was struck with brilliance.

Roxie looked unconvinced.

"What if I tell you a secret? A factoid, if you will. About me. And California," I added, enticingly. "Will you come with me then?"

She quirked her eyebrow again. "It depends on the factoid."

"I'm moving there in June."

"Really? Oh my, God, Gage!" Roxie's squeal pierced my eardrums. "You got a job?"

"I got a job."

"You got a job!" She shrieked again and launched herself at me, laughing.

"A dream job, Rox. I don't even know how I landed it."

"Gage! This is amazing. We should celebrate. We have to tell-"

"We're not telling Jendy."

Roxie stopped mid-hug. She pulled back. "Why not?"

"I'm kind of waiting on the right time. You know. She's going to Pittsburgh. She doesn't have a job lined up or anything. I can't...I feel strange telling her."

"Like you are abandoning her?"

"Jeez, Rox. You trying to rip my heart out?"

"That's how I feel." Roxie looked longingly at the UC Berkeley pamphlet in her hands. "I mean, the girl lost everything. And you know about her foster families."

Yeah. How she had about ten different families until she turned eighteen.

"I should go tonight," Roxie said, her voice thick with guilt. "Yeah. I should go."

I heard Jenna in the bathroom, singing to herself. She was in love with this Daniel guy. And she would be moving in with him in a month. "I'll buy."

"I *am* hungry." Roxie conceded, and the decision was made.

So there we sat. Roxie scarfing down all the salad. Daniel droning on and on about some kind of astrophysical event. Me asking for shot after shot of whiskey I probably couldn't afford. Jenna, stars in her eyes, nodding in agreement with everything Daniel said. Jenna looking completely opposite of everything I knew of her. Jenna in her too-short-for-this-kind-of-weather-skirt and heels that looked like ice picks meant for stabbing men's hearts instead of ice.

Skirt and heels? Who was this Jenna? The skirt skimmed her thigh, barely covering her scar. Her scar. I wondered if Daniel ever saw her scar and a startlingly jealous rage burned through me at the thought.

"Can I get another beer?" I asked the waitress.

"Absolutely, sir." She smiled, even though she should have said, *You're drunk as fuck, sir.*

Roxie was still shoving down salad, glancing everywhere but at Jenna the birthday girl and her boring boyfriend.

Daniel stopped to take a breath, and Jenna finally found her in.

"So I'm doing reading this translation of Brus for my senior thesis. And what I really find fascinating--" Jenna started before Daniel's phone rang, interrupting her.

He checked it. "I need to take this, Jenna."

"Oh, yes, of course," she cooed at him. "Sure."

Cooed? I grimaced.

"But what you were saying was great. Great," he said absently as he patted Jenna's head.

Roxie rolled her eyes at me and shoved an entire forkful of salad into her already full mouth.

I downed another shot of whiskey as I waited for my beer.

"I can't believe you're doing shots at a restaurant," Jenna hissed as soon as Daniel was gone.

"And a Happy Birthday to you, Jen!" I slammed the glass to the table. I had never called her Jen, and the word felt as alien as the top shelf whiskey stinging my tongue.

"Whatever. Never mind." Jenna held up her hands in surrender and turned to Roxie. "So what do you think of him?"

"He was checking out the waitress." I answered before Roxie could say anything.

Roxie's eyes widened as her fork clattered to the bowl in front of her. "No. No he wasn't," she argued.

"And whose side are you on?"

"Not now, Gage," she muttered. "Don't do this now."

"So were you," Jenna said flippantly, but I saw her glance over her shoulder to the door Daniel exited.

"You don't get to argue that. I'm not your boyfriend," I refuted.

"Oh, shut up. You would check her out even if you were my boyfriend." Jenna dismissed me, but I could hear the anger rising in her voice. It was kind of revolting how much I liked it. If I wasn't so drunk I would have felt shame. I would have stopped. But I was drunk, so I pressed on. "Well, we'll never know that will we?"

Roxie whipped her head around so fast, I figured it would snap off and fly across the restaurant.

"What's that supposed to mean?" Jenna narrowed her eyes at me.

I ignored the question. "I don't like him," I said and listened to Roxie groan.

Jenna's face fell. "Why?"

"He's an asshole."

"No," Jenna argued and looked to Roxie for support.

Roxie shrugged. "He is pretty abrupt, don't you think, Jenna?"

"He's being honest. Direct. More people should be like that."

"And what's this robot stuff?

"What robot stuff?"

"You're like his damn robot. Is he making you repeat this nonsense? Blink once if you need help, Jenna."

"Screw you, Gage!" Jenna replied, quite succinctly.

"Why do you even like him?" I countered.

"I...I...I--"

"Make your point, Jenna. As you can plainly see, I drank a metric-ton of alcohol, and I'd like to get home."

Jenna stammered some more.

"You don't even know why you like him. Love him." I scoffed, correcting myself.

"You told him?" Jenna, face red, hissed at Roxie.

Roxie quickly got back to eating salad.

"He's nothing like you," Jenna said.

"And thank God for that," I toasted nobody then downed the beer the waitress had just set in front of me.

"We talk about adult stuff. Sophisticated stuff."

"Says the girl with a stack of Victorian romances under her bed," I said and watched the blush spread over Jenna's face. I felt like an utter shithead for doing that to her, which meant I would dig deeper. "Do you talk about that with him Jenna? Classy stuff like that?"

"What do you care?" She threw her napkin at me.

Was Roxie sliding away from the table? I grabbed her wrist to pull her back. "People are staring," she hissed at me.

I brushed her off. "Did you change your hair for him, Jenna?" I threw the napkin back. "Did you wear a skirt for him, Jenna?"

"What in God's name is wrong with you?" Roxie glared at me. "Who do you think you're impressing?"

I barely heard her over the roar of blood rushing my ears as I waited for Jenna's answer.

"He's drunk, Jen," Roxie said too patiently as she turned to Jenna. "Don't answer him." She was obviously appealing to Jenna's sober sanity.

Jenna ignored Roxie too. Her death-ray eyes were set to full-kill on me. "I would not do that. I would never change myself for a guy." But Jenna's voice was wavering, getting high and pitchy.

"You did, didn't you?" I egged.

"Jen, ignore him." Roxie jabbed my ribs.

"You tried to get me to change my hair for a year!" Jenna exclaimed.

She was right, which meant that was something else I chose to ignore. "I don't like him Jenna."

"I don't care what you like," she hissed.

"You act different with him."

"I do not!"

"What the hell kind of Stepford act are you putting on for everyone? And what the hell are you wearing? It's ten degrees out. You look like the girls *I* screw."

"What a perfectly misogynistic thing to say," Roxie said pertly, and I knew if I ever had her on my side, I definitely lost her with that remark. "And it's thirty degrees out," she added.

"Shut up," Tears pricked at the corners of Jenna's eyes. "Everyone just shut up."

I was just telling the truth, the hard truths that nobody wants to hear. Isn't that was Daniel Baxley touted? And wasn't that the very reason I hated him? The alcohol swam through my blood, blurred my vision.

"Hey, Jenna," Dan's voice interrupted us. "Is there something wrong here?"

I snorted.

"Nothing," Jenna said, a little too cheerfully.

"Okay then." He sat.

The guy was clearly an idiot. Otherwise he would be able to tell that I nearly incited a riot, and he should punch me in my stupid, drunk face. Right there in the restaurant. Get me tossed out on my ass.

"That was work. Very important call."

Jenna smiled at him.

"I hear there are lots of astronomy emergencies right now." I said sarcastically. "There was that documentary a while back…Armageddon, I think it was called? Wasn't, like, Aerosmith in it?"

"Oh, my God. If you want to live, shut up," Roxie kicked me under the table as everyone glanced at me. No, glance was the wrong word. Jenna fiery hot eyes tore daggers through me.

But I couldn't stop. I addressed Dan, but stared at Jenna. "So, Dan, you're an astronomer--"

"Astrophysicist," he corrected. "And I prefer Daniel."

"Of course. So, tell me, what do you think about moments? Do you think we get more than one? Is it, I don't know, *cosmic*?"

Jenna turned all shades of color, ending in blotchy red. I heard, I actually heard, her sharp intake of breath, as if I kicked her in the stomach. She became very still, except for her fingers that curled hard and white over her knife.

"What *the hell* are you doing?" Roxie hissed in a tone so low, I wasn't sure if she even said anything or if it was my conscience. "Are you trying to humiliate her?"

Daniel finally figured it out. He fell quiet. I watched his fingers curl into a fist. Yes. Here it was. He was going to punch me. I set my mouth in a line as I sat up straighter. Do it, Dan. Do it.

Jenna shifted uncomfortably. "Daniel? She touched his arm. He jerked away, and she pulled her fingers back as if scalded.

He stood, jerkily moved his long limbs. He glanced around the table at all of us, his gaze finally landing on Jenna. He ran a tongue over his teeth. "Listen, Jenna. I think I'm going to cut this short."

"Oh. Oh. Okay." Jenna scrambled for her things. "Well we can go back to-"

"No, you misunderstand. I mean I'm going back to my hotel and checking out. I'm leaving."

"But--"

"You are obviously having issues with your friends. I really don't feel like I need to be a part of this little drama."

"Daniel, everything is okay."

He raised his eyebrows at her. "I have never been one for fixing your issues. You have always known this about me." He calmly sipped his wine then wiped his mouth with a napkin. "And you have so very many issues."

Roxie and I sat in shocked silence.

This time my fist was the one curling in fury.

Jenna opened her mouth. Then shut it. Then opened it again. "Yeah. I know."

He checked his watch. "Anyway, that was work, as you know. A bit of a crisis going on. They need me. There is no need to waste my time up here when you and your friends need to work out these issues you are obviously having. This one over here is drunk for God's sake." He gestured at me.

"Yes. Of course. I agree."

Roxie, who obviously couldn't feign politeness anymore, gasped. "Jenna."

Jenna held up a hand and shook her head at Roxie.

"You can take care of the bill, right?" He looked at Jenna, who looked lost.

I opened my mouth, but shut it when Roxie kicked me under the table.

He shrugged into his jacket. "I would say this was a great night, but to be perfectly honest, it wasn't. Let's hope for better next time. Perhaps without your friends." He gave Roxie and me a tight lipped smile, and I barely clamped down on my temper.

"That will be great." Jenna smiled. "Perfect, really." Her eyes were all glassy. So were mine. But for a different reason.

"Excellent." He kissed the top of her head.

"I'll call you," Jenna said weakly.

"If that's what you would like."

And with that, Daniel Baxley was gone, taking all the words and air from the restaurant with him, leaving us in a painful, sucking vacuum.

"Can I freshen everyone's drinks?" The waitress' chipper voice filled the air and we all jumped as if startled out of a coma.

I blinked twice. I turned my body toward Roxie, but my gaze stayed fixed on Jenna. "What. In the hell. Was that?"

"I could ask the same of you," Roxie said icily.

At that, Jenna's eyes flew to mine. They flamed practically red with ire. "I hate you," she said, and, picking up her purse, she fled the restaurant.

"I guess I'm paying," I said to Roxie.

She blew her bangs out of her eyes. "Oh, you're paying all right, buddy."

Outside, Jenna pulled away from my grasp. "Don't touch me."

"You're not walking home in this." The sleet had started up again. "In those." I pointed to her feet.

"I'll take the Metro."

"I'm going with you."

"You are not going with me. I don't want you to go with me."

"I don't give two shits what you want."

Jenna turned to Roxie. "I don't want him to go with me," she said with a deadly sounding calm.

"Hey, hey. What if you take the bus, Gage, and I'll go with Jenna?" Roxie played mediator.

"No!" I shouted. Was she kidding? "Are you kidding? I'm not taking the fucking bus."

"Take a cab then," she whispered furiously at me. "Leave her alone, Gage. Let me take her home."

"Wait, I know. Why don't we get Daniel to drive her back? Oh, that's right. He left her. Alone. In the restaurant. With no money and no way home," I bit out.

"Gage," Roxie warned.

"I paid for your food, Jen," I told her smugly.

"Oh, I'm so fucking grateful!" She screamed at me with a withering stare, her hands pressed against her chest like a prayer. People passing us turned to gawk, her performance was so theatrical. I had never heard Jenna curse before, and the shock of that, the shock to my system that Jenna was human and normal, threw me off kilter.

"You should be grateful," I said, ashamed of my pathetic counter to her brilliantly delivered profanity.

"Screw you, Gage!" Jenna screeched.

"Oh? Oh?" Two steps forward,and I was in her face. I moved even closer, our noses touching. "Screw me?"

"Yeah. Yeah, Gage. Go to hell. You know why he left. You know why he left!" He voice broke.

"He left, Jenna, because he's an asshole."

"He left, *Gage*," she spat out, "because you're an asshole." She pushed me. Then slid sideways.

"You see? You *see*?" I grabbed her by the elbow. "You shouldn't be wearing these shoes."

"Don't. Touch. Me." She pushed me hard on the chest with every syllable and finished with a flourish, screeching the last word in my ear.

"Fine. Fall on your ass. I won't be here to catch you. I'm leaving. You two take the Metro." Disgusted, I waved them off and started walking away, my mind swimming with thought of getting drunker and getting laid. That would make everything better.

"Idiot, Jenna. You're an idiot," I sang out. "I hope you and Dan the Man enjoy your Stepford life together."

And because my back was turned, because I was already halfway to plastered, I didn't even see it coming.

"Gage," Jenna growled at me.

I swung around ready for more, eager for more.

And that girl. She did the job Daniel couldn't do.

She cold cocked me right in the face.

Jenna

"Ohmigod! Ohmigod!" The screams ripped out of Jenna before she could stop them.

The pain ran through her hand, a fire that burned her bones and ate her flesh. A pain that radiated from the inside out.

"Jesus, Jendy." Gage's own hand covered his nose. Blood streamed down his face.

Roxie was shaken silent; her mouth dropped open and stayed there.

"Ohmigod. I can't feel my hand." Jenna felt the fat tears that had been threatening to escape all night roll down her face. "It hurts so bad."

"If you feel pain, you can feel your hand," Gage roared, then moaned and grabbed for his nose again. "Fuck." Gage, bent at the hip, gagged. He actually gagged. Jenna was certain he was going to puke all over the sidewalk. Right in front of that expensive restaurant. Good. Good for him. She hoped he puked all night and never stopped.

"I think I broke my fingers," Jenna cried. Streams of tears gathered, ugly and raw, in the cracks of her nostrils, under her chin.

"What did you expect? You punched my face." Now upright, Gage pulled his hand away and looked at the blood covering his hand.

"Don't swear at me, you ass! I don't know it would hurt *me*," Jenna sobbed. "It never happens that way on television."

"Oh, Jesus. Jesus, Jendy. What did you do to me?"

"What did *I* do?" Jenna turned to him, ready to scream again, then saw the blood pouring from his nose, oozing between his fingers, dripping onto the icy sidewalk. "Oh. Oh." She started dry-heaving now. "I don't...I don't like blood."

"And I *do*?"

"I feel kinda fff-- kinda faint."

"Don't you fucking faint. I'm not picking you up."

"You two!" Roxie finally came out of her stupor with a roar. "You two! What in God's name is wrong with you two?"

"Ohmigod. It hurts so bad." Jenna looked at her fingers. Two knuckles were already swollen and purple.

"I think you broke my nose." Above his hand, Gage's eyes flashed on Jenna's.

"I'm sorry," Jenna sobbed. She was not sorry at all. But she *was* sorry that she most likely broke her hand.

Roxie sprang into action. "The ER. We need to go to the ER. Jenna. Don't you dare faint. You need to walk to the Metro with me. Gage. You need tissues…something." She dug through her purse. "I don't have any tissues."

"Check my purse," Jenna said through her tears.

Hurriedly, Roxie snatched Jenna's purse to look.

"Tampons. Two! Two tampons."

"No," Gage warned, backing up quickly as he and Jenna watched Roxie unwrap them. "Don't touch me with those things."

She apparently didn't hear or didn't care about Gage's wishes as she pushed them against his face.

Jenna felt the bubble of hysterical laughter as Gage howled in pain. And she would have laughed. If there was one hundred percent less pain searing through her arm, she absolutely would have laughed.

"Don't touch my fucking nose," Gage erupted.

"Stop being a baby!" Jenna shrieked back. Which would have been effective, she thought, if she were not crying like a baby herself.

"You two are ridiculous," Roxie yelled. "We need to get to the Metro."

"Are you kidding? I'm not riding the Metro like this." Gage looked at her.

Jenna glanced at him. His hands, his face, his shirt, even his shoes were spattered with blood.

Roxie sighed. "You're both paying me back for this. You owe me."

Then she was hailing a cab.

Then they were speeding across town.

Then they were sitting in the Emergency Room.

Gage

After Jenna convinced the nurses it was not a domestic assault and that she did not need any kind of counseling or police help; after I got taped up and had some ugly metal brace strapped over my nose; after I ripped off said brace in the waiting room; after Roxie made me put it back on; and as we were waiting for Jenna's broken hand to be set and cast, Roxie sighed and leaned back against a hard plastic chair.

"You happy?" She raised one eyebrow at me. Fucking eyebrow.

I glared at her.

"Ha! You think you're menacing?" She folded her arms in front of her chest. "You look like a jackass."

Quickly, I looked away.

"You need to apologize to her."

"Hell, no. She broke my nose." And my pride and maybe some other stuff I could not really identify right now.

"She broke her hand."

"She deserves it."

"No, Gage. *You* deserve it. You acted exactly how you look right now."

"Everything I said was true."

"Of course it was."

Surprised that she agreed, I turned to her. "So, why didn't you back me up?"

"Are you an idiot?" She threw her hands in the air. "What am I saying? I'm sitting in a hospital with a drunk in a nose brace." Roxie rubbed her hands over her face and took a deep breath. "Gage, if you're going to be friends with a girl, you need to know a little rule. You don't say anything about her boyfriend. Nothing. Not one thing. Because then if they get married-"

"Married?! No. She's --"

"Shut up," Roxie shushed me with a finger in my face. "Because *if* they get married, you look like an ass. And if they break up, she looks like an ass. Because it's one of those "I told you so" things. So you shut your mouth and deal. That's how to be friends with a girl. My God, you even told her she changed for a guy." She shook her head.

"She did!"

"I know. But you don't *tell* her that. You *idiot*."

"This is stupid."

"Was she in immediate danger with this guy? Don't answer quick. Think about it first."

I thought about it. "No," I grudgingly agreed. "But--"

"No buts," she interrupted. "If she's not in danger, then you need to be more subtle. And you need to know that in the end, Jenna's an adult. She's been a grown-up far longer than we have."

I swallowed and looked away.

"They would have broken up, Gage. I know Jenna. *You* know Jenna. She would have broken up with him."

"They're still together."

"They're going to break up, Gage. You know this."

I sighed, and my nose throbbed. I made a mental note that I'd have to stop sighing for a while.

"You made her cry. You ruined her birthday."

"*He* ruined her birthday. Not me."

"Yeah. He did. But what do you think she'll remember, Gage? The guy who left a little early or the obnoxious friend she had to punch in the face to shut up? You know what she *would* have remembered if you said nothing? If you hugged her and bought her pizza? If you took her out? If you bought her ice cream? Anything other than starting a fistfight in the street like some jackass? She would have remembered the guy who left her there without a ride and money."

Shit. Roxie was right. "I have to apologize." I dropped my head back against the wall.

"Yeah you do."

"I don't want to apologize," I said stubbornly.

"Suck it up, buttercup."

"Rox, you are one harsh mistress." I shook my head.

"Life is a harsh mistress." Roxie looked at me. "God, you look pitiful. Buck up, Gage." She laughed patted my cheek, which made my nose throb more and Roxie probably knew that which was why she did it. "You'll get used to keeping your mouth shut. You don't even know how many times I've had to bite my tongue with stuff regarding you and Jenna."

"Yeah, but that's different. We're not dating. We don't have those feelings."

Roxie stared at me incredulously.

"What?"

"Lord Almighty, Gage," Roxie said. "I think a can of paint is more self-aware than you. And twice as bright."

"Twice as bright, huh?"

"Yep." She stretched her legs out in front of her.

"But what color is the paint?"

"Beige," she answered without missing a beat. "Very, very, *very* dull beige. Ecru at best."

We sat in silence then as we waited for Jenna.

Roxie finally looked at me. "If you don't want her, Gage, you have to accept the fact that someday some guy will. And you'll have to deal with it. Can you deal with it? Because this is the first and last ER trip I'm ever participating in with you two jackasses." Roxie pushed up off the chair. "I'm going to get a candy bar."

Sunday, May 9, 2003

Jenna

"Jenna…Jenna." The whispery voice tugged Jenna from a Vicodin induced sleep. "Hey. Jenna."

Certain it was the pain meds making her hear things, she grumbled and rolled over.

"Jendy," Now the voice had an arm, and it was poking her shoulder. "Jendy. Are you awake?"

Gage. She hadn't seen him in two weeks. Or was it three?

She could pretend to be asleep. Groggy, she rolled over. "How'd you get in here, Gage?" She grumbled, irritated with herself for giving in to him. Roxie had gone out on a date. And she had locked the door before she left.

"Rox gave me a key," he whispered.

That traitor, Jenna thought with absolutely no malice. Roxie had given Jenna space for the first week. She let Jenna hem and haw the second week. Roxie started asking Jenna about Gage the third week. *How was Gage? How was his nose? Jenna had broken his nose, hadn't she? When would they all hang out again? Such a shame their friendship had to end like this.* And on and on until Jenna felt twinges of guilt, because she would be moving to Pittsburgh soon, and they would never see each other again. Still, she couldn't bring herself to call him.

"How are you feeling?" Gage whispered.

"Why are you whispering?" Jenna whispered back.

"I don't know. You're hurt."

"It's a broken hand, not a radioactive spill that gave me supersonic hearing." Jenna's knuckles were throbbing. She must have rolled over them in her sleep. Ugh.

"My nose may have broken your hand, sweetheart, but I can see I didn't break your spirit." He grinned.

"I feel like a car ran over me and then backed up," Jenna groaned.

"What are we watching?" Gage nodded to the television.

"*We're* not watching anything. You are *not* making yourself at home here, Elliot Gageby." Jenna said. "Get out."

"What are we watching?" He asked again.

"You are so immature." Jenna rolled her eyes. "Fine. We'll play. *I* was watching a documentary on Mary, Queen of Scotts." *Before I fell asleep*, she added to herself.

"Well," he said companionably, "that sounds horrible. No wonder you feel like shit."

"Oh, for God's sake," Jenna sighed. "Why are you here, Gage?"

Gage

That was a good question.

At first, right after the hospital, I figured I would let it go. Let her go. Never talk to Jenna again. College was ending. It almost felt poetic that our strange and rocky journey together should also come to a strange and rocky conclusion. Because Roxie had been right. And Cody had been right. Somehow between my birthday and hers, I had fallen for Jenna. Maybe it wasn't love, like Cody had suggested, but it was more than friendship. I was figuring we could sleep together. That would help. Or something. And I was figuring on some way to make it happen. Then. Daniel Baxley. So really, I had to end it. Because watching her fall in love with Daniel Baxley was – literally and figuratively - the most painful experience I had with Jenna. But then it hit me. After a couple weeks. I missed her. As a friend. And I couldn't screw her. Because I liked her too much. And I couldn't disappear and screw her over like that. Because I'd rather have her as a friend for life than as a girlfriend for a minute. Because I was bound to screw that up somehow and lose her forever.

Basically, there was a lot of screwing - and a lot of not screwing - involved with my decision.

I had to deal with the fact that while Jenna was not the beautiful stunner type of girls I went for, she was not some sort of homely *X-files* lizard monsterwoman either. She was not just stomping around being an unlikable sea-creature-ish thing; she was likable, she was lovable, she was pretty, she was funny and more loyal than she ever had to be, her continued friendship to my miserable ass was proof of that. She was Jenna. Guys would want her. And she would want them back. Someday some dude would love her. And she would love that dude right back. And the revelation was like one of those family situation comedy type moments Jenna was always rattling on about – it was a downright sappy made-for-television moment that should have had swelling music and flowers attached, so I made myself chug a beer to cancel out the emotions. All right, I couldn't deal with sentimental stuff. But I could at least apologize to her. So I did. That minute. While she was kind of drugged up and groggy in her bed.

"I'm sorry, Jenna," I said, the words kind of rushing out of me.

"For what?" She prodded.

"You're really milking this."

"Go away." She rolled her eyes and started to turn over again.

"Okay," I blew the word out in a breath. "For being an ass. For saying all that shit."

"What a heartfelt apology."

"It is."

"From you? Yeah, I know it is." She sighed. "It will never happen again?"

I crouched down next to her bed. "Never again," I said.

She looked me in the eyes. Held my gaze.

"Never, Jen. I promise."

"Ok," she sighed, pulled the covers back. "Get in."

I moved to stretch out beside her.

"Look at this." She held up her arm. Her still swollen hand was covered in plaster cast up to her elbow. "I can't even wash my hair."

I sniffed. "It doesn't stink."

She bit down on a grin. "Roxie washes it. And ties my shoes."

"I can polish your toes when you need it."

She finally smiled.

"Your face broke my hand, Gage."

"Your hand broke my face, Jendy."

"I'm sorry for that."

"I deserved it."

"Does it still hurt?"

"Sometimes." I touched my nose. The black circles the punch left around my eyes finally faded to a dull yellow.

"Good." She smoothed the covers over me.

"Friends?"

"Friends."

And it felt, for the first time since I met her, that yes, we were exactly that. Friends.

We fell quiet for a minute. My hand started combing through her hair.

"He broke up with me," she said, and my hand paused in her hair. "Two weeks ago."

Don't say it, Gage. Don't say I told you so. You're not supposed to do that. But, God, did I want to say it.

"I cried for a week," she added, and my hand fisted in her hair. I was curious. And pissed. And completely right about him.

"Why'd he break up with you?"

She didn't say anything for a minute. Then, "We were too different."

Ha! I knew it. The broken nose? Totally worth it.

"Can I say something?" I asked.

"Yes," she said cautiously.

"He didn't deserve you."

I heard her exhale against my shoulder.

"And can I say one more thing?"

"Yes."

"You should have broken up with him."

"Yeah," she said quietly.

"It kills me that you didn't."

"It kills me more. Believe me."

"Can something really kill something more? Dead is dead." She snorted.

I closed my eyes.

"Can I tell you something, and you can't judge me?" she asked.

"Probably not."

"Gage!" She punched my arm.

"Settle down there, Rocky. I don't need more broken bones."

"I knew he was an asshole. But he kind of tricked me or something. Maybe I tricked myself."

Roxie was right. How about that?

"You know, it felt so good to have someone want me. To say I love you to someone. I felt like a grown-up with him."

"Yeah." I pulled her close. "Jenna, that's cheesy. And stupid. I don't know if I can be friends with you anymore."

Laughter rocketed from her. I felt it against my neck.

"It was the glasses that tricked me. The glasses. Or the beard. Was it the beard?" Jenna asked. "I think it was the astronomy."

"No. It was the beard."

Jenna laughed.

"Am I now allowed to call him a douche?"

"Yes. Now is appropriate." She closed her eyes against my shoulder.

"He was such a douche."

"Oh God, and now I have to move to Pittsburgh. Alone. That was a stupid idea, wasn't it?" Her face crumpled in sad realization.

"It's an adventure now," I corrected.

She shook her head. "What a disaster."

"We're all entitled to one."

"It's really a shame I used mine up now. So young."

"You can have mine."

"How selfless."

"I'm known for my philanthropic nature."

"Let's go to sleep. And never speak of this again."

"Ok."

Now I thought. Now is the time to tell Jendy about your job.

"I got a job." I said.

"You got a job?"

"Yes."

"Like…a real job or, like, you got one an hour ago to tend bar at Grady's?"

"A real job."

Jenna's eyes flew open. "No!"

"Yes."

"Financial planner Gage. I mean Elliot Gageby. Oh, wow. Did you realize everyone's probably going to call you Elliot?" She chattered, beyond excited for me. Even when she knew a large chunk of her life was going to be writing with a side of crummy jobs to pay the bills. I knew it. I knew she never would have faulted me for taking the job in California. My dream job. Everything I wanted, practically handed to me.

"You remembered."

"Elliot? Yeah. It's your name."

"No. I mean the financial planning stuff."

"Of course I remember." She smacked me playfully and smiled. "You want to make a lot of money."

"Huh." She remembered. I bit my lip. That would make things kind of tricky.

"What is it? What firm?"

I hemmed.

She shot me a funny look. "What one? Come on, tell me. This is going to be the only excitement I have for years of struggling writer-dom to come."

"It's a job. A good one. Steady work. Remember that."

"I know. I mean, I'm not expecting you to be a CEO. I know you'll probably start out as a minion picking up everyone's coffee for a while. That's fine. You'll be good. Really good." She beamed at me. Beaming. She was so happy.

"It's, like, not the best economy right now. It was really hard to find a job," I lied.

"I know that. That's why this is so great!"

"And I need to pay the bills. School loans, stuff like that." I was holding her off, still trying to formulate the plan, the lie, in my head. Where would be an easy place to find work?

"I know," she said impatiently. "*Tell* me. You're killing me! What firm?"

"It's not quite a firm."

"What? What do you mean? Tell me!" She practically squealed.

"Not really. I'm an accountant."

"That's...accounting." Jenna said slowly. Then she looked confused. "That's what you want? Accounting?"

"It's what I want, Jenna."

"I thought you wanted finance."

"Things change, Jenna. A lot changes."

"Yeah."

"This is a good thing, Jenna. This is a happy thing."

"Right! Yeah. Good. Gage." She looked up at me and smiled. "I'm happy for you."

"The job is in Pittsburgh."

"Pittsburgh?" The shock in her voice kind of made me happy. Like, it wasn't building houses in Haiti, but I could do something good for someone at least once in my life.

"It's in Pittsburgh, Jenna. You're not going to be alone."

She stared at me like I performed a miracle until I felt hot and uncomfortable. "Now, let's watch this God-awful documentary," I said.

I hadn't performed a miracle.

All I did was, after I went home that night, turn down a job in California, a financial firm, a huge one I had been dying to get into. I expected to feel sick when I called the recruiter. I expected my stomach to turn when I told him thanks, but no thanks, I had found another opportunity. I expected immediate regret to fill me.

But nothing.

I felt nothing.

Then I scoured the internet for a position, any position at all anywhere in Pittsburgh.

It was two phone calls, one long interview, and about an hour of paperwork.

And that was how I passed up a dream job in San Diego for Jenna.

Four Years Later

Jenna

Birthdays.

They pretty much sucked anymore, and today was no different.

Today was Jenna's twenty-sixth birthday, and she was having a mental breakdown.

Jenna spied the creamy, embossed envelope, her name scrawled across it, lying on the counter before she saw him. She was exhausted, a bone weary kind of tired that came from standing on your feet for a grueling nine hours. The kind of tired she always felt after working a shift at Bagel Plus. She was a world weary kind of tired too; her twenty-sixth birthday was passing before her eyes, she thought, and with it, the tenuous grip of still claiming "early-twenties" as her age. The phase of getting-your-shit-together-ness of her early twenties faded faster than she anticipated. It wouldn't seem cute anymore to claim she was an unpublished writer to the guys she met at the bar. She found a gray hair last week when she was staring blankly in the mirror and picking at her face. Soon she'd have wrinkles, she thought in a panic and smeared her face with dollar store moisturizer. Nothing about shift-work at a bagel shop was cute anymore. A few years ago she had read an article in the Times about the rise of the quarter-life crises and laughed. That article did not seem quite as hilarious anymore.

Jenna was deep into her mid-twenties now, and the finality of that birthday started in the morning as she had adjusted her yellow Bagel Plus visor and stuck with her through the entire day.

"Happy Birthday!" Gage called out from somewhere in the kitchen. He walked out singing. Twenty-six blazing candles stuck inside a brownie cake that was stuck inside a pink box. Twenty-six lit candles looked a lot like a forest fire. Or, in Jenna's case, a dumpster fire.

The sight, the song, and especially the glut of candles crammed on a too-small brownie hit Jenna like a sack of cement.

Had Jenna not known Gage better, she would have been mortified by the full blown panic attack that snuck up on her. "Gage. Gage," she kind of gasped, then burst into tears.

Gage quickly extinguished the candles himself, slammed the lid on the box, and moved to her. "Aw, Jendy. You're doing fine." Gage comforted her, his arm wrapping around her shoulder.

"What am I...am I...what am I--" she cried hysterically.

"Whoa, whoa. Calm down. Take a breath."

Jenna sucked in air in ragged breaths. "What am I doing with my life?" She cried some more. "I'm a mess."

"No, no. Look at this. You're always getting us free bagels." He gestured to the bag of day-old onion bagels forgotten in her hands. Jenna sobbed harder. She was twenty-six, alone - because, really, did Kaz count? - and flat broke. She couldn't even afford the brownies Gage offered her. She was sure he had bought them at some snobby shop across town.

"Should I have lit a Valium for you instead?" Gage inquired with a nudge, and Jenna laughed through her tears. After he finally calmed her down, Gage pried open the box. One corner of the pink container had crushed when he had held her tight through the worst of the panic. Jenna, her back still flat against the wall, slid to the floor as Gage followed.

"Where did you get these?" She asked.

"The grocery store," Gage answered.

"You did not, you liar." Jenna nodded. "I'm going to eat them all."

They ate the brownies there, in silence, Jenna kind of sniffling and heaving in her torn jeans and bare feet, Gage still in his dark gray suit and red tie.

"Well, I should thank you for this lovely party. I must say you outdid yourself," Jenna eventually said, her voice flat, but a hint of a smile as she met Gage's eyes, a signal that all was well again.

He laughed, full and rich, and it somehow reminded her of their last spring in college. "If it's any consolation," he said, "in my three months of experience, mid-twenties is not quite the calamity you are making it out to be in your head."

Jenna nodded in agreement, but really, Gage, he had no clue about life failure or calamities. Maybe he did understand the first year they moved out to Pittsburgh, crammed into his Jetta, both of them lugging boxes into the tiny three-story walk-up. It was then that they both had lousy jobs with worse pay, she at Bagel Plus, he as a part-time bartender and seasonal accountant, filing taxes sometimes twenty hours a day every from January to April.

Then sometime during year two, things started shifting. It was so slowly, Jenna barely noticed the changes piling one on top of the other. First, Gage got the interview at Heinz. One week later they offered him the job. Salary and benefits and a client list a mile long. It wasn't the job he had dreamed of, but *Hey, I'm not complaining*, he grinned as they toasted over cheap champagne at a dive bar as close to Grady's as they could find in Pittsburgh. *Damn right*, Jenna laughed. And they got dizzy drunk, then walked home, calling him the Ketchup Accountant. Then they went a little bit mad spending his first paycheck at Crate&Barrel.

He chased girls. He had always chased girls. But year two was a different kind of chase. These girls were different. Because they weren't girls anymore. They were Women with a capital W. Women who carried butter-soft, leather purses that cost as much as Jenna's junk car. Women whose paychecks matched his. Sometimes Women who out-earned him, which he said absently over breakfast, was the sexiest kind of Woman of all. That comment stuck with Jenna, who had been counting quarters for gas money, and she glanced up at him, but he wouldn't look at her, which meant he realized what he just said to her.

He took those Women, the Purse Women Jenna called them, to some martini bar he found in Squirrel Hill. Then they would come home, drunker than sailors on leave, and Jenna would throw on a pair of ridiculously expensive noise canceling head phones Gage bought her for her twenty-third birthday and type out her manuscripts well into the night. Sometimes in the morning she would eat breakfast with the Women, sometimes she wouldn't, and sometimes they were gone by the time Jenna woke up.

About six month after he started, Jenna noticed Gage perusing the classifieds. For new apartments, he said. Jenna looked over his shoulder and felt the color drain from her face. There was no way she could afford the places he searched.

They moved anyway.

They moved into a new place closer to Gage's office. The rent was three times higher. Gage shrugged it off, saying Jenna should pay what she always had, and he could make up the difference. It was only fair. And it was worth it, he reasoned. He was sick of the walk-up and reporting the rash of theft they had suffered. They were on a first name basis at the local precinct and typically reported the crimes to the same officer. Jenna had her bicycle stolen so often she took to buying replacements at yard sales.

Maybe Jenna didn't notice at first because she was naïve enough to assume she would follow suit. An agent would pick up her first manuscript. Then a publisher. She would sell a million copies, hit the New York Times Best Sellers list. All on her first try. Or at the very least, when Jenna was thinking more realistically, she would find a small press in Pittsburgh or Philly or maybe Toronto like that girl in Jenna's writing group that met on Thursdays in the library who found small-time success immediately and made a modest living selling romance novels. Jenna would make a living doing what she loved.

Because Jenna knew that of the two of them, she was the worker. Sure, Gage has always been the lucky one. But *she* was the high school valedictorian – the one that had a local newspaper article written about her overcoming death and adversity. She was the Suma Cum Laude one. She was the scholarship one. She was the paying-off-student-loans one. She was the one who took the knocks life handed out to her, but then knocked back harder. Jenna was the one who made things happen. Gage, the lucky one, fell into fortuitous breaks and whirlwind romances he didn't even care about, and yes, she was happy for him, but she stifled the niggling jealousy with the thought that, like always, she would eventually follow suit. Because Jenna was the one who made things happen.

And then...nothing. Nothing happened. Not for manuscript number one. Not for number two. Or three or four. She didn't follow suit. She didn't follow anything. She worked nine hour shifts at Bagel Plus; she biked home or walked home, depending on if her bicycle was stolen that week; she heated up some soup; she switched on a used laptop she bought at the Penny Saved. She typed until her fingertips burned and then fell asleep next to her bowl of Ramen.

And somehow, inexplicably, that was Jenna the valedictorian's life.

Last year, when she was still twenty-five and fooling herself about where twenty-five fell on the continuum of early-to-late twenties, she met Kaz. He was singing at an open mic night. He smells like dirt, Gage had told her. He might actually be living outside, Gage had suggested. He's not dirty, he's *earthy*, she argued. And Kaz was not living outside. He lived in cheap studio right next to the train station where he practiced his "art" and "music," but mostly slept and made fried mac and cheese for breakfast and hotdogs for dinner. Theirs was a relationship that was energy-conserving lightbulb, as much off as it was on. His was a place where Jenna visited one or two weekends a month, a place where they would sleep in a bed that vibrated with each passing train.

She was making three dollars an hour more at Bagel Plus than when she started at age twenty-two. She was promoted to night manager.

She was exactly where she was in college.

Except now she was twenty-six and eating brownies in a dark hallway with a guy in a power suit who made six-times more than her every, single paycheck.

Gage

To my great surprise, Mom and Dad were much calmer, much happier outside of their marriage. It's not like Dad was completely cured of whatever horrendous memories racked his brain all the time, but being away from Mom relieved him of two different medications he had been taking previously. And it was not like Mom became Queen of Zen or anything. She still was abrasive and harsh, always willing to give her opinion even when nobody wanted it. But four years and two new children lit something in her I never before witnessed.

Kristen seethed at the injustice of it: that she, that our old house, Mom's old job, the life Mom first chose was but somehow not good enough, but these two boys and her young husband and her new McMansion in northwest D.C. were perfect. Kristen, as a result, never called and rarely visited.

Me, I guess I thought the same things as Kristen, but in a quieter, drink-away-the-thought-of-it approach. I seldom called, and visited only slightly more often that Kris. The sight of Mom at ease with her new children and new husband - a divorce attorney that she stressed did *not* represent her in the divorce between her and my father - was a foreign one, and I never knew quite how to handle it. As a result, I never felt particularly welcome in Mom's new house. There was always this air of uneasiness; I was a solid reminder of a life nobody wanted to remember, a fact made even more painful because Mom and her new family a mere quarter-mile away from Dad and my childhood home. The unease when I visited was real, it was clear, and it was painful.

And, yet, here I was now at Mom and James' house. Visiting.

Mom's favored method – guilt – always worked with me and never with Kristen. She worked the same way every time; her script ever unchanging, and it always worked, which grated me more than I cared to admit.

First the call. Or I should say calls. The messages -- *I'm not telling you to visit, I would never tell you what to do, Elliot, but you do know you have a brother now. Two brothers, if you are inclined to include Joel.* She would say this in a way that aggravated me to no end, as if I wasn't accepting of Joel as my stepbrother. Guilt would seep through me, and I'd start to question my motives. Did I really love Joel? I'd typically delete the message, get roaring drunk that night, and end up in bed with some chick. The next morning Jendy and said chick would eat breakfast together. I'd realize, watching the two eat cereal and converse awkwardly, that yes, of course I loved Joel. I had to hand it to Mom, who could probably run for office in some cartoon diabolic, evil genius land, for manipulating me so thoroughly and so often. I'd be pissed off enough to not want to visit her, but I would, because if I did not visit, she would take this as confirmation that, yes, I hated Joel and James and her new life. So Mom, as always, got exactly what she wanted in the lousiest way possible.

When I would get there, she would always act put out, as if my visit was unexpected, and they never had anything ready, never mind the fact that I started letting Mom know three weeks in advance that I'd be visiting.

The kids were cute and most times they made the visit worth it. The older one, Joel, was eight and allergic to everything. Cheese and nuts and chocolate and kiwis and shellfish and dust and mold and perfume and six different types of trees. The house was kept spotless, the place all white and clean and smelling of mild, organic disinfectant, which probably helped Joel, but his allergies were most likely not the sole reason the house was so clean. Mom always did have an antiseptic kind of personality, leaving anything in her wake as cold and sterile as she.

Then there was Ian, the four-year-old. Really cute. There was no denying that. He'd call me Elli in a way that reminded me of toddler Kristen, with a lisp that turned the L's to W's, following me around, eyes wide and round, proudly showing me his toys and hopping on my back any time I'd bend over. *Brovers. We're brovers*, he'd say, *Mommy says we're brovers.*

There were pictures of the two kids all over the place: Ian as a baby dressed in a little blue getup all babies wore, the jumpsuit kind of thing; Joel, a toddler with James, both in basketball uniforms; family pictures all of them in matching sweaters kicking around autumn leaves, the kind of pictures Mom ordinarily sneered at; Ian's preschool pictures, his smile wider than his face, his eyes disappearing behind its crinkles; Joel's school picture, his hair messy and front teeth missing.

I loved the kids. And James was fine.

But Mom. God. It was always Mom. Our interactions were a precarious situation, with stiff conversations sounding more like hostage negotiations. Mom prying for information, dissecting my answers, analyzing the body language I perfected at hiding over the years. Then the questioning, the endless questioning, with me struggling to keep my mouth shut simply to keep the peace around little kids, which was also probably why I was dreading the next three days. Which was probably why I was wide awake at six a.m. on a Saturday, scrolling through my cell phone, checking work emails and avoiding anything on the other side of the door of my beige, beige room.

The enthusiastic pounding on my door made me jump.

It was already starting.

I'd probably have a nice case of shingles by Memorial Day from the stress of it. "Give me a minute, Mom."

I threw a hoodie over my bare chest and looked for a place to hide my cell phone. Mom barely tolerated me bringing work into the house. *You're visiting, Elliot. You have brothers now.* As if her new life of stay-at-home mom of two somehow erased the old life of Kristen, Dad, and me watching her go over briefs at the breakfast table, take calls during dinner, and skip every school event in which

Kris and I participated so that she could meet a new client or appease a current one or screw whatever guy she was seeing at the time.

The door cracked open. "Mom, seriously. Wait." I hurriedly tucked the phone under my pillow.

Joel came bounding in. "You wanna play basketball, huh, Elliot? With me and Dad? Mom got us this new hoop, and Dad's teaching me to dribble with my left hand now, and I'm so bad at it, but Mom says practice makes progress."

"Practice makes progress, huh?" That was a new one from my mother, light-years away from the perfection she expected of Kris and me.

"Practice makes progress. Practice makes progress," he sung.

"So you're into basketball?" Joel had a persistent "sick" look to him, his eyes and lips perpetually puffy and raw, his Epi-pen always at the ready, and we were constantly washing our hands around him. I wondered how he and sports would work out.

Well, that's pretty presumptuous of you, Gage, I could hear Jenna clearly in my head. *Assuming a kid is some kind of weakling because he has allergies. It's basketball, Gage. Not shellfish.* If she were here, she would have said it aloud, as if already reading the thought as it materialized in my head. And then I would have to sit there, thinking about that, coming to the conclusion that yeah, it was probably pretty asinine to assume a kid was destined suck at sports because of allergies and puffy eyes.

"Mom says you played basketball," Joel said eagerly.

"Did she?"

"Yeah."

"And what else did Mom say?"

"Mmm." Joel cocked his head and scrunched his mouth. "Uh." He scratched his ear. "That you could dribble real good! And you could teach me. Yeah, she said that!" He exclaimed, an obvious lie to get me up and outside with him.

And that seemed about right; the only thing Mom would remember was the fact that I played basketball. Mom wouldn't remember the time I made the All-State team my senior year. She wouldn't have remembered the play-off games or the state championships. She wouldn't have remembered the night I scored my one-thousandth point, the way Kris ran screaming out onto the court in her pep band uniform, jumping into my arms, her flute still in hand. Hell, Mom probably wouldn't have even remembered the scholarship Villanova offered me - the scholarship I turned down, because she wouldn't have remembered when I got sick of basketball, when I packed up everything: the trophies, the pictures, the newspaper clippings into a blue tarp and threw the whole mess into the dumpster outside of Ming Yun Chinese restaurant, then went and ate two orders of chow mein.

She wouldn't have remembered those moments. She was having an affair with some other guy for all of those moments.

Bitter much, Gage? I shook my head. God, I hated this house.

"Elliot?" Joel was staring at me curiously. "You know how to dribble?"

I gave Joel a quick grin and pulled my sneakers from the tangle of clothes on the floor. "Yeah. I think I remember how to dribble."

James joined us ten minutes later.

James, who was always James to me, and never quite a stepdad – was someone a stepfather when he stepfathered his way into your life when you were already an adult? – wasn't bad. He stayed mostly out of the way during my visits. He was a lawyer like my mother, but younger, much younger, and still practicing law at Hartly, Hartly & Fein. Only twelve years older than me, I probably would have been friends with him, went out drinking or played basketball at the Y with him, if we were colleagues.

He wasn't bad a basketball either. He didn't trash talk or lord over Joel. He let his son do whatever he wanted, whether that meant shooting free throws, wildly heaving the ball with both hands from between his legs, or making up his own drills, sprinting from one grassy edge of the court to the other on spindly legs. James conducted himself with the same laid-back patience in whatever he did, a trait I never saw in either of my parents. It made me wonder what kind of lawyer he was in the courtroom. He also made me think of Jenna, and how he would be such a better match for her than Kaz, who I was certain harbored something within his body that needed either penicillin or lice shampoo. She "dated" this "musician" – dude was worth of a lot of quotation marks – when she was lonely or got another rejection from an agent. Lawyer, I catalogued in my mind. Jenna needs a laid-back lawyer.

"Why don't you bring him in, James?" Mom hovered near the patio. "He shouldn't be running like that."

"He has allergies, Mom. He's not an invalid," I said, probably more irritated that I would normally be because 1. My mother was the one making the comment and 2. I had thought nearly the same thing an hour ago, and I in no way wanted any confirmation that I thought the same way as my mother.

"You're not here on a consistent basis, Elliot. You wouldn't know, would you?" She said it lightly, but I knew Mom's version of light. I hadn't visited in a year, and she was putting me in my place.

"We're on our way in now, Deb," James said easily then turned to Joel. "Should we make some French toast, buddy?" James ruffled Joel's hair, then draped an arm around his shoulders, and looked up at me with a quick grin. "You think your brothers would like French toast?"

As I watched them, I felt a pang of loss. Mom had always been gone, but so had Dad, in a much different way. He wasn't at my basketball games either. He had always been distant when I was a child, and he completely ended his minor involvement in my high school life after he lost it at Kris's piano recital. I took up jogging solely to have something in common with him when he went through his vegetarian marathon phase.

"How's the job?" James asked, tossing the ball to me.

I dribbled twice and tried a jump shot. *Swish.* "Oh, you know. Work is work. How 'bout you?"

"French toast!" Ian reminded us as he scrambled for the rebound and dribbled it all the way to the French doors. We followed him into the kitchen.

"Deb's not liking my hours. But you do what you got to do in that kind of place. There was this lousy firing that happened, a real scandal behind the whole thing. An affair with a client? Lots of gossip. You can imagine what a mess that was for a family law firm. I'm left picking up all the slack. You know how it is trying to get partner. You probably remember from your Mom."

Wow. Affair with a client and James always working late? That was a hell of a lot of karma getting throw back in Mom's face. Kris would have reveled in it.

"You moving up the line?" James asked.

"Yeah. Promotion in the works, I'm hearing."

"Whoa. Congrats, man."

Mom sat silently at the table.

"It might be rumor."

"Let's hope it's not." James thumped my back. "I'm taking a shower." He dropped a kiss on my Mom's head, which weirded me out so much I had to turn away. James strolled down the hall, whistling.

"How's that girl?" Mom said with an unwarranted contemptuousness as soon as he was out of earshot.

"Which girl?" I truly had no idea. I slept with a lot of girls and dated none. And I shared none of that information with my mother.

"That girl with whom you cohabitate."

"Jenna? Do you mean Jenna Gressa, the woman I've been friends with for approximately six years? The same Jenna Gressa you met three years ago?"

"Oh, is that her name?"

I resisted the urge to roll my eyes at Mom's feigned confusion. Yeah. Like Mom didn't know her name. Jenna had visited with me three years ago. She was the one who helped us discover that Joel was allergic to shellfish when she shared half a lobster tail with him. She also administered the Epi-Pen and called 911. Mom blamed Jenna, even though James was exceedingly kind about it, saying that the same thing could have happened with any one of them. They knew about the chocolate and nuts and cheese back then. They didn't know about the shellfish or kiwis yet. Or the six different types of trees.

Jenna never came back.

"She's fine." Truthfully, Jenna hadn't been fine. Not really since the last move to our new place. She was quieter now, always drifting around the place, a beleaguered look on her face, like she was lost. *Like an orphan*, I said once, jokingly then winced at my words. Why did I always have to make proclamations without thinking first?

She bought fish, these neon kind, and she named them Perfect, Free, and Taxes. She stared at them a lot, another unsold manuscript in front of her, marked up in red pen. She started drinking coffee by the gallon and smoking on the porch, neither of which she did in college. She would down cup after cup of black coffee, leaving mugs littered in her wake like her own abandoned children. That observation I kept to myself.

She visited Kaz every once in a while. She would come back the next morning looking sallow, much worse than the night before. I'm not going to see him anymore, she would insist. I'd nod and watch her shake her meds into her hands, gulp them down, then work furiously on a new novel, seemingly unstoppable, for the next two weeks.

Jenna was quiet a lot. And when she wasn't quiet, she was fighting with me, the exasperated kind of arguing, where both of us would look at the other and wonder how we ended up here in this place together.

"Jenna is fine," I repeated to my mother, as she set two mugs of coffee in front of us.

"So that's all you have to say about everything?"

"If asking about Jenna qualifies as 'everything' then yes."

"You don't need to be difficult."

I shrugged and sipped my coffee.

"You can talk to James but not to me?"

"Get off it," I said before I could check myself.

She sighed and shook her head. "I really expected more from you."

You raised me. I really expected more of you, Mom. Oh, there were so many things I could have said.

"Really?" I asked, blandly.

"I thought by now you'd be more adult. You're twenty-six, now, Elliot. I was married by twenty-six."

"And we see how well that worked out."

She ignored my comment. "I was working my way up the chain."

"You heard me say about the promotion."

No reaction.

"What do you want from me, Mom? You want me to get married?" I raised eyebrows, hoping I looked disinterested. The last thing I needed was her latching on to anything that looked like interest.

"I never said that."

If she expected to get a rise out of me that way, she underestimated me. I had been holding it all in for over a decade. I could go a lifetime. I shrugged and scratched at the corner of my lip. Her eyes instantly narrowed, zoning in on that small movement. Immediately my mind shot into overdrive. *Should I have done that? What does touching your face mean again? Lying? Hiding? Insecurity?* The woman set me on edge like no other person on the planet.

"I was always terrified you would end up with her." She laughed at the obvious absurdity of the idea.

"Jenna?" Seriously? We were back to this? There must be something more she was fishing for to let her guard down enough to tell me that.

"Who else would be talking about?"

"*Terrified* though? A little overstated, don't you think, Mother?"

"You were always mooning over her in college, always trying to save her and make her better."

"I wasn't mooning over her." Irritated, I stared into my coffee. "And I didn't need to make her better. Jenna was fine then, and she's fine now."

"I always thought you liked her."

"Yeah. I liked her."

"You know what I mean, Elliot."

I refused to answer.

"So nothing is there?"

"We're friends, Mom."

"That's not an answer."

"We're friends, Mom," I repeated.

"She is a mess, Elliot. And you don't want to mess with a mess." She laughed at her little joke, and anger rose in me at how easily she could make light of Jenna's life.

"She's a survivor, Mom," I said, a little more emphatically than I wanted to convey to my mother during this cross-examination.

Mom studied me. "Is she?"

"I'm hungry. You want something?"

"I mean, look at you, Elli," she said, and I winced inwardly at the nickname only reserved for Kristen...and now Ian. "You have a dream life for someone your age. Great job, money. That apartment move was smart. You're getting the life we always wanted."

"Mom. You don't know me."

"You wanted money. You got money." She smiled to herself and sipped her coffee. "You worked for it. Good for you. You forget I spent the first eighteen years of your life with you."

Leave it to Mom to have me irritated at what she thought was a compliment. I pushed away from the table, and stood abruptly. "Do you have milk? This coffee is terrible."

"Oh, Elliot, don't be passive aggressive. It doesn't suit you," she touched my arm, and I pulled it away quickly.

You don't know me at all. "I passed up a dream job in California for this."

"And why did you do that?" She smiled smugly to herself, because she already knew the answer. "She's a leach, Elli. A leach. She doesn't have money, does she?"

I finally understood what she was getting at. I bit down on my barely contained anger. "Where's your milk?"

"In the refrigerator, Elliot," she said with exaggerated patience, "the same place milk always tends to be."

I chewed on my cheeks and waited for it. Her closing argument. She would deliver it shortly.

Mom sat, content, pouring herself a bowl of gruesome looking rice and flax cereal then turned her attention to the Sunday paper. She carefully pulled the Arts & Leisure section from the stack. "Milk, please?" She held out a hand. "Oh, look at this, El. That band you like is playing downtown tonight. Perhaps you'd be interesting in going with me."

I slammed the container next to her, seething. "Sure. Sounds like a great time," I said sarcastically, completely pissed off.

"She a lost soul, Elliot, better to give her up."

There it was. Her closing argument. Mom had patience, he had to give her credit for that.

But, in that declaration, she had slipped up. Because I was raised by a lawyer; she had been out of my life for so long she must have forgotten that I could read into statements also. That one small statement spoke volumes about her relationship with Dad, more than she probably wanted to give away, more that I wanted to know.

"I know what you're thinking, Elliot. I'm your mother, but I'm not stupid."

"I never said you were."

"And I know what that means, too, Elliot Gageby."

I set my mouth in a firm line.

"You think I'm annoying and cold, and maybe you're right. You're thinking Jenna knows you so well. But I know you too. I know what's best for you. And this girl? She isn't best. She's not even okay."

"Mom--"

"She's going to bring you down, Elliot. I know people like Jenna. I lived more than a lifetime with people like Jenna. A life like hers is not one you want."

"I'm not you, Mom. That kind of stuff doesn't bother me."

"How many women have you dated? Seriously dated?"

"I don't want to seriously date anyone."

"You're twenty-six, Elliot. All twenty-six-year-olds want to find someone serious."

"Jenna is not the reason I'm not serious with anyone."

"She's too dependent on you, Elliot."

"Mom, you met her three times! You are embarrassing yourself here."

"And you're too dependent on her."

I sighed, and we stared at each other. "This is getting ridiculous. You don't get to unload your lifetime worth of baggage on me because *you* have issues with Dad. Making me question my life and my decisions like you know anything at all about me. Dammit. God dammit."

"You could watch your language around here."

"Jesus, Mom. You gave up all rights to mothering me a long time ago."

"You have little brothers now for whom you should be setting an example."

"Yeah. Yeah, Mom. And you have two *other* children you could be acting like a real mother to. Or do Kris and I not make the cut anymore?"

"Now who is being ridiculous? Really, Elliot. You're acting silly. Of course I know you and Kristen count. I call you both, invite you to visit. It isn't my fault you only come once a year. I have those trust funds set up in your names for when you are thirty. What more could you possibly want?"

"I don't know, Mom. Nothing I guess."

"And do you see how we have deviated from the point of this conversation? I swear, you are so much like your father. All heart, no head."

Was that really so bad?

"This is why I need to tell you these things. You're too impulsive. You never think things through logically."

"Just tell me then." Just tell me so I can leave.

"All I'm saying, Elliot, is that you have devoted nearly seven years to this girl.

"How is that bad?"

"It's not bad. But I know why you are really in it. And I'm telling you, it's not going to happen. You won't save her. You won't get the girl."

"That's not my endgame."

"Ah. So you have an endgame." She smiled.

I rolled my eyes. "Mom--" Then I stopped. "You know what? I think I'll spend the rest of my time at Dad's."

I watched Mom try to cover the shock and disappointment. Should I be upset with myself for feeling so smug about hurting her? Because I was not. Not one bit.

She pulled herself together quickly. "Yes, your father. He always gets a pass with you, doesn't he, Elliot?"

But Mom was wrong. Dad did not always get a pass with me. As I was driving to Dad's house, I thought of Kristen, of how she stayed there in our childhood house with Dad after the divorce, lived there with him for all of her college breaks and summers off. I figured she would kind of live there forever, take over as Dad's spouse. The very thought made me sad and more than a little sick.

I thought of Dad, about how he had been profiled on NBC Nightly News. The former sniper who now carved peace doves and bluebirds, painted them and handed them out to sick kids at the children's hospital. The Army veteran who rocked babies in the neonatal intensive-care unit. Kristen taped the segment and sent it to me with this little Post-It note: *Isn't Dad amazing, Elli? He's doing so well.*

I had watched the tape with Jenna and when Dad said something like, "I can't think of anything better to give back." Jenna whipped her head around to look at me and reached for my hand. Anybody else would have thought Dad's statement was sweet; how was there any fault in what Dad said? But Jenna knew. Jenna knew me well. Because a slightly guilty flare of anger flamed in my gut.

Guilt because I knew of only a small sliver of the horror Dad had gone through. And it had been hell. But anger because, well, how could I stop the anger at the injustice of it all? Mom with her new kids. Dad with his new kids. What better could you give back? *Oh, I don't know, Dad. How about your son's childhood?* I thought about that tape on my way to Dad's house, and I turned right instead of left.

Jenna

"Make me something, will you, Gress?"

She met him last year, in January, on a night when the wind blew hard and frigid as ice and the sky spit snow. He always called her Gress. Something about Gress being a much more free-spirited than the confining chains of an oppressive name like Jenna. *Jenna?* Kaz had practically spat out her name. *Sounds like some flighty character on a teenager's show. You*, he said, *the first night they met, are no Jenna.*

The statement made her all tremble-y and excited inside. I am no Jenna! His scent, his words were intoxicating.

What's your last name? He had asked her.

My last name? He was cute with his shaggy hair and flannel, and she was tipsy and giggly and flirtier than normal. Gage was next to them, grumbling about being dragged to this terrible show.

Yeah, babe. What's the last name?

Gressa. Jenna Gressa.

Jenna Gressa? Damn, babe, you might have the worst name on the planet.

She giggled again, and Gage rolled his eyes while Jenna and Kaz stared into each other's. Kaz left abruptly then, taking the stage to finish his set, singing increasingly bizarre songs. During one of his breaks he walked right over to Jenna and kissed her fully - almost embarrassingly intimately - right there in the crowded bar. People cheered, and when she tore away from him, stunned, she downed the rest of her drink. He didn't buy her a new one, but gave her the rest of his, and even though Gage said something about Roofies or at the very least, needing penicillin by the next morning, she drank the concoction.

I like your sweatpants, babe.

Really?

Yeah. Fuck society and all its norms and conventions.

That wasn't the reason Jenna wore sweatpants, but she didn't want to correct his assumptions of her. Telling some hot guy with a voice that sounded like he gargled with rocks every morning that "it's a nerve condition, actually," made her as lame as she knew she was.

And even though Gage and Jenna fought bitterly about it, throwing around casual threats and not-so-casual expletives there at the bar, Jenna went home with Kaz that night. And the love affair she built up in her mind ended abruptly. She hated herself for knowing that his apartment was the turn-off, the way it shuddered with each passing train, the way the mold collected at the edges of everything. Sheet music and art projects covered every inch of free counter space. But for a twin bed and a torn leather couch, the rooms were nearly bare. The television had been converted into a planter filled with half-dead succulents. Dishes, crusted over with old food, piled high in the sink. My newest art installation, he explained. An interpretation of society's increasingly cavalier attitude toward food waste.

Her visible cringe proved she did not believe him.

He called her a spoiled brat then. Wide-eyed, she vehemently denied it. *No, no, I'm really not.* He didn't know her history. Her dad, her mother. The revolving world of foster care. And maybe she was more defensive because she did feel spoiled now. Yes, her history was death and loneliness. But her history was also Gage. She knew that she would be in Kaz's exact position if it weren't for Gage.

So, to prove Kaz wrong and assuage her guilt, Jenna slept with him in a bed that smelled like stale cigarettes. They both smoked after, a move that was so cliché she rolled her eyes to herself and mentally wrote the scene into a manuscript. In the morning, she walked home, but not before he made her eggs that scared her when she first bit into them. Covertly, she felt around in her mouth for chipped teeth, before realizing her scrambled breakfast was full of broken shell bits.

When she made it home, Gage had made her breakfast again, smoked sausage and French toast whisked with organic milk and certified humane eggs. He all but begged for all the details, telling her he was sure she was going to be murdered by morning and that he had called up his bedmate du jour, the Catholic one, to light a candle and pray to the patron saint of one-night stands for Jenna.

She told Gage only one thing: that Kaz's real name was Cassius Kazlinski, a fact she discovered while scanning his stack of mail when he was still asleep. Kaz also had a subscription to AAA Travel magazine, which was so basic and normal and nothing like his persona. They both had a good laugh at Cassius Kazlinski's expense, and Jenna promised Gage she'd never go back.

She promptly disappointed herself when she returned to Kaz again and again, intrigued and repulsed more and more every time.

"What do you have?" Jenna tugged at the refrigerator door, which opened itself with a sticky suck and pop, fully expecting to see the usual suspects: a brick of molded cheese (cut around the mold, he'd say), a forty-pack count of hotdogs, and a dozen or so eggs rolling around on the top shelf, carton-free (free range, he'd say. They don't deserve the confined uniformity of their vessel, he'd say).

Instead, she shrieked. "Oh, my God. Oh. My. God."

Jenna never considered herself one of those shrieky squealing girls. Those girls never annoyed her, either. They were simply there, the shrieky people living amongst the non-shriekers. That changed though, the instant she saw the rats. She was already hopping around, shaking her hands, flinging them around as if the rats had already covered her body. She would have jumped on a chair, if Kaz owned any chairs.

He peered over Jenna's shoulder into the fridge. "Oh, I forgot," he said blandly.

Jenna felt the horror overtake her expression. "You *forgot*? So, you *knew* about this?"

"It's my newest art installation."

"Art? This is…" Jenna's face contorted in disgust. "This may be a health hazard."

"It was fate, Gress. I opened the door last week, and there she was."

"She?" Jenna squeaked.

"It was just the one at first." He pointed to one of the three. "The rest is assumption."

Jenna stared blankly at him.

"Meaning, I'm assuming they are all 'she's'."

The blank stare continued.

He shrugged and picked up his guitar, slinging the strap over his shoulder. "Fate."

"This is not fate, Kaz. This is a health code violation. Several, in fact." Jenna shivered, her skin itching. They were on her, weren't they? She could feel them all over her skin. She scratched the back of one leg with the toe of her shoe. Then she ran her fingers through her hair, shaking out the nothing that was in it. "You should call your landlord."

"I think they're cute." He picked a few chords. "How do you like this one? It's new." He started to break out into song, before Jenna interrupted him.

"You know rats carry the plague."

The strumming stopped. "Do they?" His voice was much more intrigued than disturbed.

"No. No, no, no." Jenna shook her head then grabbed at her bags. "Why am I here?"

His lower jaw poked out as he considered his answer to her question.

"It was rhetorical, Kaz."

"Excellent. Because, you know, I'm never really sure why you are around."

Jenna stopped abruptly. "What?"

"You're always…around. Filling up space. For what?"

"What?"

"Oh, you know. You're a bagel girl. I never thought I'd end up with a bagel girl. Really, Gress, are you going anywhere in life?"

"You are asking me this? *You*? You have rats living in your fridge. On purpose!"

"You could be my next installation. Life: Stalled."

Jenna's mouth dropped open. Then she shoved him, and narrowed her eyes when he grinned. "Shut up about your installations. You barely have running water in here."

"Showering from a bucket spoke of society, Gress. I couldn't expect you to understand."

"And I guess refusing the job at the restaurant and asking me for a loan instead was a piece dissecting society's overwhelming laziness."

"I apologize for not having a sugar daddy to buy me everything."

"We're friends!" She said, sick of explaining her relationship with Gage to Kaz. Kaz who visited once and never stopped talking about the horrors of commercialism, the pure greed and materialism of their apartment.

"I have a showing," he answered.

"Kaz," she said as if speaking to a child. "You're delusional. A refrigerator full of rats is not a showing. It's a tenuous grasp on reality."

"Not here. A showing. At the university."

"No, you don't." She shook her head. There was no way. "The college?"

"Three weeks. Booked it yesterday morning."

"The rats?"

He shrugged. "I'm not sure I should be telling you this. You have always been unsupportive of my art." He popped open the fridge again, gazing adoringly at his rats. "I think they like hotdogs." He picked up the package, which was full of teeth marks and ragged holes.

Jenna ignored his observation. "The *university*? How did you get it? How did you get in?"

"I slept with the woman in charge of showings." He closed the door and settled back into strumming his guitar.

Jenna blinked once then started. "Yeah. Okay." Jenna grabbed her bags. "I think this is over."

"You're jealous, that's all."

"No," Jenna said, rolling her eyes.

"Doesn't matter. You'll be back. You're my Free Range Gress. You come and go. You are my chicken, and I'm your keeper." He scratched his cheek, with a puzzled look. "Farmer? I'm your farmer?"

Jenna prayed for patience. "I am not coming back, Kaz. This is it."

"You're as predictable as the tides. Every two weeks." He thrummed the strings, turning the sentence into a song, singing it over and over until Jenna practically shrieked again.

"I am not predictable."

"I could set a watch to you and your time. Like a really slow watch. You can't get enough of my genius. It's why you love me. And my showing. You'll be by my side for my showing. It's inevitable."

"No. No. I'm done. This cannot be happening." Kaz had a showing. This was unreal. "And I will have you know, it is not your genius that keeps me coming back. It is because I am terrified," She regretted starting this sentence, "to die. Alone," she finished lamely.

And now, her humiliation complete, Jenna closed her eyes, took a deep steadying breath, and turned on her heel. "Goodbye, Kaz."

"Babe, wait."

Jenna, one hand on the knob, dropped her head to the door. She slid her eyes to one side and his profile filled her vision.

"Come back here." He signaled with two fingers and a pleading look. He unstrapped the guitar and set it on the cracked vinyl floor.

Reluctantly, Jenna shuffled back to him. She could at least accept the hug and apology he would give her.

He took her limp arms in his and wrapped them around his waist, and she raised his eyes to his, attempting a smile.

He cupped the back of her head, pressing into his chest into a half-hearted hug. "You got twenty bucks I can borrow? Until I get paid for the show."

Jenna inhaled deeply into his flannel.

"I'll pay you back," he added.

Gage had been right.

Kaz smelled exactly like dirt.

Gage

It was a little after one in the morning, and I could feel her standing above me before I saw her.

"Why are you back?" she asked.

"Why do you think?" I answered.

Jenna made the little humming noise she always made when she knew my problem was my mother. I called that sound her refrigerator noise. *Stop being a refrigerator,* Jendy, *and tell me what you're thinking,* I'd say. That was years ago, though. Right after the shellfish incident. I never said that anymore, because I knew what she was thinking about: the shellfish incident. It was the only thing she could connect with my mother.

"Should I leave you alone?" she whispered.

"I know you're only asking me that out of courtesy," I said.

"I can get in then?" She lifted the sheet without waiting for my answer, which would have been yes.

Kaz. It had to be Kaz. Kaz was the only reason Jenna would creep into my bed at night.

Jenna's hair was all wrapped up turban-like in a blue towel. She had taken a shower as soon as she banged through the apartment door. She had to know I was home then, saw my BMW in the drive. She didn't seek me out like I expected though. She went straight to the shower, where I heard her switch on the shower radio. The pop station she tuned it to didn't muffle out the sounds of her one-sided conversation, her occasional crying. I stayed there in bed, hot and uncomfortable while I listened, unsure of what to do; my mother's parting words about Jenna still tumbling through me.

I had listened to Jenna get out of the shower, move to the kitchen, roll open the sliding glass door, and move to the porch, presumably to smoke a cigarette or ten.

Now she was here. Next to me in bed. She smelled like shampoo and Dove soap and coffee and cigarettes. It was a new Jenna smell, a scent which I still wasn't accustomed.

"Were you sleeping?" she whispered.

"No." My mother's words about Jenna had been a dark storm suspended over me all night. "Too hot."

"It is too hot," she agreed.

"We could buy an air conditioner," I suggested.

"I can't afford it."

"I can."

"You're not buying me air."

"Hell then, I'll put it in my room. I have no qualms about buying myself air."

"There's no reason to pay for air. That's stupid."

"You're stupid," I said affectionately.

She took the towel from her head, and I saw she already had her wet hair pulled up in her signature ponytail.

"Why are you back early...or should I say so late?" I asked as she snuggled into the arm I wrapped around her, even though we were both hot and sticky in the humid air.

"Do you really need to ask?"

I half-grinned. "That usually calls for a drink." I shifted. Jenna was silent for a minute. I waited for the rant. About Bagel Plus. About Kaz. When nothing happened, I shifted up on a hip to look at Jenna. Tears were streaming down her face. I thought she got it all out in the shower. I was never good with crying. "Jendy. What's wrong?"

"I hate my life." It was as if that sentence was all she needed to leap over to full-on crying. That sobbing, heaving, ugly-face kind of crying.

"Aw, Jendy." She was on the verge of hyperventilating. I had never seen her like this. Not the first time Kaz broke her heart. Or even when Daniel did it back in college. "You're going to be fine." But I felt uneasy, holding her there in my bed while she basically fell apart next to me.

What was I supposed to do?

"Did you stop taking your meds, Jendy?" I asked, which, apparently, was the wrong question to ask.

"I'm allowed to cry," she wailed.

"Yeah," I said. "Yeah. You're allowed to cry."

So she did.

And I laid there. Awkwardly petting her hair.

"Four years. All those manuscripts. Hundreds of rejections," she eventually said. "Is it going to work, Gage? Tell me it's going to work."

"It's going to work."

"I'm fairly pathetic." She said those words a lot after returning from Kaz's place.

The wrath I hadn't felt since the year of Daniel Baxley churned in me. "Fuck him. Don't listen to that asshole," I said, never mentioning Kaz's name.

"It's not only him."

"It is him. He makes you feel like shit."

"No. It's not only him."

All right. Whatever. I turned back over to stare at the ceiling.

"It's..." she trailed off. "Gage?"

"Hmm?"

"How long can you go unpublished and work slinging bagels until you have to stop calling yourself a writer?" She asked instead. "When do you give up? What does it feel like to give up? Do you think I'll even know it, or will the giving up be so gradual I'll barely notice? Writing will be an old dream, a nothing that never happened?"

I sighed, feeling a lot of things. Pissed that she wouldn't talk about Kaz. Kind of relieved that she wouldn't talk about Kaz. Jenna and her mess of boyfriends, I had no clue about. But this job stuff, this

I could handle. This was something I understood. This was something I was good with. Hating your job. Going in day after day knowing that you aren't who everybody else thinks you are.

"You are not what you do."

"What does that mean?" She pushed her hair out of her face.

"You know. When people ask what you do for a living? I hate that."

"Me too," Jenna choked out, and I could hear the crying start up again.

"You're…you're not what you do, Jendy. You are who you are," I said quickly, trying to staunch the second wave of sobbing. I rubbed her cheek. It was probably too rough. "You're a writer. You're not the job that gets you money. You're the job that makes you happy. Just keep telling yourself that."

Jenna pulled away from me. "That's pretty deep for you."

"I heard it on PBS. Some life-guru hawking his book."

"PBS." She started laughing. "Since when do you watch PBS."

"Somebody had it on in the break room."

She laughed harder. "There's the Gage I know."

I sighed. "I bought the book," I said, "but I don't know. A bunch of words to fill the air."

"So, what you're saying is, your advice is useless."

"Yes. Exactly. I just want you to stop crying."

She laughed. "Do you hate your job?" As she asked, she wiped her cheek against the edge of the sheet.

"Why do you think I get drunk every weekend?" I folded my arms behind my head. Something I learned from the book. Vices.

"For the women," Jenna said.

Vices, the book said.

"So you're being for real? You hate your job?" She half-sat up and studied my face. "All these years?"

"Eh," I shrugged. "Not every single year. But lately."

"You make good money now."

"Would you be happy if they paid you what I made but you never got published?"

"Hell yeah," she said without pause.

I laughed.

"Here put this over on your nightstand will you?" She was holding out the hairband that had held her wet strands up a moment ago. I took it and tossed it into the drawer of my nightstand and slammed it shut.

"Nite, Jen."

"Nite, Gage."

We settled into silence.

I thought about my mother as her words flooded back to me. I fought them. No, I wasn't doing this for Jenna. I was not here solely for Jenna. *No, Mom*, I said silently, *Jenna is not dragging me down. This is me; this is my choice; this life is exactly what I choose.* Something else the book told me. Maybe that book wasn't total bunk. It seemed to make Jenna happy.

Still, why was I left questioning myself and my motives toward Jenna? Why, as much as I tried, couldn't I stop thinking about my mother's argument? And why, when Jenna wrapped her arms around me and eventually fell asleep, did I feel like everything about us and our platonic friendship was one huge lie?

Jenna

Jenna's thinking was exactly along those same lines. Gage wouldn't know it though. And Jenna wouldn't know it either, because she didn't voice any of those thoughts.

She did not say that his arm felt so different than everybody else's arms, and why was that?

She did not say that everything he did, everything he said, always seemed exactly right.

She did not say that was the reason she fought with him so much. That she was fighting with herself, fighting against herself in every possible way.

She did not say that he was an asshole sometimes, and still she loved him. In a strictly platonic way.

She did not say that she knew every time he held her like this, every time he called her Jen, it was his way of saying, *I love you. I love you like nobody else.* She had figured this out long ago. She had no idea if he had figured it out yet though. And as a result, she did not say that quite possibly for the last four years, she had been falling in love with him. In a strictly romantic way.

She would.

She would say those things she promised herself.

Tomorrow. There was always tomorrow.

And then she fell asleep in his arms.

Jenna

It seemed innocent enough, the oversized and overstuffed piece of mail, scattered amongst Gage's credit card bills and Jenna's Writer's Digest renewal form. But she had seen enough of those gold-leaf envelopes to know nothing good ever came in embossed, calligraphy heavy packages.

Jenna glanced at it, catching the *and Guest* shadowing Elliot Gageby's name, confirming her suspicions.

"I have a question for you," Gage asked.

Jenna felt the headache knock at the base of her skull.

"No," She muttered out from under the paper coffee cup gripped between her teeth before Gage even opened his mouth. "No way." The apartment keys jangled from one finger of her very full hands.

"You don't even know what I'm going to ask."

She gritted her teeth harder around the lip of the cup and slid her eyes to the envelope. "No way. Three Gage." Jenna held up, or tried to hold up, three fingers. "I went to *three* frat weddings last summer. Three."

"You're not even going to ask who is getting married?" Gage inquired. He plucked the coffee cup from Jenna's mouth. Transferred the bag of day old bagels to the counter.

"Okay," Jenna indulged him. "Who is getting married?"

Gage looked downright giddy with glee. He stalled though, not answering Jenna's question.

"Who, Gage?" Jenna hated how he could do that, make her interested in something she did not care about.

"Cody."

"Cody." Jenna parroted.

"Cody," Gage confirmed.

"You're a liar," Jenna said and turned away.

"Seriously. Kid's getting married."

"Cody Strassberger, at the age ripe old age of twenty-five, is hitching himself to some poor soul for life?"

"Cody Strassberger is engaged to a nurse. Cody Strassberger is living in two-bedroom ranch in a suburb with said nurse and her two-year-old child." Gage leaned in close to divulge the most shocking tidbit of all. "Cody Strassberger is an insurance agent in Harrisburg."

Jenna's eyes widened. "Cody Strassberger is not an insurance agent in Harrisburg."

"All of it is true. Ace confirmed it. They are all on Facebook or something. I have to get on Facebook." Gage was talking to himself again.

Ace was a thirty-year-old stockbroker in New York. Two summers ago he was living in an apartment so tiny that Jenna and Gage had to sleep on the kitchen floor when they visited. Now Ace was married to some other stockbroker. Ace's had been the first of the frat weddings to which Gage dragged Jenna last summer.

Cody, who Jenna remembered solely as a binge drinker, a generally happy-go-lucky one, but a near-alcoholic nonetheless, was engaged to a nurse and doing well. "Well then," Jenna said. "I am definitely not going. So don't even ask."

"I wasn't going to."

"You were," Jenna maintained. "I could see it in your face."

"I," Gage argued, "was just going to ask how the bagel industry is doing."

"Probably about as great as the accounting biz," Jenna answered. Except approximately sixty-thousand dollars a year less great than accounting. "And no."

"No what?" He asked innocently.

"No, I will not be your date to anymore frat weddings."

"Jenna. I would never do that to you."

"You have been doing this to me since last year. Since the first invitation."

"Well, not anymore. That's what Von is for now. I know we haven't been together long, but it's been long enough to invite her. I would think. Right?"

"Yeah, yeah," Jenna agreed quietly, her voice already distant. Jenna was in the midst of unwinding her messenger bag from over her shoulder. Gage continued talking, but Jenna abruptly stopped listening. He had Yvonne now. My God. He had Yvonne. Gage had come back in some weird mood from his mother's house at the beginning of summer, which Jenna hadn't thought much about at the time. He was always in some sort of mood when he returned from those trips. And she was having her own crisis. But Jenna distinctly remembered this one because she had crawled into bed with him, and he talked her out of her slump.

She also thought some weird things right before she fell asleep. Something about his arms and promises she made to herself about tomorrow. But the next day she felt bizarre, as if she didn't belong in his bed. She also felt lonely, even though Gage was still there, drooling on the pillow next to her head. She crept out of bed, smoked on the back porch, and promised herself new things. Things like how she would never think of Gage like that, like a boyfriend, again. Then she drank three cups of black coffee to seal the deal.

That afternoon, Memorial Day, Gage went to some work party he had originally turned down because he was supposed to be in D.C. that weekend. Jenna went up to the roof, where she drank an entire pitcher of Margaritas by herself, called Roxie when she was still a little too drunk, then took off her top and laid down on an old plastic beach lounge that had been up there since they moved in.

She came downstairs five hours later with a sunburn and dirty bare feet and asked Gage to slather aloe on her as soon as he walked through the door. She turned and peeled off her shirt, revealing the naked, pink flesh of her back. Gage was quiet for a minute. He swallowed, he audibly swallowed, the sound causing Jenna to look curiously over her shoulder at him. He shook his head then asked how in God's name had she already gotten a sunburn? Fell asleep on the roof, Jenna answered. Naked? Only half-naked, she said. Please, hurry. I'm itchy.

He left that night in a cab, returning home drunker than ever.

Then he left the next night, and the next.

At week's end, he told her about Yvonne. Yvonne Huggen who owned the Huggen Kiss Cupcakery. Yvonne who made monthly deposits into a Roth IRA. Yvonne who drove an Audi. Yvonne, who obviously was doing quite well in life. Jenna never realized the baking business was so profitable. Jenna had been sure it would not last long though; she was certain she would be eating breakfast with this Yvonne within the week. And if there was anything Jenna knew about Gage, it was that a breakfast with Jenna meant the good times were over.

One week passed. Then two. Then a month.

And Jenna heard plenty of Yvonne Huggen, but never once laid eyes on her.

She sketches cupcakes, Jendy, Gage had told her. She seriously sits down sketching cupcakes nightly and updates her business plan every single month. Who does that? He did not say it in some condescending way though; the admiration was palpable in his voice. Jenna stared at him blankly. She never saw Gage in such a state over a woman. *She's ahead of the curve, I'm telling you. She comes up with these flavors and promotions*, he'd say. *She's great at marketing*, he'd say, looking off into space. Jenna would *hmmm* and nod and feel a curious sickness pulling in her gut, a queasiness that she tried to push down far and away.

So he had Yvonne now. For weddings. Jenna had never stopped to consider that. "Yvonne," she said to herself. "Oh. Yeah."

She walked into the kitchen, Gage on her heels, and pulled a glass out of the cupboard. "Why are you being all weird?"

"I'm not being all weird," he answered.

She moved to the counter. He was on her like a shadow. "You're following me."

"I'm not following you."

Jenna stopped abruptly, and gritted her teeth when he bumped into her. Turning, she looked him up and down. "You're *not* following me?"

"Oh, Jendy, you've always been a little paranoid." But he backed off quickly, leaning against the counter now.

Jenna peered into the refrigerator, moved some containers around. "Did you drink all my apple juice?"

"Put it on the grocery list," Gage said evasively and tossed a pen at her. She caught it, one handed, while the other poured water.

"Nice. Very impressive." He nodded at her. "You have a headache."

"Yes," she answered.

"You want me to rub your neck?" He reached out, one cool hand touching the base of her head.

She shrugged him off and whirled on him. "What is all this? What are you doing?" Jenna eyed Gage suspiciously.

"Nothing. I know how you get headaches sometimes. I could get you an aspirin."

She narrowed her eyes at him.

He rolled his in response, and pushed from the counter. "All right. Fine. I have a favor to ask you."

She stared at him pointedly. "Which is?"

"I've been with Von four months now."

"Congratulations."

"I sense sarcasm."

"Oh, no. Not at all. I'm always proud of your biggest accomplishments."

Gage sighed. "Anyway. I'm going to need you to leave."

"What?" Her heart pounded. "I have to move? She's moving in? How am I going to find a place by the end of the month? Five days, Gage? Jesus, you could give me a little more time." Her stomach twisted with a new and worse thought. "Oh, God. I'm going to have to move in with Kaz. Oh. God. Gage, there is no way in hell I'm moving in with Kaz."

"Spiraling, Jendy. Spiraling." He said casually, which had become his code for telling her to shut up and calm down. "Just for the night." He held up one finger. "One night."

"Oh." Then, "Why?"

"Jendy, you know why."

She pursed her lips together. Von had stayed over a few times before. She was always sneaking in when Jenna was already in bed, and sneaking away to work before Jenna woke, so they never really crossed paths, but still, Gage had never asked Jenna to leave the house.

"Four months, Jendy. This is a big deal."

"Indeed it is." She turned from him. Was it love? Would Gage declare his love? *Declare his love?* Sheesh. Jenna needed to branch out from Victorian romance. "Indeed it is," she repeated.

"So you can leave?"

"Gage I have a chapter I wanted to finish tonight."

"You could stay with Kaz."

Jenna's eyes widened at his suggestion, and Gage had the presence to look embarrassed. "For one night," Gage reminded her. "Not even a whole night. Five hours. Six tops. He has...electricity. Right?"

"Sometimes," Jenna muttered. "He lives in a box."

"Ah-ha! I knew he was homeless."

"You know what I mean. And I'm not crawling back to him. Not for one night, not for five hours." She pushed him out of her way, and walked to the bathroom.

Gage followed.

"You want to watch me pee?" Jenna raised her eyebrows at him.

"I've seen worse," he countered, but he turned away, and she slammed the door.

"If you can't leave, could you at least wear the headphones and type in the closet?" He shouted.

Jenna already planned on trekking down to Bagel Plus to write there. Six hours for Gage. She could do that. But -- "I'll leave on one condition."

"Anything."

Jenna opened the door a crack and peeked out. "I want money for coffee. And food."

"Done." He dug his wallet out of his back pocket. It was thin and leather and matched Yvonne's purse. Okay. Jenna didn't know that for sure, but she had her suspicions. Gage swapped wallets three weeks after his first date with Yvonne, and Gage had not bought a new wallet in…well, ever.

Which made Jenna think of something else.

"And I want to meet Yvonne."

"Really?" He looked pained.

Not really. Or, maybe. I don't know. But I have to know.

"She is the only one I never met. And four whole months, Gage. That's some kind of record. Either you are smitten, or I'm a total embarrassment to your sensibilities."

"Nobody says smitten anymore, Jendy."

"So, which is it Gage? Love or embarrassment."

His face fell serious. "Okay. It's really hard for me to say this, Jenna, but I guess, of anyone, you should hear it."

Jenna watched him carefully.

He swallowed, looking nervous. "I've never said this before." He took Jenna's hand. "You're an embarrassment. I mean, really Jendy, nobody says smitten anymore. Or *sensibilities*, for that matter."

Jenna rolled her eyes. "Hilarious."

He smiled, lightning quick, kissed Jenna's hand, and pushed her toward the bedroom. "You better start packing up your laptop."

"I never heard a confirmation on that meeting."

"Fine. We'll meet. We go to the bar, like, next Saturday or something. When she has a day off. Whatever."

"To the bar? On a Saturday or something? Wow, Gage. Romance is in the air. Swoonworthy."

"For God's sake."

"This is happening? For real?"

"Yes. Just…leave."

"I'm already gone."

Gage

Jenna didn't know the particulars. She thought she did. But she didn't. She assumed I met Von at the bar that Memorial Day, or maybe during the week after, when I was drinking way too much. She assumed we started dating after that. She assumed a lot of things I let her assume. But now that Jenna wanted to meet Von – and why didn't I think far enough ahead to realize Jenna would probably want to meet her someday? – I probably should set the record straight.

I didn't meet Von at the bar. I met her at her bakery, the Friday morning after Memorial Day. I was incredibly early for work because I was trying to get my boss to notice me for promotion. I promoted not long ago, but hey, why not keep getting promoted as much as possible? So, anyway, I was a little hungover. Just a little. And early. Incredibly early. Like 6:30 a.m. early when I saw her: this compact little thing with blonde hair past her shoulders hefting a fifty pound bag of flour across the parking lot and through the front door of Huggen Kiss.

That. Made me stop in my tracks.

I didn't even know what the hell a Huggen Kiss was, but I walked across the parking lot and into the store, kind of dazed, as if a magnet pulled me through the door. She was alone, a radio playing whatever the "greatest oldies" were, and she was already in the back, but I could still see her blonde hair swaying.

"You need help?" I called out.

"No, thank you." Her reply intrigued me more. She wasn't even winded. "Can I help *you*?" She walked to me, brushing her hands against her jeans.

I looked around quickly to surmise where exactly I stood and with what exactly she could help me.

"Coffee?" I asked, even though the menu board above me was filled with cake and bread prices.

"An interesting request at a bakery that sells no coffee, but I can do that for you." She beamed as she poured a cup from behind the counter. It looked like a pot she made for herself and maybe some other co-workers who weren't working yet. She handed it to me. "You must be lost or on drugs." She turned her smile on me, and I was gone. I was gone. I was hers.

"Thanks." Did I just thank her for calling me a drug addict? "How much?"

"We don't do coffee. So…nothing?"

"Uh." It was about the first time I was at a loss for words.

"Anything else?" she asked, and I realized we had been staring at each other.

"Dinner?" I asked.

"At quarter 'til seven in the morning?" She looked at me like I was crazy. "The best I can do is day old cookies."

"No."

"Then I'm out." She laughed and leaned against the counter. "You could try the place next door. They make the dinner food of which you speak. I'd wait until they actually open at eleven. Or, you know, dinner time."

"No," I said again. "Me and you. Dinner."

Her eyes widened. "Us?"

"Yeah." It was coming back to me now, my thoughts arranging, my brain finally firing on all – or at least half – cylinders. I leaned over the counter, moving close to her, biting my lip with a half-grin. "Dinner."

"Who are you?" She tilted her head curiously, but I could see the hint of a smile.

"Elliot Gageby," I said holding out a hand, using my first name for the first time with a woman.

"Elliot." She took my hand cautiously. "You're not a drug addict?"

"No," I said simply.

And you're not lost?"

"Not anymore."

She laughed, short and sweet. "Dinner."

"Yeah," I said, with challenge in my eyes, though I wasn't sure why I should be challenging her. "Dinner."

"I guess I could do that." She shrugged, and it drove me wild. "You have a number?" I pulled out my wallet and handed her my card, and she replied, "Oh, fancy. And he speaks the truth. Elliot Gageby." Then, "You work across the street."

"Right across the street." And how did I never notice this place?

And to my surprise, she handed me a card.

Yvonne Huggen. Huggen Kiss Cupcakery. Proprietor. Head Pastry Chef.

"Cupcakery?" I asked.

"Too cutesy?" She asked.

I didn't know what a cupcakery was. "Not at all."

"Still want to take me to dinner?"

"Yes." I said

"I'll call you," she said.

I nodded once, the smile growing on my face. I backed my way to the door, holding up the coffee, my wallet forgotten in my other hand. "Thanks again."

"Oh, and Elliot?"

"Yeah?"

"You could use a new wallet." She beamed again, her eyes mischievous.

I stared at my frayed wallet. Yeah. How had I never noticed that before either?

The first date was weird as hell. Maybe it was because she insisted on picking me up. Or maybe it was the way she looked completely different at night, her hair twisted into some kind of coil all around her head, a dress that hugged her everywhere. She drank whiskey and laughed a lot, her body bowing close to mine every time. The first time she leaned in, I'd expected to be wrapped up in some scent she wore. And that's where she was different. She smelled like nothing. I was in love. In lust, I corrected.

She also interrupted me constantly to check her phone, blaming work related things. "I'm a great multi-tasker," she said in a voice that shot straight to my groin.

I shifted. "I did not realize the pastry business was so lucrative," I replied, nodding at the phone that never left her hand. Typically I'd be annoyed at the habit, the girl who could not leave her phone alone. But this woman was no girl. This woman was all business.

"Can I divulge a secret?" She asked, and I thought of Jenna. Divulge. Jenna would use that word.

"Divulge away." I leaned in conspiratorially.

"I'm looking into expanding."

"The cupcakery?"

"No, my waistline," she joked.

"You're ambitious," I said.

"Is there any other way to be?"

I thought of my own complacency in a job that paid me well on my long, slow march to nowhere. Promotions, yeah, sure, but promotions to nowhere I truly wanted to be. I thought of coming home every night to Jenna, where I watched her smoke on the porch as I downed a beer. She would tell me about her books, about the bagel of the month. I thought of the weekends. The weekends where we would drink at bars and stumble home at night, either together or in a pack of three: me, Jenna, and some chick I picked up, some girl Jenna would eat breakfast with the next morning. Yeah. Yeah, there were other ways to be.

She must have interpreted my silence as agreement, because with a smile she leaned in one last time. "Want to leave?"

Yes. Yes I do.

But when I stood up to reach for my car keys, I remembered I had not driven. Disorientation at this entire date shook through me. And I liked it.

She looked at me over the rim of her glass as she finished her whiskey in one gulp. God, she was hot. I smirked at her and snaked an arm around her waist.

She jangled her keys at me. "We can go to my place."

Her phone went off. Some cake emergency. She talked all the way home, right up until I grabbed the phone out of her hand, slammed it shut, and flipped her onto the bed. Her eye went wide. "I guess I'll call her back later," she laughed and pulled me down on top of her.

God. She was hot. She was everything.

October 13, 2007

Jenna

Jenna did end up going to Cody's wedding. As Roxie's date. Jenna was surprised to learn that Roxie and Cody had developed quite a rapport at all of those frat parties in college. They were friends. I have lots of friends, she said with a shrug when Jenna expressed this surprise to her.

Roxie and Jenna were seated at the wedding with Gage and Von – Jenna had met Von, and Von was perfectly nice, always bringing day-old cookies and bread to the apartment late at night after she closed the bakery. They went well with the day-old bagels. Lots of carbs equaled lots of happiness in their apartment. Jenna was invited to play scrabble with them or go out to the bar with them. Von even insisted on taking Jenna to the movies with them one night and splurged on The Third Wheel – a popcorn and drink combo for packs of three. Von set up Jenna on three blind dates, and Von was so nice Jenna did not have the heart to tell her how truly horrible the dates were – and there was no way she'd tell Gage how she ended up at Kaz's place after one of them, sleeping with him then eating three old, hardboiled eggs the next morning.

Von was perfectly nice. And even though he hated the word, Gage was smitten. He had to be smitten because he never seemed to mind that Von's cell phone was like a long-lost appendage. It was glued to her hand or ear most times and the stuff she was saying into it was always work related. Gage did not seem to care about that, and Jenna never brought it up, because, well, Von was just so nice anytime she was not on her phone that Jenna did not want to be the one that brought it up.

So, anyway, they were seated at Cody's wedding, Roxie and Jenna and Von and Gage, only Von called Gage "Elliot" and it was so foreign to Jenna's ears she looked around for some stranger every time the name was uttered.

"Work?" Jenna asked Roxie.

"Work is amazing." Roxie shook her head and stared into her Old Fashioned. "I never knew how rewarding a job could be." After working as a beat officer for three years, Roxie had landed a job in something she had never considered in college: forensic technician. Jenna always assumed she would be freaked hearing about crime scenes, but Roxie could make a analyzing bloodstain patterns and helping catch the bad guy fascinating. "I'm going back for my master's in forensic psychology. Did I tell you that."

Jenna smiled faintly and nodded.

"I can't believe how much is out there for us, just for the taking."

"I know," Jenna agreed, but she thought of Bagel Plus. Should she go back for her master's degree? In something else? Psychology, like Roxie? Could she be a psychologist? That wouldn't be so bad, analyzing people's thoughts and motives. Making a career. Making a salary. What did making a salary feel like?

And what does giving up feel like? The thought slammed into her, full force. Would she know, or would it be gradual?

"How about you?" Roxie swirled her Old Fashioned then sipped, and she looked so adult, so put together, Jenna actually ached. Roxie always knew what she wanted and where she needed to go. Roxie looked like a salary. "Work?"

Jenna grimaced and shook her head. "Bagels are always bagels." Jenna stared out to the dance floor, where everyone looked so adult in their expensive clothes, cocktails in hand.

Roxie must have sensed Jenna's unease discussing work – probably all those psychology classes – and dropped the subject. She followed Jenna's gaze.

"So who is this Von?" Roxie asked as they both stared at Gage and Von entwined in each other. "Do we like her?"

"She's nice," Jenna replied, never taking her eyes off the couple. "She's just so nice."

Jenna

Greta, the always reliable, steadfast - if not boring - manager of Bagel Plus went out for her dinner break one Saturday in early November – almost exactly one month earlier. Jenna barely registered the day. It had been crisp and warm, no different than the day before. The customer flow had been steady, like every other day. And like every single time before, Greta left with her brown bag that contained an tuna-salad sandwich on wheat, an apple, and a double chocolate brownie she bought every day from the Bagel Plus bakery display. Jenna always liked Greta, whose even keeled demeanor and complacency – if not love – of her managerial position was a comfort. Jenna had never met someone so predictable in her life.

During their downtime when they stacked cups and counted inventory, Greta and Jenna talked, Jenna expounding on the drama of her life, her lack of career, her new apartment, while Greta focused more narrowly on topics of cats and herbal tea. Jenna was sure Greta was more than this one-dimensional cat lover, but Greta was so private otherwise, Jenna had no clue what her other dimensions might possibly contain.

"Guess it's my break," Greta said, checking her watch. She never left one minute before five and never arrived one minute after five-thirty. "I think I'll do the bank deposit now."

"Okay," Jenna said, a little shocked, because Greta never did anything as wild as depositing the money one day early.

At 5:31, Jenna frowned. It was not as if she cared that Greta was one – or even five – minutes late, but even the sixty-second tardiness was unlike her.

When the minute hand his 5:38 with no Greta, Jenna felt anxiety rise. "Have you guys seen Greta?" Everyone shrugged. Jenna and Greta were the only long-term employees, outlasting the college kids by not months, but years.

At six o'clock, Jenna called and called Greta's phone, increasingly concerned and not hiding it well in her unanswered and panicky voicemails. Greta had all that money on her. She was alone. It was dusk. Who knew what could happen? Jenna paced, the store phone glued to her ear.

Then at 7:06, Jenna's cell rang, and Jenna dove for it. *Greta Bagel* rolled across the screen. Jenna sighed with relief and also felt kind of bad that she had programmed Greta into her phone as a Bagel. Especially when she had been worried that Greta was missing, kidnapped, or dead.

"Hey, Jenna," Greta's soft voice filled Jenna's ear.

"Greta! Are you okay? Where are you?"

"Jenna, I'm not coming back."

"What?"

"I'm quitting. I'm giving you my notice."

"Now? You're quitting now? But this is...this is crazy."

"I've been thinking about this for a while." Her voice didn't sound sad or lost, but determined.

"Greta!" Jenna had said, completely floored. "You can't give me your notice. I'm nobody."

"I'm done," she said.

Jenna tried one last time. "Pull yourself together, Gret! People don't do stuff like this." But people did. Even people like Greta, people who color coded their purses and ate the same lunch every day. And the day went on. After Jenna hung up the phone, the next customer requested a cold pressed vanilla iced coffee and Jenna, dazed, filled the order.

Okay, so the day was not completely normal. Greta's Great Escape was the talk of Bagel Plus that day, among both employees and regulars looking for Greta, who had never taken a sick day. She heard one employee whispering that perhaps this was the most fascinating thing Greta would ever do in her life.

"It's madcap, Gage. Nobody knows what to do. Corporate is coming in." Jenna told him over the phone.

"Madcap, Jendy? You're going with madcap?"

"Oh, shut up." She hung up on him, more interested now in the one wild rumor making the rounds: that Greta actually stole the bank deposit and use it to fund her new life. Jenna called the bank, frantic and also kind of shocked that the thought of Greta stealing the deposit had never crossed Jenna's mind – seriously what kind of night manager was she? – then disappointed everyone by debunking the rumor. Sure, Greta had been planning secretly planning to quit in the bagel industry, but she never shirked on her responsibility.

After exactly one day, the chatter died down, and Jenna was offered a new position as if nothing had happened. She accepted, still kind of numb. The whole thing landed like a present in her lap: a huge salary increase, vacation and sick days, health insurance. By the end of November, Jenna was finishing up her first full week as the manager of Bagel Plus.

And what a disastrous week it had been.

There was a new menu roll-out on Monday, which caused utter confusion and expected outrange. The righteous anger was not really directed at the menu change, but the upcharge in pretty much everything. If there was one thing Jenna had learned in the near decade she spent in the coffee biz, it was never to get in the way a person and their two-dollar coffee. Unless it was in the form of money handed back to them, to customers, change was a very bad thing.

On Wednesday, the bagel truck over turned on I-99, causing a comical spill that the entire nation watched on CNN. The spill led to flocks of birds infiltrating the highway to fight for hundreds of pounds of bagels. Of course, Twitter got in on it, hastagging the entire incident as Bagelpocalypse. Nobody on Twitter gave a shit about the grief the whole event caused Jenna. She tried to fill the loss of bagels by pulling croissants and declaring October seventh Official Croissant Day, a plan that backfired when they ran out of croissants by ten a.m.

And today, a promotion that meant to soften the blow of the coffee upcharge and Bagelpocalypse, went really wrong, resulting in a backlash and an actual picketing of Bagel Plus, even if it was only a handful of yoga-type blog moms who had nothing better to protest that afternoon.

"Jen? Jenna?"

"Hold on," Jenna hissed at Hannah who would not stop tapping her shoulder and turned back to the man currently snapping his fingers in front of her face. "Yes, sir?" Jenna pasted on a smile.

"I'd like a large coffee, skim, half-caf, stirred, 180 degrees, to go." He started to pull money out. "Thanks," he bit out belatedly without looking up.

Jenna punched some buttons. "That'll be 3.79," she replied.

"What?" He said tersely and looked up from his wallet.

"3.79. Please." Jenna added politely with the same glued-on smile.

"3.79? It was 3.44 last week."

"Yes, I know. I'm sorry, sir. The prices changed this week."

"Um, Jenna?" Hannah was back at Jenna's shoulder, her voice meek but urgent.

"Can you give me one minute, Hannah? Thanks." Jenna rolled her eyes to herself and held in a sigh. "Sir?"

"No," He said, obviously disgusted. "I'm not paying that. That's twenty-five cents extra!"

"Would you like a smaller size?"

"No. I want the old price."

"I can't do that, sir. The prices are pre-set in our system."

"So?"

"We are offering or a limited--"

"I don't want a limited anything. Coffee."

"I want to speak to the manager. Where is he?" The guy looked over her shoulder.

"I am the manager, sir." She said.

"You're the manager?" Coffee Guy latched onto that information. "Then over-ride the system."

"I am sorry, sir," Jenna could feel the headache pulling at her eyes. "I can't do that."

"Well, why not?"

"The prices are set by corporate."

"You could change it." That was technically true. She could easily shut him up by using the employee discount.

"I can't change prices. That would be theft."

"Theft? Ha! You're stealing from me!" An idea lit his eyes. "You probably are. You're probably making it up and pocketing the difference."

Jenna watched the line behind Coffee Guy grow.

"I would never do that. If you look at the menu behind me you can see--"

"Don't patronize me."

"I'm not." Jenna held up her hands, wishing he wouldn't have patronized Bagel Plus.

Coffee Guy narrowed his eyes at me. "I waited in line at least ten minutes for this."

So pay the freaking quarter, she wanted to scream.

Customers murmured behind him.

"Here, sir. I can give you coupons for your wait." Jenna could see his mood change immediately. She stuffed them in his hand.

And the guy tried a new idea. "So, use the coupons now."

"Fine. Sure. No problem. Discount now." Jenna rang up a random coupon and hoped one would work.

"That was easy enough," Coffee Guy grunted.

"Have a great day!" Jenna chanted cheerfully as he moved down the line. *See you in hell!*

"Jenna?" Hannah wouldn't give up.

"What?" Jenna swiveled with a snap before remembering that Hannah was the fragile one, prone to tears. "Oh...uh, Hannah? What's up?"

Hannah, eyes wide. "Sorry. So sorry."

"No, Hannah. It's fine. What's up?"

"Uh, um, you know about...you know--"

"What Hannah?"

"You know about how you had me go out and give the hippies those day old cream puffs? To make them go away?"

"Yeah."

"They're uh…throwing them at the windows now."

Calling the police on housewives was never something Jenna thought she would have to do, and yet, there she was, dialing the phone, giving statements to an officer with the same shade of brown coloring his eyes and hair. He broke up the protest using all charm and no force.

"You think they'd have something better to do," Jenna said when it was all over, and the last mom kind of trickled away with her toddler. "Like meditate in a tent or something." Then she caught herself, eyes widening. Was that a hate crime, insulting hippie mothers? She looked up to the officer with a grimace.

He looked stern, and her belly jumped. She was going to be arrested, Jenna was sure. She was going to be arrested and lose her job because of a hippie hate crime, and she have to move back in with Gage and Von, and sure, Jenna got along with Von, but Jenna would probably truly have to kill herself because there was no way in hell Jenna was going to live with them.

Then his eyes twinkled. He leaned into her. "Or, like, I don't know, buy tickets for Bonnaroo?" He whispered.

Jenna, startled, stared at him for a blank second. Then she sighed. "You're not going to arrest me."

He chuckled to himself. "You have a nice day, ma'am."

Jenna smiled and bit her lip. "Thanks, Officer, uh--" She searched at his chest for some kind of identifying nametag.

"Graham. Michael." He held out a hand.

"Officer Graham." She took his hand and felt her color rise, but wasn't really sure why.

"I prefer Michael," He said, his eyes on hers, and she felt like maybe they were flirting, but she hadn't flirted with a guy in so long she wasn't sure. "Just in case, you know, we ever end up talking again." He held a card between two fingers, passing it to Jenna.

"Yeah. Yeah." She felt her cheeks heat when she took it, and self-consciously brushing the hair from her eyes – she had cut her hair not long ago and still hated her bangs – and backed away from him. "Later." And she had never pictured herself thanking hippie mothers for protesting, and she had never pictured herself casually saying *Later* to a cop.

That evening, she closed with Hannah who could not stop jabbering about the whole incident and how hot that cop was. When Hannah finally left, Jenna inventoried their stash of cappuccino and cookies, replaying the whole conversation between she and the cop in her head, convincing herself that what she thought passed between had not actually happened. And two hours later than she planned, Jenna biked home in her uniform and climbed the stairs to her apartment, exhausted but amazed at what steady hours and a salary did for a twenty-seven year old psyche.

She took off her Bagel Plus visor, hung it over her vanity mirror, and watched the square of stock card fall from the spot on her visor where she had tucked it five hours earlier. Officer Michael Graham, printed in tiny black block lettering. She read his name over and over. Jenna smiled, stuck the card in her mirror, wedging it between the wood and glass then whistling, walked to the kitchen to defrost a lasagna.

Jenna

Dating Michael had been easy, much easier than Jenna ever imagined dating should ever be. Their first date was exactly one week after she defrosted that lasagna. Michael took her out for coffee late in the afternoon, where Jenna found out that he was only twenty-three, four years younger than she, which seemed outrageous and made Jenna feel old and uncomfortable.

"But you're so mature," she blurted out then backpedaled quickly. "I mean, of course you're mature. It's not like twenty-three is a teenager or something...not that I would ever date a teenager. Unless I was a teenager," she finished lamely, hiding her face behind the overly large coffee cups and cursing herself for her blathering. She was just so shocked. Jenna's own twenty-third year passed through her mind. Her first year out of college, Jenna had been slinging bagels and grinding coffee part-time, gritting her way through the days, drinking her way through the nights with Gage. The nights she was not drinking herself into oblivion consisted of falling asleep on top of her keyboard or her latest manuscript, waking late and running to work in a rumpled uniform. Jenna had been, in all honesty, barely functional.

Michael was twenty-three. He was so much younger. But he lived in a spacious two bedroom in the suburbs. A house. The man had a mortgage. He had a full time job and a pension and a stability Jenna was sure she would never know. For God's sake, Michael was enrolled at Pitt for his master's degree in criminology. Michael was twenty-three. He was so much younger. And somehow so much older.

"It's the uniform," he said. "People always think I'm older in the uniform."

"Ah, of course."

It wasn't the uniform.

Michael was simply different. He called when he said he would; he picked her up when he said he would; he held her hand; he laughed at her jokes; he made them both popcorn in some electric machine they searched for together online. They did laundry together and balled socks together afterward and even once they baked a loaf of bread from scratch that ended up a charred little brick in the oven because they had been too busy making out there in Jenna's cheap and disgusting efficiency.

Occasionally, when Jenna was younger, she would scrutinize the real estate section in the newspaper, imagining what kind of charmed life she could lead if she only had access to one of those houses one day. What she didn't know at the time was that she was picturing Michael's exact life. He grew up in New Hampshire. The youngest of three, his brother and sister were both doctors in New Hampshire. They all got together for two weeks in the summer, and they spent Christmas with their grandparents. In New Hampshire. *New Hampshire, New Hampshire*, Jenna repeated after his story. They were both drinking beer, and being tipsy, it seemed both fitting and hilarious at the time to chant his home state over and over. Nobody ever left New Hampshire, he added, quite animatedly, and they both dissolved into an inexplicable fit of giggles. His cheeks were red from the alcohol, it was their third date, and he leaned over and kissed her hard on the lips. When he pulled away, Jenna blushed, and he teased her. "What's this," he said running a finger down her cheek, and she shook her head. "Really?" He cocked his head and stared at her, a ghost of a smile crossing his face. "You're not going to tell me?" Jenna pressed her lips together, looked to her hands. Looked back to him. He took a sip of beer. Slowly. He set it down and leaned back to look at her. He bit his lip waiting for an answer, any answer. Nothing. Jenna swallowed hard. His eyes softened. "I'll figure you out," he said in a voice so quiet Jenna was sure he already had put the pieces together. "I've no doubt," she said, equally hushed, and everything around them kind of stopped. He walked her home then, and she held his hand, and when she pushed through the front door, she led him by that hand to her bedroom. His hands were hard and his hair was soft and his eyes never left hers. His arms fit around her perfectly and stayed that way all night.

Tonight, all these months later, she looked at him while he made chicken parmesan with fettuccine noodles he made from scratch. He looked at her, his face dusted in flour, and she smiled.

"Love you, Jen," he said.

It wasn't the first time he said it, but it felt like the first time of…something. Something she did not want to express to him, because he would try to understand, but he never could. And that was not a bad thing, Jenna decided. Some things in this world could be hers alone. In that moment, every single thing that never made sense about her life suddenly clicked.

Also, the chicken didn't burn that night.

Everything. Everything was so good. And perfect.

Gage

The past several months had sucked.

It had been a never ending shitstorm of one hellish disaster after another.

Okay, it had not all been horrible. But huge chunks of time had been horrible and, mostly, looking back now, it was much easier to remember the horrible chunks and not the small and good things that happened

Everything had been fine, more than fine. I had been dating Von who was beautiful and perfect and hardworking and goal oriented. Jenna and I were getting along fine. Hell, even Von and Jenna had been getting along fine.

And then it all kind of imploded and collapsed at once.

First of all, Jenna left.

The whole even still confused me.

It was a shock to my system, Jenna moving out. The decision seemed rash and made absolutely no sense at the time, and I definitely remembered the exact time. The morning after Cody's wedding Jenna tapped on my bedroom door. Von's legs and hair and arms were still wound around me. "Hmm?" I mumbled at the tapping, barely awake. The door creaked open and Jenna's head popped in.

"Whoa!" I jumped, fully awake then, and flipped the comforter over my lower half. Beside me, Von grumbled then tugged at the sheets and rolled over. Von rarely stopped to rest, but when she did, the woman could out-sleep a coma patient.

"Oh, don't be such a prude, Gage," Jenna said flippantly. "I've seen you naked and vomiting with the flu. Can we talk?"

And that was it. Over coffee, Jenna informed me that she needed to move out.

"Need to?" I asked.

"Want to. Whatever. Same difference," she said with a flip of her hand. "I found a place."

I could not see the "same difference" in that statement, but whatever. I moved on. "You found a place?"

"It's not the best, but it's - it's something, Gage. I need to do this."

"Are you sure?"

She didn't answer, but looked away. "I need a cigarette."

"You quit," I reminded her.

"I know. How tragic."

I shook my head. "You're sure?" I tried again, mostly because I couldn't imagine living any other way.

"Do you want eggs?" Jenna asked, which seemed like a perfectly Jenna type of answer.

Von padded out to the kitchen then, and we all ate eggs together about half an hour later.

The move never made any sense to me, especially not after Jenna had the meltdown to end all meltdowns not long after moving. She was crying and cutting hair crying some more because she hated the way she cut her hair. Von and I were over at her new place constantly: making her tea and cookies (Von), begging her to just move back to the old place (me), sleeping on the floor next to her bed (Von and me). Then, just as quickly, she was not only better but thriving. A new position at Bagel Plus. Michael. It was so fast our heads practically spun. Jenna was doing well, so well, in fact, that when my lease was up, Von suggested moving in together. So we did. And though I could previously not visualize living any way without Jenna, there I was in a new apartment filled with so much Pottery Barn, our life looked like an advertisement.

Three days later Kristen called. I had been brushing my teeth at the time, a mundane event I never would have remembered had it not been for the two very different pieces of news she delivered.

"Are you brushing your teeth?" She asked, incredulously.

"Hmph," I answered, because I was brushing my teeth.

"Stop brushing your damn teeth! Who brushes their teeth on the phone?"

I spit and took great care in wiping my mouth. "Jeez, Kris, what's your deal?"

"I'm pregnant, that's my deal."

I spit again, because the news was so shocking I had forgotten I already spit. Kris was pregnant? How could she be pregnant? Well, okay, I knew *how* she could be pregnant, but I hadn't talked to her in so long. How had she even been with someone long enough to get pregnant? And I asked exactly that question.

"Just because you don't call me doesn't mean I don't live a life. We're not languishing down here waiting on your calls, Elliot."

"God damn, you're moody."

"It's not the pregnancy," she said, a warning for me to not blame the mood on the pregnancy.

I never planned on doing that, because, as I said, "I know. I've lived with you before, Kris." Kris could be one moody person.

"He's wonderful, by the way. The father. Brecken Stoltz. We've been together six months, in case you're wondering."

"I was. I thought it better not to even ask. He's a lawyer isn't he? You met him in law school."

"Good. Because he's good. And we're not getting married." She said the last part defiantly, as if I would even dare to suggest it. "And he *is* a lawyer. Well, a law student. How did you know?"

"Because his name is Brecken Stoltz. That's the lawyery-ist lawyer name a lawyer could have."

"Hmm," she contemplated. "I thought it sounded more California-dude than lawyery. Or maybe, like, a German beer."

"Eh," I conceded, because I had nothing more to say about Brecken Stoltz's name.

"I'm staying in law school. I'm not dropping out."

"Good," I said, because I was genuinely happy she was staying in school. "I'm sure Mom is proud," I added, voice dripping with sarcasm because there was no way in hell mom was proud of this turn of life events for Kristen.

"Mom's pissed."

"Of course she's pissed." We were silent for ten seconds, which feels really long when you are on a phone and late for work. "Are you pissed?"

"No," she said, and that was when her voice finally changed. "I'm happy." I could hear the smile in her voice.

"Then I'm happy too."

"Really?"

"Yeah. Sure. I'll be an uncle. I'll be an awesome uncle. It's pretty cool." And it was pretty cool. For the first time since I answered Kris' call, I felt something good. Something good and pure ran through me. My sister. A mother. Me. An uncle. "I love you, Kris."

"I love you too, El."

I thought that would be the end of the call then. I thought maybe she would bitch about Mom a little bit more, fill me in on all the shit Mom laid on her about getting pregnant. I would sympathize and tell her I'd visit soon, and then we would hang up.

That isn't what happened.

"That's not the news though, El."

At this point I was chucking stuff into my car. Keys. Messenger bag. A file I forgot to put in my messenger bag. Gym clothes. I set my mug of coffee on the roof of the car. "You being pregnant is *not* news?"

"It's Dad."

That. That was one of the horrible chunks, the chunk that covered up the fact that I was happy about being an uncle.

"What's Dad?" I asked and could already feel the icy fear fill my belly. "What?"

"It's not terrible."

But as it turned out, it was terrible. Dad had needed surgery. Something so routine, it was practically a nothing, Kristen had said. Kris figured she could take care of it. She could take him in for the surgery, help him out afterwards. No need to bother me, since I was so far away. Practically a nothing. Then they messed up his pain medication which wasn't the terrible part, but it did lead to some complications. And then he contracted MRSA. And I did not even know what MRSA was, so as Kris was still talking, I was Googling and when I saw that MRSA was pretty fucking serious and people could actually die from it, I was screaming, *What the actual fuck, Kris?* And, *How could you keep this shit from me?* And then we were screaming back and forth as I made the quick decision to drive down to D.C. instead of work, and I heard my coffee mug fall and shatter by the time I hit the end of the driveway. We screamed some more back and forth until Kris started crying, and I felt like a complete asshole and apologized. We hung up then, agreeing maybe Kris being pregnant and me zipping eighty miles an hour down a highway wasn't the best time for a death-scream match.

I ended up taking off more work than normal, driving and sometimes flying back and forth from D.C. At one hideous point, Kris and I hovered over Dad's hospital bed basically waiting at for him to die. It was horrible the way Kris was whispering in his ear that it was okay, he could let go, we would be all right, we loved him.

No, Dad. We will not be fucking okay, I wanted to counter. *Don't listen to her, she's basically insane with hormones and nothing will ever be okay about this.*

Simultaneously, things with Von started going down the toilet. The fighting with Kris transferred over to Von, and we were screaming at each other practically every weekend I was home. Von and her fucking work. The constant cell phone was irritating beyond belief. *My father is dying*, I told her, *and you can't get off your fucking phone for one minute to freaking sit with me.* She threw her phone at me then, and raged that she had sat with me - for practically the first two weeks of this ordeal – and unlike me, she did not have a trust fund to rely on when she took sick time from work. And that was the wrong fucking thing to say, and the fights whiplashed to screaming matches of privilege and trust funds and money and who worked more and who slept less and couldn't I just fucking fold the towels after they came out of the dryer for God's sake instead of letting them wrinkle in the basket?

We did not speak then for another week, not until the deathbed scene with Dad. I cried all night then, and Von sat with me, and our fights ended, but nothing really felt the same with her after.

Dad ended up not dying, but recovering. I don't know; rather than hearing Kristen's vocal spiritual acceptance of his inevitable death and her peace with it, he must have heeded my silent bitching about how he would fuck everything up by dying. His recovery was slow, and I took a medical leave to live with him because Kris was fairly pregnant by then and looking ready to explode. Dad and I sat a lot outside, and he was quiet for most of my stay. Most of his comments were about trees and woodworking and how he missed them both when he was in the hospital.

Kris had her baby then, and I stayed for that as well. She had a girl she and her boyfriend named Leslie Elliot Gageby Stoltz because according to her, nobody was named Leslie anymore.

Elliot? I asked her. *Her middle name is Elliot?* And Kristen bit her lip and smiled a tiny smile at me, and I nodded instead of saying anything because I could feel tears filling my eyes. Kris hugged me and started crying – we cried a lot those six months, and my usually non-crying family blamed it on the lack of sleep - then we ate a birthday cake Mom bought for Leslie at that deli that sold all those freaking flavors of olives. It was the first time I had been with my entire family in forever: Mom, Dad, Kris, and me in Dad's backyard (along with Mom's entire family and Brecken Stoltz's entire family). Dad sat back and watched us all together at the picnic table he built the year before. He watched quietly, a faint smile on his face, and when I looked over at him, his smile grew. I smiled back, not nearly as wide, but just as heartfelt. We both shrugged at each other, and I kind of felt like something important happened.

And then, everything felt normal again. Or as normal as it would ever be.

"Von?" I called out as walked through the front door and Bruster, the cat we – mostly Von – adopted from the shelter five months ago, came running at me meowing like he had not seen another living thing in days. I spared him a pet or three then dropped my keys on the table next to the door even though Von was forever nagging me to hang them on that key hanging thing she bought at Pottery Barn. I set my messenger bag on the Oriental rug Von picked out from some catalogue, and then ran both hands over my face and back through my hair. I sighed as Bruster stretched up on two legs vying for my attention. I picked him up, and he purred manically. "Babe?" I called again as I passed through the living room and dropped Bruster on the couch. Von hated when I let Bru on her furniture…our furniture?

Truth was the place always felt more Von's than mine…or ours…or whatever.

"V?" I yelled again. Probably in her office. I made my way through the living room to the kitchen. Grabbed a banana and peeled and bit into it in record time. "Thought we could go out tonight. Jesus, what a week. I'm--" I stopped when I saw the yellow legal paper, her writing scrawled across it.

Hey Babe,

Had to run back to the bakery.

Gonna be a late night. Don't wait up.

Made you a little treat!

Dream of me!

C ya tomorrow.

—V

She drew some little hearts and kissy faces around her initial. The note was on top of a plate of brownies covered in plastic wrap, the brownies filled with chocolate fudge that she knew I loved. The anger rose up in me faster than I expected. Faster than yesterday, or the day before. With a loud curse, I balled the note and hurled it across the kitchen. Bruster skittered away. "Sorry, Bru."

I grabbed my phone and punched buttons. "What's up?" Skipping the formality of hello, I dove right into the deep end when she answered.

"Elliot?" Von sounded rushed and confused.

"Yeah, babe."

"Didn't you see my note?"

"Yeah, it's right here."

"Uh…" She paused, either still busy or at a loss for words. I could feel the thoughts clicking in her brain - what else could she say? She left a note.

"You coming home or what?"

"Did you read my note?"

"Yup."

"It's gonna be a late night."

"Yeah. I know."

"Babe? Are you mad?"

"This is day seven, Von."

"Day seven?"

"Seventh day in a row pulling an all-nighter."

A long silence. "Oh, babe. I'm sorry. You know it's not personal. I'm a workhorse."

"You need a break."

"I'm clearing my schedule tomorrow. But, hon, I'm sorry I really need to finish this. I don't have time to talk."

"Yeah. I'll see ya then." I pulled the phone away from my face, my finger poised over the End button when I heard her voice.

"Babe?" Her voice sounded tinny and very far away.

With a sigh, I held it to my ear again. "Yeah?"

"I love you."

"Same," I said, and we both hung up.

I looked at Bruster who had forgiven me for the outburst and was winding his way around my legs. "It's just you and me, bubs."

Bruster stopped. Looked at me for two unblinking seconds, then turned around and licked himself.

Thursday, April 15, 2009

Jenna

She wanted a blue dress.

She wanted Gage to be her best man.

And she wanted Roxie to walk her down the aisle.

Michael did all the things Jenna would have wanted him to do. There were no big declarations or shiny rings. That would have killed her, and he must have known it. They were alone, in the kitchen, she with a cup of tea in her hands, he leaned over a pan or a pot, cooking something. He was always cooking something. Spaghetti? Jenna could not remember all the details. She could remember the way he turned to her, the seriousness painting his face. She had just said something about horses or dogs or some kind of animal with four legs. "What?" she teased. "Am I boring you?" "Never," he replied. Her eyes flicked to the clock hanging over the oven. Jenna had been doing well.

Her eyes followed his. "Are we late for something?" She racked her brain.

"Not really. I'd say right on time." He moved to her. He moved around her. His hands circled her hips. Hers circled her cup of tea. "What?" She looked up to him, eyes confused and full of questions. "Michael, what?" She waited a beat before an anxious laugh escaped.

They stared at each other, nerves and something else Jenna couldn't identify buzzing between them. "Are you breaking up with me?" This didn't feel like a break-up, but then again, Jenna had no clue what else this quiet tension could be.

"I'm thinking about something, Jen. I can't think about anything else."

Jenna couldn't form the question she wanted to ask, so she waited, her pulse beating her in throat.

He looked down at her hands, then back up to her worried gaze. "I want to marry you, Jenna. I want to marry you. I want to marry you so much. And I want to be your family, and I want to make family for you, with you. All that. It's all I can think about, Jen."

Her lips parted in disbelief. She laughed then, because the relief was so physical, so deep, she felt it flood and fill her body. She wanted to cover her face, to cry, to laugh. But she couldn't because she was still holding that stupid cup of tea. She was in shock maybe, but the good kind that ended with a dream and not a nightmare.

"That's an agreement then?"

"Was that a question?" She managed.

He laughed then too. He nodded.

So she nodded, her face flush. He stole the cup from her hands and took a celebratory swig and set it down with a clatter to the counter. Then he whopped and picked her up. He twirled her. He actually twirled her. Jenna didn't know until that moment that she was a woman who wanted to be twirled. She thought of everyone she would tell, which in the end boiled down to about two people. Roxie and Gage. They would look at her crazy, she knew. Because Michael was young, and she was not quite steady in life yet. And because they had not even been together a year yet.

It's a big change, Roxie would say. A huge change. Was she sure she was ready?

But she had watched When Harry Met Sally. She watched it at her last foster family's house, on, she wasn't sure, the ABC Family Channel or Hallmark or something like that. There was that line. *You want the rest of your life to start as quickly as possible.* Back then and for a long time after, there was nothing she saw that made her want to start the rest of her life as quickly as possible.

And now there was. There was so much.

A blue dress, she told Michael. She wanted a blue dress.

Absolutely, he said without hesitation. Get a blue dress. Get whatever you want. Get everything you want.

Sunday, June 7, 2009

Gage

"Do you have any gauze?" Jenna's frantic voice filled the space between us.

"Gauze?" I tucked my cell between my ear and shoulder and licked the spoon of the sauce I was stirring in my kitchen. "Yeah, I think so."

"Good." Jenna sounded only a little less frantic at my confirmation. "Bring it over."

"What in the hell do you need gauze for?"

"Just bring it over, Gage!"

"For what?"

"I cut my leg shaving."

"So, get a Band-Aid. I'm in the middle of spaghetti." Von would not appreciate me leaving in the middle of a mess and half-cooked spaghetti.

"Gage, I shaved like a three inch strip of skin off my ankle, I'm hopping around the house with a towel rubberbanded to my leg, and my bathtub looks like a crime scene. "

I cringed. The spaghetti sauce looked a lot less appetizing. "Jesus, I didn't need to know that."

"Apparently you did."

"Chilling."

"Just get your ass and your gauze over here."

And because Von was one of those always-be-prepared people in an over the top kind of way, I knew we had not only guaze but medical tape, anitibiotic cream, antiseptic, elastic bandages, calamine lotion, cold and hot packs, a splint, and Von's certificate verifying her completion of first aid and CPR classes right in the trunk of our now shared BMW.

"Okay, so what do you need?" I yelled out as I swung myself and Von's kit through Jenna's front door.

"What do you have?" She yelled back.

"Could I interest you in a tooth preservation kit?"

Jenna was wearing a miniscule pair of shorts, a tank top, and had blood seeping through the towel that was haphazardly attached to her leg.

"Thank God for Von." Jenna said in a voice that told me exactly what was in her medicine cabinet: expired aspirin, unused sunscreen, and three old knock-off brand Q-tips probably called Kotten Swabz that were covered in eyeliner. The same things that were in the medicine cabinet at our place.

She grabbed the kit and dug through it like a looter in a riot.

"You're welcome."

Jenna rolled her eyes and unrolled the gauze.

"That is," I said as she peeled the towel away from her ankle, "horrific. Do you need stitches?"

"What are they going to stitch together?" She gestured to the skin, or, well, her missing skin.

"Good point." I tried not to gag. "You want me to wrap it?"

"Nope."

Thank God. I heaved an audible sigh of relief, and Jenna laughed.

"So," I said, sitting down next to her.

"So," she replied, not bothering to look up.

We sat in silence while she tended to her leg, and I looked everywhere but her legs.

"You good?" I asked when she finished.

"As new," she said. She used two rolls of gauze, which might have been excessive, but I wasn't complaining.

"Okay, then," I said, trailing off mostly because I had no clue what to say next. And that was a strange feeling. Had things gotten weird between us? Is this where we were? We rarely were alone anymore; now anytime we saw each other it was for couple-y things like drinks or appetizers or game nights that did not involve copious amounts of drinking. Some days, I would be showing Michael my new grill and Von would be in the kitchen with Jendy. Some days I would come home to notes that Von was already at Jendy and Michael's place, could I please stop for wine on my way over? Michael and I started running together every morning; Jendy and Von joined a book club and then missed most of the meetings because of work or because the books were boring. Jenna and Gage had turned in to Jenna and Von. Gage and Jenna morphed into Gage and Michael.

So, I wondered again, had things gotten weird between us?

Then Jenna looked up with a grin, and everything seemed normal, and I refused to speculate where that creeping anxiety of being alone with her had ever come from. "You want a drink?" she proposed. "I think we both deserve a drink for getting through that one."

"Yes, please."

"What's your poison?" Jenna asked as we walked to the fridge.

"Same as always," I answered.

"So," she said, handing me a beer.

"So," I repeated. Things weird? Ok, yeah. Things maybe had gotten a little weird.

"How's Mike?" I asked.

Jenna   "He's good. Same Michael, different day."

"Yeah," I said.

"Yep," she said.

"And you?"

Jenna shrugged and nodded and gestured as if to say, can't complain.

"How's your leg?"

That's when Jenna sighed and kind of laughed. She looked at me, exasperated, eyebrows raised. "You want to talk about my leg? The thing that happened five minutes ago? That's what you really want to ask? That's what you want to talk about?"

We sat in silence, me rolling my bottle of beer between two palms, Jenna alternating between staring out the window and staring at me.

"You're working up to something," Jenna finally said.

I glanced up. Took a gulp of my beer.

"So, why don't you say it," she suggested oh-so-helpfully.

I took another gulp. I ran my hands through my hair. Scratched my chin. Finally, "When did things get weird?" I asked.

"About the time I got engaged," Jenna fired back so quickly it was as if she had prepared in advance.

I looked down.

"This is not Daniel all over again." She said this, but it was more like a question. Was I going to lose my shit? This is what Jenna was really asking. Was I going to pick a fight, throw punches, end up in the hospital?

"No."

"You like him."

"We're friends."

"Me and you? Or you and him?"

"Both," I said, because I wasn't sure what I meant.

"So ask me," she prompted.

How did she know?

I asked. I exploded. Not anger. Confusion. "Why are you getting married? You've known him for what, six months? What the hell is going on? You're marrying him, Jen. Marrying."

"I know."

"Have you even seen him with the flu?" I thought of my fights with Von. Have you seen his father dying from MRSA?

"He's had the flu. He puked in the bed. I had to wash the sheets, and it was the most disgusting thing I've ever accomplished."

"Oh," I said, deflated. And then, "So, why? What makes you so sure? Marriage," I said, like a curse.

Jenna swallowed hard. She looked away, and then back. Straight into my eyes. "He was nice to me."

My jaw dropped. It had to. *"Nice?* That's what you are going with?

"Yeah. He's nice. You don't think he's nice? You don't think he's good to me?"

"Well, yeah." I couldn't argue with that. "He's nice to you."

"He's the first guy who treated me like this."

But what about me? Almost. It was almost out of my mouth and right there in front of us. Jesus, thank God I stopped myself. Because, one – I wasn't always nice to Jenna, and two – did I really want to say that? I mean, really? Did I want it to sound like I somehow felt cheated out of marrying Jenna, that I, in some way, considered myself in the running of lifetime commitment? Yeah. Okay. As if I needed that out there dredging up even more issues between us.

Also, because it wasn't true.

So I said, "But, seriously Jendy, *nice? That's* why you are marrying him?"

"Are you making a case against me marrying Michael?"

"No."

"Then, no, that's not why I'm marrying him, you idiot. Nice is not the only reason I'm marrying him."

"So, you don't know why you're marrying him at lightning speed."

"That's not what I said."

Jenna was being confusing as hell. "Then it's true what they say. You're gonna go with that."

"What are you talking about? What do they say?"

"'When you know you know.' And that's all there is to it. You're going with that. When you know, you know. He's the one. That's what they say."

Jenna laughed. "They're full of shit."

"You're on a roll tonight."

"I'm feeling sentimental. Wedding and all."

I stared at her. Hard.

"They are!" Jenna insisted, "Full of shit. It's because they aren't thinking about the *why* of it all. Or because all their friends were getting married. Or because it was the right time. They had nothing else left to do. It's the After effect. They have finished everything. So they get married. That's why they have no real answer."

"So, your answer to that is *nice*. Because he's nice."

"And with Michael, I matter. All of me matters. We're good together."

"You matter." I wasn't telling her this; I was merely repeating what she said, because I could barely follow her logic. She made a life altering decision on *nice*? And *mattering*?

"And I grow. We grow. The way we grow together...there's nothing like it. The way I grow with him? I couldn't do it with anybody else. I don't know, maybe I'm not making sense. But it makes sense to me, you know?"

And there it was. There was my answer. Maybe because Jenna was right about some people. Some people had no answer to *why*. Why they did the things they did. Why they loved the people they chose to love. Why they married the person they married. Because for some people, marriage was simply one more event that happened to them. To the right person at the right time. Or because everyone else was married. That was the answer to why. And when I thought about it, that answer was a lot weirder than *nice*. Because everyone else is married? That was somehow a better answer? Because I finished everything else and this happened to be the person I was with? That was somehow better? So, yeah, Jenna made complete sense.

"You never thought about it with Von?" Jenna interrupted my jumbled thoughts.

"Marriage?"

"Yeah."

"No," I said, almost too quickly.

Shock crossed Jenna's face. "Never?"

"Are you making a case for marriage to Von?"

Jenna shrugged. "Just surprised is all. Never once?"

"I can honestly say it's never crossed my mind."

"That's fine."

"I'm glad you approve," I said as I shoved the beer away from me. I rolled my eyes. "Thanks so much."

Jenna gave me a funny look. "Why are you acting all pissy?"

I did not answer because the answer was this: I expected Jenna, the one who was getting married, to argue the case for marriage to Von. I could fight back then; I could make my case against it. But Jenna was fine. She didn't care at all. She left me hanging, all bottled up with my half-baked ideas. And also because the second part of my answer was this: I was one of those people Jenna spoke of. I was one of the After People. Marriage was for After. After you got your degree. After you backpacked through Europe. After you got the good job. After you got your promotion. After you got your raise. After you bought the house. After you moved across country. Marriage was for whomever you happened to be with – who had a both a good 401k and personality – after all those things were accomplished. Marriage was for when you ran out of things to do. And children were for when you ran out of married things to do, whatever those things were.

The right person. The right time. I could easily see myself answering the question of *why* with, "When you know, you know."

I was one of those people. And Jenna was very much not.

And that made me pissy.

"Has Von said something to you about marriage?" I asked.

"So that's why you're pissy," Jenna incorrectly guessed.

"You're not answering my question."

"Because she didn't say anything," Jenna assured me. "She never said anything about marriage either. I was just curious is all."

I didn't believe her. Why else would Jenna have brought up the idea of me marrying Von? Because the topic had to have come up between them. They had all that time alone together, all that time to talk. A lot of that time Jenna had been thinking about being engaged or actually being engaged to Michael.

I stared at Jenna.

Jenna stared back.

We stared long enough for Jenna to start laughing, an uncomfortable sort of chuckle. "What?" she finally asked.

"You're bleeding through," I said, nodding to her bandaged leg.

Gage

Gage!" Roxie's voice cut through the conversation Cody and I were having. "Gage, you need to go talk to her. She is freaking out."

"Freaking out? About what?" I was already following Roxie through the complicated twist of hallways that filled Michael's parents' house. Correction: mansion. Apparently, Michael had grown up freakishly rich. "Where is she?"

"Back here. She keeps talking about her dad. I can't get her to calm down. Just...just do something. Okay?"

"Okay. Okay. I'll figure it out."

Roxie stopped outside the door, wringing her hands nervously. She looked like she was biting her cheeks. What the hell happened to Jenna?

I pushed through to the overly quiet room. A bedroom, I surmised quickly, a powdery pink one, filled with ceramic knickknacks and lace pillows. I felt big and awkward and way too male to be in this room. To be stumbling my way through it. To Jenna. Only Jenna. Jenna alone, sitting on the bed in a light blue dress, one of those tiny little veils over reaching over her forehead, stopping just above her nose. I stopped. She looked amazing.

"Jenna."

She glanced up, and it was then I saw her face. Puffy, raw, red. "What is going on?"

A wracking sob escaped her, and she shook her head, unable to speak, and covered her face with one hand. She looked embarrassed. I had not seen her this bad in a long time. Gingerly, I sat down next to her.

"Do you need—do you want something?" I asked in a voice that we both knew referred to pills.

Jenna shook her head. "I am not taking a Xanax on my wedding day. I should not have to take a Xanax on my wedding day."

"I'm sure Cody has some weed."

"Cody's an insurance agent."

"And insurance agents don't smoke weed?"

Jenna let out one snort of laughter over her tears. That could be a good sign. She rubbed at her eyes, and I started to breath a sigh of relief, my hand sliding to her back, ready to make some other smartass remark and get her down the aisle, when she stopped me with a determined look.

"Gage," she said.

"What?" My hand stopped the figure eight motion it was making on her back.

"I can't do this."

"What?" Panic mixed with something very strange, some emotion I could not identify, ran through me.

"I don't know." Then she kept repeating the same thing over and over and over while I sat there, stunned. Silent. Still. I hoped my body didn't give away the racing thoughts that ate at my brain.

Jesus. Is she serious? Do I go out there and grab Michael? Do I make some announcement? My God, this is insane. She can't be serious. Shit like this doesn't happen for real. "What about him being nice? He's a nice guy. He's nice," I kept repeating like an idiot.

"I need my dad," Jenna said, interrupting the ice flow of panic coursing out of me. "I want my dad. This is so much, and there's nobody here for me. I'm alone, God, I'm alone and right after this I'm moving and I want my dad and --"

"Jendy. Stop."

She fell silent immediately and stared. Expectantly. Quietly. Waiting for me to save the day.

I had absolutely nothing to say.

We stared at each other.

"This," I began then stopped. Took a breath. God, if you're actually real, give me some word. "Jendy," I said again. "This shit is fucked up."

We stared at each other again as the words sank in.

A giggle, a small, kind of lunatic sounding giggle escaped her lips. She moved a hand to cover her mouth.

I chuckled with her. "You're not the kind of girl who does this on her wedding day."

"Do you have brain fever?" She exclaimed then barreled on while I wondered what brain fever was. "I'm exactly that kind of girl, Gage!"

"Okay. So we go from there. You are that kind of girl. The girl who wants to run on her wedding day."

"Oh, my God. How strangely cliché of me."

"I don't think that's cliché. Most people do get married on their wedding days."

"Thanks. Thanks for your amazing support."

"What am I supposed to do?"

"What am *I* supposed to do?"

"I don't know, Jendy," I said. "*Marry him?*" I suggested, as if it were a novel idea.

"Oh, my God. I hate you. Get Roxie."

"No. *You* get your shit together," I said forcefully. "What the hell do you think you're doing?"

"If I knew what I was doing, you would be the first person I would inform." She snorted then, laughter mixed with tears.

I touched her back. "You have us," I said. "You have me. You have Roxie."

"I don't have my dad."

"You don't have your dad," I agreed, more matter-of-fact than sadly. Did I lose points for that? Should I comfort her instead? "You have Michael. And he's nice." I reminded her. "You matter to him. And he matters to you." The sentiment sounded so trite, so stupid that I don't know why it made her smile. But it did. A smile bloomed on her face.

"We're here," I reassured her. "We are right here. Like, seriously, next to you. Roxie and I are literally right next to you up there."

She rubbed at her face once more and looked at me.

"Good?" I asked.

She nodded, her eyes still a little wild looking, her breath still shaky.

"Yeah, you're good." I smoothed my hands over the back of her hair, the part not covered by that birdcage looking veil. "You're hair looks a little shitty," I said, and she laughed then blew her nose. "But you're good."

"I'm good," she agreed.

I touched her shoulders, rubbed my hands up and down her arms reassuringly. "You're good."

"You're here."

"I'm here." I cupped one hand behind her head and kissed her forehead.

"I'll be okay." She closed her eyes at my touch.

"You'll be okay." I kissed one eyelid. "Okay?" I rubbed my thumbs over her cheeks then kissed them.

She opened her eyes. "Okay," she said, her breath hitching.

"Let's go?"

"Let's go."

I smiled at her then kissed her on the mouth, only once, a calming, platonic kind of kiss. "You matter, Jen. Don't forget that."

She shifted and looked up at me, her face flushed. "I'm going to miss you, Gage," she said softly. Her breathing slowed, the soft, shallow pants rising and falling against me.

My hand curled into hers, tugging her toward me. Everything I did felt nothing like a choice and everything like compulsion. It was nine years - hell, it was a million years - pulling me toward her.

My eyes flashed to hers. *I'm sorry. I'm so sorry.*

I searched her face, waiting for the *No, Gage* or the *Stop it, Gage* or the *What the hell is wrong with you, Gage?*

Jenna's eyes never left mine.

I watched her bite her bottom lip then close her eyes. Her chin inched upward, close enough to my mouth to know what she expected. The breath I didn't realize I was holding released in one swift whoosh.

I shifted, swallowed hard. I dropped my forehead to hers. Closed my eyes. Our mouths were an inch away. Less than an inch. My hands drifted toward her hips and squeezed.

And then I felt it. The moment, and the fact that it changed.

"Gage," she said, her quiet voice stopping me. I could feel her breath on my lips.

I opened my eyes.

She stared back at me, her eyes wide, unblinking. They were clear now. They were certain.

"I can't do this. We can't do this."

"Why not?" I asked.

"I'm not that kind of girl. You're not that kind of guy. And," she said with a truth that stabbed like a knife, "he's not my consolation prize. You were right. He's the one."

I took one deep breath. Our eyes met one final time.

"You going to go get married," I whispered.

"I'm going to go get married," she agreed, her words soft, almost not there at all.

If God were badass enough to send anyone deserving to their own personal hell, I knew what was waiting for me in the afterlife. And it wasn't ice and Jenna's tedious boyfriends. No. It was Jenna herself. An eternity of Jenna. Walking down the aisle. To another man.

And I stood up there.

With Roxie, who was clueless as to what happened with Jenna in that guest room five minutes earlier.

When asked by the minister, I handed Jenna the ring.

When asked by the photographer, I smiled.

And Jenna smiled.

But her eyes never quite met mine for the rest of the night.

She said not one word to me.

And nobody noticed.

Well, almost nobody.

"What did you do?" Roxie asked later as she danced with me.

"Let's not talk about it."

I didn't have to say anything else. Roxie knew. She was a damn psychological expert now. She knew.

"You had nine years," she said.

"I love Von."

"I know you do," she said sympathetically. "It'll be okay, Gage. Everything will work out."

But when we looked at each other, we both knew.

I would never see Jenna again.

Part Three
The Way We Weren't
Three Years Later

Sunday, January 1, 2012

Jenna

There was nothing like kicking off the New Year with a pregnancy test.

Jenna waited anxiously in the bathroom, sitting on the edge of the tub, jiggling her knees anxiously, like she had every month for the past year: full of trepidation and excitement and fear and terror and hope. Full of everything every single time; full of everything except one thing: the baby she and Michael wanted.

The box said it took a minute to deliver the results. But after the first one last January, Jenna realized it really didn't take that long. The plus or minus showed up almost immediately. But after the first five negatives; after shaking it like an old-timey thermometer then confirming to herslef the result would change, Jenna didn't want to see it instantaneously anymore. So she would wait the full three minutes without peeking, sure that was the trick to getting a positive. You had to trick this inanimate object into thinking you did not care one way or the other what it said about the contents of your uterus. But not even that had changed anything as the next six were negative. For Jenna, it was always a No. No, Jenna. No baby baking in this oven. But still, Jenna performed the ritual monthly like a painful religious rite.

It was getting to be worrisome.

The negatives. They took Jenna back to a place she never wanted to go anymore.

All the negatives. Their first year together was hard. Nobody had warned her about that. Nobody told her what it would be like to lose a friend. Nobody told her what it would be like to gain a husband. How both thrilling and depressing moving away from everything she knew in Pittsburgh, back to everything she kind of, sort of remembered in D.C. How strange it would be to live so close to her college town as an adult, as a real and functioning person in society, not a half-way kind of grown up person on a campus. Nobody told her what it would be like to be married to a police officer. She didn't know that she would feel connected, bonded to Michael in a way she never felt when they dated. She didn't know that she'd jump every time she heard sirens at night when he was on duty. Nobody told her what it would be like to get a call. A call that Michael was shot on duty and she would need to get to the hospital right away.

All the negatives.

But, Michael was quick to remind her, there were all those positives.

There was that call, that terrifying night that she as she raced to the hospital and braced herself for terrifying news. Michael could be paralyzed. Michael could be dead.

Except.

Except he wasn't. He wasn't paralyzed. He wasn't dead.

Michael had been shot. In the back. Once. And he was fine. Not even critical. Michael was stable. Sore. Resting. Then he was recuperating. The doctor said he would probably always have back pain, the way the bullet nicked his spine. But for now - and forever - he was fine.

And there was that other positive, Michael reminded her. The positive Michael's doctor gave Jenna, a gift completely unexpected. The neurosurgeon, Dr. Newhouser, notice Jenna's limp once, casually asked what happened, and Jenna told him. About the fire, the jumping, the fence, the nerve damage. "Wow," he had said, "that's quite a story. I must say I was expecting something much more mundane." They all kind of laughed, because his tone was so funny and they were all feeling so good because Michael was doing so well. But then Dr. Newhouser said – out of nowhere – he said, "Oh, and by the way, I know what that is. I know why you feel that pain. And I can fix it for you. If you are ever interested." Jenna and Michael – who was eating green Jell-O at the time – stared incredulously.

And he fixed it. Not in, like, one day or anything. But over the course of a year and three surgeries, Dr. Newhouser fixed Jenna's leg. Like Michael and his back, she still felt occasional twinges of pain.

But she could wear normal jeans and run without pain, and that was something.

And there was that other thing. Being published. Jenna had been published. Her first novel had been published over a year ago. Jenna and Michael plodded to the local bookstore to stare in shock her name, Jenna Gressa-Graham, printed across the front of a yellow hardback book shelved in the Local Author section. They stared. They ran their fingers over the pages, fussed over the beautiful cover art. They placed it back on the shelf. Gently. They stared some more.

"I want a baby," Michael had said.

Jenna then turned to him. He was still staring at her novel on the shelf, a little bit dazed. "Me too."

He reached for Jenna's hand and their fingers twined around each other like branches of a growing tree, and they smiled, eyes never leaving her novel.

That was before. Before they knew anything about the future of Jenna Gressa-Graham, the author.

So all of that made Jenna wonder. It made Jenna agonized. What if she proved equally unsuccessful at raising a small human? Perhaps the trouble with getting pregnant was the universe telling her she would be a horrible mother and perhaps it was best to not even try. A few months back Michael suggest fertility testing. Jenna resisted the idea. All because of That Thought. That was the thought that brought terror to her heart.

Jenna did want a baby, right? She questioned it every time she took a test.

Yes. Sure. Absolutely she did.

Jenna tapped her fingers. Checked her watch.

Three minutes. Done.

Jenna picked up the test.

Negative.

She padded down to the kitchen.

Michael sat at the table, a mug of coffee in his hands. He used to sit in the bathroom with Jenna. Until test five. Then she needed some alone time. He raised his eyebrows at Jenna.

Jenna shook her head.

"Aw, Jen." He stretched out a hand, and Jenna took it. He pulled her into his lap. "It's okay, babe. It will happen."

"I don't know," she said.

"It will."

It won't, Jenna thought, but she stopped short of arguing. What good would it do?

"Have you given any more thought to…you know," Michael sounded almost reluctant to bring up the fertility testing Jenna knew he was dancing around. And for good reason. Jenna always said no.

"I don't want to." Jenna shook her head resolutely. "If it happens, it happens."

"But we could know, you know, if something is…wrong."

"Nothing is wrong with me!" Jenna cried and tried to push away from him.

"No. No." Michael pulled back, not letting her get away. "Jen, nobody ever said it was you. I never said that."

"It's always the woman."

"Says the feminist?"

Jenna stifled a chuckle. "I'll think about it," she relented.

"We're still young."

"Speak for yourself," Jenna grumbled.

"Aw, is my ball-and-chain a little grumpy about her age?" Jenna felt Michael's smile in her ear. "You're still hot."

"More like Icy-Hot," Jenna corrected.

"You know how to turn me on," Michael said and nipped at her ear.

"Shut up," Jenna laughed. "We need dinner. Let's go out. I need to get out."

"How could you say no to this?" Michael teased and pressed his fingers into Jenna's hips, bit her neck. Memories of Gage squeezing her hips the night before her wedding came flooding back and Jenna cringed inwardly. Why now? Why now, when you haven't thought about him in months? Jenna took a calming breath. It's okay. It was nothing, and that nothing was a long time ago.

Jenna turned her face to Michael's mouth and kissed him, full and aching and until she was flushing.

"Whoa," Michael breathed. "That was unexpected."

"I'm starving."

"Me too." Michael's eyes were wide with desire. His arms wrapped around her waist.

"Let's eat."

Michael sighed and dropped his head. "You're killing me."

Jenna laughed and kissed him a second time. "I'll make it up to you." She leaned into his ear. "Tonight," she whispered.

"Oh, well, in that case." He kissed Jenna back and then straightened, still holding Jenna in his arms. "Ow." For a second Jenna thought he was teasing her about being heavy. But then he set her down and pressed a hand to his back.

Jenna's smile turned to a frown. "Your back?"

"Yeah. It's not bad. Off and on. Twinges. Nothing big."

"You should call the chiropractor. Or Dr. Newhouser. It's been acting up more than normal."

"Eh." He grimaced and twisted his torso back and forth. "It's nothing."

"You run too much."

"I don't *run too much*," he said, mimicking her concern.

"Don't make fun of me."

"I'd never," he said, then smirked and wrapped his arms around her. "Give us a kiss there, Killer."

Jenna relented and gave him a peck on the cheek. "You're not going to call, are you?"

"I'll call, I'll call. If I don't call, you'll nag me to death."

"What?" Jenna stuck out her lower lip. "I'm not a nag."

"Speaking of calling," Michael said, "your agent called."

"Good deflection there, Officer."

"That's my job," he grinned. "I told her you would call back."

"Was it urgent?"

"It was about your new book deal."

"Oh?" Jenna said, trying to sound nonchalant, even as her stomach exploded in butterflies.

"Yeah," he said, matching her tone.

They both stared at each other a long time finally before Jenna erupted in with a squeal. Michael laughed and pulled her onto his lap.

Jenna smiled. "It still doesn't feel real."

"I don't know if it ever will."

Jenna laughed. "So we going out to eat or what?"

"Is my big-time author wife paying?"

"You mean the one with horrible reviews?"

"Of course," he said and Jenna laughed. Michael laughed and kissed her. "Let's get the heck out of here."

Gage

I finished my five miles and sat panting in sand. Dover did his little circle thing then, tongue hanging, sat panting beside me.

"Thirsty?" I fished he collapsible bowl from my pocket, took a swig of water then added the rest to Dover's bowl.

He drank, sloshing water everywhere.

"Pig," I said, and he kept drinking now making snorting and snuffing sounds as if to mock me. He was no Bruster, who was back home and probably meticulously licking his paws for the fifth time this morning.

I sighed and laid a hand on Dover's huge head.

I stared out into the ocean.

California stared back at me.

My limbs started to twitch. I stretched out one leg. I rolled my shoulders.

I stared into the ocean some more.

I thought about running fast, jumping in. Dover would love it. All I'd have to ask was, "Swim, boy?" and he would already be in the water. Me, I'd take a little longer. But then I junked the idea. Today was a work day. I fished a hairband from my pocket, and pulled my now longer hair into it. Desperate Bachelor is what everyone at work now called my hairstyle.

I rarely thought of Jenna anymore, but sometimes, every great once in a while, I was on the beach, and then suddenly I was gone, and it was the week of Jenna's wedding.

You'd think the first week after Jenna's wedding would have been the hardest. And if you asked me at the end of that week (before everything else that happened a month later), I would have agreed, yes, hell yes, that was the worst week.

That was the week I stupidly decided proposing to Von was a whip smart idea and the only thing left to do after Jenna and I ended contact with each other.

"What should we do tonight?" Von asked on her night off, her first night off in weeks. And because Von was always so busy working, she had not noticed my off mood, because I was asshole enough to think kissing – or at least trying to kiss – Jenna five minutes before her wedding was a great idea.

I was full of great ideas that week.

"I have an idea," I answered.

"What?" She at the table hunched over her new iPhone.

"You marry me."

Von's blank face stared back at me. Then, with a start, her eyes lit. "Oh," she laughed and hit me playfully. "Don't kid like that. I almost believed you." She hunkered back down over her iPhone.

I pulled the ring box from my pocket, opening the lid with a flick of my thumb and forefinger. "I'm not joking." Three stones, diamonds that glittered under the kitchen light. Three stones that followed all the rules that really made no sense to me. Carat and cut and something else I couldn't remember. Three months' worth of paychecks I had taken out of my savings account. All the rules. I followed them all.

Von's mouth dropped. I, at that time, could not decide if the coloring draining from her face was good or bad. She looked at the ring, then to me. Then back to the ring. "Elliot. Oh, my God." She stared at the ring, her eyes wide and round. She pressed her knuckles to her mouth. I couldn't read her expression, but the silence, the wordless full minute was at best described painful, but more accurately described as a rusty, guts-being-torn-bodily-from-me quiet. A knob of fear twisted through me.

"Does this have anything to do with Jenna?" Von asked, her voice low, her gaze not fully meeting mine.

The knob of fear twisted into a tight ball of anger. Of everything she could have asked, anything she could have answered, this was one thing I had not expected. Because it was true? I pushed that thought from my head. "This has nothing to do with Jenna."

"Really? Jenna - Jenna your best friend; Jenna who got married, like, ten minutes ago--"

"It wasn't ten minutes ago," I interrupted, frustration slipping into my words.

Von gave me a look that said, *duh, Elliot, but it might as well have been ten minute ago.*

"No. It's not about her. It's about you. About us."

"You're not losing Jenna."

Guilt replaced the anger. Von had no idea what she was saying. "Oh, my God, Von. This has nothing to do with her!" I snapped to box shut and threw it on the table. We both watch it skid past her and clatter to the floor. Neither one of us reached for it.

"Okay, okay." Von's voice took on that overly patient tone, I was used to hearing her use on stressed out clients. "Maybe I'm wrong.

Irritated, I shrugged her off. "Don't pull that shit with me, Von. You don't need to placate me, and you sure as hell don't need to play therapist."

Von's eyes flamed. "Don't need to play therapist? Ha!" She jumped up without warning and poked one finger into my chest. "That's hilarious."

"What the hell are you talking about?"

"Everything in your life has something to do with Jenna. What she does or what she doesn't do. What she needs when she's sad. What she needs when she's happy. I'm not a therapist, but I'm a human being with eyes and a brain. Jeez. Sometimes *I* need a therapist."

"You're not making any sense."

"Do you know how excruciating this is for me? To watch you two like I'm the other girl in some rom-com, the oblivious idiot waiting for you and Jenna to come to your senses. Except I'm not oblivious. Try living that life. And worst of all, I like Jenna! I like her." Tears started rolling down her face.

"Von. Von, what the hell is wrong with you? I'm proposing to you. Proposing." I drew the word out. "Do you understand that? You're not the other girl. You are *the* girl."

"Of course you say that. Of course you do. Because you're wonderful. Blind as a cavefish, but wonderful."

I smiled a little, laughed softly, because maybe this would turn out all right.

"Von." My hands dropped to her waist. "Von, I love you. This has to do with you. Only you. This is our life. Our future. Nothing else. This is about forever."

"I have a future, Elliot. I'm living my life. I made this business here. It's all I can focus on right now." Her cheeks were tearstained, but her eyes were clear, her voice firm. She dropped back to the chair, looking, I don't know, shell-shocked? How could I have screwed everything up so badly that the woman I thought I would marry looked shell-shocked at the idea?

"Why did you have to do this now, Elliot? It was going so well."

"It still can. We can do this." I laid my palm on her thigh, shook it. "We can do it together."

She looked down. Her eyes refuse to meet mine. She exhaled a long, shaky breath. "Can we go backwards? Back to before you asked this?"

So, yeah, that week sucked. Especially when it ended with an awkwardness so thick between us, nothing seemed to break it. She spent more hours at work. I spent more hours at work. We spent so much time away from each other, away from the awkwardness of each other that the only natural step was, one month after I proposed marriage, to break-up.

So, no, apparently we could not go backwards.

The week Von moved out, that was the week I thought was the worst. It was at the very least the drunkest week I had in a long while. It was easier assuming I was throwing up from whisky rather than torment and misery. That assumption made the alcohol go down that much smoother and come back up that much quicker.

The hardest week? In retrospect, the hardest week was the one that snuck up on me. Months later.

"OMGeeee!" Brittany, the girl I met four hours earlier celebrating her twenty-first – twenty-second? – birthday, squealed and fell back to the bed.

OMGee? Were people really saying this now? How old was I? I scratched my face. She fanned hers with both hands. "Woo! It's so hot," she complained, twisting her long curling hair over one shoulder.

"You want some water?" I tugged on a pair of shorts.

"You should get an air conditioner. Can't believe a guy like you doesn't have conditioned air." She grinned up at me.

I gave her a lopsided grin, but something was twisting in my gut. "No reason to pay for air." I swallowed hard.

She giggled. "I guess that's true."

"I'll get you that water."

I stumbled out to the kitchen, still a little tipsy.

"Where did you get this?" Brittany called out somewhere behind me. Ugh. She was one of those girls. The wanderers. The ones that felt it necessary to walk around your place and comment on everything.

I turned to see her touching the painting on my wall. "Spain."

"You went to Spain?"

"Once in college."

"Wow," She said, impressed, like it was some great feat that took more than a passport and a few grand.

I shrugged and turned to the kitchen.

"You have a nice place." She pushed herself to sit on the counter and then took a sip of the water I handed her.

"Thanks," I said and did the whole nod and look around thing, like I was seeing my place for the first time.

"I thought it would have been…bigger."

The water glass stopped half-way to my mouth. I narrowed my eyes at her.

But she glanced around happily, totally oblivious to my scrutiny.

"Well, ah," I coughed. "I'm going to bed."

"I'll come too," she said and bounced down the hall.

I smirked at her, but a much larger part of me wanted to beg her to leave.

"Hey, what's this room?" Brittany started to push on the door to Von's old office. It was cleared out, empty, and depressing.

"That's just," Quickly, I covered her hand on the knob to stop her, "a spare bedroom."

She looked startled and her eyes darted back to the room, like maybe I was crazy and it was full of severed heads and hers would be next.

"There's nothing fun in there," I said, shaking my head with a little grin, trying to let her know I wasn't a psychopath.

"Nothing?" She pouted a little and ran a finger down my chest.

"Nah," I said with a grin, and I fisted my hands in her hair to give it a little tug. "But there might be something fun in this room," I raised my eyebrows, nodded at my bedroom.

"Oh, is there?" She bit her lip and grinned.

"I don't know," I teased and backed her into the room. "We'll have to see."

She squealed happily as I picked her up and flipped her onto the bed.

Later in the night though, Brittany asked, "Do you have a rubber band or anything to pull up my hair? I'm still so hot."

"Yes, you are," I said with a grin and smacked her ass. She shrieked with laughter. "There's probably one in here." I pulled open a drawer and fished around for one. I pulled it out. I squinted at it. It was not a rubber band; it was a hair band. Confused, I rolled it through my fingers wondering what girl would have gone to the trouble of putting a hairband in my night stand.

Then it hit me. It was Von's. The one thing, the only thing, she forgot.

I tried to stuff it back in the drawer before Brittany saw it, but it was too late.

"Oh, awesome! Even better." She grabbed the band and twined it through her hair as she chattered on. "You really know how to take care of the ladies, Gage. Rubber bands. They get all stuck in your hair. They're like..." She chattered, but I had stopped listening.

I stared at my hand as if the band were still there.

Brittany leaned over me with a smile and turned the light off.

The next morning, as I watched Von's hairband bob away from me in Brittany's hair? That week. That was the hardest week.

And the next week?

That was the week I packed my bags for California.

I was not sure why Von and Jenna and the week following her wedding cropped up in my mind. Enough time had passed that I rarely thought of either Jenna or Von. So much time had passed, in fact, that it felt downright foreign to think of my life three years ago. I almost kissed Jenna? I actually proposed to Von? The events of that time felt ancient and false, as if the incidents happened to someone else, as if I were remembering a story once told to me by a friend or co-worker.

Dover and I ran the beach every morning. Seven days a week. Today was no exception. Soon we would make our way home. I would drink a green shake, turn on the television for Bruster and Snuggins –the cat that was bought, named, and gifted to me by my last ex-girlfriend exactly two weeks before we broke up, the cat that officially made me one of those weird-o "animal collectors" or whatever was the male equivalent of Crazy Cat Lady. Dover and I would leave in my Audi – an Audi that when I first bought reminded me of Von and now reminded me of California – then I'd drop him at Dog Gone, the doggy daycare down the street. I would spend exactly nine hours at the office, still accounting and still hating it. I'd flirt with Emily at the photocopier; she would recap the last episode of The Bachelor I did not care about. Emily moved to San Diego from Denver about six months ago. Sometimes we would sit on the beach and eat fish tacos at lunch; sometimes we'd have sex on weekends.

She was built nicely; her calves were impressive, and she laughed when I told her that the first time we slept together. She missed Colorado, and she wasn't sure why she even moved here. A bad breakup, a new start, she would say with a shrug. Tell me about it, I'd agree with one of those world-weary sighs. You're a morose son of a bitch, she would say, and we would both laugh. She would smoke a cigarette on my porch, saying "I only smoke after sex." Sometimes I'd stare at her through the double paned glass of the sliding door and wonder what Jenna was up to. That only happened the first two or three times. After that, I would watch Emily and wonder when she was coming back to bed.

Week nights were the loner nights, though. Scotch-and-a-book nights. Nights spent doing things my frat boy past would have laughed about, and laughed gleefully. What a douche, they would have said.

Tonight, Dover sat at my feet, and I looked at him curiously. "What do you think, Dov? Should we finish Jenna's book?"

Dover's tail thumped twice. It always thumped twice no matter what I asked him, and I took the action to mean yes, mostly because I only asked him questions that I wanted yes for an answer. Should I call Em tonight, invite her over? *Thump thump.* Are we sick of green shakes, boy? Do we want a Baconator for breakfast instead? *Thump thump.* Dover was the definition of man's best friend.

I pulled out Jenna's book. I had found it on Amazon about three weeks ago, and God, did it suck. In a good way. A spiraling, depressed sort of book I could imagine Jenna writing, she convincingly laid out the story of a woman diagnosed with psychosis as she tried to decipher whether she was still alive or now dead. Jenna published it a year ago, but I did not find out about it until I was in the breakroom reading one of Em's old magazines, those gossipy kinds that had all the celebrity news. It had some article about upcoming movies, and I kind of skimmed it, looking mostly for the pictures, when I saw *Gressa-Graham* float before my eyes. My eyes flashed back a paragraph. Her newest book had been optioned for a movie.

I immediately Googled Jenna's name. Amazon reviews were mixed. Some horrendous. They were the ones proclaiming that Jenna Gressa-Graham was dumb cunt or that she was the shame of the nation or how she got a three picture movie deal out of such drivel nobody would never know. I felt terrible for Jenna, having to read that shit, but then I wondered, well if some bigshot movie producer thought your drivel was actually fantastic, and you signed a movie deal, did it matter what the pleebs thought? Probably not. Jenna probably cared though. Or not. I had no idea. I didn't know her anymore.

Dover and I finished another chapter. I sighed and set the book down.

"Am I pathetic?" I asked Dover.

Thump thump. Two thumps could mean *no* when I wanted it to.

"Should we call Em?"

Thump thump.

"It's Thursday, though, Dov. Do you think that will mean something? Or, more importantly, do you think she'll think it means something?"

Thump thump. Two thumps could mean *I don't know* when I needed it to.

I chugged the rest of the Scotch then wiped my hands on my pants. "All right, all right. We'll call Emily." Yes, I needed to call Emily. Not only was I turning Dover and me into a couple, but I was turning us into a "we" couple.

"You want me to come over now?" Emily's voice registered surprise.

"We could carpool tomorrow."

"Um...yeah. Sure! Gimme, like, half an hour or so?"

"Sounds good."

"You want me to pick up something to eat?"

"Sounds great."

"Any preference? Chinese? Tacos?"

"Surprise me."

"Okay...um...okay. See you in a bit."

I hung up the phone and reached down to Dover.

He met me halfway, stretching his golden head close to my hand. I scrubbed his fur a little more enthusiastically than I planned. "She's on her way, buddy." I smiled. In the beginning, three years ago, I felt terrible most days. But that time was ancient, and this time was different. Most nights I felt great. Especially on the nights Emily stopped over. I trudged off to the bathroom to splash some cologne.

Sunday, October 9, 2012

Jenna

Elliot Gageby was staring at Jenna.

In the privacy of her own home office, Elliot Gageby was right across from her, and he was smiling.

From a computer.

On Facebook.

Friend Request from Elliot Gageby popped up under a little red notification. Jenna jumped up and away from the computer as if it had thrown a bucket of ice water at her.

She paced the room. She crept back to the computer, took in his face which was staring back at her, smirking back at her.

Then she logged off.

Turned off the screen.

Run, Jenna, run.

She ran.

To the kitchen. For tea that she never poured.

To the bathroom. To brush teeth she had brushed already.

To the kitchen again, wondering where she set her mug of tea until she realized she had never poured one.

Jenna paced the house, lapped the house, practically marathoned the house.

To the kitchen again. Finally poured some tea.

Then she proceeded to do the whole routine all over again.

I hate you, Gageby, Jenna thought as she jumped up a third time, leaving her mug of mint green tea steaming on the marble countertop. Jenna hurriedly logged back onto Facebook.

Friend Request. Elliot Gageby.

Still there. Of course it would still be there, Jenna. Duh.

She had set up the Facebook page not even two weeks ago. How did he find her so quickly? Roxie. It had to be through Roxie.

Jenna tapped a finger against her teeth.

Elliot Gageby. Accept. Deny.

Jenna chewed a thumbnail.

Accept.

Deny.

Her hand twitched on the mouse. Hovered over the options.

Accept.

Deny.

Michael banged in through the door, back from his long run in preparation for the Marine Corps Marathon in a couple weeks.

Jenna jumped and hastily turned off the monitor.

Then she made a face at her dramatics.

What was she doing? There was nothing for her to worry about. She was not doing anything wrong. Michael knew she and Gage were (used to be) friends. Michael always liked Gage. He asked her about Gage's whereabouts occasionally. He mused once or twice about his disappearing act after the wedding. Jenna switched the monitor back on.

"Jenna?" Michael panted in the doorway.

Why was Jenna thinking of Gage in that bedroom, close to her on the bed, the way she felt when he lifted her veil and kissed her forehead, her eyelid, her cheek. Jenna shook the memory from her head. *Now, Jenna. Now is when you feel bad*, she thought sarcastically.

"You have a good run?" She turned her face up to Michael's for a kiss as he walked over.

"Always. I'm all sweaty," he apologized and pecked her quickly. "I kept getting these back cramps almost the whole time."

"Still?" Jenna turned in her chair. "You run too much."

"You can never run too much," he said. "You writing?"

Jenna ignored his attempt to change subjects. "You need to--"

He held his hands up in defense. "I called the chiropractor. I called the neurologist. I called them all." He said before she could finish.

"All right then. I'm done caring about your health."

"Thank you," he said magnanimously.

Jenna punched his arm.

"Ow, Killer, calm down." He said leaned over Jenna's computer. "Whatcha doing?"

Jenna tapped her fingers on the desk. Best bet was to be honest. Then she would have nothing to feel guilty about. "Look who sent me a friend request." Jenna nodded at the computer.

"Elliot Gageby?" He took a swig from his water bottle. "Who's that? The publisher?"

"Gage."

"Oh, yeah. Gage. I forgot his real name." His face morphed into one of those considering, don't-talk-to-me-until-I'm-done-reading looks. The one Jenna thought made him look so cute.

Michael touched the screen. "Look at that. He lives in California. So that's why he disappeared."

"Hmm. Yeah." Jenna vaguely remembered Gage bringing up California once or twice. She'd have to call Roxie, see what was up with Gage and California.

"And he's in a relationship."

"Really?" Jenna's head swiveled back to the profile. *Status: It's Complicated.*

"That says *It's Complicated*, Michael."

"It's complicated," Michael sing-songed back. "It's complicated."

Was it Von? Could it still be Von? Gage pulled the disappearing act on Michael, and Jenna pulled the disappearing act on Von. None of them talked or knew anything about each other anymore.

"Well," Jenna thumped hers hands down on the desk, "good for him." She nodded.

"Yeah. Good for him," Michael agreed companionably. "Odd how he kind of fell off the map after we got married."

"No, it's not," Jenna said. Did that come out too defensively? She deliberately calmed her tone. "We live far apart. It's not *that* strange."

"Yeah, but, Jen, you two were, like, sewn at the hip." He bumped Jenna's hip with his.

"No, we weren't," Jenna rolled her eyes as she brushed off his comment.

"You weren't?" He chuckled. "You lived together for years." He kissed Jenna lightly on the nape of her neck. "You're forgetting I was there."

"We were just friends," she snapped.

"Killer." Michael gave Jenna a strange look. "I know that. I am just making conversation."

Jenna took a deep breath. What was wrong with her? It had been years. She loved Michael. "Sorry, hun. I'm stressed. Thinking about a million things."

Michael patted her back and meandered out to the kitchen. Jenna listened to him open the refrigerator, pictured him pouring his protein shake like always. "You going to friend him?" She heard his voice drift in from the kitchen.

She stared at the screen, at Gage's face.

Accept?

Deny?

Saturday, November 10, 2012

Gage

"Rox, I can't believe you're leaving us." I swooped in for a hug. "Have you lost your mind?"

Roxie laughed deeply. "Mr. California. Puh-lease. You left me years ago."

"Oh, yeah. That's right. It's the fact that you're being stupid and moving farther north into the dark and snow that makes you crazy."

"Speaking of snow, you're covered in it. Get off of me." She pushed me away playfully then brushed at her clothes.

"I can't believe you actually came in from California. It means a lot to us." Lance said good-naturedly as he took my coat. Lance was the reason Roxie was moving. Lance took a job up north, and Roxie had found work at a college up there. Professor of forensics or forensic psychology or something complicated and ambitious and smart like that. "It means a lot to us."

"I figured I'd take a few weeks off. I won't be able to get in for Christmas, so I'm going to see the parents." Dad had gotten married last month to an artist from Arlington. A courthouse type of wedding nobody expected. Kristen drove down from New York, but with such short notice I had not been able to book a ticket. Kristen played them some sonata on a keyboard she insisted on bringing to the courthouse, signed their wedding certificate as their witness, took a million pictures she posted to Facebook, and broke down at least three times crying when she rehashed the whole ceremony to me later.

"Well, aren't you the sweetest son," Roxie said with no trace of sarcasm. She kissed my cheek. "How is your dad?"

"Doing great," I said. "We'll probably do Thanksgiving."

"And did you bring the girl?" Roxie looked expectantly behind me.

"It's complicated," I said.

She screwed up her face. "Oh, boo. I wanted to meet her."

Now I gave her a look. "So do I get to come in or are you going to let me freeze my California ass off here in your foyer?"

"Oh, my God," Roxie shrieked. "What am I thinking? Come in, come in! And speaking of Thanksgiving, do you remember the bacon turkey? Lance, did I tell you about that one time in college, like what, a week for before Thanksgiving, Gage? We had this-"

"The bacon turkey and the Tofurky showdown? Yes, you did tell me." He looked at me. "Several hundred times."

"My Tofurky won. It definitely won." Roxie taunted.

"Babe, that Tofurky only won because Jenna felt sorry for you. She and I ate the entire bacon turkey after you left," I whispered tauntingly.

"That's a lie you lying liar." Roxie turned to Lance. "That's a lie."

"What about that roommate chick of yours? What was her name again?"

"Terri," Roxie answered.

"I can't believe you remember her name."

"How could I forget?"

"What happened to her? Get caught under a pile of magazines?"

"She's a professional organizer in Tulsa."

"Are you kidding me?" I laughed. "How do you know this stuff?"

"The power of social media."

"It's sick really." I hugged her again and realized how much I missed home.

"She's going to be here, Gage." Roxie whispered as her cheek pressed against mine.

I nodded. I knew that. Or at least what I last knew of Jenna, I knew that. Jenna moved to Georgetown with Michael not long after the wedding. Roxie had known back then that Jenna and I were no longer speaking. She also knew exactly why we were no longer speaking and was benevolent enough to never bring it up with me.

Ever. While Rox never dished out too much information with regards to Jenna, she would text me any particularly important bits. *Get this, G* - Roxie had a penchant for shortening names to single letter – *M took a new job as a detective.* I texted back a simple *Whr?* Then I held my breath, even though I had no reason to hold my breath. *Grgtwn.* Georgetown. Jenna was moving back home. Or to what I thought of as home. I wasn't really sure where Jenna considered home anymore. Now, Roxie and Jenna lived minutes apart. After that update, I started refusing any Jenna information from Roxie years ago. I wondered if Jenna refused the same.

"Does she know?" I asked Roxie as my heart pounded. I wondered if Roxie could feel it through my chest.

Roxie chewed her cheeks thoughtfully. "She doesn't. I didn't say anything. She doesn't like...well, you know."

Talking about me. Knowing about me. All of the above.

Roxie looked so nervous, I laughed and pulled her close. "Jeez, Rox, calm down. We're adults. We'll survive."

"You changed, Gage."

"Yeah?"

"So relaxed. So grown up. It suits you much better than your college douche-bro act."

"Thanks so much," I said, rolling my eyes.

"All true," replied Roxie, who never minced her words.

I had to agree.

"You want a beer?" Lance offered me a Labatt.

"Sure, man."

"I'm glad you're not such an," I could practically see Roxie search for the right word, "asshole anymore."

"Nice assessment," I laughed. "You either," I said and clinked my beer against Roxie's while she howled with laughter.

"I was never!" Roxie countered.

"A little bit," I argued. Then I leaned it and whispered, "In a good way."

She laughed, and then we both looked up as Jenna, wrapped up in a bright red coat, pushed through the door without knocking.

Michael trailed her, huge crockpots in both oven mitt covered hands. "I know, I know. We're late, and you're all waiting for the buffalo chicken dip. Well, except Roxie. Roxie, I have this vegetable concoction for you. I never made it, so d-don't… expect much."

I knew the exact moment Jenna noticed me. It was the hitch in her voice nobody else detected. It was the way she stumbled over the end of her sentence. But, I had to give the girl credit. She knew how to cover the biggest - and possibly shittiest - surprise of the night. Me. In Roxie's living room.

I knew exactly when Michael noticed me too. He was a little less subtle.

"Gage!" Michael shouted. "Jeez. Where have you been, man?" He set the crockpot down in the living room.

"California."

"Yeah! We saw on Facebook," he said. "Jenna showed me your friend request."

Never in my life had I seen a look of panicked embarrassment. Jenna delivered quite nicely. I pretended not to notice as Michael plowed on. "But come on. You could have called. Poor Jen. She was like a lost puppy that whole first year without you." He swung an arm around Jenna while she winced. Her smile was tight as she lifted her eyes to Michael.

"Was she?" I asked and raised the bottle to my mouth, needing a swig of liquid courage to be able to look her in the eye. "Well, Jenna," I finally said, and lowered my voice. "I'm sorry." I watched her face until her eyes were on mine. "Really. I'm sorry I ruined it."

Jenna flushed.

"Eh, it wasn't that bad," Michael jovially punched my arm. "She survived."

"At least she had me when we moved down here," Roxie cut in and hugged them both.

I silently thanked Roxie for the topic switch. "You liking it here?"

"Absolutely. I wouldn't have ever thought to move here, but man, as soon as I graduated and saw this listing, Jenna was jumping on it." He laughed. "For as long as you two lived up in Pittsburgh, Jeez, she couldn't get out of that city fast enough."

Jenna flushed again. We looked away from each other.

"You ever think of moving back?" Michael asked.

"Come on in, guys," Roxie interrupted, clapping her hands, saving Jenna. "Eat some food. Michael, bring that in here."

"Sure. Sounds good." Michael turned and balanced the crockpots on his hands again.

And then Jenna was rushing past me. "Everything looks good, Rox. I'm starving. I haven't eaten all day saving up for this."

Then Michael was chiming in behind her. "I don't know, Rox. My stomach has been a mess lately."

"It's stress. He's working way too much," Jenna insisted. "I keep telling him he needs…" Jenna's voice drifted away into the kitchen.

I wondered around doing all the things people do in other people's houses. I stared at all the pictures of Roxie and Lance and their families. Roxie's family apparently still took the annual Christmas skiing trip. The picture of Jenna and Rox caught my eye. Jenna's wedding. Her blue dress.

My hands in her hair.
My hands on her hips.
The feel of her skin.
My mouth one breath away from hers

"So how's the accounting business, Gage?" A friendly hand patted my shoulder, and I jumped. "You still in it?" Michael had wandered out of the kitchen and over to me, some protein shake in hand.

"In what?" I took a deep breath. It was not hard to conjure up the stinging slap of her words, the truth in them. *He's not my consolation prize. He's the one.*

"Accounting? You still in the biz?"

"Oh, yeah. Accounting. Same old, same old, Mike. You know how it is." He had no idea how accounting was; he had no idea how the same old, same old was. He was a detective, everything was different for him every single day. But Michael, he was nice enough to nod in agreement.

"And how's the running going?" I pointed to the protein shake he held with my beer.

"Still looking for a good running partner," Michael said. Then he started saying something about split times and personal bests, and my gaze drifted away. Out of the corner of my eye, I spied Jenna. She was deep in conversation. Except for her eyes. With those, she watched Michael and me intently. She must have become comfortable with the idea of me, though, because she didn't even look away when I stared at her. She gestured with her hands, expansively, the same gesture I had seen her do a million times before, but she seemed different. I could not place it. Why was she so similar and so different at the same time? Then when she laughed and her eyes darted, I knew. Her eyes. Her eyes were different. They looked different when she laughed. Where her skin used to be smooth now crinkled at the corners. And her mouth. It creased at the corners, creases I never saw before. Laugh lines. They were still soft, barely detectable, but they were there.

It crossed my mind that I didn't really know Jenna anymore. I didn't know what she thought about or what her favorite sweatshirt looked like. I didn't know what she ate for breakfast or even what kind of car she drove. I didn't know if she and Michael wanted kids or what they argued about. I didn't know what they laughed about. I didn't know what jokes gave her those lines around her eyes and mouth. I used to know everything. Now she was practically a stranger. She was the girl I found in the bushes in college. Except.

Except she wasn't.

Emily, I thought. I had known Emily only a little more than six months, but I knew her better than I knew Jenna now.

Jenna looked good, though. No. She looked great. She looked heathy and relaxed. She didn't have the sickly skinny look that she sported through college and right after. Michael was still talking about running. I nodded in agreement when appropriate.

Through the glass of the sliding door I saw her, alone on the back porch. Her feet were bare, and she was sipping a Corona. Alone. Some things stayed the same. Jenna always liked to be alone.

The sound of fifty different conversations going on around me grated my nerves. God, I wanted to be where Jenna was. Alone. And with her. At the same time.

I stood up from my chair, still staring at her.

She caught my eye, gave me a surprised deer-in-the-headlights look, and then turned away quickly. I moved to the door. Slid it open with a silent swish.

"Hi." The door clicked shut behind me.

Jenna did not answer. She wiggled her toes instead and inspected them. I bit down on a grin.

"The light in there. The sound. A little too much for me."

She smirked to herself and snorted. "Doesn't sound like the Gage I know."

"You don't know me anymore," I said, and she visibly winced.

I contemplated that wince. Did it hurt her as much as it hurt me to lose our friendship? Did I screw her up royally by trying to kiss her, basically trying to sabotage her wedding? Did she think about our last moments in the bedroom as much as she thought about her wedding vows with Michael? Was I overanalyzing everything? Maybe she never thought of me at all. I sat down next to her and when our knees bumped, she shifted with a jolt.

"I am sorry," I said quietly. "I am."

She stared ahead. Her eyes looked glassy, and it took a long time for her to answer. "Yeah, I know."

We looked at each other and our eyes asked everything we could never ask each other. At least not now. Not yet.

Are you good, Jenna? Are you good? Are you okay?

Her eyes clouded over then, and I couldn't read her answers. She glanced down to the beer in her hands. She was picking at the label, shredding it with nails painted a bright blue. *You paint your nails, Jenna. You always thought that was a waste of time.* I opened my mouth, but I never said the words.

"You look different," she said finally, never looking up. "Older. Yeah. Older."

"Same to you," I shot back, but there was no edge to it. We were older. It was as simple as that.

"I didn't think you would, somehow. Gage is always golden," she said, mostly to herself. "You got these," she rubbed an index finger near the outer corner of her eye, presumably pointing out the wrinkles, "what are they called?"

"Wrinkles?" I suggested.

"Crows' feet, I was thinking," she said wryly.

"You get them from the sun."

"The California sun," she said, and I thought she was going to ask me about my job, or about California, but she did not. "So you're old then. You have wrinkles," she stated so abruptly I laughed.

"You too," I said. "Right here." Without thinking I reached for Jenna's face, for her mouth, for the laugh lines that now framed her smile.

She flinched a little, and I hesitated. The touch. It meant nothing. This was the girl with whom, not long ago, I slept through nights, my arms wrapped around her, her hips curled into my. *Spoons*, she would say, sometimes when we were drunk, and I would tug her to me, and we would have long outlandish conversations that we barely remembered the next morning. Now, I couldn't even touch her face.

We sat there, together but separate, beers forgotten, knees close but not touching, eyes staring into opposite ends of the night, waiting in an uneasy silence for the moment to pass, wondering if it would. Hoping it would. Praying it would.

"I'm sorry too, you know," she said.

I turned to her, confused. "For what?"

"Roxie told me the big secret a couple weeks ago. And believe me, she didn't want to tell me, you know, because of some sort of Roxie and Gage Secret Handshake Club, but," Jenna sighed and rolled her eyes, "she told me. So you can't get mad at her."

"What in the actual hell are you talking about?"

"About California. About how you wanted to live there. That job you turned down. Gage, you turned down a job, a career," she corrected, "for me. They don't just hand those thing out. And you turned it down."

I shrugged.

"What in God's name were you thinking?" Exasperated, she turned to me.

Our eyes caught, and I looked at her. I watched her bite her lip before she turned away.

"Yeah," she said, closing her eyes as if it hurt to think about my decision. "I don't want that burden on me. I'm supposed to hate you for my wedding day. It ruined all the pleasure I got out of hating you." She laughed and looked at me, obviously trying to lighten the mood. "Also, you know, the wedding day shit was as much my fault, too."

But I could clearly see the burden she put on herself for my decision. She was wearing it right now. "Stop thinking about it, Jen," I said softly.

As if alarmed, her eyes darted back to mine.

"Not just the kiss--"

"The almost kiss," she interrupted, correcting me.

Not just that. But the California thing too. You do things. And you regret them, or you don't. That's life." I bumped her knee with mine. She looked up at me. "I don't regret not taking the job. It was for the best."

"It was the best," she agreed. "Mostly," she added with a side-eyed for me.

I lifted my nearly empty bottle to me lips, and Jenna mirrored me.

"It's kind of weird to think that all those years were because of Daniel," she said. Jenna closed her eyes. "Seriously. I am so sorry you did not take the job you wanted because of me."

I nudged her again. "Jen. I'm fine."

"I barely remember him anymore. Feels like a completely different life. Do you even remember him?"

"Remember him? I still breathe funny at night." I rubbed my nose, which was never quite straight after that night.

"I can't believe I wasted a good punch over that guy." Jenna said. "And on top of that, you were *right*! God."

"Jendy, my girl, I've been waiting to hear you say those words my whole life."

She laughed, sweeping a hand through her hair, brushing it back behind and ear. The gesture was so familiar suddenly, I knew. I knew what made her laugh. Maybe I never did forget.

"You seem good, Jendy. You seem stable." I wondered if it was okay for me to say that now that I was not close to her anymore.

"I've been living a very average life now for a very long time." She indulged me with a grin and shrugged. "All that drama in college and after. All those meds I couldn't take and wouldn't take, all the bouncing back and forth. It's not worth the bullshit."

"I guess so," I agreed. "And we get wrinkles."

I expected her to laugh, but she didn't. Jenna fell silent for a long enough time for me to start to worry. *Was* she average? Was she truly all right?

"We're trying to have a baby," she said suddenly.

Shocked, I waited to answer so I did not stammer.

"I know. It's crazy." Her smile almost looked like a grimace.

I nodded at her face, her frown. "What's that all about?"

"I can't--" she started then must have changed her mind. "It's not happening."

I sat in a wordless silence. I had absolutely no idea what to say.

"How do you make it happen?"

The question was so absurd, I had to stifle laughter. "Well, Jendy," I started, "I think you figured out how to make a baby happen by now."

"You know what I mean," she said, and I saw the tears prick her eyes. "Gage, I want a family so bad. God, I want a family."

Yeah. I knew what she meant. But I had no clue what to say, even less of a clue as to how she felt. It's not like I could not hear the desperation in her voice. But I could not relate to that particular desire.

"I couldn't tell Michael. I could never tell him how bad I want it."

That moment was back upon us. Awkward. Painful. Unending. I opened my mouth to say something, but Jenna beat me to it.

"I should," she nodded at the sliding glass door, the party inside.

"Yeah, yeah. Go." I said a little too anxiously, surprised that for all the times I had thought of her over the years, all the times I had wanted to be with her, sit with her, see her, talk to her one last time, I was surprised that now I wanted her gone. I watched Michael inside with Roxie on the other side of the glass door. They were laughing about something. I wanted Jenna to be with them, laughing. I wanted her desperately to be with Michael.

"I'll see you later, I guess?" She asked, her voice tentative.

"Yep," I answered, even though we both had no idea if there would ever be a *later*.

I ended up in downtown D.C., a place I hadn't been, in, well, I could not really recall the last time I had been downtown. It was like trying to remember the last movie you had seen. Pictures, flashes of the familiar, was all I could recall. But when exactly and for what reason? I don't know. I thought it had been summer; it had not been more than a decade ago. Trees. I remembered trees. Cherry blossoms? Kristen would have dragged me to something like that. Kristen was the only person raised in D.C. who actually wanted to participate in all that touristy type shit no local would ever do. She'd even be asking people to take our picture in front of monuments, and they would be asking where we were from. Oh, across the river, she'd answer.

I walked a little bit more. Bought some kind of ice cream, frozen yogurt, chocolate chip cookie dough. Threw it away after three bites because it had that gritty not-quite-ice-cream taste I never liked.

I pushed through the doors of Seven Eleven, grabbed a coffee, poured in way too much creamer. No, I thought suddenly, it couldn't have been cherry blossom season; that wasn't in the summer. That was the spring. I was here, downtown, doing God-knows-what in the summer. It was hot that day, practically sizzling. What was I doing here?

I walked around some more, staying out later than I planned, wanting to avoid my dad and Racca, his girlfriend - no, wife - who liked to drink chamomile tea at night with him on the porch and discuss the day. If Kris were around I could tolerate it, but alone? And now, after the night of Jenna? No. I needed to be alone right now. I couldn't tell them about Jenna, about how there were no more *laters* with us, how that conversation definitely felt like some kind of closure we both needed, but did not really want.

So Jenna was going to have a baby. Or trying to have a baby. Uncle Gage. My stomach clenched. I would never be Uncle Gage to her kids. Her kids. Jesus, Jenna would have kids with Michael. Why couldn't she tell him how much she wanted a family? He knew about her father, her mother. Of course he did. He had to know how much she wanted a family.

I jumped on the Metro, coffee in hand, and sat next to a pack of college students clad in Catholic University hoodies and torn jeans. The girls were a loud and giggling pack, obviously drunk, and the guys were drunker. They bounded off at the next stop, the girls jumping onto the guy's backs, the guys staggering and hiccupping with laughter. God, they were young. They looked so ridiculously young.

Why didn't Jenna ask me about my job? Or about my relationships? Why nothing about California? That stupid comment about the California sun and nothing else? She didn't want to know? She never accepted my friend request on Facebook either.

I rode three more stops in seething silence.

Fuck that, I thought. When I got off at my stop, I shook my head angrily and whipped my cup into the night. Immediately I felt guilty for littering, for wasting some mediocre coffee, and for getting pissed at Jenna for absolutely no reason. Why the hell are you mad at her Gage? You haven't talked to her in three years.

Why didn't I ask her about her marriage? Why didn't I mention her books, her novel that I searched for on Amazon and had shipped to my house? The fact that I read that magazine article that mentioned her. If that moment at Roxie's was going to be our last moment, why did I waste it? Why did we both waste it? And dammit, why couldn't I remember the last time I was here? I jammed my hands into my pockets, irritably searching for my keys. When I looked up, I saw her, and stopped dead in my tracks.

She was sitting on my porch, or rather, my dad's porch. I should have known she'd be there, though I had no idea how or why she got there. I should have known, because my entire night had been leading up to this moment.

She saw me and stood, slowly, haltingly.

I took her in. I took in everything. Then I said it. Her name, a question I had wanted to ask for a very long time.

"Von?"

She bit her lip; I could see her face, half shaded, the light spilling out over her, over the porch.

"Jesus. Von. What the hell are you doing here?" I asked, my voice full of the warmth and shock only a little bit of alcohol and a night of reminiscing could bring.

And then I remembered. The last time I was downtown.

Von.

It was with Von.

Jenna

"What if I'm all shriveled up inside?" Jenna climbed into bed and situated herself. "What is my womb is like four hundred degrees and cooks anything that dares enter it?"

Michael shook his head with a smile. "We are going to be fine, Jen." He kissed the top of her head.

"Wendy. All she had to do is look at Eric, and they're pregnant," Jenna said about Wendy, Michael's sister, who was currently pregnant with their fourth child, a girl.

"They're different." Michael started to pull out a book.

"Your mom probably hates me because I can't spawn progeny."

"Spawn progeny? I don't think those words ever came out of her mouth."

"Michael," Jenna warned.

"My mother loves you." He set down the book and motioned to her.

Jenna laid her head on his chest. "I could be all dead inside."

"You're not dead inside."

"Your mother probably thinks I'm dead inside."

"Aw, Jen," Michael laughed. "My mother would never say that. I don't think Mom has even admitted to me yet that sex exists."

Jenna smiled.

"I read this article that said fertility peaks at twenty-seven, and it's all downhill from there."

"You're only thirty-one."

"Almost thirty-two. Four years dead already. My insides." Jenna waved her hands over her stomach. "All dead. Zombie babies. It's all I can give you."

"Lucky me. Zombies are all the rage right now." Michael smiled.

"This is not funny," Jenna said even as she laughed. She grabbed pillow and socked him.

"Come here, Killer." Michael commanded with a laugh and rolled over to Jenna, pulled Jenna by the waist, slid her easily beneath him. He kissed her until she was breathless. "You are way too obsessed. If you relax--"

"You better not be saying what I think you are saying." She squirmed out from under him. She couldn't bear to hear it. Those platitudes. *Give it time.* And *It'll happen when it happens.* And *You're probably all dried up inside.* Oh, no, wait. That last one was all Jenna.

"I was going to say if you just relax, I will give you a back rub."

"Oh, yeah. I'm sure you were," Jenna said suspiciously. But she wasn't going to pass up a massage. She flipped over onto her stomach.

"You should start running with me. It'll give you something else to obsess over." He kneaded Jenna's shoulders.

"I'm not obsessing."

His hands stilled on her lower back. With rough hands, he flipped her over.

"Wow. Thanks for the three-minute rubdown," Jenna said with sarcasm, "It was magical."

"I need to give this to you now."

"I'm not in any kind of mood for 'giving it to me.'" Jenna snorted.

Michael rolled his eyes then reached into the nightstand. "I was going to take you there as a surprise on your birthday, but," He pulled an envelope out of the drawer and handed it to her, "I think you need this news now."

"News?" Jenna's voice rose curiously, as she flipped the blank envelope in her hands. "What is this?"

"Open it."

Jenna opened it.

Two tickets to a resort outside of Pittsburgh.

"Pennsylvania." Jenna pressed the tickets to my chest like a love letter. "Be still my heart. You do love me."

"It's a tough job, but some guy has to do it."

"When are we going?"

"For your birthday. On your birthday."

"You really know how to woo me, boy. I can't believe we're going on a trip. To Pennsylvania." Jenna glanced over her shoulder at him.

"To a resort. A really nice resort," he added.

Jenna fanned herself dramatically.

"I figured I better start spending my wife's movie money."

Jenna laughed.

"You are way too easy to please," he said.

Jenna smiled at him, hoping he could not detect the sadness, the emptiness she knew still lingered in her. "Thank you," Jenna said sincerely.

"Seriously. The best thing that ever happened to me was you, Jen," he said as he moved to her.

"Same goes," Jenna agreed as she wrapped her arms around his neck.

Gage

"Elliot. I don't want to alarm you," Von said over the phone, which of course, put me on full alert.

So, Von.

Yeah.

We had sex that night in November.

I took Von up to the guest room I used at Dad's place, and something about seeing those college kids on the metro was so piercing – I missed Jenna who I had just seen, and Roxie who had not even moved yet, and Von, God, Von who I loved so much so many years ago. And then there she was, materialized right in front of me, and I wasn't even drunk or otherwise out of my good senses. We talked a little bit, and I thought about Emily even as I wrapped Von into a huge hug. I thought about Emily and how she and I did not cross over the border to dating each other yet, but we were sleeping together fairly regularly, and if I slept with Von that would pretty much end any chances with Emily.

I took Von upstairs.

I didn't even ask why she was in D.C. or how she knew to come to my Dad's house. Not until after.

"How did you know I was here?"

"Twitter," she answered, sheepishly. "I saw your tweet. And I was in the area."

"Whoa. What a stalker," I commented. Von stammered. "Kidding. Glad you showed up. Want a drink?"

"Coffee if you've got it."

"Decaf?"

"Regular."

"At midnight?"

"I have a long drive back," she replied as we snuck down to the kitchen. Sex with a girl in my room. Sneaking into the kitchen. God, I felt great. I was twenty again.

"Tonight?"

"Yep."

"After this?"

She patted my shoulder. "Don't worry, chief. You rocked my world."

I snorted with laughter. "To where?"

"Pittsburgh," she replied as if I was an idiot.

"You're still in Pittsburgh, but you're here?"

"I was at a convention."

"I don't believe it."

"Someone's got a big ego."

"Why didn't you say yes, Von?"

Her eyes went soft, and I knew she was remembering the night I proposed. "You know why." She looked at me with such pity I wanted to puke.

"Whatever," I waved my hand.

"You still friends with Jenna?"

"No," I answered honestly, and it hurt because that was the first time in all these years I ever had to tell someone I was no longer friends with Jenna.

"What happened?"

Now I looked at her.

"You slept with her," she answered.

"No," I said. "Jesus, Von. I didn't sleep with her. She's married. She's happy. She's fine. They're trying for kids, actually." I said the last part brightly.

Von propped up her chin on one hand and studied me. "Okay. I'm done asking."

"Good."

Von looked at her watch. "I better get going. I have to open the bakery in four hours."

I shook my head. "You're a machine. Always were."

"You too," she said.

I watched her gather her things. "Bye, chief."

She reached for the doorknob.

"Von," I called out, stopping her.

She turned around, eyebrows raised in question.

"You'd say yes now."

She smiled sadly. "I'm married to my job now, El." Then she left without another word.

And we didn't talk again.

Until now. Until *Elliot I don't want to alarm you.* I counted the months in my head. And I knew. I just knew.

"You're pregnant." I looked up from the mound of tax work on my desk. The mound seemed like the most important thing in my life thirty seconds ago.

A moment of stunned silence greeted my statement then, "Whoa. You're a good guesser."

"So you *are* pregnant?" The pen I was holding slipped from my fingers and bounced to the floor.

"It's possible."

"Did you take a test?" I stood abruptly and began pacing.

"I took four. Five," she corrected.

"And they said you're pregnant?"

"They didn't say anything."

Now I was confused.

"They were broken?"

"They didn't say anything. But they displayed a positive sign."

Jesus. I wanted to strangle the woman. I wanted to scream and shout and swear at her ability to drive me insane.

"That means you're--"

"Pregnant," she finished for me. "Yeah. Like we've kept saying over and over. I'm pregnant."

"Four months pregnant?" I asked.

"It's yours," she replied. "I've been to the doctor. Had the first sonogram."

Regret filled me immediately. This is why you don't act twenty when you're thirty-two. You do stupid, stupid shit. Reckless shit. "We probably should have--"

"Yeah. Condoms would have been a great idea."

"Why didn't you call me sooner?"

"I think about calling you. We're swamped at the bakery. Wedding season coming up. You know how I work."

"Like a machine," I said drolly.

"Yeah. So I never thought about it until all the puking. I thought it was nerves from the--" She stopped abruptly, and I wondered briefly how she had planned to end that sentence. "Anyway, the point is, I never thought about it."

"Oh, shit, Von."

"Shit indeed. Diapers full of it."

"So, what now?"

"Listen, you don't have to do anything. I'm telling you because I thought you should know so for future reference--"

"Von. Von, stop." And how was she going to end *that*? For future reference, you can tell all the women you sleep with you have a kid? For future reference, you now have a tax break? For future reference, you are a father? A dad. A *dad*. Someday somebody, some kid, was going to call me Dad. Ohhh shit. The panic. The never ending panic. I needed a Valium. Where was Jenna and her Valium when a guy needed it? That's when it really hit me. Jenna who so badly wanted a family. Jenna.

"Are you there? Elliot? Are you okay? Are you...breathing? Are you dying? Elliot?"

I swallowed the panic clawing at my throat. I thought about my dad. Crying at Kristen's recital. Rocking babies at the hospital. Shooting people in the desert. What the hell kind of father would I be? And what kind of kid would hope to be me someday? This kept getting worse.

"You don't have to do anything," Von reiterated. "I'm serious, Elliot."

That statement pulled me back to reality. "Are *you* serious? You think I would do nothing? That I'd contribute nothing?"

"I don't think you would do nothing, no. But it's an option. I know we are really far apart right now."

"It's not an option."

We sat in silence.

"This is going to be hard," Von said.

"You're right. I am really far away," I said. I felt even farther.

"And I'm moving."

"Now?" Why the hell was Von thinking about moving now? Did women move when they got pregnant, some kind of biological need? Like nesting or whatever that was called?

"I wasn't completely honest with you back in November."

"What?"

"I lied."

"Why would you lie? About what?"

"You're in California. I'm here. I never thought I'd see you again."

I said nothing.

"So, anyway, I've been expanding Huggen Kiss. I have an option for Arlington. I'm planning a move there. God, this is so weird to be telling you this stuff. We haven't seen each other in almost four years and now I'm—this is weird." She paused to wait for confirmation.

"I agree. This is weird."

She sighed. "The night I saw you I was checking out a new place nearby. I remembered your dad and your crazy mother. How are they doing, by the way?"

"They'll be thrilled," I deadpan.

"Oh, my god, your mother. She already hates me."

"She hates everyone," I said casually, as if Von's concern was nothing new.

"I was checking out that place, and I thought about your family. And you. And I looked. And saw you had said something on Twitter about D.C. I saw you checked in on Foursquare. I thought,

Jeez what are the chances? We are both here at the same time? I was nostalgic. I never thought this would happen." She said this as if she was profusely apologizing.

"Nostalgia isn't for the faint of heart."

"Or for the ovulating."

"My God, Von." I couldn't help it, I laughed hard and for a long time.

She listened for a little bit. "Are you okay? Elliot?" She asked this a couple more times before dissolving into laughter too.

"I don't know. I don't know why - why I'm laughing."

"Me either."

"This is kind of awful." I laughed. "No offense."

"This is the worst." She laughed harder.

God, we were a mess. And we were going to be parents.

Parents. Somehow, together we were going to raise a child. Imagine that.

"And the best, Von," I said when the maniacal, panicked laughter subsided. "It's kind of the best."

Jenna

The resort was exactly what they needed. Even though the week was winding down, Jenna had not felt this relaxed in months. Her rush to finish her next manuscript, her baby obsession, it all faded into the background of luxury massages, hiking trails, and mini bars. Except for the first night when Michael got sick – which they blamed on his recently diagnosed ulcer, food poisoning, too much whipped vodka, or all three – the vacation had been fantastic.

"What do you want to do?" He asked over breakfast in the restaurant. "Last day, babe."

"A run?"

"Too much exertion. I'm kind of tired." He contemplated a forkful of eggs. Set it back down.

"You just woke up," Jenna teased.

"It's vacation! You're supposed to sleep the whole time."

"We could kayak around the lake."

"You are supposed to be suggesting couples' massages."

"And you're supposed to be talking me into charity runs and geocaching. We've somehow switched bodies."

"I think I've been catching up on about five years of sleep deprivation."

"Ah, see, that's our difference. I'm too far-gone to even try to catch up."

"Maybe a walk. I could probably do a walk."

"Sounds good."

Michael pushed his plate away.

"You're still not hungry?" Jenna asked.

"No. Not much of an appetite."

"Your ulcer again? We need to talk to your doctor about a new prescription. This one's definitely not working."

"Calm down, Jen. Probably still food poisoning."

"Or a hangover," Jenna suggested cheerfully.

"Or both!" He raised his glass and clinked it against hers. "But, I'm thirsty as hell. So, there is that."

"That's a good thing," Jenna said.

"More coffee?" Michael held the pot over her cup.

Jenna nodded and watched him pour. She reached for her napkin and unfolded it. Then she folded it again. She curled the edges.

Michael stared at her curiously.

"What?" Jenna touched her hair self-consciously.

"This isn't going to be good." Michael replied.

"What?"

"You need to say something. And it isn't going to be good."

"How do you know?"

He nodded at her napkin. "You always play with stuff when you are nervous."

Jenna's hands immediately stilled. "Do I?"

"You should have seen the way you shredded that label on your beer at Roxie's place. When you were talking to Gage," he added.

Surprised, Jenna's eyes flicked to Michael. "You saw me? Us?"

"I glanced out once or twice." He shrugged like it was no big deal.

Jenna changed the subject quickly. "So, I was thinking…"

Michael grinned. "So what do you have to say, Killer? Spit it out. Off like a Band-Aid."

"I'm going to call the doctor when I get home. It's been long enough. I didn't want to know before. But now I think I need to know."

"I think that is a great idea." Michael circled his fingers around Jenna's wrist. "I'm going to go too. It's probably me, anyway. Or it's nothing at all."

"Nothing at all." Jenna repeated, mentally crossing her fingers. "Who knows? This could be our babymoon, and we don't even know it."

"I like that idea."

"And you could get your back checked again," Jenna said gleefully. "And your ulcer!"

"Nice. Aren't we the perfect couple? Falling apart together." He stood and pulled out some money from his wallet, and tossed it to the table.

"Now let's do something other than talk about the shriveled up organs of your elderly wife."

"Elderly? No way. I won't let you say that about yourself," Michael chided. "Senior citizen. I think that's the politically correct term."

"You want to race to the end?" Jenna jerked her head to the end of the trail.

"See? Running. New obsession. I told you." He lifted her hand to kiss it.

Jenna grinned. "If you're too pansy--"

"Whoa! I think I created a monster."

Jenna laughed.

"Ok," he panted. "I'm game."

Jenna noticed then how his face looked waxy and pale. "Oh, hon, I was kidding. You look pretty worn--"

"Ready-set-go," He hollered like a child and took off.

"No fair!" Jenna called, immediately forgetting her concerns, and caught up. Then passed him. "Hey!" She teased after a few seconds. "How am I winning here? I'm the one with the wonky leg." Jenna threw a smile over her shoulder as she glanced back.

Michael had stalled in the middle of the path. His hands clutched his abdomen.

Jenna squinted, and hand shading her eyes. Michael looked like he was breathing hard. Too hard.

"Are you ok, babe?" Jenna stopped and, also breathing hard, started to make her way back to him. "Ulcer?" *I shouldn't have challenged him. I knew his ulcer was bothering him. Why would I do something so stupid?* "Babe, I'm sor--"

Then it all happened so fast.

Clutching his stomach, Michael dropped to his knees with a grunt.

Jenna, dread pitting in her stomach, took off, tearing down the path like a wild animal. "Michael! Michael!" She had a million thoughts, but his name was the only thing she could say.

He was on his back by the time she reached him, moaning. "Oh, God. God. It's killing me." Sweat beaded over his brow, and Jenna could tell it wasn't solely from the run. Panic crowded her chest.

"Oh, my God." Gingerly, she touched his forehead. As overheated as he looked, and thought his skin beaded, his skin felt cold and clammy. "Michael?"

"Jen," He moaned and clutched his stomach. "Some - something," he tried to talk through the pain. "It's wrong."

Heat exhaustion? Why did she goad him? She pushed his hair back from his sweaty face. Then it hit her. His loss of appetite. His nagging stomachaches. It was his appendix. Jenna knew it. Jesus, it was probably bursting.

"Oh, my God." Jenna covered her mouth. "Michael, you're going to be fine." She pushed off the ground, her eyes searching the trail for any stray runners. Cursing herself for not bringing a cell phone, she knelt over him again. "I'm going to get help." In a blind panic, Jenna started to run before changing her mind and doubling back. "I don't want to leave you," she cried.

"Jen, go!" He pleaded.

Jenna took off again, and tried to ignore the groans coming from him, the one that pulled at her heart, tugging her back to him.

Gage

Roxie's phone call woke me in the dead of night.
And that's when I realized something.
Cancer. It doesn't really give a shit who you are.
You could run a hundred marathons a year.
Or you could smoke a pack a day.
You could build a thousand houses in Haiti.
Or you could burn them all with a match.
You could love old people and adopt kittens and pledge your fortune to telethons.
Or you could hate babies and kick puppies and defraud charities.
But cancer?
Cancer doesn't give a shit who you are.

Thursday, May 9, 2013

Jenna

"Buzz my head, Jenna," Michael said, holding the clippers out to her.

There were all of these steps with cancer. Step one: everyone cry. Everyone. Just cry and cry and cry. Then, the step that kind of fits with crying: deny. Cry and deny. It's a sport, really. Deny everything. Nah. Could not possibly be Michael. Not Michael who runs every day. Not Michael who thought kale was cool before it was cool. And also: not them. Surely cancer could not happen to them. Not Michael and Jenna. They were young. Not long ago, Michael had blown out twenty-eight candles on his birthday cake. They had been married not even four years. Didn't they get their wedding album, like, yesterday? And Jenna. She knew it was selfish; she felt the guilt and pain for even thinking it, because Michael was truly the one suffering. But Jenna still thought of it in the secret of the night. She already lost both parents. Could life be so cruel?

So, Jenna and Michael spent those first raw days staring at each other as if they were new creatures who had floated into each other's lives. They barely talked on the ride home from the first doctor's appointment. They said nothing over dinner. Silence was one deep void that plagued Jenna and Michael for days.

And then there was this other step, the one Jenna did not expect. The acceptance.

At first, Jenna awoke in a panic nightly, sure Michael would be dead next to her. She would roll, check him. But there he lay, breathing normally and evenly like any other night. And he'd eat in the morning. Not much. But that was no different than the entire month before the diagnosis, back when cancer was merely stress.

And he would take a handful of pills. And Jenna would drive him to chemotherapy. And she would drink coffee while she waited for the cycle of toxins to kill his cancer. He was still the same old

Michael. Jenna was the same old Jenna. They were the same old couple. With a twist.

And suddenly, an acceptance they never expected filled their silent void.

Then came the hyper acceptance. The manic Googling. The obsessive reading. The chants, God, the chants. *We'll beat this, we'll beat this, we'll beat this.*

Yeah, the hyper acceptance was really, in the end, another form of denial, Jenna now thought as she stared at the clippers Michael held out to her. Because there was no way in hell she was going to shave Michael's head. That was simply one more thing to add to the pile of reality being thrown at them. Not that cancer didn't look real every time she wiped up chunks of his hair from the bottom of the bathtub. But shaving a head? There was no going back. She was back at stage one. Cry and deny.

"Come on. It will make me more aerodynamic. For the marathon." He rubbed his head, and Jenna noticed how easily clumps of hair shed into his fists.

She swallowed hard. The marathon he still planned to run. In October. In five months.

"Ok. I'll do it." Steeling herself, Jenna thrust out an open palm.

Michael clapped the buzzing razor into her hand with a salute. "God speed."

Jenna bit down on her lips. He seemed to be in such a good mood. She didn't want to sour it, but everything felt so real now, like they shouldn't be joking and smiling. He sat on the toilet. Jenna shaved Michaels head over a towel as tears streamed down her face. When she finished, he stood and Jenna passed him a mirror. She shook the shavings off the towel and into the toilet.

"Thank God I have a head that can pull off this look." He ran a hand over his now bald head and smiled at her. "Damn. I'm gorgeous."

Weakly, Jenna tried to work up a smile.

He glanced at what was left of his hair floating in the toilet. "So." He nodded at it. "Should we have a funeral?"

"No," Jenna answered, too quickly.

"All right. No funeral. You just want to go to bed and do me then? I'm pretty hot now. And I could use a break."

A shocked laugh rocketed out of Jenna but she stopped herself. She bit a knuckle and looked at him sadly.

"Jen," He said seriously, reaching out to rub a hand across her back. "You can laugh. It's ok to be normal."

We're not normal, she thought, but Jenna nodded at him, as he pulled her close and tucked her head under his chin. Jenna stared at their refection in the mirror, she tear-streaked, he pensive. She watched Michael's reflection raise an eyebrow and ask her reflection, "So? Do me? Or no?"

Jenna clapped a hand over her mouth and laughed. And kind of cried. Because even now, especially now, when Michael was being so funny, the words rang in her head.

Six months.

The doctors, even the second opinions, even the third opinions, said six months. Six months at best. The chemo, the medication, the surgeries were only meant to prolong Michael's life, to make him comfortable. But in the end, Michael was given six months.

Jenna had written the number, scribbled it down on the notepad she took to his appointments.

Six months at best.

Pancreatic cancer. It's a silent killer. That's what all those pamphlets said. All those internet websites. All the survivor stories.

It's a silent killer, they all said. And it did not kill only inside the body – pancreatic cancer killed a lot of Jenna too. It silently killed her along with Michael, because how could there be six months at best? *At best?* There was no way his body would ever give out. He ran marathons. Six months was Michael's death sentence, but Michael was so much more, so much stronger than six months. That's what Jenna kept telling anyone who would listen: Roxie, the doctors, the nurses, the therapy group one doctor suggested.

Some days Jenna cheered for Michael because there was so much hope. He had had a chance! They had a chance. A new treatment center in Texas. A new drug trial in Phoenix.

Some days Jenna screamed because she hated that everything she read told her it was true: Michael would be dead in six months.

She would panic.

Then she would sob hysterically.

Then she would dry her eyes because she didn't want Michael to see the tears, the despair.

She had worried so much, for so many months, about her insides dying. She had worried out loud. She had worried out loud to Michael about her dying insides.

She wished she could take it all back.

She wished her insides *were* dying.

Because Jenna's husband, Michael – wonderful Michael – it had been his insides dying the entire time.

Gage

After hearing about Jenna and Michael, I freaked.

I paced the house day after day. Night after night.

Von called occasionally. When silences would engulf our conversation, Von asked what was wrong. I didn't know how to tell her about it. I tried. I tried once when she Skyped me during dinner. *The baby loves chocolate milkshakes*, she said. She grinned and patted her belly. I tried while she was once again Skyping me. She was getting ready for bed, smoothing cream over her belly. I tried to tell her. But I could not do it.

I picked the phone up and tried to call Jenna a dozen times. More than a dozen times. Six months, Roxie had told me.

Six months.

I thought of the baby, my baby, growing in Von while Jenna's husband died.

Von had her second ultrasound about the same time Michael was being diagnosed with cancer. She had not had one since then, and I was surprised to find out she probably would not have another until the baby was born. I didn't know anything about babies. Apparently you did not get a third ultrasound when the doctor thought that everything looked fine and declared the mother healthy. You didn't get a third even if you called once a week and demanded one.

They didn't understand. I couldn't wait fourteen more weeks to see our baby. I wanted to see that baby. I needed to see that baby. I needed to hear its heartbeat flood my ears.

I itched all over.

I wanted to throw things.

I freaked out internally for about ten minutes.

Then I decided to move back home. To Pittsburgh. Or Arlington. Or wherever the hell she was, wherever the hell my baby was.

I needed to move.

To Von.
Right then. It was that easy.

Jenna

It was late when the phone rang, very late. Hurriedly, Jenna grabbed her cell, answering it without looking at the caller ID, and hoped the sound did not wake Michael who had finally fallen into a pain medicated sleep less than an hour ago. She pressed the phone to her ear and whispered a quick greeting, fulling expecting Michael's mother to answer her.

"Jenna?" Gage's voice whispered back to her.

"Gage?" Jenna had not slept, had barely eaten, and had been staring at a computer screen for the better part twenty-two hours, so she was sure she was hearing things wrong.

"Did I wake you?"

"No." Jenna put the laptop to sleep and closed the lid. "I was just doing some research."

"Roxie told me."

"Oh, good. Thank God. I'm glad--" Jenna stopped short. "Not glad, but--"

"I'm so sorry, Jenna," Gage interrupted.

Jenna could not find the strength to answer. Truth was, she was sick of everyone's pity, sick of their sorry's. She felt her throat start to close and drew in breath so sharp it hurt her lungs.

"Is he up for visitors?" Gage finally asked.

Jenna forced the false brightness she had learned to pull out for anyone and everyone asking about Michael. "Oh, yeah. You wouldn't believe it. He's totally normal." *For now*, she thought darkly and tried to shake the shudder away. "He's on these great pain killers. And his appetite is a little bit better--"

"Jenna," Gage stopped her midsentence. "I know we haven't talked in a long time, but Jesus, it's me. Say what you want. Or not. You want to sit in silence, I'm fine with that."

Jenna was stunned into silence. But not for long. "Oh, please. Stop acting like Mother Teresa. I'm not an idiot. You don't want me to sit in silence. Why the hell would you have called me at three in the morning if you wanted me to sit in silence on the phone with you?"

He laughed, and all the years of silence between them seemed to fall away. Everything felt as normal as it could have between them, considering.

"Listen. This sucks, and I hate it. I'd do anything to take it from him. And also," she lowered her voice, "I have to tell you something I haven't said to anyone ever, and if you ever breathe a word of what I'm about to tell you to anyone, I will do worse than murder you: I'll let you live with my wrath."

"Holy shit, Jendy, what are you about to confess?"

"I feel tricked, Gage. I feel tricked and duped and dammit, it's not fair. It's not fair that he was shot in the back years ago, and that was when I was supposed to lose him, and then he was fine, perfectly fine. I was tricked. And sometimes I hate everyone. I hate everyone so much. And do you hate me? Do you think I'm the worst ever?"

Jenna had no idea if Gage knew about Michael being shot in the back, but if he did not, he did not show it. He stayed silent, obviously processing her whispered outburst of shameful thoughts that had been building for way too long.

"Yes," he said finally. "Yes. You're pretty damn awful. I'm scandalized, and I wish I never called you."

"I hate you," she retorted, but she laughed and realized it was the first time she had laughed in over a week.

"You think I could stop by some time?"

"Oh, my God, Gage, of course you can. He loves you, you know that, right?"

Gage didn't say anything, but Jenna could almost see him nodding.

"When do you think you can fly in?" Jenna played with a pen, clicked the cap on and off.

"I'm already here."

Startled, Jenna jumped up to jerk the curtains away from the window. "You're here?"

He chuckled. "I mean I'm in the area. Arlington. Not like stalking your driveway or anything. I moved back."

"You did?" Jenna sunk to the floor beneath the window. The carpet was thick. And covered in lint. God, she needed to vacuum. When was the last time she had cleaned the house?

"Jenna?"

"What?"

"Are you sleeping okay?"

Jenna was silent. "Yes," she lied.

"Which means no."

"Don't even start, Gage, or I swear to God--" She couldn't take one more person calling, asking if she was okay, if she was sleeping, if she needed anything. She knew they meant well, but all it did was reminded Jenna that she and Michael were a couple of those people. The unwell people.

"It's understandable," he interrupted.

"Oh."

"You'll sleep when you need to," he said. "Listen to your body."

Jenna made a face. "Listen to my body? What creature inside you just said that to me?"

He laughed.

"Seriously. Who are you? Didn't I nearly get alcohol poisoning with you five or so years ago?

"Things change."

"Tell me about it. We don't speak for three years and somehow you move to California and become some kind of Zen master? What do you eat now? Pita bread?"

"Oh, Jenna," Gage said patiently, "nobody eats bread in California."

Jenna ran a hand over the carpet. "When did you move back?"

"Like a month ago."

"Really? Wow."

"Yep."

"For a job?" she asked.

There was a long pause. "Something like that. I would have called, but…"

"And I would have called you about Michael, but…"

They fell silent.

"Jenna. I'm so sorry. About everything. I never should have--"

"You don't have to apologize. It all seems so stupid now." Jenna shook her head. "Michael and I? We used to fight about laundry. And the proper way to load the dishwasher." She laughed sadly, but felt her jaw quiver. Her eyes filled. She did her best to contain them. "I have to go, Gage," Jenna said.

"Okay," Gage said, without questioning her. "I'll see you soon."

"Yeah," she said, the word coming out short, her voice quivering, and she hung up without saying goodbye.

She sobbed for about an hour. Gage had done his best to comfort her, but it wasn't the same. Jenna was living a different life, a very different life than Gage lived. And they had been living very different lives for a very long time. He was here in D.C., probably with some fancy new job and title, probably a beautiful apartment. Gage was a single guy without a girlfriend or a family. He was free. Gage had no clue about life throwing you curveballs for which you never practiced.

Saturday, June 29, 2013

Gage

Von had changed.

I had originally pinned her whole change on the pregnancy, something neither of us had planned, which we said out loud often in the midst of another argument. But then I watched her carefully over the weeks of living with her. Von was not absorbed in work like years ago, but now almost obsessed with it, and no, I realized, Von's change had occurred small peaks and valleys. Her change was something that happened over years and very slowly at that. I guess that was the natural way of personalities: they changed so glacially that the only people who noticed were the ones absent the longest.

Which meant I had changed in Von's eyes as well.

Her favorite argument was one involving my hair. She took up that one today.

"You just look so--" she stared at me.

I knew exactly what was coming. She had been looking bored earlier. She was texting frantically with the Pittsburgh branch. Then suddenly everything died down. She was itching for some kind of excitement, I could tell almost immediately, and I was the only person around to fulfill that need.

"What? I look so what?" I asked, giving her the argument she wanted. Maybe it was also the argument I wanted. Maybe I was bored too.

"Different," she filled in, but the word was weak, as if she was searching for one better, one that dug a little deeper, stung a little harder.

I touched the ends of my longish-shortish hair, as Emily once called it. "The hair?" I asked. It always came back to the hair.

Von stared at me, eyes cloudy and half-confused. "It is…strange to see you with long hair. But no. Something…different."

She turned back to her soup, chicken and dumplings this time. Soup was the only thing Von had been able to stomach for the last three weeks. She ate so much of it I was starting to get morning sickness by merely smelling it. She stirred the soup. She spooned up one bite. She brought it to her mouth. Then she stopped. Her eyes flashed to mine. "You're really not going to cut your hair?

"It *is* the hair." I pointed a finger at her with a smile as if I caught her red-handed.

"No," she said, "it's really not."

We sat quietly, Von eating her soup, me kind of staring off into the distance.

"You should really cut your hair, though," she suggested.

"It is the hair," I said, and I wasn't smiling this time.

"You're back in D.C. now. Nobody gets promotions with your kind of hair. You have to pull it back into some kind of stubby ponytail thing, for God's sake."

I had taken a job as an accountant at Cagney Co. a few weeks after I moved back. It was an easy placement, and a higher placing than I had in California. I hated the job and the city more than I remembered. Sure, San Diego was a city, but it was a different kind of city. A city in which I lived alone as a bachelor with no attachments, no promotions I tried for, no children to take care of. A city where I worked some weekends in a surf shop across the street from my condo. A city where I started living with my trust fund as a back-up.

But now I was in D.C. On you own volition, I reminded myself. Von never would have minded you staying in California. You chose this, and quite willingly. But when a chance at promotion came up here at Cagney Co., Von was itching for me to make a run for it. I was less than interested. She stared at me, waiting for my rebuttal. My eyes met hers. I stayed quiet.

"God, that irritates me."

"My ponytail irritates you," I said, with measure.

"No, when you're quiet. You never were quiet. And now you're quiet, and you don't answer me, and what the hell is that all about?" Her voice rose, egging me on. She was desperate for a fight.

I could not give her one. I was sick of fighting. Not with her, but with everything. I was sick of fighting with everything, fighting for everything. All that fighting. And for what?

"You're really not taking the promotion?" she asked.

Ah, I had realized then what for what word Von was searching. Ambitious. I was no longer ambitious. I was no longer ambitious in the way she remembered. And suddenly her fixation on my hair made sense.

"I'm not taking the promotion," I said.

"We're having a baby," she countered.

"I have plenty of money. I've been on my own for years. I've saved forever. I have the trust fund," I added.

She shook her head then. "It's not that," she said.

"Then why did you say it?"

Fire lit her eyes. "When did you become so...so--" she let out a frustrated cry. "I can't find the word to describe you."

"Sorry."

"Oh, don't say that like I'm hurting your feelings. You could care less." She started to roll my eyes, but stopped. They flashed with an almost giddy desperation. "California!" she shouted accusingly. "That's what you are. When did you become so California?"

"Probably since I moved to California," I answered.

"Well, you're in D.C. now."

"I guess that's a problem I don't really care about."

"Why?" she asked, exasperated.

"Why should I keep fighting for a promotion in a field I don't even like?" I asked.

She gave me a blank stare. The she shook her head. "God, you're irritating. Get away from me." She pushed at the space between us.

I laughed.

"It's not funny."

"It kind of is."

She shook her head, and huffed out a breath. Then she grabbed her work laptop from the kitchen counter. "I need to work," she muttered.

"Then you should work," I said, and leaned down to kiss the top of her head. "I love you Von. And I love our baby," I said. "I'll take care of both of you. And I don't even need a promotion to do it."

She blinked up at me. "I don't understand you."

I didn't know what to say to that. "I'm going for a run." I grabbed a water bottle from the refrigerator. Then I thought of something. I turned back to Von who was already lost in her phone. I was going to say something, but I wasn't sure what. A rebuttal? A farewell? I had no clue. But then I saw it. Von stared at her phone, completely engrossed in whatever she read. She opened her mouth once then closed it. Her throat convulsed, and she nodded. It was the throat thing that gave me pause. I cocked my head to study her, but she had already looked away, a hand covering her mouth as she read another incoming text. She worked her fingers over the phone quickly, texting whatever reply the bakery needed.

I left, a little reluctantly then. Had I been too hard on her? Too glib?

Maybe I should change back. For her. For the baby. It would make everything easier. I squinted in reflex of the blinding sun and kept walking.

Jenna

She never should have clicked on that video, the video that talked about the guy who gave a heroic fight against the cancer that ravaged his body.

And then died.

Because then Jenna clicked on the next video and then the next, each one more devastating and heroic than the last. She did not want Michael to be a video, or a hero, or whatever. She wanted Michael to be alive and strong for a very long time.

She wandered then, the way she had started wandering around when Michael was sleeping. In her robe. In the dark. Sipping first coffee, then whiskey. Whiskey was still as disgusting as it was in college. Jenna grimaced and tossed the remains down the sink. Michael was sick constantly. Tumors were everywhere. Like doctors originally predicted, radiation wasn't working.

Jenna stared at the clock.

It wasn't that late, maybe only nine o'clock, but she felt spent.

She watched Michael after that. She stared at him sometimes, willing his body back to health. It never worked.

He was on the couch, remote in hand. Asleep. Waxy and ashen. And sweaty.

Jenna's stomach turned.

She knelt and placed a hand on his cheek.

"Ugh," He moaned. "I'm hurting all over, Killer."

Jenna's heart clenched at the nickname. "What can I do, Mikey?" She ran a hand over his head. Jenna never called him Mikey. Never. Where had that come from?

He smiled weakly. "Mikey?"

Jenna laughed softly and shrugged with a look of bewilderment. "I don't know."

"You're cute," he whispered, his voice hoarse and almost floating, as if already detached from his body. He reached a hand to her and Jenna imagined his voice and his hand tangling together in her hair. "Can you get me some Vicodin?"

"Yeah." In an instant, Jenna scrambled to her feet. She liked having something tangible to do for Michael. She felt so out of control most of the time. She dashed to the kitchen and searched the cabinet, the one they cleared of the good china they never once used and filled with Michael's medicine and other cancer paraphernalia. She shook the bottle into her hand. Only one pill left. Oh, God, how had she missed that?

Jenna handed the last pill to Michael.

"You are so good to me, Jen." He looked so relieved, as if she walked through the desert to give him a drink.

She kissed his cheek.

The smile he offered her was faint and almost gone before it started.

"I'm going...to…" Jenna choked back tears. "I'm going to the pharmacy. Get you a refill."

Michael was already asleep.

After picking up more pain pills, Jenna drove aimlessly in the car for an hour, sobbing. How would she do this for five more months? How could she not? What would she do after?

You won't Jenna. You won't. He'll beat this.

Today was a bad day.

Tomorrow will be better.

She thought of the guy in the video. His family talking about his last day. His family talking about his last good day.

How would she know when it was Michael's last good day?

She would not. She would never know his last good day until it was over, until he was gone.

She needed to be alone. She needed to be with someone. Gage, she thought as the rain started, as she flicked the wipers to high speed. Gage was here now. She could find Gage.

Jenna pulled over and flicked through her phone. Google search. White Pages. Look-up. Elliot Gageby of Washington D.C. Georgetown, he had said. That was all Jenna really knew.

It was all she needed to know.

Elliot Gageby. The only one. In all of the area.

Gage

I had to do it.

Because, really, I did not know what else to do.

Today was the day. Tonight was the night.

"Von, I need to tell you something." I said this to her as she poured over paperwork at the kitchen table.

"Can it wait?" she asked, absently. "I have this inventory on the Arlington site. And Pittsburgh is--"

"If I don't do this now, I never will." I must have sounded serious, or even bordering dramatic, because Von, looking stricken for the first time in all the years I had known her, stared up at me, lips parted in shock.

"Von, I need to be with you, and I need to be with this baby, with our baby."

"You are with me," she said slowly, giving me a curious look. "Elliot, what is this?" She glanced at her phone again, long enough to have me wondering what was going on with that phone.

"Michael has cancer."

"What?" Von's face registered alarm. "Michael? Our Michael? Jenna's Michael?"

"Nothing's working.

"Babe, why didn't you tell me this?"

"I don't know. I don't know. I'm freaked out. This is insane, and this kind of stuff shouldn't be happening. I thought it was…I thought it was…I don't know. I thought it would get better."

"Well, what kind is it? What are they doing for him?" She stood abruptly, panicked, not waiting for an answer, and I felt terrible for saying nothing sooner. "I should see them. I should see Jenna. Is she okay?"

"No," I said. "She's not okay. And Michael's not okay. And I just need you and our baby and we need to be together."

"Oh, my God, Elliot." She pulled me to her. "Of course. We are always with you. Of course we are."

"It's not getting better."

"What's not?"

"His cancer. It's not getting better. The treatment, I don't know, the chemo, I guess, isn't working."

"It's not?"

"He's dying, Von."

"Oh, my God, Elliot." She held me tighter. "Oh, my God. I'm so sorry."

"I need to know you are here, and you're not leaving."

"I'm not leaving."

"And the baby."

"We're not leaving, Elliot." The sound of tires crunching outside our house interrupted anymore conversation we might have.

"Who could be here now?" Von looked up from my arms to the car lights shining through our front window.

"I don't know. Someone from the bakery?" I suggested.

"Doubtful. They would text me, not drive over in the middle of the night."

I flipped on the porch light, looked out the window. You see those movies with the double takes, and well, that's what I did.

Jenna. Looking like she had pulled herself out of a pond. On my doorstep. In a bathrobe?

"Gage," she choked out, and her hands stretched to me, ready to wrap around me.

"Jen?" It was all I got out before Von moved behind me. "Elliot? Who is it?"

Jenna jolted. She seriously and literally jolted. Her body tremored so hard I almost reached out to her. Her eyes darted from me to Von. They settled on Von's obviously pregnant belly. *Shit. Shit shit shit.* Why did I decide it was a great idea to keep both Von and her pregnancy a secret? Jesus.

Under the porch light, I could see the red flush spread across Jenna's cheeks. Then she realized her hands were still in the air, hugging nothing. She dropped them to her sides, two lead weights.

"This…this…is Von." I said, stammering, epically failing. I pulled the door open wider.

Jenna said nothing. Her lips still parted as if she was going to speak. Nothing.

"Elliot. We *know* each other." Von said with an exasperated shake of her head. She turned to Jenna. "Men are so bizarre. Come in. Come in." Von took Jenna's hand, and Jenna moved as if in a haze through our front door.

Jenna stared at Von's belly, the black maternity shirt pulled taut across it. Her belly button had popped out a week ago, and now it poked through everything she wore. We had laughed about it that morning.

Von pulled Jenna into a hug, and their bellies touched. I winced. But then Von was pulling away, studying her. "Can I get you anything? A drink? You are soaked. I could get you a shirt…might be a little big." She rubbed her belly.

"You're pregnant," Jenna finally got out.

"Yep. We are due in August. Elliot, you didn't tell her?" Von gave me a strange look.

I glanced up to see Jenna's reaction. The red blush deepened across her face. "Oh. Oh. Oh, wow." Her throat convulsed. "Wow."

"Why don't you come in? Get dried off?" Von, always a hostess, directed me. I did not move. I stared at Jenna. I never in my life wanted so badly to pull her away, to explain everything. "Elliot? Hello? Why don't you get her a coffee? Something hot." She pulled Jenna close to her. "Elliot told me about Michael. Jenna, I'm so sorry."

Jenna

She hugged and hugged Jenna until it hurt. Until Jenna pulled gingerly from Von's grasp. "I'm sorry. I'm sorry. I shouldn't have come." Jenna shook her head and backed away. "It's late."

"It's not that late," Von insisted.

"Jen," Gage pleaded.

"Jenna?" Von's voice interrupted his. "Stay. Stay with us. Do you need help? Elliot can help. I can help. We'll do anything. Let us know what you need."

"No. No. This was a mis-…I should….go." Jenna started shaking her head, backing away, trying to look a little less psycho-stalkerish. "Congratulations, Von. Gage."

"Jendy, wait. Jenna!" Jenna heard Gage behind her, but she had already run back to her car; she was already pulling it into reverse.

Jenna

"It's probably time to start getting him comfortable," Dr. Lee told Jenna one bright and sunny day in July. Eric and Wendy were with her; they left their four kids at the hotel with Michael's mother.

Jenna's face fell at Dr. Lee's advice. This couldn't possibly be happening. He had a marathon to run in October. She felt her hands go numb. "I thought he had six months?"

"At most. It's not looking like much progress is happening. I would be happy to continue treatment, but at this point it would only be prolonging the end process. As always, it is Michael's decision." He reached into his desk. "Here are some cards you might find helpful." Because Jenna sat numbly in front of him, unable to move, Dr. Lee passed the cards about grief counseling to Wendy and Eric. "I am so sorry, Jenna."

Jenna nodded as the numbing cold spread to her legs.

Wendy and Eric's faces mirrored grim expressions as they stared at the cards in their hands.

Jenna pressed fingers against her temples.

Then Wendy was hugging Jenna in the hall, both sobbing hysterically.

Jenna looked to the only other doctor she knew. "Eric?" He had to know something this one didn't. "It's not…it can't be that soon. Do you know anything?"

"I don't know anything more than Dr. Lee, Jen." Now it was Eric's turn to fold Jenna into a hug while Jenna. "I'm not his doctor. I'm not even an oncologist."

"But he is twenty-eight. Who doesn't--" Jenna choked on her words and pulled out of his grasp. "Who doesn't get to be thirty?"

Wendy wept harder, and Eric reached for her, held her. Tight. Very tight. Jenna watched his fingers dig into her the soft skin of her arms, watched Eric's knuckles turn white. Jenna realized then that nobody would hold her anymore. She was alone now.

"How are we going to tell the kids?" Jenna heard Wendy ask nobody in particular.

The fights she and Michael had all those years ran through Jenna's head. She regretted them now. The baby she never had. Jenna wanted it desperately now. Her dad, even her mom. Jenna wanted them back. Jenna wanted them now.

A do-over.

Jenna wanted a do-over. And over and over and over.

"Jenna, we have to talk about some things." Michael was sitting on a wheelchair next to her in the kitchen.

"Sure, hon." Jenna dried a dish and stuck it in the cupboard.

"I don't have much time left."

"No." Jenna turned sharply as he took her hand. "Don't start talking like--"

"Jen. If I can't be honest with you, then who?" He shook her hand lightly. "Let me stop pretending."

"It's your decision, Michael. Dr. Lee said you could try--" Jenna realized how idiotic she sounded when he gave her a wry smile. Jenna had not repeated to him what Dr. Lee had divulged, but Jenna could never hide Michael's own body from him. In the end, Michael would always know better than anyone what exactly was happening inside him.

"I need one thing. I need you to do one thing for me, okay?"

"Anything." Jenna settled her head in his lap. He was so frail. He hadn't stood on his own in a week. It hurt to look at him sometimes.

"You're going to have to find someone new to love, Jen. When it's time." He stroked her hair.

"No." With a shocked start, Jenna immediately righted herself. "No. I don't want to talk about...about th-this." Her face crumbled. The tears she forced back fell freely now into the sweatshirt that hung from his body.

"I know. This sucks, Jen. But I want you to know I'm okay with it. When you're ready to love someone again. I'm okay with it."

"No. Don't tell me to find someone else. Please, Michael."

"I'm not letting you Havisham on me," he argued weakly.

"This isn't funny." She snorted through her tears. "Also, that's a terrible comparison. It doesn't even work in this situation." She rested her head on his lap again.

"That's my Jenna." He was silent then, still for so long, Jenna thought he fell asleep. He did that a lot lately. Right in the middle of conversations. Then his hand began stroking her hair. "Okay. You do what you want, Jen. I want you to be happy."

"You're the one, Michael," Jenna assured him with everything in her. He had to know that she loved him fully and completely. That she never settled.

"You're the one for me, too." He smiled, pulled her close for a kiss. "But it's okay to have another one."

Gage

I read all the books, but it was nothing like I planned.

At quarter 'til five in the morning I was packing bags into the car. I counted on Von to be freaked, nervous, anxious, or something along those lines, so I woke up early to let her sleep in a little. She would need her rest. And also, I needed a little alone time, time to sit in the car awhile breathing, because my nerves were a little jangly.

But when I walked into the house fifteen minutes later, I found a scene I did not expect. There was Von, sitting at the kitchen table, her hair pulled into a bun and clad in her company polo – a special maternity one she splurged on for herself - and sweatpants. She was also completely engrossed in texts. "Hi, honey." She smiled and flipped her phone upside down. I made a face and incline my head at that strange behavior. "What's that all about?"

"I figured I could get some work stuff out of the way before we leave."

It wasn't really what I was asking, but I let it slide. She was probably nervous. "What could you possibly be swamped with at work on the day you're giving birth?"

"Work doesn't stop for a baby," she argued, rubbing her belly. "It's the Reager wedding, by the way. I know, I know. You don't want to hear it," she conceded at my look, "but that's what we're swamped with. Beth told me the fondant is apparently falling apart. She also told me to stop texting her and go have our baby." Von laughed. "But how can I do that when the ice sculptor won't return our calls?"

"The ice sculptor?"

"I told you about how the Reager bride wants the cake intermingled with an ice sculpture? Yeah, so it's up to us to work with the sculpting company they chose, and the guy is being a total prick about everything. I told Beth we should have gone with the other guy."

"Well listen, I'd love to talk shop with you," I said as I checked my watch, "three hours before the birth of our son, but I need to finish getting ready."

"Okay, yeah." She waved me off with one hand, which meant she was not even listening anymore.

I raised my eyebrows and turned to the bathroom. "Just a quick second."

"Take your time," she called after me.

Take my time? Jesus. I thought I'd be spending the entire morning and half the car ride calming her down, and here she is talking about the imminent birth like we were off to a movie.

I slipped into the bathroom for a hurried breakfast. I hid the food there last night. Von wasn't supposed to eat before the c-section. I had planned to starve myself with her in solidarity, until Von's doctor told me that probably was a bad idea. She didn't think Dad passing out on the delivery room floor was the best idea.

I downed the granola bar in two bites and grabbed a second. Then I chugged the coffee I had poured in the kitchen and sneaked with me. One last granola bar, polish off an apple. Okay. Good to go. I looked at myself in the mirror. Today you're a dad. My heart pounded in my throat, but my reflection smiled at me. I sloshed cold water onto my face, wiped it dry with the hand towel that Von was forever telling me to stop wiping my face with, and headed back to the kitchen.

"Okay, babe, you rea--" I stopped mid-sentence to catch Von sipping wheat was left of the coffee. She was toying with a banana.

I eyed her. "You probably shouldn't eat. They said not to eat."

She screwed up her face in contemplation.

"You might puke," I suggested grimly.

"You really think so?"

"It's a possibility."

She considered some more. Then, "Oh, screw it. I'm hungry," and she chomped into the banana.

"All right then," I said. "Let's go."

"One last text," she said, still chewing and leaning over her phone.

By 6:30, Von and I were in delivery, covered head to feet in blue scrubs. I stood dutifully at her head like the doctor instructed me, my heart exploding in my chest, my feet almost numb from the endorphins coursing through me. I shook my hands nervously under the operating table Von lay on, and took what I hoped was a surreptitious, calming breath. Von had ranted non-stop about work and fondant and that tyrannical ice sculptor and how he damn well better call her back. She chattered the entire way to the hospital, the entire way through her prep. She talked so much that I started getting pissed off. On the day the Von was giving birth to our child, I was annoyed with her. It also grated on me that she was completely cool about everything, while I was a nightmare inside. I did not want her to see me like this when she was so steady.

"What do you think about that ice sculpture? You think it's going to be a catastrophe?" She looked up into my face, which was covered in a sanitized cap and mask.

"Von." I looked at her. Her arms were strapped to the table. She was in a sterile white gown. "Do you see where we are right now? Really. This work stuff can wait."

"Elliot."

"What?" I bit off, fairly irritated over her work.

"Can you come here?" she asked.

I bent down close to her.

"I am freaking out down here. Freaking. Out. I didn't plan this, I didn't plan us, I didn't plan anything. And now we're here. I'm having a baby. A baby! And this c-section felt like the only thing I had any control over. And now I'm strapped to a table."

"Aw, Von," I rubbed a thumb over her cheek, disgusted with myself for being secretly pleased she was also scared out of her mind. "I'm sorry."

"So, please, can you tell me this ice sculpture is not going to be a catastrophe? Is this going to be one huge disaster?"

"Babe," I whispered, "Everything will work out perfectly. *Nothing* is going to be a disaster."

"Okay," said Dr. Warner. "We're ready to go. Are Mom and Dad ready to meet their baby?" I couldn't see her smile through her mask, but I could hear it in her voice.

"Don't you dare peek over that thing," Von whispered fiercely.

"I have no desire to see your innards," I countered, and she smiled.

"And don't get me in the picture. I look terrible."

We both laughed nervously before falling silent.

"I'm making the incision, Yvonne. You are doing great. You too, Dad."

Von looked up at me. "Elliot," she whispered.

"Hmm?" I crouched down close to her.

"I wish you could hold my hand."

I gripped what I could, which ended up being her fingertips. And right when I did, a high pitched wail punctured the room.

I saw the baby, a flash of pink fleshy legs, a patch of dark hair.

"Brown hair," I said to Von.

"Oh, my God," she whispered, and her voice sounded like a shaken up soda, which is exactly what I felt like inside.

"You have yourselves a boy," Dr. Warner announced.

I grinned. A boy. We knew this information months ago, but the formal announcement stole my breath. I smiled down and Von as she smiled up at me. "We have ourselves a boy," she said, her voice shaking with tears. I kissed her head.

"And my God, you should see his legs!" Dr. Warner exclaimed. "This is going to be one tall boy!"

"Soccer player," Von said.

"You think he's going to play soccer?" I turned to Von and smiled.

"I'm cold. Can I get a blanket or something?" Von asked, teeth clattering. "One minute, Yvonne. We'll get you all put back together and get you warmed up." Dr. Warner nodded to a nurse who hurried across the room with our baby.

"She's cold. Is that okay?" I worried over both Von and the baby now.

"Totally normal," a nurse informed me.

"Congratulation, Mom." Another nurse turned to us. "And Dad."

Everyone congratulated us. Some nurses clapped.

"What's he doing now?" Von asked me, her voice rising. "Is he good? Can you hold him for me?"

"He's good," I said. "He's right across the room."

"Can you see him?"

"I'm watching him right now."

"Go hold him, Elliot."

"I don't think I can yet."

"But he's okay? Is he supposed to cry like that?"

"Yeah, babe. He looks really good." I rubbed a hand through her hair then noticed a tears gathering at the corner of her eyes. Some rolled down her cheeks. "Oh, babe." I hunched down. "He's really okay. I promise."

"I know. I believe you." Her voice caught. "I just didn't think I would cry."

I sighed and kissed the corner of her eye. "Honestly? I didn't think you would cry either."

That made her laugh, and I felt a little less out of control.

The nurse called out a bunch of information, none of which meant anything to me.

Then she was smiling, carrying our baby to us. He was wrapped in yellow and now some pink and blue striped cap covered that patch of dark hair I saw earlier.

Adrenaline coursed through me, and when she laid him in my arms, I realized I had no clue how to hold a baby. Are these doctors and nurses supposed to do this shit? They just hand over this baby like he is ours, as if we have any clue as to what we are doing? We just take him home and that's it? Holy shit. This baby is in my arms. Our baby. Our baby is in my arms. Oh, my God, he's amazing. He's amazing and perfect and so little and he weighs nothing. He weighs nothing! How is this even happening? How in the hell is this moment even real?

But it was.

And he was.

I bent over Von, our tiny package in my arms. "Here he is Von. Here he is."

"He's perfect," she said, echoing my earlier thought. And it was crazy, I thought, how terrifying beginnings could be.

Jenna

Maybe it sounds weird to call it perfect, but considering how terrifying endings could be, it was as close to the best ending a guy and the ones he was leaving behind could have.

Jenna was not sure how it happened that she was the only one in the room, being that every family member and close friend had crowded into their house for the past two days. But Michael's mom and dad left an hour before to refill his pain meds, and Wendy and Eric had arrived with pizza. So, while everyone crowded in the kitchen grabbing slices, Jenna snuck to Michael's bed. Alone in the room, she lay beside him. When her hand touched his smooth scalp, Michael abruptly turned his head. His eyes focused on Jenna, and Jenna was shocked how clear and certain they looked, considering he hadn't opened them in forty-eight hours.

Michael, she mouthed, wondering if he would recognize her in his morphine induced fog.

"Jenna, my Jenna." His hand weakly reached for Jenna's face. But when the effort proved too great, Jenna placed her hand on top of his and laid their entangled hands on her cheek. "My girl."

No, she wanted to say. To scream. To plead. To beg.

But she knew he was asking her permission to leave, just as the hospice counselor predicted. So Jenna nodded.

"Do you see it?" He pointed at a closet across the room, a closet Jenna had not cleaned in six months. Six months. An explosion of clothes littered the floor. "It's going to be great."

It was funny. It was hilarious.

And it wasn't funny at all.

"Do you know what I mean?" He whispered this into her ear as she curled her warm body around his shivering one. Jenna had no idea was he meant, but felt some sense of relief knowing that somewhere in Michael, he knew whatever came next was going to be wonderful.

Jenna pressed her face close to his, her mouth against his ear. "It is," she whispered, as she threaded her fingers through his. "You, Michael, were everything to me. I will love you always."

And about twenty long minutes later, as she heard his final, labored breath rattle out of him, Jenna realized she had not cried everything out of her like she previously believed. She turned her face into his pillow, the pillow that smelled exactly like Michael, and knew she would never stop crying.

Gage

Nearly everyone was gone by the time I made it to the funeral home.

I was already suffocating, and I pulled at my tie.

How was I going to do this?

Jackass. Stop thinking about yourself. Don't be a selfish douche.

How the hell did Jenna do this?

And right as I thought it, there she was.

In the front. Flanked by two older people I guessed were Michael's parents. Talking quietly to Roxie.

Jenna Gressa.

Jenna Gressa-Graham, I corrected myself. Then realized it wasn't quite so true anymore. The enormity swamped me.

Her back was to me, and feeling younger and stupider by the minute, I shuffled to the back of the room, hands in my pockets.

Lance walked up behind Roxie, two coats in hand, and when Roxie turned to take one she spotted me. A sad smile crossed her face. I acknowledged her silent greeting with a nod.

"How is she?" I asked when Roxie made it back to me.

"I think she's still in shock. She hasn't cried yet."

I shook my head and crossed my arms. *Aw, Jendy*, I thought staring at her back.

"Don't say anything stupid."

"Jesus, Rox, I'm not a fuc--" Then I stopped myself, realizing if I was going to drop an f-bomb in a funeral home, maybe I couldn't finish the sentence the way I intended. "I'm not the idiot I was ten years ago," I whispered furiously. There. That was better.

Afterwards, as I sat alone on the steps outside the funeral home, it occurred to me why smoking had been so appealing to both my father and Jenna. I could really use a cigarette. Instead, I propped my elbows on my knees and dropped my head into my peaked hands.

Do I pray? Should I pray now?

I sighed into my hands. In the funeral home only minutes before, everyone was whispering, and I did all the things I was supposed to do. When I hugged Jenna, she returned my hug stiffly with a robotic, *Thank you, Elliot.*

Elliot?

Jesus. She was a mess. *I'm sorry, Michael,* I prayed silently to Michael, wherever he was. *She's a mess.*

"Gage," Jenna said, startling me.

I jumped up, brushing my hands nervously over my jacket, my pants. She looked startled herself

"Hey, Je--" I started to say before she was collapsing into my arms. "Oh." I caught her and sunk back down to the cement steps.

"I wa-wanted…to wait. Until th-they were g-g-gone," she sobbed.

And kept on sobbing while I felt utterly useless.

"How am I going to do this?" She wailed.

Would she ever be okay again? What if she cried and cried and never stopped? Terror filled me, but still, I said nothing.

And while I was staring into the night, contemplating her future, my future, and everything else in the world, I felt her breathing slow, her wracking sobs fade.

"Thanks for not saying anything," she said, her eyes were red and nose was running all over my tie. "Everybody. They say so much," she explained wiping a tissue over her face until it looked raw. "I can't stand it."

"I bet," I said, then cringed. *I bet?*

"You're better when you're not talking," she said with a little smile.

"I need to tell you something, Jendy, and this is the absolute worst time to tell you and the worst place to tell you, but I need to tell you because I don't know when I'll see you again and I don't want to mess it up like last time with Von being pregnant and you seeing all that--"

"Gage," Jenna interrupted, impatiently.

I stared at the ground in front of us, her feet next to mine on the cement step. "We're engaged," I said quietly. "Von and I are engaged."

She was silently nodding the entire time I spoke, as if she expected the news. Then, "I'm happy for you," she said. "Really. I always wanted the best for you."

Jesus, did she want to break my heart? Because she was doing a wonderful job. "You have always been too nice for your own good," I said and squeezed her shoulders. I kissed the top of her head.

"I'm going home alone tonight," Jenna sighed, breaking my drifting thoughts.

"You can stay with me," I offered, "and Von. She would be happy to see you."

"And the baby," Jenna added. "I don't think I'm up for that, Gage. No offense."

"Yeah," I agreed.

"I really should go home," she stood, but didn't move. "I don't think I can."

"Are you sure you don't--"

"Can you give me a push?" Jenna asked.

I almost laughed. I stood next to her, put my hands on her shoulders. Then I turned her to me. "I'm not pushing you, Jen."

"Stop trying to make me cry," she said, her eyes welling up again.

"I hate that this happened to you. I hate that this happened to Michael. I hate it. If it had a face, I'd punch it. That's how much I hate it."

She started breathing hard again, and I could feel the tears start to charge out of her. I pulled her tighter to me. "That was perfect," Jenna choked through her tears. "Dammit. That was perfect."

Gage

Von looked ragged and desperate, her shirt smeared with water and some sticky substance that looked like maybe old formula. I was so used to seeing her straight from the gym, showered and fresh, clothes neat, that the sight of her like this threw me. "Hey, guys," I said slowly, remember all the nights I binged on Netflix after Ryan fell asleep, contemplating exchanging my crusty sweatpants for jeans to look like an actual human being, but never actually getting around to it.

She pounced quickly. "How was it? What was it like out there? It was nice wasn't it? The weather guy said it was a high of eighty today. Unseasonably warm weather, Elliot! *Unseasonably.*"

I shrugged. I had jogged in the park, read a book, picked up a new iPhone, sat down with the iPhone in a Bagel Plus and thought about Jenna. Thought about Jenna and how she was doing right now. I thought about how I should call her or stop over, but I was always with Ryan, and I had no clue if I should attempt to pull that kind of visit off with Ryan in tow. I attempted to call into work and check my voicemails, but as soon as I heard the first ring, I got that puke feeling creeping up the back of my throat and hung up hastily. I had called Jenna instead, but got her voicemail. The voicemail made me worry that something was wrong with her if she was not answering her phone anymore. Basically, except for the bagel and a flashing memory of Ryan curling his little fingers around mine that morning before I left, my day sucked in general.

"I kind of missed him," I said, nodding to Ryan who was bundled in Von's arms.

Ryan was currently screaming so hard his face bypassed red and went straight to purple.

Von's expression at my statement read like she might be having that puke feeling. "Have at it, Daddy." She immediately handed Ryan over. "I was going to take him out, but, God, he pitches a fit as soon as I strap him in. He's been like a banshee on Red Dye 40 today."

"Freedom." I said. "I shouldn't have shown him Braveheart straight from womb."

"Huh?" Von asked but didn't wait for an explanation. "I can't deal right now. He's been screaming his head off for the past hour – ever since the strapping-in debacle. It's like the kid's holding it against me or something."

"He's just like his mom," I said with a grin.

"Ha," Von said with little humor and barreled on. "I have these papers to go through. Something is messed up with deliveries. Devin called to tell me every single thing I'm asking for is on backorder due to some flood. I don't know."

"Why don't you go? I'll take care of him, and you go do what you do best."

"What does that mean?" she asked, a sudden irritation in her voice.

I screwed up my face as I looked for Ryan's bottle in the refrigerator. "Nothing, babe."

"You think I can't take care of my baby? You think I'm a bad mom?"

I turned to stare at her, incredulous. "Babe. I never said any of that." I popped the bottle in a glass of hot water.

"I can manage three bakeries, but I can't handle my child for half of a day, a measly eight hours?"

"I never said that."

"You implied as much."

"You're going off the deep end, Von."

"I know what you're saying, Elliot." He voice grew with every word.

"I'm not saying anything." My voice matched hers. I would have held up my hands if they weren't full of Ryan and bottles.

"I hate this," she whispered.

"You hate what?" I asked carefully. I stood there with Ryan, waiting.

Von didn't answer.

"You hate what, exactly, Von?"

"Never mind."

"I'm not going to never mind that. You hate what? You hate this?" I gestured to Ryan and myself.

"No!"

I cocked my head at her.

"I don't want to fight in front of him."

"Then I'll go put him down. He's ready for a nap anyway."

"Of course you would know that, Superdad."

I narrowed my eyes at her. "What's that supposed to mean?"

"What do you think?"

"I don't know what to think. I had a day off, I come home in a decent mood, and then there is this." I gestured to her.

"This? *This*? What?"

"This mood swing. It's insane."

"So, I'm insane now."

"You know what, Von? I'm done. I'm done with this. Whatever. You are right. I'm wrong. I'm the best, you're the worst. That's the way I think all the damned time. You're a real mind reader, Von. A real fucking--"

"Don't talk like that in front of him!" Von yelled. "Watch your mouth, for God's sake."

I sighed. "Again. You're right. I'm wrong."

"You don't need to be that way!" she countered.

I started to walk away.

"Where are you going?"

"I'm putting him down," I said. "He needs to sleep. And I really have no idea what to say."

"Fine! Whatever!" I heard her keys jangled and the front door slam behind her. "I'll go do what I do best."

Jenna

Jenna sat in the pile of Michael's rubble clutching a book.

Michael's mom recommended the book to her three weeks ago. She said it had helped her immensely. She said a lot of things. Jenna had stared blankly most of the time, cups of coffee forgotten between the two women. I'm worried about you, Michael's mother had said. Jenna had nodded.

Wendy stopped over not long after that, recommending the same book. She told Jenna the hospice counselor recommended it.

Jenna nodded. She had been nodding a lot lately. She said things, what she hoped were the right things. Things like, *I'm doing better. I'm sleeping. I'm taking care of myself.* Lies like that. She took the book, nodding, but thinking, *please leave so I can go sit in Michael's stuff.*

His stuff. His college sweatshirt. His favorite running shorts. His Marine Corps Marathon medals. His pile of books, some that smelled like mildew because they had still been packed away in the garage from the move. His wedding ring wrapped in tissue paper. Jenna would take it out, flip it over and over, try it on. But it would fall off every time and remind her of Michael and how sick he got at the end and how the ring would not stay on his finger anymore. None of the stuff smelled like Michael anymore, but still she would pick it up in her arms and inhale deeply.

At night she'd take a shower, washing her hair with a dime-sized amount of his shampoo, the Dove kind that smelled like cologne. Sure, she could have used as much as she wanted and bought the same scent over and over. But this, this was his.

But now she sat again in his pile of stuff. Every day she would add to it. Today she added that book. The book was not him, but the book had touched his mother, his sister. Michael had always looked so much like Wendy.

Jenna looked at the book.

Starting Over: Life After Death.

Starting over?

A few months ago, Jenna was obsessing over pregnancy tests and Michael was training for a marathon.

She didn't even know which reality was true: the one where Jenna pined over baby clothes and complained about the never-ending changes her agent wanted for her latest manuscript, or the one where Jenna sat like a zombie in the dark in front of a blank Word document, blubbering about Michael and talking to the shrine of his pictures she had set up in the hallway.

Starting over?

Jenna didn't even know where to start.

A knock on the door startled her enough to drop the book.

The door. Jenna supposed she could start there by answering it. She stood up and moved away from the make-shift shrine to Michael, picking her way through the piles of debris on her way to the door. When she tripped over a Lego set Michael had built in third grade, she curse and rubbed her toe. It was then Jenna realized she was still in her underwear and a thin camisole she might not have changed in three days. And she was going to open the door. She cursed again. Jenna sifted through the pile and found Michael's favorite pair of basketball shorts. She hastily pulled them on and threw on his college sweatshirt.

Five more impatient knocks.

I'm coming, she thought irritated. Who would be coming over here anyway? Wendy? Michael's mother? No, they usually called first. And they had gone back to Maine two weeks ago. Right? They were gone, weren't they? Jenna stumbled over more of Michael's clothes that littered the floor. Jenna typically had time to pick up. Probably the FedEx guy. Or the cable guy. Didn't Michael call about the cable back in March, and they never showed? Yeah, he had.

Jenna recalled the grumping conversation about it. So, it was the cable guy. Only about eight months late.

"What?" Jenna grumbled as she swung the door wide.

A gaping stare greeted her. "Okay. You look...good." Roxie stood with two bags of groceries in her arms.

"Roxie," Jenna, thrown off-guard, stared. "What are you doing here?"

"What? I can't visit my friend unexpectedly to secretly check up on her welfare under the guise of a road trip?"

Jenna chuckled. The act felt foreign to her, which made her wonder briefly how long it had been since she laughed.

"So..." Roxie said.

"So?" Jenna asked.

"I can come in?"

"Oh. Oh, yeah! Absolutely." Jenna moved aside as Roxie moved into the house.

"What have you eaten today? And also, when were you last out?"

"I ate a bagel this morning," Jenna lied. "And I went out for a run yesterday night."

"You're lying."

"Yes. Yes, I am."

Roxie sighed.

"I'm fine, Rox."

"What have you been doing?" Roxie nosed around Jenna's house and stopped abruptly at Michael's shrine. "Oh," she said slowly. "Is that a—is that a nest?" Roxie

Jenna slumped to the couch. "Don't judge me."

"I would never. But I think that might qualify as a nest."

"It makes me feel better," Jenna said.

"Does it?" Roxie asked.

Jenna felt Roxie's survey of her and blushed. She had not showered in maybe a week. Her hair, pulled into a greasy ponytail, hung limp. She had looked into the mirror when she woke up and was shocked at her gaunt cheeks, her red-rimmed eyes. "I've never felt better."

"And those are Michael's clothes you're wearing?"

"Perhaps."

"God, Jenna."

"What?"

"You need to eat. I'm making you food. You're eating it, and then we are getting out of this cave."

"I'm not leaving."

Roxie gave Jenna a look.

"I'm not eating, and I'm not leaving," Jenna reiterated.

Two hours later, Jenna stood in Neiman-Marcus with Roxie. Jenna needed a new sheet and comforter set, Roxie had determined earlier while Jenna picked at the food Roxie served her. Mainly, Roxie concluded that because Jenna had confessed that she mostly slept in what Roxie called The Nest because it had been too hard to sleep in her and Michael's bed. It reminded her too much of Michael. Jenna agreed with Roxie, telling herself it was easier to agree with Roxie, but also knowing deep down Roxie was right. Jenna wanted new sheets. Jenna wanted desperately to sleep like a normal person again.

"What about this one?" Roxie held up a flannel set.

"I hate it," Jenna grumped. "Too hot."

"These?"

"What kind of company puts a pattern on a pillow when you cover it with a pillowcase anyway? What a waste of dye."

Roxie's eyebrows shot up. "Okay," she said slowly. "What's really going on here?"

"I hate this," Jenna said. "I don't want to do this."

"You're in the anger stage."

"Of course I'm in the anger stage. What stage would you be in if your husband died?"

"Jenna," Roxie said. "I'm trying to help you. You said you wanted new stuff for the bedroom."

"I changed my mind."

"Listen, Jen, I'm trying to work with you."

"I want to go home."

"It's so nice out. You don't want to stay out?"

"I hate this. There's too much stuff here." Jenna was on the verge of tears. Why was she crying? It was only bedding. But trying to calm herself only made her angrier. Stupid pillow company, she thought bitterly. Stupid waste of dye.

Roxie set the pillow back on the shelf.

"It's too fast. All of this…" Jenna was crying now. In Niemen-Marcus.

A little girl who had been entertaining herself while her mother contemplated sheets stared at Jenna, entranced. Her mother pulled at her hand and gave Roxie and Jenna a smile somewhere between sympathetic and weirded-out. "Come on, honey. Let's go."

"What's wrong with her, Mommy?"

Jenna cringed. She was scaring the children. Horrified, she swiped at my tears. She needed to be at home. She needed to be with Michael.

"Why don't we get food? The food court," Roxie suggested.

"I already ate."

"You barely ate," Roxie corrected.

"I'm fine," Jenna said angrily, yet somehow still sobbing.

"I'm trying to help you," Roxie said gently.

"It's only been two months." Jenna slid to the floor and dropped her head into her hands.

"I'm sorry." Roxie sighed as she hunkered down next to Jenna. "I don't know what I'm doing here."

"I don't know either." Jenna glanced up only to see shoppers stare curiously as they passed.

"I don't want it to get worse."

"Is it going to get worse than this?"

"Don't tempt fate."

"I hate fate." Jenna, in fact, hated everything lately.

"Maybe if you start…like…doing normal stuff again. Living normal life."

Jenna wanted to do exactly that. She also didn't want to. She wanted to wallow in misery forever. She wanted everyone to feel sorry for her. She wanted strangers to stare. She wanted sympathy to be offered. Basically, Jenna was a walking, hoarding, hiding-in-a-nest-of-old-clothes mess of a human right now.

"Have you tried writing again? Or running? Or anything?"

"I don't want to do anything."

"Ever?"

Jenna shrugged.

"What about that book Michael's mom gave you?"

"That book is stupid."

Roxie glanced around, looking completely lost.

"I'm such an ass," Jenna wailed. "You drive all the way down here. I know you're taking vacation days for this. All of you. I know what you're doing. Visiting me. I'm like this little baby who can't even take care of herself."

"Don't be so hard on yourself. You are alone down here. Everyone else has someone. You are doing way better than expected. You are going to be fine. You need time." Roxie said this very convincingly, but Roxie could not see the way she was staring at Jenna.

Jenna could see the doubt in Roxie's eyes, like she didn't quite believe anything coming out of her mouth. Roxie, Jenna decided, was very uncertain of Jenna's future.

"What about Gage? Have you seen him?"

"Not since the funeral."

"What?" Roxie looked incredulous. "You have not seen him since then? What is wrong with him?" Obviously fuming now, she whipped out her cell phone. "I'm calling him."

Jenna's head popped up from her hands. "No." One hand darted out to cover Roxie's fingers poised over her phone. "No, no, no. Don't call him. Please," Jenna pleaded. "He has his own life. And that baby. He's probably so busy with his baby. And Von."

The absolute embarrassment of Gage having to come over and rescue Jenna devastated her. Oh, Lord, Gage seeing her house, that shrine, the nest? No. No way.

Roxie chewed her cheeks.

Jenna's eyes pleaded with her.

"Fine. I won't call him," she agreed. "But what are we going to do?"

"I don't know."

"We could start with standing up, maybe?" Roxie suggested.

Jenna let out one mournful laugh. "And that pillow." Jenna bit her bottom lip. "It wasn't really that bad. I could, you know, I would be fine with buying that pillow, I think. Only the pillow. That's all."

Gage

"It's Roxie," Von said as she tossed the phone to me. She turned back to Ryan, who was screaming in his car seat.

"Rox, what's up?" I asked Roxie as I cleared plates from the table.

"She's not doing well, Gage," Roxie said, and I immediately knew.

"Um, yeah. Hold on a minute."

I glanced over my shoulder to Von, who looked desperate and lost in her quest to calm Ryan. She shook a rattling stuffed monkey in front of his face. He screeched and kicked. I reached into the fridge and tossed her a teething ring. "He's teething," I said.

Thank you, she mouthed back.

Von again became absorbed with screaming Ryan.

I ducked out of the kitchen and into the hallway, where I was sure Von would not hear me talking to Roxie about Jenna. Von and I had been basically a mess lately, especially anything concerning Jenna and Michael. The fight we had about me not telling her about Michael sooner and also never telling Jenna about Von and her pregnancy had not blown over. She raged any time I brought up Jenna or Michael. She raged even more after he died. None of it directed at Jenna, of course, she was sure to let me know. Jenna is innocent. She felt terrible for Jenna. She felt terrible for Michael. She felt terrible for herself. There was no sympathy left for me. I had mistakenly - quite stupidly mistakenly - suggested her rage over the whole thing might be post-partum hormones. Yeah. That theory sunk like a brick. *Michael's cancer, Elliot? I knew nothing about it. You decided to say nothing. Yeah,* Von stated dryly, *it's my hormones.* She walked away muttering under her breath; I heard her ten minutes later on the phone with Devin, the Pittsburgh branch manager, discussing a new menu direction.

"How bad is she?" I asked Roxie once I was safely half-way down the hall.

"Terrible."

"Really?" Well, shit.

"What did you expect?"

"I don't know. Not that bad. Isn't his mother staying with her?"

"She left last month."

"Last month?" Michael's mother had been gone a month? Jenna had been alone an entire month? How could I have lost track of time so badly?

"She doesn't eat. I can tell. She's like a little twig."

"Aw, hell."

"I had to buy her new stuff for the bedroom."

"Why?"

"She won't sleep in the bed."

I groaned.

"She hates leaving the house."

"Oh, shit."

"I went there a week ago and stayed for the weekend. She seemed better when I left. You know, I made her eat and go outside and all that stuff. She said she'd make sure to go for a walk or something every day. But now I've been trying to call all week and she won't answer."

"Jesus, Rox, she could be--"

Roxie interrupted quickly. "I know she's there. She calls me back and leaves messages when she knows I'm at work."

"Oh, shit," was all I could say again.

"I know. She doesn't even want to talk to me anymore. Maybe I'm trying too hard. And you? Why haven't you been there? She needs you."

My stomach lurched. "I...I don't have an excuse." Even though I kind of did with Ryan teething early and crying constantly, with me going back to work on approximately three hours of sleep a night, with Von acting strange all the time, alternating between crying on me, raging at me, ignoring me, and then acting completely fine and normal.

"I lied to Jenna. I told her she would be fine. I really don't know though," Roxie said.

"I'll go see her," I said resolutely.

"And don't tell her I told you any of this. I wasn't supposed to say anything. Yeah, right. Like I'm not going to tell you."

I smiled. Thank God for Roxie. "Okay."

I hung up the phone and turned. And out of the corner of my eye saw Von's ponytail swing out of view. She had been listening. I braced myself for the worst.

"Von?" I called out.

"I'm leaving," she called back from somewhere downstairs.

"Where are you going?"

"Out."

"Where?"

"I have work to do, Elliot. No big deal." She wound her purse strap over her shoulder. "You okay with Ryan? He hasn't cried in at least five or six minutes."

She seemed normal. Maybe she hadn't been listening. "Yeah, sure. No problem." I tried a smile.

She smiled back. It didn't reach her eyes.

I narrowed my eyes at her. "Were you listening to me? On the phone?"

"Yes."

I wasn't surprised at her answer. She never had been a liar.

"And you're pissed?"

"You're not keeping secrets from me? Again?"

"No. I...I didn't want to upset you again. I'm walking on eggshells here, Von."

She sighed. "I'm going to work. I don't want to talk."

"I already apologized. I don't know what more to say. I didn't know how to tell you. I was…I was stressed out of my mind back then," I called out as I watched her bob away from me. "I still am."

It was late, really late into the night, when Von finally walked through the door.

"Where were you?" I asked, flicking off the television. My voice was flat, in preparation for another fight. "You could not have been at work that whole time."

"I'm sorry," she deflected and trudged up the stairs to me. "Where's Ryan?"

"Asleep. It's almost midnight."

"Where did you go?" I asked again as she turned to hang her coat in the closet.

"Out," she said vaguely.

I moved to her. "I was worried about you."

"I'm sorry," she said.

"For what? I'm the one who screwed up."

"No, no. Don't say that, Elliot," she said, averting her eyes. "Don't put this all on yourself."

"What are you talking about? None of this is your fault."

"Elliot, I need to tell you--" But she stopped. Closed her eyes. Shook her head. "You should see her. Jenna. Go see her. Tomorrow. You should see her tomorrow."

"What are you talking--" my words were cut off in my throat when I saw Von's tears. I swallowed hard. "Do you want to come with me?"

She shook her head. "I want to, but I have so much to finish up tomorrow. All these pie orders. Thanksgiving." She shrugged. "Then Devin is stopping down to go over numbers from Pittsburgh. Tell Jenna…tell her I'm thinking about her. Okay?"

"Yeah. Yeah, sure. Of course." I wrapped Von in my arms and pulled her close when she started crying. Confused, I stared at our refection in the mirror. Were we fighting? I was not sure, but I had a strong feeling I had wrecked something very important.

Gage

"Ah, I was wondering when you'd show up." Jenna leaned against the door she just opened. I don't know what I was anticipating – a slammed door in the face, a hug, a sigh, a sobbing mess – but this was not it. She looked nervous; she looked jumpy; she looked too skinny. But she did not look crazy.

"What are you talking about?" I asked.

"You two don't think I am that dumb, do you? Roxie conspiring with everyone about some schedule to make sure I was brushing my teeth every day?"

"I conspire with no one," I said easily.

"Ha!" Jenna spared me a short laugh and walked into her house. I was obviously supposed to follow. The strangeness of her house, which I only saw once before when I stopped to visit Michael, had me reliving memories of college. How I knew so very much of her then. How I knew so very little of her now. Pictures of Michael filled the entryway. I wonder if Jenna even registered that she lightly touched the top of each one as she passed.

"I figured she'd talk you into it. You're the reinforcements, huh?" Jenna

"The reinforcer. I like that title." Was I supposed to keep it light? Maybe Jenna was a ticking time bomb, set to explode and take everyone with her without warning.

"What do you want, Gage? To save me?" This must be the bitter stage, I thought.

"I'm supposed to get you out of the house."

"Too late. I'm already back."

"From where?" It was seven-thirty in the morning. She was still in sweats and a tee-shirt, the same outfit she religiously wore in college.

"Bagel Plus."

"Do not tell me you are working there." Roxie was right. Jenna had not only gone off the deep end; she dove in head first.

"I'm not working there," she answered, much to my relief. "Why are you here?" Jenna asked.

I cocked my head to study here. "What kind of act is this?"

She laughed. But I caught the melancholy that flickered in her eyes. I caught it and then I watched her bury it.

I squinted. "You seem…odd."

She rolled her eyes, the same ones that hid her despair. "I am odd. That's all I ever was. How many thirty-two-year-old widows do you know, Golden Gage?" Something caught in her voice.

That's when I walked to her. When I tried to pull her into a hug, to comfort her, she ducked easily from my reach and gave me a watery smile. And said the last thing I expected. "No, thank you."

I stared at her.

She stared at me.

I thought of something. "Can I use your bathroom?"

Jenna gestured grandly with her hand as if to say, *be my guest.*

As soon as I shut the door, I rifled through her medicine cabinet. "Zoloft, Zoloft, Zoloft," I muttered under my breath as I twisted medicine bottles and read labels. Most belonged to Michael. Insanely high doses of painkillers, old prescriptions for infections. I found exactly one bottle labeled Jenna Gressa-Graham. It was Zoloft, and it was the maximum dose.

I emptied the bottle into my hand and began counting the pills. My brain went into over drive. *She is prescribed a month's worth of pills, and she should be taking one a day, and today is the sixteenth, and if she already took one today, there should be, what, how many left? Fourteen?*

I counted. Exactly fourteen.

I sighed, and leaned against the counter. So, Jenna was on schedule. I flushed the toilet and washed my hands, since technically that was the reason I used her bathroom.

I meandered out to Jenna who was standing at the sink, casually waiting for me, a glass of water cupped in her hands. "Are they all there?"

"Hmm?" I raised my eyebrows in what I hoped looked like an innocent gesture. "What's that?"

"My pills. You counted them, didn't you? Am I doing a good job? Do I pass?" She took a sip of water then set her mouth in a grim line.

"Jendy. Come on."

"I've lived a lot of life without you. I'm not that girl anymore, Gage."

"I never said you were."

Jenna gave me a look that said she did not believe me. "I'm not crazy."

"Jenna. Jesus. I never said you were. Never."

She pursed her lips together. I watched her tongue run over her teeth. "Yeah. Okay." She turned to the sink. Then she whipped around suddenly. "No. No. You know what, Gage? I'm not doing this."

"Not doing what?"

"You don't get to waltz back into my life like we are BFF's. You barely know me anymore."

"I know you," I countered.

"No you don't!" She shouted the words at me, and they pierced like the bullets they were meant to be. "For God's sake. You counted my pills!"

"I'm sorry. I'm *sorry*. Okay? What the hell am I supposed to do Jen? I'm trying to fucking take care of everyone here!"

"Then why don't you go home and take care of them. Why don't you go home to Von. And your baby," she added bitterly.

"Wow. That was mean." I raised my eyebrows at her. But Jenna had not been wrong. I definitely did not know this Jenna.

"Mean?" She laughed at shook her head. "What is this, junior high?"

"Jenna," I said with as much patience as I had left. "Please…come here, okay?" I tried to pull her into a hug.

"No!" she screeched and pulled back. "We are not friends, Gage. We are not friends anymore."

Stunned into silence I could only stare. I ran my tongue over my teeth. "Who is being junior high now?"

"Shut up."

"Jendy, this is ridiculous. I'm trying to help. You're not being fair."

That was what set her off. She spun, a tornado of barely contained fury. "Not being fair? I'll tell you what's not fair. This! *This* isn't fair. I get Michael for five years. Not even! Not even five years. Michael, the man who was supposed to be the love of my life. Supposed to love me forever. We were supposed to get--" she choked on a sob, but winced when I tried to touch her. "We were supposed to get wrinkles and arthritis together. *We* were supposed to have the baby. And what did we get? Five years! That's it. Congratulations to Jenna. And you." She turned on me.

"Jenna," I interrupted.

"No! And you! I get you…and your…your Mommy issues and your--"

"My Mommy issues?" I bit out. "What?"

"Don't interrupt me." Jenna poked her finger into me to emphasize every word, "And your girls…and your Alaskan-sized load of baggage for thirteen years. For the rest of my life. And Von," she said, looking up at me. "Von gets everything else."

"Jenna."

"So don't tell me--" She pushed at my chest.

"Jenna." I grabbed her wrists. "Jenna, stop."

She pulled out of my grasp. "Don't tell me about what is fair and what isn't." She pushed me hard, catching me off guard, and I stumbled back. My hand reached out for balance; I caught her wrist again and tugged her with me. She bumped up against my chest as we fell against the counter.

"Don't!" Jenna shrieked pulling at her wrist. "Don't touch me. I can't—I can't stand when you touch me!" She pushed at me again. And again. Then she stared at me, the breath heaving out of her.

I tried to find my equilibrium. Everything swayed around us. "Jenna," I said calmly. "I'm giving you a pass here because of what happened, but--"

"I don't need your stupid pass," she interrupted and pushed me again, sending me off kilter once more. "Screw you, Gage, for even coming here. Screw you for ever finding me. Michael," she spat out, "wouldn't even want you here."

Something in me snapped at that. Angrily, I swiveled.

Jenna's eyes flared. Out of the corner of my eye, I saw her ball a fist.

"Seriously?" I choked on a bitter laugh. "You wanna fight me? Is that what you want Jenna? You want to punch me in the face again? Break my nose? Watch me bleed?"

I watched Jenna's flaming, desperate eyes narrow on me, her target.

"Go ahead, Jen. Break my nose. Do it. Just do it now. Because I'm already bleeding." My voice cracked.

Jenna's eyes went wide. She hesitated.

"Do it, Jenna. But let me tell you one thing. You can hate me. You can punch me. And it's not going to change anything. Michael is gone. Ryan is here. And I never should have tried to kiss you on your wedding day, and I feel like the lowest level of scum for doing that to Michael. And the past is the fucking past. It's gone, Jenna. And there is nothing I can do about it."

The silence that followed enveloped us, it gathered around us, it held us captive. The only thing I could hear was the faint breath from Jenna's earlier exertion escaping her otherwise still face. I swallowed, and the sound echoed in my ears, and I wondered if Jenna could hear it like I could hear her. I looked her dead in the eyes. "And I miss him, too."

Jenna broke then. The sob was deep and slow and it wracked her body with an almost unnatural force. She turned inward then; she folded into herself, her shoulders shrinking, her knees twisting as her body slid to the floor.

I watched it. I watched Jenna break apart in front of me. I felt myself break apart with her.

And then I sat down beside her.

When Jenna finished crying, when we both finished crying, she looked at me, her face torn apart, her hair wet with her own tears.

I reached out, tentatively, because I wasn't quite sure how she would react. She still might be itching to punch me, and just because I invited her to crack me in the face earlier did not mean I actually wanted it to happen.

I placed a hand over hers.

She looked down at our hands. Then she stared straight ahead, her eyes cloudy. She closed them, almost as if she was in pain. My body tensed, waiting for the worst, bracing for a final blow. Finally, with one long, strangled sigh, she twined our fingers together and dropped her head against the cupboard behinds us.

"You feel better?" I asked.

"I feel worse," she said resolutely. She looked exhausted.

I nodded. "Me too."

She surveyed me. "And you look like shit, Gage. I mean, really. Are you even sleeping?"

I felt the sharp pang of laughter. "The irony of you asking that," I said and rubbed a hand over my face. Jenna looked like she gave up sleep on a bet. And was winning.

She rested her head on my shoulder. I kissed her forehead then shifted, and Jenna fell into me. Without thinking, I wrapped my arms around her.

And we sat there like that until my fingers tingled and my arms went numb, until the sun dipped low, until the sky blurred pink.

Jenna

After Jenna's fight with Gage, she tried to be normal again. Really, she did.

She made dinner. Her favorite: Penne with Vodka sauce and one of those bagged salads with cranberries and almonds in it.

But then she sat with her plate at the table and waited for Michael to walk through the door.

She went for a jog.

But Jenna kept glancing over her shoulder, certain Michael was behind pacing her.

Finally, Jenna tried sleeping in their bed again, fresh and new with different sheets and a big fluffy comforter Roxie bought online and had delivered to her as an early Christmas present. But Jenna woke up in the middle of a nightmarish sleep, drenched in sweat. She moved to the couch and vowed never to go back to the bedroom again.

Jenna visited with Wendy and Eric, who were kind enough to drive in almost every weekend with the kids. But she came to dread their visits. The kids shrieking and playing around Jenna. Little Matty who looked so much like Michael reaching up his pudgy little hands to her. "Aunt Jen-Jen," he asked once, "when's Uncle Mikey coming home?"

When they invited her to Thanksgiving dinner, she had to decline. The thought of a holiday with everyone but Michael was torture. *How will I do this every year?* She thought bitterly as she ate one-third of a Hungry Man turkey dinner on Thanskgiving.

One day, she tried to write.

She typed and typed and typed for pages.

But when she got out of her writing trance, she looked up and realized she was alone.

So alone.

I'm sorry, Michael, she thought as she choked back tears. *I can't do this alone.*

Gage

"I'm meeting Jenna at Bagel Plus tonight."

This declaration was met with an apathetic *Hmm* from Von and a squeal from Ryan. The squeal probably had less to do with Jenna and more to do with the fact that he had reached under the couch and found a fistful of old Cheerios.

"Can you get those from him?" I nudged Von who was staring at her phone.

"Hmm?" She answered again. She punched in a message and smiled to herself.

I pushed myself away from our lunch and caught Ryan's hand before it disappeared into his mouth. He screeched in protest then burst into tears.

His wail pulled Von out of her trance. "Oh, baby, what's wrong? Is Daddy a meanie?" Von smiled sympathetically at Ryan, but made no move to scoop him away from me.

I bounced him while he sobbed. "So do you think you want to come with me? You and Ryan. It could be fun."

She finally acknowledged me with a confused glance. "Come where?"

I gave her a look. "To Bagel Plus," I said slowly. "To see Jenna."

"Wait. You're going to see Jenna?"

"At Bagel Plus. Yes. I thought you could come with me."

"I have a meeting with Devin."

"On a Saturday evening?"

"It's about the renovations," she said quickly.

"That's not what I asked," I said. "Why on a Saturday night?"

"It's the only time he could come."

I stared at her.

"It's important, Elliot."

"So is what I'm doing."

She tilted her head and pursed her lips. *Really?*

"Yes, really." I answered her unasked question.

"So, call Reggie," she said of our babysitter.

"Reggie is New York City with her boyfriend this week."

Von shrugged. "I don't know what else to do."

"I thought we could go together. Jenna would be happy to see you."

"I do miss her." Von did seem to consider that. "But, I can't cancel now."

"You could take Ryan," she said. "Boys night out. Tell Jenna I'll see her next time."

"You could take him. You don't get too much one-on-one time with him."

Von's expression fell. "That was mean."

"I didn't mean it that way." I bumped her hip. "You know that."

"And anyway, I'm not taking a baby to a meeting."

"It's just with Devin."

"It would hardly be productive."

"Devin wouldn't care. Where's the meeting?"

Von colored deep red and looked away.

"What's that all about?" I nodded at her reddening face and grew suspicious. All the lightheartedness I fought to keep fell away instantly. "Where is this meeting, Von? This meeting on a Saturday night?"

"It's a meeting!"

I stared at her hard. Ryan shrieked some more.

"I'm not your mother," she said.

"Where is it?" I pressed.

"At his hotel."

"Yeah. That seems innocent. Why would I be worried?"

"For God's sake, Elliot, this is ridiculous. I'm just meeting with him. It's about the renovations!"

"So you said already. If you won't come with me, then give me a night off, Von. Take Ryan to the meeting."

"Come on, El. You know what I'm like when I'm alone with Ryan. It's better when you are around."

"You are fine when you are alone with him."

"I'm a mess. I never know what to do when he starts freaking out."

"Why are you so worked up about getting to this meeting?"

"He flew in from Pittsburgh! Jenna's here all the time. You can meet her tomorrow."

We stared at each other silently until Von broke. "This is pathetic. We are fighting over who has to stay with our child. It's so selfish."

Ryan took that opportunity to grab a fistful of my hair and pull hard. "Ow." I struggled to untangle my hair from his hand while Von tried hard not to laugh. I gave her a look while I put Ryan in his bouncer.

"Oh, come on. It was kind of funny."

"Yeah. Hilarious."

I could tell by Von's expression that she was struggling to find our couple's counselor's advice, because I was doing the same thing.

"I feel," she started then paused. Then she gave up. "Don't be an asshole."

"Good try," I said bitterly.

"Oh, shut up," she slammed her phone to the table.

She stalked out of the room, leaving me alone with Ryan who was chewing his fist now and her phone which

I walked over to it. Six messages from Devin. My hands itched to touch her phone, to slide my finger across the screen, unlock her phone. I wanted to see those messages. And that was something I had never thought before to do.

They were meeting in his hotel.

I put my empty hands on my hips

I'm not your mother.

No, she wasn't my mother. She was Ryan's mother. She was the woman I loved. Even when we fought, even when we could not resolve anything, even when we were seeing a counselor twice a week.

So what should I do?

My hands reached for her phone. Then they stopped. They reached for Ryan instead.

What should I do?

Trust her.

Trust her?

Jenna

Starting out, they tried to meet once a week. They realized quickly that was setting the bar a little too high; Gage had a child and a fiancé now, plus work. Jenna had even more work and deadlines she dreaded. They were no longer in college. They did not live the single life in Pittsburgh any longer.

Gage and Jenna did not do much other than meet at Bagel Plus, she on her laptop, typing away, he, eating a bagel or a cookie or whatever and silently reading the paper or a novel or scrolling through his phone. Occasionally, he'd laugh out loud and show her whatever article he was reading or read a passage aloud. Both took advantage of the Bagel Plus Free Refill Guarantee and drank lots of coffee with lots of sugar. Once or twice, they drank too much coffee, felt jittery, and took a break to walk around the block. Sometimes during these walks, they would talk. Catch up. Jenna told him about her latest manuscript and the parts she was stuck on. She told him about a spin class she was taking and how she hated the instructor, but he was hot so she guessed she would keep up with it. He *was* hot, after all. Gage showed her pictures of Ryan, short videos he took of him crawling and squealing. *My God, he's the spitting image of Von*, she'd say and Gage would nod silently and put the phone away. They would walk some more, past cars and people, the clutter fading away, the noise quieting around them. Jenna's favorite part about talking to Gage was that he never once asked her how she was doing, how she felt. She loved it. Everyone, every single person around her, asked her constantly how she was doing. Not Gage. Most times, Gage simply walked silently beside her, hands jammed in his pockets because he always forgot gloves.

That was all.

That was enough.

Her writing had never been better.

"You seem happy," he said to her once, seemingly out of nowhere.

Jenna thought about it. "Yeah. Yeah, I'm happy." She smiled, surprised with herself and her answer. "And you? Are you happy?" Jenna asked as an afterthought, because of course Gage was happy.

"We're back," he said and nodded at the entrance to Bagel Plus and opened the door for her.

Gage

"It's not that difficult." I said as Ryan screamed over us.

Von practically choked on her tea and stared pointedly at him. "Really?"

"It's not what I thought it would be," I corrected. "But, babies have a lot in common with my old frat brothers."

Von raised her eyebrows so high they disappeared behind the fringe she was constantly saying she regretted cutting into her hair.

"They puke. They sleep. They try to make terrible decisions, and you have to stop them. Rinse and repeat."

"Is that it, Elliot? Is that all it is?" Von asked bitterly.

I gave her a look. "Von. Come on, I was kidding. It's a joke."

"No. Don't give me those stupid Golden Gage sympathy looks. Yeah. I know all about Golden Gage and his golden life. Jenna and I talked back in the day. So, no Elliot. Screw this."

"What are you talking about?"

"You, Elliot Gageby! Screw you and how easy this is for you," she spat. "Of course it's easy for you. Everything. You're whole life is handed to you. You don't even have to work if you don't want to. You can live off the trust. Must be nice."

"You think I had an easy life? Are you kidding me? You've met my family. Do you know what it was like growing up in that? I barely touched that trust fund. I have worked years, years, Von, in a business I can't stand and you don't get to harp on me for wanting that hell to end."

"You have a child."

I laughed bitterly. "You are going to use that against me? Me, who took twelve weeks of family leave so you can go back to your buttercream bullshit in less than a month? Three weeks?"

"Buttercream bullshit? Whoa," she said incredulously. "That was unnecessary, Elliot."

"Are you kidding me, Von? I know you can't wait to get out of here and away from me. You can't wait to leave. You are out late. You are on your phone constantly when you are here."

Von's eyes went wide.

"Look at that. You have your phone right now." I had come to hate that phone. "Can't let it go for one minute. At least put it down for our fight."

"No."

"Come on, Von. Put it down."

"I said no," she repeated forcefully.

"Why are you afraid for me to see your phone? Always flipping it over, always locking it. Password protected, Von? What is going on in that phone?"

She turned as white as the fingers she had death-gripped around her phone.

The idea slowly ate my brain. I cocked my head as I eyed her. "What *is* going on in that phone, Von? What was the meeting about? Devin, was it? What did Devin have to say to you at that meeting?"

Tears started rolling down Von's cheeks. She shook her head.

I walked deliberately toward her. "Von. What is going on in that phone?" A dead calm fell over me, my voice was quiet enough that Von's weeping echoed loudly through the house.

I put my hand over hers. "Von. Let me see the phone."

Her breath hitched through her tears. "You," she started before she gulped down a sob. "You have to know, Elliot. You have to know I had a life before we slept together that night. I didn't plan this. You have--" she sobbed uncontrollably, her face burned red and wild. "You have to know. I was with him before the baby. I had a diff—a diff—I had a different life."

I blinked slowly. "You're cheating on me."

"No. Yes. I don't know. Elliot, I was—I was with him before you. You were one night in November. He was a year, an entire year before that."

Her statement twisted through my gut. "You cheated on him. With me. That November. You cheated on him."

"I thought it would be one time."

I remembered Emily and what I did to her that November with Von. The fight that I felt for the first time in a long time ripped through me like a storm. But now it was gone. Immediately dissipated. I could feel the wreckage all through me, but there was nothing I could do about it. Because I also had a different life before Von. One in California. One that would have eventually included Emily? I don't know. Because I screwed that one up before it even had a chance to materialize. Von had cheated on her boyfriend. I had cheated on my girlfriend. We were both in the same boat. In the same house.

Saturday, February 22, 2014

Jenna

"Gage, hey! I wasn't expecting you!"

He stepped silently through the door, hands in pockets. It was then Jenna noticed his face was red and wind burned.

"How long were you out there? Are you cold?" She immediately took his hands in hers and blew into them. "You don't even have gloves on! You want coffee?"

He said something, but his gaze was so intent on Jenna's lips pressed against his hands, she heard nothing but a dull roar charging through her head.

Jenna dropped his hands quickly and though she was not sure why, wrung hers together. "Well, come in," Jenna waved him in and charged to the coffee table where she picked up a steaming mug. She drank deeply then looked over the rim only to realize Gage was watching her. "Oh. Shit. Did you say yes or no to the coffee?"

"Are you working? Maybe I should go."

"No!" Jenna reached for his hand to stop him. "Gage, don't go. I'm sorry. I wasn't working, just thinking. I'm pretty excited--" Then she stopped to look at his face. Something was off. He swallowed thickly. Jenna watched his throat convulse. "Are you ok?"

"Yes." He ran a hand through his hair and the snow that turned to water in the heat of Jenna's house rained down onto the carpet. "No. I'll take that coffee."

"Ok," Jenna said warily as she pulled another mug from the cabinet. "Do you need to talk about something?" He was silent as she handed him coffee. "Lukewarm. Only the best for you."

He shrugged. "It's fine," he said without drinking it.

"Gage, what's wrong? Talk. I'm a good listener."

He raised one eyebrow – the move he finally perfected – as he dropped to the table.

"I will be," Jenna amended. "Starting now." She smiled broadly. Gage sighed. Jenna's smile faded as she cocked her head and patted his hand.

He was silent for a long time. He twisted the mug. Finally, he turned and looked out the window. "She cheated on me."

Jenna stared uncomprehendingly for what felt like forever. "Von? Cheated on you? *Von*? Our Von?"

"Our Von." He laughed sadly then shrugged. "And I guess technically she also cheated *with* me."

"What?"

"And Emily." He looked past Jenna, his eyes lost in thought. "I'm not really sure if I cheated on her, because really we weren't together at the time. Mostly weekends, you know? Sometimes during the week. I think about it and, well, what's the difference really? Everyone is fucking hurt."

"Who is Emily?" Jenna felt like she was deciphering an unbreakable code.

"Nothing is good with us," he replied.

"With you and…Emily?"

"No, with Von.

"Nothing is good with you and Von. Nothing? Ever?"

"Ryan. Only Ryan is good with us," he corrected.

"Gage, you are going to need to rewind this story about one year. I have no idea what you are talking about."

"I wish I could rewind it." He paused. "No, I take that back. Then there would be no Ryan. And how can there be no Ryan?"

Jenna, still lost, felt her mouth move but no words escape. Then finally she formed something. "Gage? Where is Ryan?"

"With Von. Visiting her family in Pittsburgh. They haven't been there in a while. She wanted him to visit."

"For how long?"

"I don't know. They left almost a month ago."

"A *month*? This happened a *month* ago? This happened a month ago and you haven't said anything? And you haven't *seen* them? What have you been doing?"

"Thinking."

"Gage, what the hell is wrong with you?"

"I was thinking a lot."

"Gage, this is crazy. This is insane. They are in Pittsburgh? And you're here, *thinking*? What are you *thinking* about?"

"How I messed up."

"What did *you* do?"

He didn't answer.

"Gage, what did you do?" Jenna asked insistently.

"Fell in love with the wrong girl."

"No! You cheated on Von too?" Jenna could not stop her mouth from dropping open. Her heart sunk. "You cheated on her?"

He laughed at that, the low and hollow sound escaping him. "You have no clue. No clue how funny that is."

"What are you saying?" Jenna eyed him suspiciously.

"She cheated on me."

"She cheated on you." Jenna parroted back in the same low, dry voice, as she tried desperately to find her bearings. "I know that. And you did not cheat on her, but you may have cheated on Emily, who now is irrelevant to this story. Because she is back in…California?"

"Yep."

"But you are in love with someone else?"

"Yeah."

"How is that not cheating, Gage?" Jenna was not going to let him off the hook. "Being in love, in my book, is pretty much cheating."

"The girl doesn't know."

"What?" Jenna's face screwed up. "I am so lost."

"I can't blame Von. It was mostly my fault." He sighed.

"It was your fault that she cheated on you?" This entire conversation was so morose, so gloomy, so unlike Gage. "Who is the girl you fell in love with?"

"This coffee is not enough." Pushing his coffee away, Gage ignored Jenna and walked to the refrigerator. The move looked so familiar, Jenna expected him to take a swig right out of her milk carton. "Can I have a beer?"

"It's really old. It was…" *Michael's.*

"Right." Gage started to put it back.

"No." Jenna stopped him with a hand on his arm. "Michael would want you to have his old, bitter beer."

Gage finally laughed. It wasn't his normal laugh, Jenna thought, but at least it was something.

"Nothing was right. For a long time."

"But I thought…you seemed…and she was so…pregnant," Jenna finished weakly.

"I couldn't tell you everything, Jendy. She cheated, but maybe I'm to blame too. We fought constantly. I proposed after Ryan was born. I took it too far. And she accepted because, I don't know, exactly. But, whatever. I screwed up. I don't know what I'm doing half the time anymore."

"Who was it? Who did you fall in love with? Even if you didn't do anything about it, Von had to pick up on that. Maybe that's why she cheated." Jenna said, already in problem-solving mode. If they could figure this out, they could get Von back.

Gage set his beer on the counter. "I'm not going to talk about that, Jen. I should not have even brought it up."

"Why not?" Anger flamed in Jenna. They could fix this. They could fix it, and Gage was refusing. "Who? Emily? Tell me."

"No," he said resolutely and took one of Jenna's hands. He reached for the other. Jenna felt his fingernails dig into her palms.

"That's crap," Jenna said, her voice breaking. "I thought we were friends."

"I can't, Jendy. I'm not going to…" He looked away from her.

Jenna tugged against his hands. "Let me go then."

He held tighter. "No."

Jenna narrowed her eyes at him. She pulled harder. Struggled until they both fell back against the marble counter. Struggled even as his hands pressed hers into that same cold marble behind her.

Struggled as he boxed Jenna in between his feet and the counter without a word. The anger that flamed was now blazing through Jenna, shooting through her chest, prickling down her legs, flaring in her eyes.

"Why did you even come here?" Jenna spat out. "For pity? Because you screwed up another relationship? Just leave. I have enough to deal with--"

"Jenna." Gage stopped Jenna with the three fingers he pressed against her lips. Her eyes, wide and wary, shot to his. The anger that engulfed Jenna rapidly twisted into confusion. "You don't want to say these things, Jen," he whispered shaking his head.

It was his hands. The way it slid a warm trail from her mouth to her cheek. The way his fingers, long and lean, curled around Jenna's chin, held her still. The way the other slid from her hand to the small of Jenna's back, rested right there at the base. It was his eyes. The way they burned into her, through her. It was her name. He called her Jen.

"What are you saying, Gage?" The questioned trembled out of Jenna. He had said nothing at all.

"I've been thinking so much," was all he said.

I fell in love with the wrong girl. His words echoed through her.

"You're not saying that," she choked on a sob.

He shook his head. "I'm not saying anything," he said.

Jenna was lonely. Jenna was alone. In this house. With Michael haunting her.

Jenna looked up into Gage's eyes.

God, Jenna thought, *I am so lonely.*

Gage

I knew it when she knew it.

Her eyes darted back and forth.

Her breath, unsteady, tumbled out of her parted lips and onto my hand.

Her bottom lip quaked. Did she know she was biting it? Did she know she was killing me?

She was going to kick me out.

I lost the girl I loved. And then I lost another one. And I'd keep losing and losing and losing until I was broken.

But in all the years I knew Jenna Gressa, she never failed to surprise me.

A sob shattered out of her.

And then her hands were in my hair, pulling my mouth to hers.

Jenna

Jenna's hands were in his hair.

Gage's hands were everywhere.

His body pressed into Jenna as he backed her through the room.

Blindly, Jenna groped around behind them, fumbling for light switches, searching for…what? What was she searching for?

His hands were on her face. On her neck. Running down the length of her back. Pulling Jenna closer and closer until she thought she would melt into him, melt through him.

They were tripping on things. Slipping on scraps of paper with novel ideas scribbled all over them. Stumbling over the mess Jenna left in one of her three-day writing benders. The chair they crashed into wobbled precariously. Gage's hand shot out to steady it before tangling its way back to Jenna's hair.

Was this what it was like when you teetered on the brink for thirteen years? You stumbled around blindly listening to everything fall around you?

"I missed you. I missed you." Jenna repeated the words over and over. But this declaration wasn't an apology or a fact. It was a revelation. Jenna had missed him. All these years. All these misses.

"I missed you, too," he said into her mouth.

For the first time in months, Jenna was happy. She was free. She was floating.

And then she was falling with Gage onto the couch.

His fingers were threading around her hips, pushing into her skin. They found her stomach, hot and quivering, pulsing under him.

He pulled away for one second to look at her, to see her face, her eyes.

Jenna thought she must have looked crazy, maniac even, with her eyes wide and searching his. She did not care.

Jenna's hands shot up, gripping his shoulders as he shifted above her. Gage's muscles bunched and tightened.

A shot of desire, dark and heavy and liquid, shook her. Jenna closed her eyes against the longing she felt deep inside, an ache that was so familiar. And Gage, he was so familiar. And so different.

Jenna's breath caught then stuttered as his mouth took hers again.

Gage groaned.

Jenna had missed this too. This feeling. This wanting.

Jenna hadn't felt like this since…her eyes flew open and flashed to Michael's shrine of pictures watching them from their place on the coffee table.

Gage

Something changed. And like all those years ago, I felt it immediately.

I opened my eyes in time to see Jenna's darting glance.

I stopped to follow her gaze. My hands, half-way to ripping off her shirt, halted abruptly. I focused on Michael, whose face beamed back at us. Jenna's fingers, still on my shoulders, flexed once before they fluttered away. Her eyes changed. I swallowed. Closed my eyes. Dropped my forehead to hers. Her fingertips were now on my chest, pressing lightly. I opened my eyes and waited. She looked like she wanted desperately to say something. She said nothing.

I was glad. I didn't want to talk. I didn't want one word to come out, not from her, not from me. I wanted the silence that engulfed us to go on forever. Because at least then, I'd still be here and she'd still be here and everything would be the same.

But then she was shifting under me. And I knew what she was going to say, because I was thinking the same thing. "This would be wrong wouldn't it?" I lifted my head to look at her.

She looked like she couldn't decide. I sighed and sat up. She followed, tugging at her shirt.

"Does it feel wrong?" she asked.

I felt the breath ripple from my lips. I paused. "Honestly, I don't know. But, yeah. Probably."

Jenna said nothing.

I thought of my life. How I had planned for it to go one way, how I had flipped it over in one kiss. I thought of Von. I wondered what she was doing right now. Was she alone? What was Ryan doing? Involuntarily, my hands clenched.

Jenna spoke first, her eyes shining into mine. "I did love him, Gage."

I closed my eyes. The pain was unbearable, a flood ripping through me. "I love her. It makes no sense given, this," I gestured to the space between Jenna and me, "whatever the hell we just did, but I want it to work with her."

"It makes sense," Jenna said.

"I need--" But I stopped because I had no idea what I needed.

Jenna helpfully filled in my list of needs. "You need to go home, I think. You need to talk to Von. And you need to see your baby. You really need to see Ryan."

There we sat. As awkwardly as we had ever been with each other. Jenna smoothing her hair. Me fumbling with my keys.

Jenna looked at me. "We probably--" she swallowed audibly. "We probably shouldn't see each other."

I turned to her. "For how long?" I asked, already knowing the answer.

She bit her lips and looked into the expanding space in front of us. "Gage," she said gently, "If you are going to work things out with Von, I think you know the answer."

I nodded. She knew how to call me on my selfish son-of-a-bitchery without ever really hurting me.

I walked to the door. And I could see us.

We were nineteen and Jenna was staring up at me, the ground soft and cold beneath her.

We were twenty-one, and Jenna was in my bed smiling, laughing, giddily drunk.

We were twenty-five, and I loved a different woman.

We were twenty-seven, and Jenna loved a different man.

We were thirty-two, and we loved each other enough to finally let go.

And that was it. The story of us. In five short sentences. In thirteen long years.

"Bye, Jendy," I said, opening the door.

"Bye, Gage," she whispered.

And I shut it.

Two Years (and six months) Later

Jenna

And that was it.

Gage would live his life, Jenna supposed. And Jenna would live her life. Separately.

He would get married, she supposed. He would laugh and cry and eat and work and live and breathe. All with Von and Ryan and whatever other children they had together.

And that was it.

Jenna would sometimes laugh and sometimes cry and sometimes eat out alone and sometimes eat out with dates and most times spend a great chunk of her day sitting in Bagel Plus writing.

Six months after she last saw Gage, she would date a man she met online, a man named Trace. Trace was a banker in New York who wore mostly suits, but sometimes khakis. Jenna felt safe with him, mostly because he was so far away, and they only saw each other one weekend a month. And she knew that was pretty messed up reasoning, but she was happy that he was the first after Michael, because everything about him was distant and easy. They spent two weeks on a Florida beach. They spent a long weekend in the Hamptons. But like the way of anything too far away for far too long, the two slowly fizzled, slowly faded, until Jenna finally pulled the plug.

And that was it.

She would visit Roxie in Rhode Island often; she would be her maid of honor in Roxie and Lance's tiny beach wedding. She would look for Gage, but wouldn't see him. She would ask Roxie, but Roxie would say that she lost touch with Gage a long time ago, and wasn't that sad and wasn't that the way of things: you have these grand ideas of who will be your friend forever and how your life was going to go, and one day you would wake up and realize you had not spoken to him in two years.

And that was it.

Jenna would write more manuscripts; Jenna would turn those manuscripts into books. She would sign contracts, and sign books, and one last time sign the rights to a movie deal. She would watch the movie at a premiere with a date named Charlie who she dated a lot more seriously than Trace, but when everyone started asking when they would get engaged, they ended it instead.

And that was it.

Or, that would have been it.

That would have been exactly it.

If it wasn't for one day.

Three months earlier, Jenna had started getting these migraines, these terrifically horrible migraines that incapacitated her for twenty-four hours straight at least once a week. And because of what happened with Michael, Jenna immediately predicted a tumor. She was dying of cancer, and she had already updated her last will and testament in her head as she waited for the MRI. At the doctor's appointment one week later, she steeled herself for the news. She held a tape recorder in her shaking hands; she knew all too well from Michael's appointments that there was going to be stuff she missed, and since she had no family or friend with her to record the important notes, she brought the recorder. And Jenna was more than shocked to learn that she did not have cancer. She was not dying. Jenna was having run-of-the-mill migraines. Jenna did not need chemotherapy and radiation. All Jenna needed was some anti-convulsant medication, a semi-annual appointment with a neurologist, and a pat on the back.

On August the nineteenth, Jenna was scheduled for a neurologist appointment at one o'clock.

On August the nineteenth at noon, Jenna was running ridiculously late. She sprinted out the door of Bagel Plus, balancing her Everything Bagel and keys and latte and cell phone in one hand and hoping she would not miss the Metro. It was that exact moment when she got the call that would change everything.

She answered it and spilled her coffee all over her white canvas flats, turning them tan and caffeinated. "Shit." She drew the word out as she bent over to scrub at them. That was her greeting, and she was embarrassed to find her neurologist's receptionist on the other line.

"Mrs. Gressa-Graham? Is that you?"

"Yes? Yes, sorry. I just spilled something. Sorry," Jenna mumbled, completely mortified.

Jenna found out then, as she was staring at her shoes, that her neurologist was in a motorcycle accident – neurologists rode motorcycles? – and they needed to reschedule her monthly appointment because he had broken his leg and was in surgery.

"Sure. Of course." Jenna made mental note of the new date and time. *Don't forget this, don't forget this*, she repeated, crouched there on the sidewalk as she scooped up her coffee and blotted her shoes with napkins she dug out of her purse.

When she hung up, she blew out an unsteady breath and looked around. Jenna felt weird, jangly all over. One minute ago she had been running late and now she had absolutely nothing to do. She blotted her shoes some more. A couple of teenagers bumped into her, cursed, told her to move out of the middle of the fucking sidewalk. Jenna stood uncertainly, still contemplating the notion that neurologists rode motorcycles. She spotted a garbage can and waddled over to it, her shoes uncomfortably squishing against her otherwise bare feet, and shoved the cup and napkins into the trash.

Coffee. Jenna supposed she could get more coffee. And a new bagel, she thought, as she realized she had accidentally stuffed her bagel into the trash as well.

Jenna turned back to Bagel Plus and grabbed the door handle.

And immediately froze in place.

Because standing at the counter just inside, she saw Von.

Not only Von. Von. And Gage. And two young boys.

Jenna's eyes went wide. Her hand, still glued to the handle, turned cold.

She watched them through the window. Von was even more beautiful than Jenna remembered. The younger boy had Von's fair looks. His hair, like feathers, haloed his head, framed his blue eyes. Jenna smiled wistfully at him. Ryan. It must be Ryan. He looked the right age. But who was the second boy? He was older. Jenna scrunched her face, deep in thought. Who could he be?

"Hey! You coming or going?" An irritated voice blasted in her ear.

Jenna jumped with a start. "Oh. Oh. Sorry. Sorry. I'm going."

"Whatever." The guy rolled his eyes and jammed past her through the door.

She caught a snippet of Gage's conversation through the now open door. "Strawberry or blueberry," he said to the younger boy.

"Peanut butter," the boy shouted, triumphantly.

Von's voice rose over the din. "That's not a--" The door slammed, cutting her off.

Jenna gaped. Jenna stared. And then Jenna turned to run.

"Jendy?" She heard the familiar nickname and the familiar voice attached to it, which meant Gage had not merely noticed her, but shouted her name so loud she heard it through the door.

Wide-eyed, she turned back. Eyes bugged, smile plastered on her face, Jenna raised her hand in stiff greeting. All through the glass.

"Jen? That you?" Gage, laughing good-naturedly – apparently at the sight of her – ran to the door, ducking and dodging people and chairs along the way. "That's Jen! Von! You were right. It's Jendy."

He pushed the door open with little regard to the fact that Jenna was standing close on the other side. The door immediately smashed into her forehead. Her head bounced back, and though she barely felt pain, her hand robotically moved to inspect the damage, which was none.

"Whoa!" Gage reached for Jenna and deftly pulled her through the door and into his arms. "Crap. You okay? I'm sorry, hon." He rubbed gruffly at her, his palm against her head, and Jenna did nothing but stand there, frozen, at the absolute absurdity of the situation. All Jenna could think was that he smelled the same. Exactly the same as he had in college. Exactly the same as he had two, no two-and-a-half, years ago, when he was boxing her in at her counter, when he was pressing her into her couch.

Jenna felt her face go hot.

He pulled her away to examine her head. "It's red," he declared, and she felt her blush deepen. "But I think you'll live." He kissed her bump without reservation, and Jenna's eyes went wide again. It was such a Dad thing for him to say, to do, that Jenna nearly giggled like a schoolgirl.

What is wrong with you? Jenna scolded herself. *Perhaps you did sustain some type of brain damage.*

If he noticed her embarrassment, Gage said nothing. He towed her along behind him. "You should eat with us, Jenna."

"Oh." Jenna looked frantically to Von, to the boys, then back to Von. "Um." Jenna searched for her bearings, something that seemed to have fled her the second she spotted Von.

"Elliot," Von hissed, "she might have other plans." She gave Jenna a sympathetic nod.

"She's fine. She's a big-time author with movies, what could she be doing?"

"A neurology appointment, maybe," Jenna mumbled.

"What?" Gage turned to her with a start. "Neurology? What is wrong with you?" His gaze fell on her head again, the spot where the door met her face.

"It's none of your business, Elliot. Jeez!" Von shook her head.

Jenna, completely overwhelmed, felt the giggles start again. "Nothing is wrong with me. Absolutely nothing, actually."

Gage stared at her, a mixture of confusion and concern on his face that somehow looked like disgust to Jenna, making her laugh harder. "Does she look okay to you?" He looked to Von.

"Why don't you slow down, Elliot? Give her room to breathe." Von said, the only voice of rationality in the group. "You clocked her with the door. She needs a minute."

"Yeah. Yeah. Jen, take a minute."

"You're an idiot," Von said to him, but her voice was light and teasing.

"So, um, what are you all up to?" Jenna asked hoping she sounded casual because she could feel the quaking of nerves under her skin. She remembered her last conversation with Gage, the one about never seeing each other again, not if he wanted to work it out with Von. Did Von know about that conversation? Most likely. Jenna squirmed.

The little boy in the stroller began to whine. "Daddy," he whimpered, drawing out the second syllable as he tugged at Gage's shirt.

Von elbowed Gage. "What?" he asked.

"Introduce the kids," she said quietly.

Gage's eyes lit up. "Oh, yeah. I forgot. You haven't seen us in so long, you wouldn't know." Gage turned to the older boy. "Remember this guy? It's Ian."

"Ian?" Jenna smiled remembering Gage's brother. "Oh, man. Ian. You probably don't remember me."

"Nope," Ian said. "It's my birthday. I'm ten."

"Wow! Double digits. That's an important one. Well, happy birthday, Ian."

Gage smiled, and it was a stab to Jenna's heart. "We are out for his birthday. Zoo. Lunch. Maybe ice cream. You know. All that fun stuff."

"All that fun stuff," she repeated and their eyes locked, held. Jenna's felt her heart crush; she felt her mouth move, mouthing his name to him. *Gage.* The corner of his mouth quirked into a smile. She blushed again. Think of something and quick, she told herself. "Oh…um…where is Joel?"

"He is at summer camp," Von answered.

"He's a teenager. Can you believe it?" Gage added.

Jenna nodded. She shifted uncomfortably, trying to think of conversation.

"Oh! Jendy." Gage, obviously excited and completely unaware of Jenna's discomfort, seized Jenna's hand as he hunched down. "You never had a chance to meet him. My boy. Our boy," he corrected, glancing up at Von.

Jenna found herself face to face with the boy with an angel's halo of hair.

"Ryan." Gage hunkered down by the boy, pulling Jenna with him. "This is Jenna."

Jenna felt the heat of Von's gaze pour over them. Jenna was certain Von was as uncomfortable as she, but when Jenna glanced back, Von was smiling easily. Confused, Jenna turned away, her attention on Ryan. "Hi, Ryan."

"This is my fire truck," he said, never stopping to look up.

"It's very cool."

"I know. Mommy got it. It's mine now."

"It's very nice."

"And I'm getting peanut butter. No strawberry. Or blueberry," he said, sticking a pouty lip out.

"Can you say hi to Jenna?" Gage prompted. "She's daddy's friend from school."

"Like my preschool?"

"Kind of like that." Gage stood and swung Ryan up to his hip.

Jenna stood with them. Even as she felt stilted and awkward in their conversation with Von right there taking it all in, Jenna's could not stop her heart from swelling. Gage. He was a dad. Of course she had known it, she had even seen pictures of Gage with an infant Ryan, but had never seen him in action.

"Hi, Jenda," Ryan said, much more interested in his truck.

"Ha! That was close! How 'bout that?" Gage looked at Jenna, and they smiled at each other. "And I never even talk about you!"

"Like father, like son," Jenna said, even as his last declaration knifed through her.

"And you know Von." Gage, his hands full of Ryan, nodded in Von's direction.

"Of course I do." Jenna nodded at Von and stuffed her hands into her pockets. "It's really nice to see you Von. He's beautiful. He looks so much like you."

"Jenna." Von grinned. "I'm glad we ran into you." She rushed to hug her quickly. "I'm so sorry about Michael. I can't imagine. I'm so sorry I wasn't around more. I, ah, I was a little lost back then myself." She whispered this part in Jenna's ear, and when Jenna pulled back, she caught the tinge of pink coloring Von's cheeks.

So, Von had been lost back then, but she and Gage had obviously worked it out. They seemed happy together, comfortable together. They were insanely lucky, Jenna thought, because life and love did not always work out the way it did for them. Jenna couldn't help but feel a rush of envy. She did her best to push it down.

Jenna smiled as she squeezed Von's hand and felt Von's wedding ring dig into her palm.

Everyone got quiet again, with Von's gaze carefully volleying between Gage and Jenna. Jenna's self-consciousness got the better of her. "I was going to get some--" She pointed to the counter. "Maybe I should--"

"Hey!" A man clad in jeans and a Polo shirt jogged toward them, a baby in his arms. "Hey, did you get me a turkey on rye?"

"We were just getting ready to order," Von said as she took the tiny girl from him.

Jenna studied him. He didn't look familiar at all. She hadn't seen Gage in years though. Some new friend? A single dad tagging along? Von had those brothers didn't she? A sudden realization dawned on Jenna. My god. The baby. It could be Gage and Von's baby. And that guy could be their nanny. Didn't Gage say something once about Von not enjoying the newborn phase? Jesus. It was bad enough imagining over the years what Gage's life was like now. Now that it was shoved in Jenna's face, she wondered how much worse this encounter could possibly get.

"Oh, yeah. I forgot this guy." Gage said patting the back of the man. "This is Jenna Gressa. Graham. Jenna Gressa-Graham. It's still Gressa-Graham, right?" Gage looked to Jenna, and she nodded in a sort of dazed confirmation at Gage's excitement. "A friend from college. And well, after college." Gage smiled at Jenna and winked.

Jenna bit down on her tears and blew out a breath. She could do this. She could make it. She had made it through much harder stuff. "You have such a beautiful family, Gage." She forces a smile and stuck out her hand. "Hello. Nice to meet you."

The man took it, and they shook hands politely. "Jenna." He smiled.

"Jenna?" Gage said. "This is Devin. Von's husband."

Jenna's hand stalled. Shock replaced her rigid formality. "Von's hus--Oh. Uh…yeah. Yes. Devin." Jenna stammered. "Oh. Devin. Hi."

"And our baby." Von added. The baby squealed and reached out for the sunglasses that sat atop Von's head. "Rebecca."

"Yeah. Of course. Rebecca. Hello, Rebecca." Jenna struggled to keep up, but she could barely think over the whirring in her brain, the blaring shock of cold confusion buzzing in her ears. Von was married. But it wasn't to Gage. Von was married to Devin, and they had a baby named Rebecca.

Um. Yeah. You miss two and a half years and, apparently, you miss everything.

"Yep. Just the typical American family." Gage grinned, a smile that seemed to know everything Jenna was thinking. Her eyes caught in his. His gaze took on a very different look this time. Jenna swallowed hard and tried to read it.

"Von's husband," Jenna repeated.

"Yes. My husband." Now it was Von's turn to smile. She looked away, but Jenna still caught it. The look on her face. The way she glanced to Gage for a fleeting moment. She ran one hand through her hair, catching it at the ends and pulling it over her shoulder. Her eyes lit up. "Hey," she said in a much more excited, kid-friendly tone. "I have an idea. Who would rather have some ice cream?"

Ian let out a cheer.

"That sounds fantastic," Devin added, even though his eyes were on a different customer's sandwich.

"Mommy says I run on sugar," Ryan said to Jenna.

"Come on, Elliot." Ian grabbed Gage's hand and tugged.

"You know what, I think your brother might want to stay here and catch up with Jenna. It's been a long time." Von said.

"Yeah," Gage agreed absently, his eyes never leaving Jenna's face. "I'll be over in five minutes, okay?"

"I'll order you one, Elliot." Ian looked up at his brother with hero-worship. "Mint chocolate chip?"

"You got it, buddy." Gage patted Ian's shoulder.

"We'll see you, Jenna." Von trailed after the group, facing Jenna and Gage, tucking her hair behind her ears. "Soon." Then she spun around and swung her hand into Devin's waiting one.

Ian and Ryan jabbered excitedly. The baby squealed.

Suddenly, everyone was gone. And the silence that replaced them jarred Jenna.

After a beat, Jenna looked at Gage. "I think I'm dizzy."

Gage

I admit I had not had the purest intentions when I suggest Bagel Plus to the family that morning.

And my only defense was this: how could you blame a guy who was knowingly – and sometimes unknowingly – off and on in love with a girl for fifteen years? How could you blame him?

Okay, I guess you could blame him. You could say get over it man. Stop being a pussy. Move on. Find a hobby. Quit your weird-ass stalking, you weird ass.

And what could I say to that?

Not much more than the fact that I love her.

And does stopping by a bagel shop once in two – no, two-and-a-half years - count as a stalking? It's not like I *knew* she would be there. I hoped. But there was no way of knowing.

And if she wasn't there, I was going to call her anyway. I was going to wait a week or two, but it was going to happen. Because I was going to make it happen this time, and make it happen right.

And really, who cares? Why do I have to explain myself to anyone anyway?

Whatever.

I love her.

"Okay," Jenna said after her pronouncement of dizziness, after I found us a table, and after we spent a sufficient amount of time staring at each other. "I have to ask. Her *husband*? Her husband is *not* you?"

"Her husband is Devin."

"So…"

"She married him."

Jenna gave me a look that said *Duh, Captain Obvious.* "And they have a--"

"Baby," I finished.

"Jesus."

"Not Jesus. Rebecca."

"This isn't funny," Jenna said as she laughed.

"It's kind of funny," I argued.

"It's kind of funny," Jenna conceded. "But a baby? She has another baby?"

"Yeah."

"But didn't she--"

"Not really want children? I know." I shrugged. "I'm nearly as lost as you are on that one. Believe me."

Jenna shook her head incredulously. "Wow. And you are-"

"Single."

I saw Jenna blush for the third or fourth time since I accidentally slammed her with the door. Which, yes, I felt awful about. Slamming her with the door, not noticing her face go bright red every fifteen seconds.

"I didn't mean--" Jenna cleared her throat.

"You need a water?" I suggested. "A tea? A cold compress? You got the vapors, Jendy? You still read those Victorian romances?"

"Shut up." She blushed harder. "I've moved on to Game of Thrones, if you're going to be so nosy. And what I was going to ask, smartass…I meant are you…okay?"

"Oh, yeah. I'm that too." I shrugged. "I'm fine. I wasn't. I was horrible, actually. It was…it was a bad year. And then I was okay. You know all about that."

"Yeah. I do."

She looked down at her hands. I nudged her foot with mine. "Hey."

She looked up. "Hey," she replied softly. A crash of dishes rang out, a stream of swearing from an employee, and the spell was broken. "God, I do not miss working here," Jenna commented.

I grunted in agreement.

"So, you're single," Jenna said. Her question was casual, but did she know what I saw in her eyes?

I laughed. "Yep. Ryan and I are visiting. We come up once a month to visit."

Surprise registered in her eyes before she quickly tucked it away. "You come up. Which means you don't live here anymore?"

"Not too far. Virginia Beach."

"What are you doing down there?"

"Did I ever tell you about working in a surf shop in San Diego?"

Jenna stared.

I rubbed a hand through my hair self-consciously and realized I had not felt like this in a long time. "What?"

"Gage," was all she said, her voice skeptical.

"What?"

"A surf shop?"

"Yeah," I confirmed. "I'd go farther, but I couldn't do that to Ryan. He should be close to Von."

"That," Jenna shook her head, "seems like it came out of nowhere. I can't believe how much I don't know you."

"I remember thinking the same about you not long ago."

She smiled a little. "And you come up here once a month?"

"More if we can. Von stops down in the summer for a few weeks."

"So everything is good between you two?"

"Aw hell, Jen. That happened so long ago. I barely think about it."

"Yeah." The sadness in her voice nearly drilled a hole in my chest.

"Some stuff I think about more often," I corrected. I pressed my foot on top of hers again. She looked at me.

Jenna cleared her throat again. "I think I might need that water." She lifted her gaze and her eyes smiled at me. "The vapors," she said quietly.

I laughed. "You want to go get some ice cream? I hear it's better than the water around here."

Jenna glanced out the window. "You think we could? They wouldn't care?"

"You'll fit in just fine. Have you *seen* my family?"

Jenna stood and stretched. "Well, thank you for that fine compliment."

"You're welcome," I said with a grin as we made our way through the shop. "And you know what I meant."

"And forgive me if I don't believe you all are the Brady Bunch all the time." Jenna reached for the door. I put a hand over hers. She looked up at me.

"I was pissed for a good while. A good, long while."

She clapped her hands victoriously and pointed at me. "Ha! I knew it! I knew you were!"

We walked out into the crowded sidewalk.

"You are way too happy about my misery," I complained.

"I meant to say 'Ha. I knew it. I knew you were.'" She repeated this in a sober monotone.

I looked at the ground, shaking my head with a laugh. I looked back up. "I mean, you pull yourself together for your kid, but, man, I kept thinking, damn, if I could get Devin in a room alone with Jenna and her left-hook." I rubbed my hands together gleefully.

Jenna punched me playfully in the chest. "Hey! No. No way. You can't bring that up. We swore we would never speak of that again."

"I definitely do not remember any sort of promise." I looked into the distance and waved a hand in front of me. "God, what a show that would have been. I would have sold tickets."

"I think I might remember a promise."

"You know, one good jab." I hooked one arm around Jenna's shoulder and punched the air. "I'm willing to nurse your broken hand back to health to witness that kind of misfortune happen to a different man."

"How magnanimous of you," she said. "I do remember a promise though. Like, maybe we were in a bed together and promising something or other-"

"Oh, you remember it so clearly. And you *didn't* happen to be on a ton of Vicodin at the time, is that correct?"

"Stop lawyering me!" Jenna protested. "I remember! I remember my dorm room and the bed and maybe some kind of movie--" She was ticking off the facts on her fingers.

"The documentary, Jenna. We watched that horrible, horrible documentary."

"You liked that documentary!" She countered.

"No. No, I definitely did not. I clearly remember you punched my face and then made me watch a boring documentary as punishment. As *punishment*! For you punching *my* face!"

She shook her head. "That's not true."

"And which one of us was high on Vicodin again?"

"Oh, for God's sake," Jenna pushed at me. "Just shut up."

"I love you too, Jendy," I said and pulled her close and wrapped her hand into mine, when I pulled her in for a kiss, a quick kiss, a friendly one right on the cheek, then on the lips, I knew she felt it. Because she sighed. And because she leaned into me.

And because I felt it too.

And when I felt it, I knew it, instantly and immediately.

And that was it.

Jenna

She could not look at him and say, *It was you. It was always you.* Because it wasn't. For a time, it was Michael. For a short and wonderful and tragic time, it was Michael. And she knew he could not look at her and say, *It was you. It was always you.* Because it wasn't. For a time, it was Von. For him, for a short and wonderful and confusing time, it was Von. And between them, there would always be Von, the mother of Gage's child; and there would always be Michael, the friend and husband and perfect memory.

But she could put her hand in Gage's hand. She could kiss him right back. And they could look at each other and say, *It is you.*

Now. It is you.

And that? That was it.

Amy Spade is a writer living in central Pennsylvania with her husband, Tony, and their four cats. She is the independently published author of young adult novels Hope Rising and Summer Unbroken, which was a semi-finalist in the 2016 Kindle Book Awards.

Acknowledgments

With many thanks to –

Aaron Patalune for his hours (and hours and hours) of reading and editing. So much appreciation. You have no idea.

Lydia Dobrowolsky and Jen Onder for their first reads and first impressions, without which, I would have been lost.

Everyone who asked, "So, when is the next book coming out?" -- you keep me going on the days I don't feel like going.

CH for the encouragement, always.

Tony for his endless confidence in me, which is uplifting and astounding all at once.

37600099R00215

Made in the USA
Middletown, DE
03 March 2019